Honor At Stake

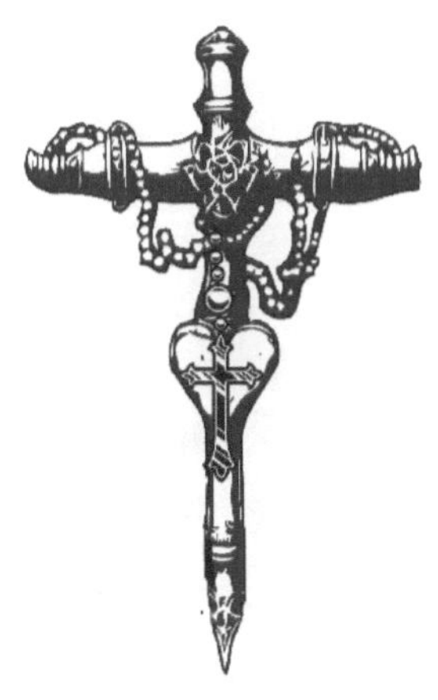

Love At First Bite

Book One

By Declan Finn

Three Ravens Publishing
Chickamauga, GA USA

Honor At Stake: Love At First Bite Book One By Declan Finn
Published by Three Ravens Publishing
threeravenspublishing@gmail.com
P O Box 851, Chickamauga, Ga 30707
https://www.threeravenspublishing.com

Credits:

Honor At Stake: Love At First Bite Book One was written by Declan Finn

Honor At Stake: Love At First Bite Book One by: Declan Finn /Damnation Press - Caliburn Press 1st edition, 2015

Honor At Stake: Love At First Bite Book One by: Declan Finn /Declan Finn – 2nd edition, 2016

Honor At Stake: Love At First Bite Book One by: Declan Finn /Silver Empire – 3rd edition, 2018

Honor At Stake: Love At First Bite Book One by: Declan Finn /Three Ravens Publishing – 4th edition, 2023

ISBN Ebook: 978-1-951768-69-0
ISBN Trade Paperback: 978-1-951768-70-6
ISBN Hardcover: 978-1-951768-71-3

Table of Contents

Prologue

ily Sparks was a standard issue girl with a non-standard issue boyfriend. She was short and cute and what might be called "bouncy," while he was tall, clean cut, and cut a nice, trim figure in his army uniform. The way she was draped on his arm almost made her look like a fashion accessory, though she tended to think of the fellow as something that really looked nice on *her* arm.

Lily was happy and had considered getting even happier a little later on. In fact, there was a nice, private alley that looked just perfect for getting the rest of the evening started. Her date was prim and proper, a perfect gentleman since they met.

Maybe it was time for that to change.

Lily changed direction, pulling her man to the alley. It was out of the line of sight for most foot traffic, and dark enough for her purposes. He was caught off guard by the maneuver. When she pushed him up against a wall and wrapped her arms around his neck, he was slow to respond.

The first noise she heard that wasn't from either of them was a cough, followed by a wheeze. Then she saw him out of the corner of her eyes—someone with a knife. The face was young, but the eyes were worn out and old. The only visible teeth were worn away, as though ground down over time.

Lily screamed. Her date turned towards the attacker, and only stared at the new arrival a moment.

"You want to mug us?" he asked, shaking his head slowly. "That's a mistake."

The mugger smiled as much as he could without a full set of teeth and came straight for Lily's date. The two men met in the middle.

Lily screamed again, at first in fear for her date, then in fear for her life.

Then in fear *of* her date as he turned on her, fresh blood around his lips.

Her screams still echoed in his ears five minutes later, as the man in the uniform stood in the alley, his mouth covered in blood, the coppery taste fresh in his mouth.

He smiled the whole time. He was perfectly happy.

Marco Catalano had enjoyed that.

Chapter 1:

Love At First Bite

September 22, Hudson University, New York City

Amanda Colt looked across the college classroom and hesitated. Something was off. Something in the room felt extremely threatening.

Amanda thought she might have found what it was when she saw him. Blond hair, blue eyes, looked nice enough—5'9" and well-built—though more like a dancer or a gymnast than a weightlifter. There was nothing effeminate about him, however. Quite the opposite.

Amanda slid into the only remaining chair, which the law of Murphy dictated *had* to be right next to this guy. He sat in the front row, in the corner nearest the windows, not the door—two good reasons why the other students would avoid the seat next to him.

Maybe she wasn't the only one who sensed something off.

The annoying thing was that she couldn't tell what was off about him. He didn't look unpleasant, smell strange, or make any weird noises. In fact, Amanda noted as she took the seat, he didn't do much of anything. His things were all laid out in proper order in front of him, his book was open and ready for notes, and he held a silver pen in his hand. Other than that, he was simply still. His focus was tight on the notebook, and his pen hovered over the page, waiting for a lecture to start.

"You might want to take a picture," he said, voice deep and resonant, but just loud enough for her to hear. "It would certainly last longer."

Amanda blinked, then shook herself. "I am sorry," she said, her light Russian accent coming out like a kitten's meow.

He looked up, and she saw how dark his eyes were. Only because of her exceptional eyesight could she tell his eyes were blue. His face was almost locked with an eternal smirk of amusement. It occurred to her that he smiled when she came into the room, and when she sat down, and the smile hadn't ever flickered.

This man took her in with one sweep of his eyes, and then kept his face locked on hers. She was about as intimidating as a chipmunk, which was unusual enough for New York, but as sexy as the one that got away—you know, that one—only better looking. She was average height with long, red-gold hair that brushed the small of her back in a golden waterfall.

Her eyes were a warm, liquid Frangelico brown and her skin Siberia pale. Her outfit today was casual, but form-fitting. Tight jeans and a sweater that should have covered her thoroughly, but they both somehow managed to be quite snug.

"Don't worry," he said. "I'm sure that I'm not half as bothered by stares are you are."

Amanda felt a smile tug at her lips but ignored it. She did not have the fabled "beauty of a supermodel," mainly because she was above a size zero.

"I am used to it," she answered.

"I'll take your word for it," he answered, his stare as unwavering as his smile. She realized what was wrong with him. He was utterly *controlled*. "Can't imagine being stared at often."

"Why not?" she asked. "You aren't ugly."

He arched a brow. "Nor am I Leonardo DiCaprio pretty," he said dryly. "Trust me when I say that I am not in the top ten male models for the year, or for the neighborhood."

"Neither am I. I am too fat."

He blinked, possibly for the first time since she laid eyes on him and went over his scan of her body once more, not leering but reassessing. When he met her eyes again, he said, "If that is your idea of fishing for compliments, you need better bait."

She nodded, allowing a small smile to slip in. "Good response." She glanced at the whiteboard with *Fencing* in big black letters. She was in the correct room. "You are joining the fencing team?"

"I'm here, aren't I?" he replied. He glanced over his shoulder, out the window. The day had been heavily cloudy since dawn and had only gotten worse. "At least the day's almost over."

"For me, it is just beginning," she answered.

He looked back at her and cocked his head. "Truly?" He broke eye contact with her, the gaze moving to her hands and her cheek, and even her neck—going for exposed skin, she realized. "Night classes all the way, is it?"

"Yes." She raised her white hand. "Am I that obvious?"

"Yup."

She held her hand out towards him. "I am Amanda Colt."

"Have any relatives in Pennsylvania?" he asked jokingly. He took it firmly in his. "Marco Catalano."

"Pleased to meet you."

He nodded. "Likewise."

Marco and Amanda walked out of the building and onto the campus plaza. The great lawn of the campus was bracketed on three sides by buildings. Its southern end was butted up against one of the numerous parking lots on campus. They decided to cut across the middle.

As they passed by the large cross in the middle of the lawn, it seemed that Marco kept Amanda between him and the cross.

"So," she asked, "what is a Physician Assistant?"

"The marines of the medical profession," he replied. His smile was still frozen on eternal amusement, as though ignorance of his profession was more joke than offense. "We learn nearly everything that a doctor does in two years, rather than four of med school. We're writing prescriptions after we graduate with a master's degree, and, on average, making six figures within six years."

She furrowed her pretty brow. "Really? Why have I never heard of them?"

"Because it's something created by the Vietnam war, and most doctor shows on television have yet to catch up to it."

Amanda frowned at the two items linked together. "Do you think everyone gets their information from television, or just me?"

Marco sighed, but the expression didn't waver. "The dissemination of information is linked heavily to popular culture. Vietnam wasn't popular. The one major show that tried to deal with it was China Beach in the 1980s, and their history was frighteningly bad at times. Physician Assistants were a way of dealing with combat nurses who had learned more practical medicine in the field than major trauma centers."

"Well, thanks for the history lesson. I can see why you would go into that field. Fencing, though…"

Marco gave a short laugh through his nose. "I could say the same of you. You deal with blades before?"

She almost laughed. "Oh yes, more than once. You?"

"High school, when they let us play with swords."

"Ah, good. It should be interesting."

Marco hefted his briefcase a little higher. "I'm headed to Brooklyn. I'd offer to give you a lift, but obviously you're just starting your classes for the day."

"You're driving?"

"My family needs the car off the street during daylight hours. My father walks to work, my mother takes the train, and I'm the last man standing. Hence, the car. You?"

"I live in the city." She looked around the campus and considered skipping her classes and leaving with him. She had her books and syllabi from online, and little was going to happen on the first day. Despite his occasionally disturbing directness, she found him interesting.

"Nice," he said. "Rich family?"

"You could say that."

"In which case, I won't say it too loudly." As he stopped near the parking lot, he nodded to her. "Again, it was a pleasure making your acquaintance, Ms. Colt."

"The same for me, Marco."

He gave a deep, old fashioned bow, then turned and walked away.

Maybe he worries people because he seems like he's out of time and place, she thought.

Amanda Colt walked into her apartment and looked around the quiet flat. There was little in terms of color. The furnishings were basic. The only part of her life that wasn't frugal was the location, and anything in Manhattan was expensive.

She slipped into the chair at her computer, warmed it up, and typed in a simple name.

Marco Catalano, Brooklyn…

She found nothing.

It was like he didn't exist. *How is that possible? In an age when even cats have Facebook pages, how can Marco not have even a single mention online? Where is he from? The Dark Ages?*

October 15th

Marco Catalano appeared to have one goal in mind. To cut Amanda Colt's head off.

The student went after her with frequent attacks. She parried and attacked immediately, but his weapon was almost always there, waiting for her. It was practically magical.

However, Amanda's major asset was speed. Marco was quick. She was quicker.

Her next attack was a thrust. He twisted his body to deflect it past him and lunged forward. She pulled back in time, bringing her sword down on his, nearly sending it into the floor. One flip of his wrist used that momentum to arc the sword around towards him, then overhead, for her face. Her sword came up to meet his, but he pulled back until the sword slid off, then thrust for her collar.

Amanda's blade came down, sweeping his away. She didn't give him time to pull his sword back to first position. She lunged for his center mass. His sword stayed with hers as he retreated, gliding along its length, deflecting the thrust as it came at him. She withdrew, but his sword stayed with hers like glue. The tip went over, down and around her blade like a snake before he flicked his wrist in a flourishing disarm.

"That's enough," the instructor said.

He pulled back for a thrust that would skewer her, but she grabbed her own sword in mid-flight and used it to parry him. The swords crashed, came down, around, and back up, starting in first position.

"That's enough, thank you," the instructor bellowed this time.

Marco pulled back, then gave a quick salute with the sword. She returned it, and they both withdrew to the same side of the gym, letting the next two fencers have time on the floor.

Amanda took off her face mask, her long hair tumbling down her back. "That was impressive."

Marco put his mask in the crook of his arm. His smile was still there. "It's easy when you have a computer-like mind."

"What do you mean?"

"I mean I fence like I play chess. I try to think several moves ahead."

"You cannot account for everything."

"Usually, I can," he answered, slipping his gloves off. He paused in the middle of removing the second glove. "Well, there are always surprises. When you suddenly sped up, you almost had me a few times before I could compensate. If you had just gone that fast at the start, I'm sure I would have been in trouble. Especially when you caught your sword as it was flying. That was a nice touch."

She blushed a little, slightly mortified that he noticed that. "No one else saw it."

"That's because they've gotten used to not seeing anything that we do when fencing. It's like they're just waiting for us to get a draw."

"Then why don't they just let us fight other students?"

Marco arched a brow. She assumed that was a sign of greater amusement, but it was hard to tell. "This semester is, what, a month old? In that time, we were both upgraded from beginners, to advanced, to dueling with the instructor. It's the only way to run the class and get everyone to practice. If they make us duel the others, we'll essentially be teaching them. If they start making us instructors, I will probably quit. I came here to practice, not sit, watch, and correct."

Amanda nodded. "I agree. Though, let us face it, we are not exactly fencing."

He cocked his head, saying nothing.

She smiled and elaborated. "Have you seen professional fencing? It is boring."

"True, but then, I like to practice as though someone is actually trying to kill me." He stared at her for a moment, like he tried to read her mind. "Would you like to hang out at some point this weekend?"

"Why wait?"

He glanced at his watch. "Odd, I would have thought you had classes right now."

"I do, but I know what they've been teaching lately."

Marco's smile expanded a moment, then snapped back to the standard smirk. "Heh. Funny, I have the same aversion to core classes—required for the University, yet utterly useless."

She cocked her head, her long red hair falling over one shoulder. "I thought that your degree made every course necessary?"

"Yeah, but they're still rather basic."

She studied him a moment, this time trying to read his mind. She came up blank. "Do you realize that you seem, hmm, different?"

He stopped and stared at her a moment, and then laughed. He laughed so loudly that the two fencers on the mat both stopped and stared at them. He kept laughing so long everyone wondered how he failed to run out of breath.

"That's a good one," he said at last. "Where would you like to start?"

"With the two of you," the club moderator shouted, *"outside!"*

Marco, dressed now in a full suit and tie, and Amanda, dressed in her usual sweater and jeans, looked like an odd couple as they emerged from the basement level gym where the fencing club had been banished to after an incident involving a rapier and the car of the University President.

"Shall we stay to the left, in the shade of the trees?" he asked.

"Why? Are you allergic to the sun?"

Marco's smile of amusement turned into a smirk, even though not a single muscle in his face moved. "I'm actually assuming that your white, Russian skin is sensitive. Otherwise, you wouldn't bother with all that suntan lotion."

"You do not exactly tan either, for someone who is Italian."

"You mean 'Catalano'? The family is from northern Italy, and close to Switzerland, and especially close to Celtic raiders who popped in and out of the area a lot, back in the old days."

"That's interesting. That old, hmm?"

"Sure, that's why I'm a freak."

She touched his arm lightly, a fleeting motion of comfort. "I didn't say you are a freak."

He sighed, looked at her, and gave her a sad smile. "You didn't, but I have been hearing that on and off for, well, a very long time. I might as well be a local vampire."

"I thought that they were all the rage nowadays."

Marco scoffed. "Mainly because no one ever thinks about it."

"About what?"

"Vampires."

"That would be odd, considering that there seems to be a hundred variations on the theme."

"Yes, but nothing *coherent*," he objected. "Forget the mythologies; at least they have a lot of commonalities, but the modern stuff…feh."

Amanda stopped and sat on a bench at the edge of the great lawn, staying just in the shade. Marco took two steps past her before he noticed. She motioned to the seat next to her. "So, tell me your thoughts."

"Why? It's just vampires."

She patted the bench. "I want to see how your mind works."

"Slowly, and with WD-40." He chuckled and sat. "Well, vampires…on the one end, you have the original mythology. Even in the Middle East, with the Ghul–their name for a vampire, singular–they were a type of undead, possibly demon spawn. They survived by drinking blood and had the ability to shape-shift. They also hung out in cemeteries. Sounds familiar, doesn't it? When you get to the European version, they could be repelled by crosses and sunlight and stakes, that sort of thing. Those stories, at least partially, take into account the existence of Free Will."

"Free will?"

He leaned back against the bench, his arms spreading out along the back. "Think about it. Almost every traditional vampire in fiction is evil, automatically and with little in the way of reservation. Turn a good human being into a vampire, and they're automatically not much better than your average rabid dog. In the original novel, aside from Dracula and his three girlfriends in the basement, there was only one other vampire. That was Lucy, girlfriend of Mina Harker. As a new vampire, she could have been easily controlled, or feral, or what have you. Now, the original Vlad the Impaler, who inspired the fictional Dracula, was not a nice fellow. Take that how you want.

"When you get into more recent novels, everything becomes a mishmash, usually with bad metaphysics. Laurell K. Hamilton is one of the worst offenders—practically everything she does is conditional. You know, vampires are dead during the day, unless it's a powerful vampire, which depends on a whole bunch of factors I'm not even totally certain of."

He paused, then smiled. "Sorry, I over think sometimes. Hence the freak portion."

"I still do not agree," Amanda said, tucking a strand of hair behind her ear. "You are intense, but not freakish."

"I'm a freak who reads too many books. I don't sleep with everything that has a skirt, especially since I go to school near Greenwich Village. I live in Brooklyn and don't sound like Tony Danza. I can go on forever."

She patted his shoulder. "Don't worry. Those things do not make you freakish."

Marco looked at her hand on his shoulder for a long moment.

For a long moment, Amanda wondered if she had done something culturally objectionable, and then he rolled his eyes. "And don't worry, I'll be happy to be your friend."

"What?" He reached up and gave her hand a squeeze, gently lifting it from his shoulder. In a voice more dry, cynical, and sarcastic as usual, he drolled, "I'm certain you heard me quite clearly. You do not strike me as deaf."

Amanda said nothing for a moment. She realized she was staring at Marco again, more than she had at any other person.

He was also the first man in a very long time to get close to her and *not* try to get into her pants. Most women in her position almost seemed inclined to take that lack of interest as a challenge. As though, if he didn't want her, she must make him want her.

In many ways, she was glad she wasn't most women. In the long run, his attitude was probably for the best anyway. "I'll take it," she said. She leaned over, kissed him on the cheek, and looked out over the sky. There was little sun left. "Sundown. Do we have to get you home before you turn into a pumpkin?"

"No, my parents trust me, the poor fools," he said cheerfully.

"Why do you ask?"

"I wanted to know how much time you have."

Marco smiled, leaned in, and said, in a conspiratorial whisper, "I have all the time in the world."

Chapter 2:

Always Date Inside Your Species

October 15th, Manhattan

Amanda opened the door to her apartment, and Marco watched her walk inside. He didn't immediately follow.

She stopped a little past the threshold and looked back over her shoulder. "Not coming?"

He frowned in thought, as though being invited into a woman's apartment was the first warning sign of some sort of trap.

"You may come in. Don't worry, I don't bite." She flashed him a smile. "Much."

Marco stepped forward, more at ease now with the invitation. "Yes, but you don't know if I do."

"I doubt it," she answered. "Besides, I think I can handle you if I need to."

"Okay." He stepped further inside and took the room in with one glance. It was borderline spartan, with a couch and an armchair, the coffee table, a television, and a computer.

The whole living room was probably the length of a short yellow bus. "Nice place. Rather small for a family, isn't it?"

"There's just me." Her eyes flickered to the floor. "Only me. For a long time. I am a little older than I look."

"Ah, understood," he said casually. "I'm guessing you don't have many parties."

"Nor friends."

Marco blinked, then looked her over one more time before moving to examine a Van Gogh reproduction on the wall. It looked like it was from *A Night on Bald Mountain*, but with the Milky Way galaxy in the background. "Not bloody likely."

"You're sweet, but it's true. Men are mostly interested in things other than friendship, and women are…"

"Jealous?" he said, not looking away from the painting, still smiling.

Ah, poor Vincent. If only someone had better stitches and found your ear in time or had better psychoactive drugs... Amanda shrugged. "I suppose it is the easy answer, and the one best held onto."

Marco nodded, glancing around the place once more. "I find it interesting that you manage to hold onto a place on the Upper East Side while going to college, with no other means of support."

She gave a small, dismissive shrug. "As I said, I have money. I have a scholarship as well."

"Ditto on the scholarship," he said, moving away from Van Gogh's *Starry Night* to a print of a Hubble telescope capture. "Though in my case, they weren't certain which one to give me."

"You are that smart?" she teased.

"I am multitalented. That's an advantage of having useless trivia stuck up here." He turned to face her, tapping his skull.

"However, I'm not sure what I'm doing here. I came because I like you. Also, you're one of the few people who will seem to tolerate my…"

"Intensity?"

"Bluntness."

She nodded, then nervously combed her fingers through her hair, trying to find anything to look at except Marco.

"You are here for much the same reason. You are the first person I've brought home in a long time."

He gave a short, medieval little bow. "I'm honored. I assume that all this–bringing me here, taking me this much into your confidence, is because of my 'let's be friends' lecture?"

"More or less."

"I must give that one more often. I've never had this reply before. Friends, then. Should be fun."

She smiled. She was tempted, as she took his outstretched hand, to pull him to her, just to see how he would react.

Honestly, in the long run, she could see herself with him as more than friends. Every time she tried something like that, however, it always ended badly. Though Marco was certainly something different. What kind of something was the question.

"Yes," she agreed, "it should."

His eyes slipped to another part of the room, landing on a set of crossed swords over the television. "Are those cavalry sabers?"

Amanda glanced over her shoulder and could all but feel his eyes on her neck. "Yes, they are. They're family heirlooms."

"Ah, isn't that grand? Which war? They don't look like

anything the United States Army would have had. With your accent, I can only assume that they're Cossack?"

She nodded. "Very good. They were taken from some Russian officers."

"Taken, huh? Fun." He wandered past her, looking over the rest of her collection, down behind the television. It was an odd place to put them, but without company to show them off to, they were, he guessed, colorful dust collectors.

Under the Russian sabers were several rifles. He blinked in surprise. "Why do you have a 1914 Enfield Rifle? The sabers, I get, but the rifle?"

"The British arrived in Arkangel shortly after the 'revolution,'" she said, walking up behind him.

"I remember something about it. They left behind a few souvenirs, huh?" Marco glanced down the wall. "A Sten gun? I've only seen these in books and World War II films. So, your family had Veterans of the Great Patriotic War? I can only assume this piece went from Britain to Russia to this apartment."

"Good." She touched him lightly on the shoulder. "How do you know so much about weapons and history? I thought you were studying to become a Physician Assistant."

Marco turned towards her, and his smile seemed to Amanda old and sad, as though he'd seen things in his young life that he really shouldn't have.

"I read a lot. I can understand the Remington from the same period, and even the Thompson submachine gun." He sidestepped out of the way and pointed at the extra-long assault rifle on the bottom. "But that's a Vietnam era M-16, notorious for jamming, which really went over well in the jungles. I think the Russians were on the wrong side of that war. Your family are collectors?"

She nodded. "Definitely. You could say they had a habit they could not break. I'm still surprised you know so much.

If I didn't know better, I would have thought you lived all of those wars."

"I'm just full of surprises."

November 4th, Hudson University Campus

"You have thought a lot about vampires," Amanda Colt said as they walked along the campus.

The sky was dark again. That was nothing new. From what she could tell, he had never been in bright sunlight. It was odd, but nothing that stood out.

"I think a lot about a lot of things," Marco said dismissively.

"I received a classical education. Vampires are almost a running theme in the history of mythology.

There are Greek, and Persian vampires. There's the Jewish myth of Lilith. Egypt's Sekhmet drank blood. India's Kali had fangs. The Romans had the Lamia. The Middle East had their ghouls. The so-called 'Enlightenment' had an increase in people who believed in vampires. Come to think about it, that would make sense. If God was 'not reasonable' and the Church was 'evil,' then there aren't many crosses to fend them off, now are there?"

He shook his head, coming back to the here and now.

"So, anyway, there are a lot of vampires. I read, I naturally pick up random facts here and there: discrepancies, inconsistencies. My education included a lot of home schooling, so I knew more about Thomas Aquinas when I was ten than most philosophy majors do when they graduate."

"I can tell." She walked through the door Marco held for her, moving outside. "So, what are your inconsistencies?"

"Crosses, for one thing. Do they work or not? If all vampires are evil, it makes sense if they do. If vampires aren't inherently evil, then there's something wrong with crosses as a blanket defense against them—surely God could recognize His own. And let's face it, if they were changed into a vampire unwillingly, is God honestly going to punishing them for something they didn't choose? How badly, and how fast, does the sun destroy them, if it does?"

"If?"

Marco arched a brow. "You prefer that they sparkle?"

Amanda's face went flat. "Do not even joke."

"In any event, one cannot manage to get relatively coherent information about vampires. At least, not in modern fiction."

She smiled at him and patted him on the shoulder. "You're right. You are the only one who would think about such things. Most people just read them and move on."

"Indeed. So, what's your next class, and what are you doing this weekend?"

Marco's home was in the middle of Greenpoint, Brooklyn. It was decent enough, as neighborhoods went. He also had a fairly nice brownstone.

Marco walked into his room and closed the door as soon as he slipped in. His room was simple. He had few pieces of furniture: a bed, a desk, a dresser, and bookcases. The bookcases covered every free inch of wall space, and even the dresser was stacked high with books. There were books about myths and history. There were medical journals and textbooks. If someone were to divine his interests from his reading selection, Marco was one part feudal lord, one part medicine man, one part serial killer, and one part mythological creature.

Well, it's not all inaccurate.

Marco still smiled as he sat down at his computer. He had an appointment to associate with Amanda Colt over the weekend. This was a good sign. For normal people.

He sighed and turned on his computer. *Well, there are worse things in life than being so medieval. One could be a predator like me.*

Marco went to work. There would be plenty of time later, to reflect on the blood he had spilled in his life. Right now, he had a few things to write up. He couldn't afford to be distracted by memories of her intelligent eyes, her musical accent, her long red-gold hair…or her graceful, soft neck.

Amanda gazed into the webcam that reflected her image back to her on her computer screen. She had been invited out. For a date? Had she been asked on a date? Was it a meeting between friends? Did he expect something from her? Did she expect something from him? Was she putting her trust into the wrong hands?

Take a breath, and try not to go insane, she thought. *We are friends. We are staying friends. He said so himself. Just friends.* Her own digital reflection stared at her accusingly. *I know what can happen. He doesn't know the half of it, but I do.* She shook her head clear. She had her secrets, but they were buried in her past. The more current secrets weren't a problem. They couldn't be. It was simply something she had to keep under wraps, and there wouldn't be any issues.

Of course there wouldn't be. Marco is smart. I like that about him, so why do I suppose he doesn't suspect something is amiss already? "I have money," like that is a good reason. He should think that something is wrong with me somewhere. Thankfully, he won't possibly imagine what.

Marco even smiled to himself as he waited for a website to load. He knew there was something up with Amanda. He didn't care.

She had money. So what? Money took one only so far. She didn't flaunt it, except in her choice of residence, and there were flashier houses in different boroughs of the city. It was a nice, security-conscious building. Considering her looks, that was a good thing.

Yes, she's sexy as hell, and smart enough to know that it's not exactly an asset. I wonder if she carries any weapons on her person. Well, she better, for her own sake. She looks good enough to eat. He sighed to himself. *Marco, if you even think of biting her…*

"Oh well," he said aloud. He stood, walked to the closet, and opened it.

There, on the floor, was his personal sword.

Amanda isn't the only one who collects weapons. Though I doubt she has ever had occasion to use them, like I have. He glanced back at the computer. It had fully loaded the website on red blood cells.

The coming weekend would be interesting.

Chapter 3:

Journey Into Brooklyn

November 4th

The day had gone well. Very well.

So well Amanda started to worry.

She met Marco at the Museum of Natural History, which he referred to rather snobbishly as "the Museum." He waited for her in the underground entrance to the museum via the subway when she arrived, though he came by car earlier.

Over the course of the day, they walked through each exhibit of the Museum. Together, they bounced back and forth over various and sundry areas of expertise. He apparently knew more about various types of weapons than anyone had a right to at his age, and she knew a little bit about everything else.

"Most knives," he said, staring at one stone-age knife, "are easy to defend against. Relatively. They're more reliable, and harder to defend against than guns, but easy to deal with if you know what you're doing."

Amanda smiled. He was almost cute with the way he was just so…blunt. It wasn't boasting. It wasn't a brag. It was just how reality was.

"Where did you learn this?"

"Out on Long Island, believe it or not. You ever hear about Krav Maga?"

"Yes, I have. Created for Israelis, right?"

"The Israeli Defense Force, you mean?" He nodded. "It's supposed to be simple and quick, effective, but not at all complicated. It's easier for me than for most people."

"Because of your three-dimensional chess?"

"Exactly. I use it in fencing, close combat, and sometimes conversations. It helps for when I want to talk people into doing things they don't want to do to start with. I can't threaten *everybody*, after all."

"*Really?*" she teased. "I must try to threaten *you* one of these days. Where did you learn this?"

"Like I said, Long Island. You'd be surprised how well it all works. I mean, hell, strangle me."

She paused, wondering if he was serious. Most of the crowd moved by, not even paying attention to them. Well, they weren't paying attention to Marco. They all paid attention to her, whether she wanted them to or not.

Amanda humored him and put her hands on his neck. She even pushed a little, stepping forward. He shot his right arm straight up, pressing it against his ear, trapping her left hand between his neck and his bicep. At the same time, he stepped back, and planted his left foot, stopping all backwards motion. Marco twisted, breaking the grip she had on his neck. Amanda's left hand bent backwards, still caught between his neck and arm. He then bent at the knees, almost in a squat, dropping his weight, and pulled her forward. He brought his elbow down like it was part of a hammer elbow, sweeping both of her arms down and into the waiting grip of his left hand. The left hand trapped both of her arms against his chest. Marco's right elbow swung up, and he easily jabbed it towards her chin in a slow motion side elbow, and then segued into a side hammer blow that only patted her cheek.

His left hand held her against him, her hands on his chest, their bodies close together, and their faces not eight inches apart. His expression finally changed. Marco's smile was wide, his eyes were bright, and that may have been one of the biggest displays of emotion she had ever seen from him. It was less about the simulated violence, and more about the sheer joy of teaching. He liked demonstrating something for her.

He was so happy about it, she didn't have the heart to tell him she was already an expert in Krav Maga, and could probably hurt him, if she had to.

"You know," she whispered. "At this range, I could possibly bite you."

Marco upgraded to a full grin. "Promises, promises." They had obviously lingered too long when other people around them started to give them strange looks. He let go of her, and she reluctantly pulled away.

"Funny that all of it was invented by a short, squat fellow with a police background in Eastern Europe," he said casually, heading back into encyclopedia territory as though nothing happened. "Can you imagine trying to train those fresh recruits? They had no background at all but were forced by circumstance to stand out in the hot sun, and burning desert, trying to figure out what this guy was trying to tell them. *Strike. Strike! Strike!* All the time wondering just how bad it was really going to get."

Marco fell into a wistful look, almost as though he were recalling a distant memory.

"Recalling your youth?" she teased.

Marco shook his head. "Nah, thinking of another good memory. Come on, the dinosaurs are this way."

Amanda watched him walk away with long, brisk strides. Without even thinking about it, she said something that made Marco come to a dead stop.

"Would you like to show me your neighborhood?"

Marco jerked and pivoted and blinked. "The last thing I'd want to inflict on you is Brooklyn."

"I would like to see where you come from," Amanda said.

"I come from the Twilight Zone, but if you insist…"

A quick car ride later—Marco insisted that the trains were nice, but he had already taken advantage of the alternate side of the street parking rules for the day— they had already moved on to their next stop.

"This is an interesting place," Amanda said, looking through an area of Brooklyn where it seemed like the property values could have improved drastically if they just invested some money in upkeep. It was just off of Manhattan Avenue, but she thought it looked nothing like Manhattan. The streets were dark, the residences were interlinked, and the local idea of a doorway must have come from designers who forgot to plan for a door, and just pounded one into the wall, and then installed one of metal and steel bars.

"I know people here. You wanted to see, didn't you?" he asked her. Marco knocked on the door once, then twice, and then kicked the door in with a loud metallic gong.

The place looked unfinished, with exposed brick face. However, it was clean, and relatively neat and tidy. The furniture was obviously secondhand, but serviceable. The only complaint was the sporadic lighting.

Marco waved her through. "After you."

"You do not need an invitation?" she teased, remembering the first time he was at her place.

His amused smile flickered a little wider for a second.

"I've been invited in before. They haven't been smart enough to revoke the invite."

"Who the hell?" Someone stepped out into the front room, a short, sturdy fellow, bald with a tattoo of a green Chinese water dragon tattooed on the back of his scalp. "Marco, don't you call first?"

"Zeng, honestly," Marco drawled, "you should know me better by now. Amanda Colt, Zeng Nyugen, head of a gang, believe it or not. The Dragons."

She shot him a sidelong look that clearly asked him if he was serious. He nodded. "Just think of them as my minions." Marco looked back to Zeng. "You're not hanging out with your lesser half?"

A tall Hispanic fellow stepped out behind Zeng. "Who's the chica?"

Marco's eyes narrowed, and his smile widened slowly. Amanda felt the temperature drop several degrees, and it looked like her friend was about to turn the newcomer into lunch. "The lady's name is Amanda Colt. She will be treated as such. Señor Hector Vega, head of the glorified street gang *Los Tigres*."

Now Amanda had to work hard on maintaining her poker face. "Tigers and Dragons…"

"As in Crouching and Hiding, yes," Marco said with a nod, his humor obviously drained as he stared at Vega. Vega raised his hands and took a step back, almost a sign of submission she had seen in wolves. "No offense, Marco."

"Good." Marco's eternal smile returned, and he turned back to Amanda. "Before you ask, yes, they did watch *West Side Story* growing up, and too many other bad films from the seventies. They have their pretenses, and I indulge them."

Zeng sniffed. "Come on, man. Why you have to be like that?"

"Because I remember how we all met. Don't you?" His eyes flicked back to Amanda, less tense. "That's a long story."

"So, Marco," Vega said, "she your new girlfriend?"

"She is a lady, and she is a friend. That is the extent of it. Take a picture, if you like, Zeng, it will last longer."

"Hey, man, I meant no offense—"

"I mean it literally. Take a photo, pass it around to everyone. If she's seen, she is to be helped in any way she requires. You will not try to pick her up, you will not do anything stupid around her. You will simply be perfect gentlemen whenever she is around. Period. Understood?"

Amanda smiled. *How sweet, I think this is his way of being chivalrous. The feudal lord commanding his serfs. Perfectly medieval. I wonder what comes next?*

He nodded to them both when they had each taken one

picture apiece, and then sent a quick text message to the others in their gangs.

As the two of them walked out, Amanda asked, "What was that all about?"

"You asked to see where I come from. They're a part of it, whether they like it or not." Marco shrugged. "Not to mention that if you're going to be sticking around for a while, and coming through Brooklyn, then you're going to be glad you have a *carte blanche* from those yo-yos. They're mostly harmless, but a large group of young males with a woman like you…well, I prefer to be safe."

She smiled. "You think I cannot take care of myself?"

"I'm sure you can, but wouldn't avoiding complications be easier on everyone?"

"If you say so. Where to next?"

"Welcome to beautiful downtown Greenpoint—or, as the locals have called it for the last seventy years, Greenpernt." Marco gestured out over the water of the East River, at the section called Turtle Bay. Across the bay was the United Nations, along with the rest of the New York skyline. "Despite all of the grief Brooklynites receive, there are some advantages to the area. Some nice sights. Ignore most of the rumors of mafia activity. We haven't had those sorts of problems since at least the eighties. Not around here, anyway."

Amanda gave a deep, happy sigh as she looped his left arm with her right and brought them closer together. He was nice and warm, and not so rock hard with muscle that he was uncomfortable to hold onto. She leaned her head on his shoulder. "Thank you, Marco. It has been quite some time since I have gone out and enjoyed myself."

"My pleasure, madam. I must say that I've enjoyed it,

too."

Amanda could feel his heart pumping harder. Was it merely her proximity, or was he intending to do something about it?

And how do I feel about it?

"Yo, dude, your money and your girlfriend."

Marco wheeled right as Amanda turned left. There were four men, and with a quick sweep of her eyes, Amanda caught a glimpse of four knives.

"I am single," she said. She looked over the four of them. "But guidos like you are not what I enjoy playing with. So...go...away."

"You're not grunting enough," Marco said, his own eyes keeping track of the two on his left. "You also need to use phrases and quotes from Pacino and DeNiro movies."

Guido Number One sneered. "Let's start with some money."

"Let's start with giving you a higher education," Marco said easily. "We'll talk after that. I don't speak Guido."

"That's it!" the knife guy took a step forward, raising his knife.

Suddenly, Amanda was in front of Marco, taking the knife to the stomach.

The knife wound was all the way to the hilt and lodged deep in Amanda's gut. He quickly diagnosed it as fatal without immediate medical attention—by immediate, he meant *right this minute, damnit.*

Marco took a step forward, ready to hold the knife in Amanda's stomach before it was pulled out and left the wound open.

Doing that took his attention off of the other two losers behind him. One grabbed him by the shoulder and spun him around. Marco blocked with both arms as the attacker swung a knife straight for his guts.

Marco met the wrist of the knife hand with the blade of his forearm. His other arm came around in a roundhouse punch into the attacker's face. The fist clamped down onto the same shoulder as the arm holding the knife. The arm that blocked the initial strike came up and around, wrapping the arm up in Marco's own—the wrist was caught between forearm and bicep. Holding him by both points, Marco drove his foot straight up into the attacker's groin, driving his genitals into his abdomen. He twisted his entire body around, bringing the thug with him, putting his body between him and the next attacker. He snapped the arm with a sharp rotation of his body, grabbing the knife as it fell.

The other guy tried to leap over his comrade. Marco sidestepped the blade, and the attacker tripped over the disabled knifeman. Before he could get off the concrete, Marco stomped down on the back of his head, bouncing it off of the sidewalk.

Marco spun around, ready to dispose of the other two and get Amanda to a hospital, when he stopped in his tracks. Amanda had already disposed of one of them, and was disposing of the other, her mouth clamped down on his throat. A trickle of blood ran down the man's neck.

"What the—?" This was the only reaction he could manage before Amanda whirled on him too.

Everything went black.

When Marco Catalano awoke, he had some serious issues. Being bound and gagged wasn't that bad. He could handle that. The problem was that the knots were well tied all around. That was the annoying part.

Granted, it would have been easier if he was in a room, held hostage in a building. Unfortunately, he was on a roof with no visible access, short of climbing the side of the building. That was common with older buildings in Brooklyn, built before roof access was required so repairmen could deal with the HVAC systems.

That was disturbing.

Marco replayed the final images before the world went black. The conclusions to be reached were not encouraging. He rolled over from his shoulder to his back. Sitting on the edge of the roof was Amanda, her nice sweater ruined with dark red stains and a hole in the stomach. If he didn't know better, he would have concluded she was crying. It was hard to tell in the dark.

"You're awake," she said flatly. "Good. We need to talk."

Chapter 4:

Dating Sucks

November 4th, On a rooftop in Greenpoint

A manda Colt was crying.

She couldn't help it, really. The horror of that night's events had nothing to do with her being stabbed, or Marco Catalano's somewhat savage counters on two of their attackers, or that she had attacked two of the thugs, sucked their blood, and even bit Marco while nearly feral.

The most horrific part of it was that the night had been going so *well.*

Twenty years. She'd been alone for twenty years, not counting the men who had spent more time trying to get into her pants rather than trying to get to know her. She hadn't exactly been a social butterfly for the previous decades *before* that, either.

Amanda faked "normal" so very well. The sunscreen let her extend her mobility by hours, at dusk and at dawn. Then she met Marco.

He was impressive. She tried to remember the last person who had such a wide variety of interests. When he started discussing historical events, she actually thought he had been there. Marco had intense focus, and an inability to care what others thought of him. He even made certain to stay in the shade when they were together, noticing her suntan lotion. He had been considerate of her the whole time.

Mind "like a computer" or not, he could anticipate her to such an extent that not even her vampire reflexes were able to sneak past his defenses.

In fencing…Of course in fencing…

Amanda, do you even believe that? Not really.

Also, he actually *cared* about what she *thought*. The last time she had discovered someone like that, he was a Soviet spy, and she had to eat him.

Now so much work, so much effort, had all been undone by two muggers. She had even been tempted to tell Marco, to explain to him what she was, and how that differed from all of the vampire stuff the culture was subjected to. She'd been so tempted.

Now what would he do? Report her? He had his friends take a picture of her. He could send that to anyone he liked. He could easily blow her cover as a vampire by posting her picture online. Facebook. YouTube. The Internet would not be her friend.

Things could only get worse from there.

Amanda heard Marco's heartbeat start to accelerate. He woke up. Amanda dried her eyes. She didn't have much makeup on, but there would be enough to streak. She hated that she had to use a digital web camera to apply makeup, but mirrors were sort of out of the question for her.

"You're awake," she said flatly. "Good. We need to talk."

Marco's extended silence spoke volumes, mostly a thousand decibels of "no kidding!"

Amanda cocked her head, studying him a moment, much like during their normal conversations. "You are not having the overreaction that I expected."

"O-r-re-a-on?" he muttered through his gag.

That was easy to expand into an entire thought: *Is there a way to overreact to this sort of thing?*

She nodded. "*Da*, I suppose you are right."

Marco sighed in irritation, then rubbed his face against the roof, trying to get the tape off of his mouth. Amanda approached him.

"Stop that. I will get it if you promise not to bite."

Marco looked at her in…his eyes read irritation, though she would have sworn that he was still smiling beneath the tape.

She smiled awkwardly and gave a little shrug. "Poor choice of words."

When she pulled the tape off of his mouth, Marco's first words were, "You wouldn't have caught me if I were aware that you were a vampire. You cheated."

Amanda was startled this time. This was *not* the response she had expected. "That is it? Your complaint is playing fair?"

"I've tried to not brag, but, while I am a little crazy, I'm *genius-level* crazy. I'm smarter than Wile E. Coyote, and I can make my own ACME devices from scratch." He rolled on the roof so he could get himself into a sitting position. "I've come to the conclusion that you're not going to eat me. You've had plenty of chances before now, but you chose to subdue me only after I noticed you eating your attacker. I figure I'm safe, unless you've decided that knowing is enough to get me killed. If that were the case, though, I think I'd be dead already. So, if the remaining discussion consists of whether or not I could keep your secret, my reply is: who would I tell?"

Amanda stared in wonder for a moment. His voice was calm and matter-of-fact. His manner was more annoyed than frightened. In fact, there was no fear in his voice at all. He wasn't scared. His heartbeat hardly increased since he regained consciousness.

"You are remarkably calm."

Marco scoffed. "Do you know what a secondary sociopath is?"

"Sociopath under certain conditions, like natural disasters and soccer games."

"Right. I've always suspected I'm some flavor of sociopath, which explains a lot." He looked around at their surroundings. "Now, I can be untied, and we can have this conversation somewhere else, or you can let me sleep. I'll find my way down in the morning."

Amanda nodded and sat back at the edge of the roof.

"Pull on the ropes. Hard."

Marco did, as hard as possible. The ropes snapped. He pulled his hands in front of him, staring at his former bonds as they dangled from his wrists. The bonds were the thick rope one would find on boats.

"That's a cute trick," Marco muttered. He looked up at her. "You better not have turned me into a vampire while I was sleeping, otherwise, we really *will* have to have a talk. Possibly with sharp objects."

"I promise, you can work on your tan in the morning."

He held up his hands, palms towards him. "Like I ever tanned well in the first place."

"This is true. But *you* have the option."

Marco stood, dusted himself off, and stuck his hands in his pockets. He studied Amanda for a long moment and frowned thoughtfully. "You have any thoughts on getting us the hell down from here?"

Amanda nodded, stepped forward, and then hugged him. He was about to comment when he saw the world blur, and felt himself falling, as though from one landing to the floor a few steps below him. It took a split second, but they were back on the street.

Marco blinked. "You should be grateful that this area has yet to catch up to a video camera on every corner."

"They do not catch me," she said into his chest. "I am too fast for them."

"Good to know."

"Mm-hmm." She nodded, again while hugging him. She could feel his warmth, his solid body. He was so very real. So alive. She could feel his heart beat against her cheek, the nice, steady rhythm.

His amused smile turned wry. "Either we should each take a step back, or we should start making out. I'm up for either."

Amanda not only released him, but she burst back so fast, she was nearly two meters away in an eye blink. She would have blushed if she didn't have such tight control over her own circulatory system.

He glanced at her for a long moment, and then he sighed. His amused smile turned tired. "May I make a suggestion? I'm going to go home and get some sleep. I don't think you're going to want to have this conversation right now with me half cranky, and late getting home. If I'm too much later, my parents will suspect that we're actually dating. I wouldn't want them to get the wrong idea. Neither would you."

She nodded slowly. "We will talk tomorrow then."

"Do I have to wait for the evening, or are you up in the morning?"

She allowed herself a smile. "Do not sleep too late. You may want to have breakfast first. Be careful about patting, hitting, or slapping anyone on the back. You might jar something."

He raised a brow. "Really? This should be interesting."

"*Da.* It should."

Marco was about to turn, but paused, keeping an eye on her. "By the way—you didn't *let* me win in all those fencing matches, did you?"

"*That* is what you are worried about? I am a vampire, who has bitten you, yet you worry about whether *I let you win?*"

"I worry about little," Marco answered. "We would need to refight every duel we ever had."

She shook her head, a smile tugging at her lips. "I don't let anyone win. Ever. We had draws. You are good."

Marco's eyes flashed wildly, and he gave her a broad, almost manic grin. "Oh, Miss Amanda Colt, I am very good."

As Marco Catalano drove home, he replayed the last conversation with Amanda in his head. It felt all wrong. When he had stared into her eyes, he had noted faint streaks of mascara down her cheeks. The tracks were only visible because she hugged him so close after jumping off the roof. She apparently spent some time cleaning it off, but she hadn't gotten all of it.

The odd thing, in retrospect, was she was quite warm for a vampire. He had been acutely aware of several sensations: her feel, her scent, all of which were comfortably close—though in that situation, enjoying her proximity would have been a *really, bad, idea.*

Marco pulled up to a stop light, and internally winced. *Did I leap to "let's be friends" so I could protect her from me, or so I could protect myself from the same heartbreak Lily gave me?*

He closed his eyes tightly and tried not to think about that evening eight months ago. The true horror of it had not come with the grimy knife, or with the blood, or the gore. Those had only lasted minutes. The weeks after, however; that was a true horror show. Those were weeks he would give nearly anything to forget.

There was a honk behind him. Marco needed to start moving. The light was green.

Marco made it home, to the brownstone where his family resided, and moved inside. He was surprised at the light on in the living room.

Doctor Robert Catalano was slender, stopping a few pounds before "thin" could settle in. His short hair had once been a solid black but was now heavily salted. His features were sharp, and the only hint of the Italian in him was his generally dark coloring—coloring which had skipped Marco entirely. "It's not yet midnight, you sure you're not early?"

"You'd be surprised," Marco answered his father. The doctor closed his book and patiently waited for his son to elaborate on the evening.

Marco stood there and shrugged. "It went well." Marco couldn't think of anything else to add to that really, except one phrase that would encapsulate the evening. "But we're just friends."

"Oh, that phrase," the doctor sighed. "Okay. Sorry. High school and no dating I can understand. College, though?"

Marco grimaced. "Dad, I did date, remember? Walesia? Lily? Raquel?"

Robert leveled a gaze at him filled with unleashed sarcasm. "One dumped you when you wouldn't sleep with her. Another tried to slip you something so that you would. Then that thing with Lily…"

Marco shook his head, trying not to think about it. "She couldn't handle it, Dad, that's all. Making her put up with it would have been—"

"At least a courtesy," his father interrupted. "I'm assuming it wasn't a walk in the park for you either."

Marco sighed. "It's over, I've moved on. Now, may I ask a question?"

"Sure, ask away."

Wow, this is going to be such a jump in conversation, it's not even going to be funny. "You have any thoughts on vampires?"

Doctor Catalano didn't even blink. "Rabies."

"Rabies?"

"Think about it," the doctor said, slipping into lecture mode. "The symptoms: hydrophobia, fear of water, holy or otherwise. The dislike of bright lights, which would include the sun and the reflected glare of a mirror. They also tend to bite, and I think strong odors, like garlic, hit them hard."

Marco nodded. That at least all made a certain kind of sense. "And the crosses? The stakes?"

"Religious artifacts have been dragged into superstition forever. Stakes were supposed to pin them in their graves, but, really, if you ram something through anybody's heart, they'll stay dead. The ability to transform, their advanced speed and strength get thrown in as part of any other fairy tale. Why the curiosity? You usually dislike vampire tales because of how poorly they stay coherent."

Marco shrugged. "It just came up tonight, that's all."

Robert Catalano smiled broadly. "So, no biting was involved?"

Marco did his best to blush. He thought it worked. "There may have been."

"Just friends, huh?"

"Believe it or not, yes."

"Well, why don't you bring this 'just friend" around sometime?"

"Be happy to," Marco said with a straight face. *As long as she doesn't eat me in the morning.*

Amanda Colt walked into her apartment and sighed. Why him? Decades of being alone without much in the way of any company, all of the people in her path over the years, she got someone who, well, someone who was not normal, whatever normal was supposed to be. No matter how she fed, she was still a predator. He still smelled like food. As he noted, he was a genius, he would have some sense of that.

Hell, he saw Amanda *eating* her attacker.

A sociopath, he said. Normally, a human predator. Somehow, he didn't seem the type. A hunter? A stalker of people? No, that was her job.

Amanda thought of Marco and wondered, *What will morning bring; his friendship or his enmity? Which would be worse?*

If he saw her as his enemy, he seemed the type to hold a grudge. He knew where she lived. He knew where she went with her evenings. He knew enough to be deadly. If he turned his single mindedness to her destruction, she would need a backup plan. She had one for years, but maybe a new one would be required to deal with Marco Catalano.

Chapter 5:

Vampires And Philosophy

November 5th

At ten the next morning, Marco stood at the bottom step leading into Amanda's apartment building. She was on the east side of Manhattan, in the mid-70s. She was so far east that the next stop was York Avenue, and right after that was the East River.

Marco smoothed down his shirt, feeling the cross from the rosary around his neck, and gliding his fingers along the butt of a knife handle—a wooden knife he had quickly modified that morning after breakfast. It had originally been a simple letter opener, a bit of sharpening did wonders.

He stood there, pondering what he should do next. Suggest they have this talk inside of a church? Nah, that would be tacky, and since she didn't eat him last night, or any time before then, it would be a serious overreaction.

Then again, it's not like we were dealing honestly before. If this doesn't go well, I will need a backup plan.

The door to the apartment building opened. Amanda Colt stood there, her red-gold hair in a ponytail. "Hello."

He gave her a little finger wave. "Hi."

"Would you like to come in?"

"I'm good here," Marco said, "in the daylight."

She smiled slightly. "Sunlight" was such a flexible term in

the city – especially since her street was narrow enough that parked cars turned it into a one-way road, and the buildings across from her apartment made it a valley of shadow. "You are so certain you would be safe?"

"I rarely see you before sundown on sunny days," Marco stated in a manner that reminded her of Sherlock Holmes, "and usually under moderate cloud cover. That may or may not include shade from buildings. I would have thought of it sooner if I thought that 'vampire' was an option."

"For a time, I thought that of you as well. I mean that you were a vampire."

"Really? You can't tell the difference?"

"There is always the possibility that you are older than you look and could camouflage it. It is not impossible. And you felt so much older. It is difficult when I smell you as possible food, but it feels like I should know you as one of my own."

"Well, I guess being borderline medieval has some advantages. But, where are my manners?" He offered her his hand to shake, she took it.

She looked down, and saw that Marco had palmed a crucifix, and now their hands both covered it. She looked back at his face. His only reaction was to arch a brow. He withdrew his hand, tucked the cross away, and stepped across the apartment building threshold.

"Now, I think," Marco stated, "we should have a serious talk."

Marco entered the apartment first this time, not hesitating, and went straight to the wall of her "family heirlooms" behind the television. The entire apartment seemed like a new entity, now that he knew just a little more about her background. Viewing the room with new eyes drew him to those first.

He stood next to that part of the wall like a showgirl on a game show and waved at the collection. "Let me guess, family heirlooms that you yourself collected?"

Amanda nodded, only mildly apprehensive over where this was going.

He motioned around the apartment itself. "You 'have money.' Investments are good, obviously, when you're investing for a long haul of at least a few decades. What did you do? Get in on the ground floor of IBM? Apple? Microsoft?"

"Yes," she said simply. "AT&T as well, before it was broken up."

That means she had stock in the ground floor of most national phone companies. Yeesh. "You have no family remaining because the rest weren't vampires, I assume. That makes sense. You are not affected by crosses, so I'm concluding that there's a loophole in there somewhere."

"Are you done?" she asked.

Marco frowned, looked around, thought a moment, then nodded.

"Then sit."

Marco took up a position on the couch, with Amanda taking the armchair. "You know St. Thomas Aquinas."

"Narrow that down a little, would you? He's only written about a few dozen feet of shelf space worth of books, and that's with the small-print edition."

"His thoughts on Christ after He died?"

Marco took a moment to think it over. "Oh, you mean Aquinas on the effects of resurrection?" he asked, as though he had recollected a famous sports game, or a popular black and-white film. "I know of it. Aquinas had a theory that Adam and Eve would have had total control over their physical form. Aquinas even patterned what Jesus must have been like post-resurrection. Essentially, after Jesus" —he bowed his head slightly at the name— "Himself came back from the dead, He could rearrange the molecules of His body and walk through the spaces between molecules of a wall, disappear into thin air…"

He drifted off slightly, pondering the ramifications of such abilities in relation to Amanda's living impairment.

"If they could do that, maybe they would be able to turn into mist or a bat, a dog perhaps?"

Amanda nodded. "You understand. After resurrection, souls are linked with bodies, so there is such tight control, at least in theory. With us, with vampires, it is similar. Imagine vampires as an imperfect after-death living." She paused and chuckled, shaking her head. "We did not quite die, but we are not quite alive. We have *elements* of resurrection. We have certain abilities. A vampire begins first as a blank slate, and we choose how we act from then on.

Think of it like the dark side. Our actions become part of us. Literally."

Marco thought through the implications. "No matter how badly you screw up, the body and soul will stay united. So, actions which affect your soul impacts your body as well."

She nodded. "Sin affects us vampires on a *physical* level."

"It affects normal people too. Gluttony makes us fat, wrath does things to blood pressure, lust–"

Amanda held up a hand to stop him. "Let me rephrase. Our bodies are the picture of Dorian Gray— only the stains of *all* our sins appear on our bodies, *as well as* our souls. God purges sin. For those who have committed large, egregious, unrepentant sins…let's just say it does not go together well with religious artifacts. With venial sins, however, mixed with contrition, religious artifacts do not necessarily have an effect on us that we can feel."

Marco put up his hands in a T formation, for a time out.

"Okay, hold on, let me process this. The more actions you commit, good or bad, the more you are formed as a vampire. These actions dictate the kind of vampire you are, both in terms of looks, power, abilities, and whether or not you can get fried by a crucifix. The better or worse you become–the more you are formed–the closer your souls become linked to your bodies. The more good or ill you commit, the more powerful you become, one way or another."

She nodded. "If I were evil, and ate someone on purpose, your rosary against my skin would not be pretty, but I would still be stronger than when I first became a vampire. Press it on the skin of some vampires for three seconds, there's scarring. Press it on them for nine seconds, they scar all over. Twelve seconds, you are facing a pile of ash."

"Just crosses?"

A smile flickered across her face. "He uses anything, and I mean anything—wafers, crosses, Torahs. He made the world, sustains it and sets rules, and meddles. Not a lot, just enough."

Marco frowned, trying to connect the puzzle pieces about the more secular rules. The sunlight was still effective, apparently, for holding back vampires. If they were an "imperfect resurrection," though, what would kill them?

"So, I'm guessing everything I know about vampires is wrong?"

Amanda shook her head. "No, everything you know about evil vampires is right, for the more… demonic vampires, shall we say? They react to all the same things that Dracula the novel character reacts to. God apparently set rules to nature, and vampires, though unnatural, have similar rules. The more evil a vampire commits, the more mobility he sacrifices for the power. An evil vampire needs to be invited in, cannot be around religious artifacts, and becomes more physically deformed the deeper they go into sin."

"Huh," Marco muttered. "*Evil* vampire. Always thought that was redundant, like 'evil lawyer.' So, the 'good' vampires are therefore immortal?"

Amanda shrugged. "Not quite. We can be killed by starvation, decapitation, dismemberment, fire, as well as sunlight and wooden stakes to the heart." She shrugged slightly. "As I said, we are *im*perfect resurrections. Though, technically, you could say that it is imperfect *death*. For blood, however, all we need is a pint a day, sometimes less, and blood banks are public spaces, after all."

"If all you need is a pint a day…?" Marco deliberately trailed off, hoping she would fill in the blanks of questions he didn't want to try asking.

"Power goes to some heads, and some have seen too many vampire flicks and they go a little crazy," she answered, pronouncing the word "*cray-zee*." She crossed her legs and stretched out like a cat, arching her back and thrusting her chest out a bit before relaxing. "Think serial killers: they are formed by their actions, and choices. *Da,* some were abused as children, but they *choose* to deal with it by killing. True with vampires, but more so. Those who were afraid to kill in life because of the consequences no longer fear them. Some choose morality, and some choose *Lord of the Flies,* where society and morality do not apply."

"Of course, because people are generally goldfish," Marco said with enough sarcasm to melt glass. "I should probably ask, and now is a little late to be asking: What about mind control and such? Telepathy?"

"It happens. Half of vampires have various levels of it." As the conversation went on, her accent thickened slightly in an almost melodic fashion. "Stronger vampires are, obviously, better at mental powers. Sometimes it just requires someone of intelligence."

Marco winced. *That would be bad.* "Any defenses?"

Amanda gave a Gallic wave of her hand. "It is mostly enough to just know about the vampire's ability. Even the strongest vampire cannot do anything unless they have absolute concentration. They need subtlety, some, or at least only one target. It is not a combat weapon."

"That's good." He looked over her body. "Let me guess, a heavily clouded day and lots of SPF50 sunblock keeps you from frying?"

"And I am…good?" she said, as though questioning her own moral standing in the universe.

"So you don't fry as easily," he concluded.

She nodded. "It provides resistance. The farther along on the good and evil spectrum, it is harder to kill us in general, but we tend to keep a low profile. Even exceptionally evil vampires do not want people hunting them with thermal scopes, seeing if we have a few degrees difference here and there. Thankfully, most people know of ways to restrain evil vampires. The more evil, the more restrictions come on them. Some people have no problems exchanging freedom of movement for more power."

Marco thought back to the meeting yesterday with his gang leaders. It was a private house, and she didn't wait for an invite before stepping in. "Which is why you could follow me into a private residence? You're 'good,' therefore you don't need an invite?"

"Precisely."

Marco leaned back into the couch and forced himself to relax. Now that she was no longer a threat, her looks were again intoxicating, her accent hypnotizing. As she opened up to him, letting him in on her deeper, darker secrets, she became more even attractive. He forced himself to take a mental step back. "Hmm. It seems like you have a tightly regulated little community, when even the bad guys play by certain rules."

"Except for Charlotte."

"Charlotte?"

"*Da.* Charlotte Harris, a trucker vamp. She liked truck stops because, well, she called them meals on wheels."

"Is that so?"

Amanda smiled. "She could exsanguinate a trucker while giving him a well, let us say, she called it a 'suck and suck.' She drained a four-hundred-pound trucker once and nearly died from indigestion."

"I guess you folks give some really major hickeys."

She smiled. "Ah, yes, James."

What? "James?"

"James Hickey, Irish representative to Romania in the 1920s," she said with a sly smile. "Where do you think the term came from, anyway? Your turn."

"My turn what?"

"You have questions to answer, Marco."

Not Lily. Not Lily. Not Lily, Marco thought frantically as he kept his outward composure. "Such as?" he drawled.

"You nearly killed one of our attackers last night," Amanda said. "I only nibbled on them a little. You did…more damage."

"As I said," he answered quickly, "I take Krav Maga." He cleared his throat and leaned forward. Marco was eager to deflect her curiosity, hoping to dodge anything that might touch on that part of his past. "Actually, I have another question: why did you bite me, and why can I break ropes with a tug of my arms?"

"I bit you because I had been stabbed. Feeding heals me. You were there, and I know what I am doing. The strength is a side effect. Now, my question."

Marco glanced at his watch and thought a moment. "You have your SPF 5000? I think we need to go for a walk. We're heading into Brooklyn."

A quick train ride later, Amanda and Marco were at a hospital. Amanda had followed Marco at a distance, dashing from shadow to shadow. He moved as quickly as he could without attracting attention from the local police. This was Brooklyn, running looked suspicious.

He opened the door to the hospital, and she appeared at his side. They both moved into the building as though nothing strange had happened.

"You are adapting to me quickly," she said, coming up alongside him.

"Evolve or die. It's sort of like living in Brooklyn. Only the strong survive." He pointed. "This way."

She made the turn with him, wondering what was going on. She followed him as he approached a tall, thin fellow in a doctor's coat. The man glanced his way, his eyes flicking to her, and he gave a small smile.

"Marco, that was fast. Is there something I should know?"

Marco nodded easily. "You know how I like to get things done early. The last thing I need is to hold onto another item on my checklist."

"Indeed." The older fellow stepped forward and offered Amanda his hand. "Doctor Robert Catalano. Ms. Colt?"

"*Da.* You are his father?"

Doctor Catalano smiled. "That's what his mother tells me." He looked over the two of them. They weren't too close together, they weren't touching. They weren't even looking at each other, but both at him. "Nice to meet you. Marco's not annoying you too badly, is he?"

"If I were annoyed," she said plainly, "I would bite him."

With a complete deadpan expression, and flat monotone, Doctor Catalano said, "Kinky." He looked around the floor. "I suppose I have a few minutes to spare the both of you."

"Just her, for the moment," Marco interjected, already stepping away. "I need to find some of the usual suspects."

Doctor Catalano rolled his eyes. "Those boneheads? Try the coffee shop next door."

"Thanks." He touched Amanda on the arm. "Be back soon."

"Bye," she said, watching him as he wandered off.

"Don't worry," the doctor said, taking her lightly by the shoulder, out of the line of traffic. "He's a little energetic, but he always keeps his word."

Amanda looked off in the direction Marco darted down. "That is good to know."

"My son is quite interesting."

She looked up at him. "That is not encouraging."

A smile. "We're similar in our word choices, unfortunately. My bedside manner needs work. Possibly surgery." He waved her over as he started to move down the hall. "Come, let's make sure you aren't run over."

"Thank you." Amanda was aware of the people staring at her; some at her legs, others at her hair, or chest. "I am not comfortable with people, either."

"That would explain a few things—like Marco."

She maneuvered through the door he waved her to. Apparently, it was the break room. She took a seat, and he sat across from her. "How so?"

"He doesn't make an impression on normal people," his father said, "or he leaves too much of one. Possibly with a tire iron."

Amanda nodded. She didn't even need that explained. The people she had seen talk with him were few and far between.

Come to think of it, I don't think I've seen anyone else talk to him but me and those two gang fellows.

"What about his gang friends?"

The doctor snickered and sneered. "Those idiots? Please. They call themselves gangs, though they're more like the neighborhood watch. They don't make it official because that means they're real 'rebels.' They're harmless. Granted, they'll occasionally apprehend a suspect after he 'fell down.' Aside from that, well, I have to patch them up as much as I have to patch up anyone they're apprehending. They're just overgrown kids who are well organized."

"Oh? What does Marco have to do with them?"

"Who do you think did the organizing?"

"Oh?" she said again. "Did he leave me with you because you would talk about this?"

He shrugged. "Possibly. My son doesn't like to brag, and he thinks stating facts about himself is bragging."

She smiled shyly. "Last night, he said he was a genius. Doesn't sound like someone who doesn't like to brag."

"Really?" Doctor Catalano chuckled. "Well, usually, when he says that, he tends to do so in a Wile E. Coyote voice, so no one takes him seriously. Marco enjoys telling the people the truth as a joke. It makes it easier for people to swallow, or so he says. I think it makes it easier for him to actually say."

"Is that why he won't tell me where he learned to fight so…eagerly?" she said cautiously.

Doctor Catalano studied her. "You know about that?"

"One of his friends from the gangs played around with him last night," she lied deftly. Somehow, mentioning that Marco had taken a mugger, armed with a knife, and broke parts of him, didn't seem like a good idea. "He looks like he has had some practical experience, not just training."

"He better have. He was a subway commando for four years."

Amanda thought over the term for a moment. She remembered the students from Xavier High School were in the Junior Reserve Officer Training Corps. They were known as the Subway Commandos, wearing full uniform and officer's sword on the trains into and out of the city. "He went to Xavier?"

"Yup. Even has his own cavalry sword." Doctor Catalano's eyes flickered to the Keurig. "Coffee?"

"Sorry, but I do not drink… coffee."

"Good idea," he said as he rose, "I shouldn't either, but you have to stay awake somehow." He chuckled and filled a mug. "Given how late you and Marco were out last night, I'm surprised either one of you has a pulse."

Amanda merely smiled. "I am good for days at a time."

He raised his mug in her direction in a "cheers" motion. "You should try being a Physician Assistant. Endurance is always welcome."

"So I have heard from Marco. Why does he not want to be a doctor, like you?"

"Because he's smart?" The doctor laughed. "Please, PAs are more useful around here than doctors. Half of them think MD means Medical Divinity, and the other half, I suspect, want to kill each other. No, PA is a far better job. Nurses and doctors look down on them, no matter how smart they are, and therefore never see them as a threat. They're also the ones sent out to deal with the drug reps who visit doctor's offices; therefore, they're up on the latest drugs and techniques, since the doctors are always 'too busy.' Meaning Marco will be up on the cutting edge of available medical technology. That's not bad. A medical degree, lots of money, lots of time, less than half the debt, and Marco isn't patient enough to do med school with this as an option."

"But Xavier?" Amanda asked. "He wanted to be in the military?"

Marco's father laughed. "Actually, I think he wanted the sword and the uniform. The education he, mostly, gave himself. If he ever wanted to go into the military, he never mentioned it."

The vampire nodded slowly. That would be best. She couldn't imagine Marco surviving in a military command structure. Either they would break him, or he would break them. Though a discharge for insubordination could have been amusing, since his facility with logic and thought processes would do a lawyer proud.

"Funny thing," Doctor Catalano continued, "is that I

think the uniform got him all the attention. He had plenty of people gravitate towards him, mostly in public. Most of the people in high school weren't exactly part of his fan club."

Amanda cocked her head to one side. "His classmates did not like him? What about the fencing team?"

The doctor let out a sharp, barking laugh. "Oh! Yes, the fencing team. They found him so insufferable that they kicked him out his last year."

Amanda laughed. "Oh, God. They may do that in college, too."

"Oh yes. It gets better. He could only work with the instructor, and even he tired of dealing with Marco. Though they didn't mind inviting him back for tournaments."

"Oh, of *course* not," she said with proper sarcasm and cynicism.

"So, he had to go outside Xavier for friends. There was Lily, a collection of others, but it all fell apart last year."

"Who's Lily?"

Robert hesitated. "Oh. He hasn't told you? Reasonable."

He thought it over a moment. "I think I'll let him do that."

At that moment, appearing as though the name had conjured him, Marco opened the door to the lounge. "Let me do what?"

His father looked at him with a smile. "Oh, I'm just going to let you explain things to Amanda. You should have updated me about what you tell who, that way I don't need to perform a foot amputation from my mouth."

Marco's mouth bunched, processing the new data. "Um, okay."

"I know. The last thing you need is the old guy telling your girlfriend all about your dark and sinister past," Robert said jovially, rolling his eyes.

"We're not dating," Marco and Amanda said as one.

With a smile, Doctor Catalano stood. "Sorry, just hopeful. I should get back to rounds. We've got some odd stuff going on lately."

Marco cocked his head. "Really?"

"Yes. Strange even for Brooklyn. If I have to deal with more bite wounds, I'm going to go crazy."

The doctor's son kept a perfectly straight face. The only indication that it was anything of note was that his eyes flicked to Amanda. "Bites, huh? The usual allotment of noses and ears and such?"

"No. Throats and wrists, believe it or not. Some of these guys are so rabid that I'm considering getting the bite victims tests for actual rabies.'"

"Yes?" Amanda said. "That might be. Have you considered swabbing the wound tracks? If it's in the saliva, it might show up better that way."

"Possible. Usually, we tend to be too busy keeping the patient alive to worry about that, and by the time we're done, the amount of blood would probably wash anything away. These are some nasty, messy wounds. Anyway," he said, patting his son on the shoulder, "thanks for bringing her by, Marco. Maybe you should bring her to dinner. You know, as *friends*."

The doctor looked out the door, checking both directions of the hallway, and stepped out.

Chapter 6:

Anatomy Of A Vampire

Marco Catalano looked back to Amanda. "What was that about, when I came in?"

"Long story," Amanda said. "Maybe later. Was there something you wanted to show me? I assume that is why you left before."

Marco frowned in thought, doing the math on what just happened. "Well, I left because I wanted you and my father to have some alone time. That way he can grill you directly instead of through me."

Amanda shook her head. "He does not seem like an interrogator to me."

"'That' was just the first round. Every woman in my life is someone he wants to set me up with. He's afraid that if he doesn't, I'm going to become a hermit, so focused on a profession that I avoid having a life. I can't imagine where he gets these ideas, do you? Don't worry, I'll keep him as far away from the topic as I can."

"Why will you keep him from that topic?"

"Didn't we already have that conversation not long after we met? The 'let's be friends' talk? That was an agreement. I wasn't going to try and change your mind, and letting him try seems, I don't know, rude."

Amanda smiled. He didn't say that it was because I am a vampire, or that he didn't date predators, or that he wasn't interested, just that it would be rude. "Why do you think so?"

He blinked, and his mouth bunched again in confusion. "Because we already covered it. You accepted the terms. Bringing it up again after an agreement is just … rude. Frankly, now that I know your background, I can't imagine that you're into younger men. Now, come, let me show you where I've been."

Amanda followed him out the door, through a sea of patients, and into the lobby. Beyond the waiting rooms, there were the two men that Marco had introduced her to last night: Hector Vega, and his shorter colleague, Zeng Nyugen.

"Lizard, Pussy," Marco said, belittling the names of both of their gangs, "you remember Amanda from last night."

Hector Vega frowned. "We remember. Why?"

"She would like to know why I'm associating with degenerates like yourselves." Marco's smile touched his eyes a little brighter for a moment before he said,

"Or, maybe why proper degenerates like you are hanging out with a nutjob like me."

Vega smiled. Obviously, Marco was in one of the better moods, one where people won't be killed. "Oh, hey man, that's easy. You're good to us…"

"When you're not a psycho," Zeng added.

His compatriot nodded. "Yeah, that too."

Amanda looked from one to the other. "Just because he can fight?"

It was a leading question, she knew, especially since she had seen what Marco had done to his two combatants from the previous evening. It had hurt to look at the aftermath. He had broken bones without hesitation. If she hadn't dealt with the other two, or if she had really been in danger, she suspected that all four of them would be left on life support. Marco was not someone to get on the bad side of. That much was certain.

Vega and Zeng exchanged a look. They knew something but were obviously worried about triggering a "Hulk Smash" moment from Marco.

"They've seen me in action," Marco answered for them. "Tell her how we met."

Vega smiled. "Oh, he came upon some of our guys working over an idiot we found. When Marco… "

"—Inquired into their activities," Marco supplied.

"Um…sure. Our guys told him to screw off. It didn't

work."

"I only put the two of them on the ground."

Vega shot him a glare. "You broke one of their wrists."

Marco scoffed. "He didn't know how to fall. Not my fault. He broke his own wrist."

"You nearly let the drug dealer they had get away."

"Yes, but I bounced him off the alley walls a few times."

Vega sighed, and looked to Zeng, who nodded. "He instructed Hector's guys to bring him to their leader. One stayed with the dealer, and Hector's other guy thought he'd be funny and bring Marco to my headquarters."

Marco cleared his throat. "I made an impression."

"On Jimmy's face," Zeng complained.

"Oh, it's not like he had anything going for him anyway. At least his face has character now."

Zeng smiled at the vampire. "You see what his general attitude is."

"Yes," Amanda said, nodding. "History is rife with small groups of professional soldiers outmatching larger groups of superior numbers."

"Exactly. That's why I spent the next summer training them. I wanted them to at least be able to march in formation." Marco glanced at the hallway clock. It was two o'clock.

Amanda could almost see him doing the math: *"If sundown is five, and Amanda can go out in low light without becoming a crispy critter, we have about two, two and a half hours to kill indoors." Or something like that.*

Amanda leaned over, and asked, softly, "Are you their leader, or are you just for emergencies?"

"I'm *legitimate*," he replied. "My father takes care of their wounded, the local cops like *him*, and I work on that reputation because I've put in more hours here than some med students have in their years of rotation. There's a reason I'm here with you on a Sunday and not at home doing my five pounds of homework."

"Oh? I thought it was because you are a *genius*," she teased.

"PA programs fail out people who Harvard accepted. Smart is one thing; handling pressure is another. I'm good at handling pressure."

"And everyone else who gets in your way, it seems."

After several hours of Vega and Zeng cautiously telling Amanda about their times with Marco, with occasional commentary, they had to depart. By then, the sun was already sinking behind the horizon.

Marco asked her, "You good to go?"

She nodded. "*Da.*"

The two of them spent their time darting from shadow to shadow, putting enough space between them and the hospital. Marco wanted the next part of the conversation to be more private.

Marco stopped at an alley, leaning casually against the

wall. His smile was still there, and she was tempted to take it as a cue to relax.

I should know better by now, shouldn't I?

"I assume I should start with what I've already figured out," he said. "Some of it I knew before I met you, and some of it I've guessed since then."

"What is that?"

"Vampirism is a virus, transmitted through contact with fluids." He moved his hands apart in a motion that said *obviously.*

"We know this from all the 'create a vampire by an exchange of blood' myth. Therefore, it generally lives in the bloodstream. Only in the blood is there enough concentration of the virus for it to be transmitted into a new host. But, like any other virus, it comes out in the saliva as well. How much do you know about viruses?"

She shrugged. "I have a medical degree."

Marco stopped, blinked, and said, "How recent?"

"Twenty years old."

"Good enough, I suppose. Are you familiar with a minor paper—actually, a Philosophy dissertation—of Doctor John-Emery Konecsni, out of NYU, in the late sixties?"

She blinked and thought a moment. He pronounced the name 'co-ness-knee,' but it sounded wrong. "K-o-n-e-c-s-n-i?"

"That's the one."

"It is pronounced 'co-nyech-knee,' she told him. "It is Eastern European. I may have heard of it. I audited some of Sidney Hook's classes when he taught there. This Konecsni you mention, he was a student of Aquinas in a class of Secular Humanists, but I've heard of him, nothing more."

"Well," Marco continued, "I read parts of the dissertation. It's quite straightforward. If you follow

Aristotle's definition of life, part of the requirements for something to meet the threshold is that reproduction comes from using an organism's own parts. Humans create sperm and egg from their own matter, and the DNA itself is what makes us 'us.' But, since a virus duplicates itself like a Xerox machine copies paper, it does not give of itself, but uses materials from other cells to create duplicates."

Amanda could see where he was going. "You mean, viruses duplicate like vampires."

"Exactly. If you want to be rather technical, while a virus comes close to meeting Aristotle's definition of life, it's just on the threshold."

The vampire laughed aloud. "So, a virus is undead."

"Exactly. If a physical virus can be undead, then why not a metaphysical one?"

Amanda arched a brow, studying him a moment. She hadn't considered that he would give quite this much thought to it. But then, he over-thought fictional vampires, why not real ones? "Interesting way to put it. What makes you so certain, however, it can live in other fluids? ...that sounded better in my head."

Marco waved it away. "I know what you meant. Trust me, the number of jokes that go around biology classes about fluids aren't fit for polite company." He stopped a moment, looking over his shoulder down the street.

Amanda followed his gaze. With her enhanced vision, she could see clearly, all the way down the road. Two men with guns were backing out of a liquor store, with a third man in a car outside. It looked like the muggers were carrying bottles in plastic bags—she could make out several as Johnny Walker Blue, easily two-hundred-dollar bottles. Someone was smart enough to access the inventory from the back room.

Marco looked around as he pulled out a glove from his back pocket, slipping it on. "As for why I'm certain the vampire virus can live in fluids other than blood…" He walked into the middle of the street, stopping at a manhole. He reached down with the gloved hand and grabbed the cover.

With one hand, he lifted the hundred-pound manhole cover, took aim at the getaway car, and flung it like a Frisbee. The cover found its mark, smashing part of the undercarriage of the car on its way to slicing through the rear wheel. Marco turned back to her and said, "I think I just proved my point. The virus is symbiotic, isn't it? Unlike the parasitic nature of a normal virus, this does everything it can to keep its host *alive*. Since it comes out in the saliva, the virus *also* wants to make certain that the food stock doesn't run low. It acts like some viruses that influence the behavior of their hosts. One virus I've heard of can manipulate an ant to seek high altitude, because then, the ant can get eaten by the bird that the virus came from originally."

Amanda laughed, shaking her head. "Where do you *find* all of this?"

"I read a lot of medical trivia."

"That is putting it mildly."

"Yup." He moved closer to her, taking her hand in his naked one. "I can feel the pulse in your fingers, and the warmth of your body. You're not a corpse. You don't *need* to be. Then again, given that you have complete control over your body, you can maintain your heartbeat and breathing for as long as you like. Or shut them down." He held her hand still, looked deep into her amber eyes, and asked, "So, are you undead because you died, and are animated, or are you only undead because you're somewhere in the middle?"

"I would think that was obvious," she said, her voice at a whisper. "Comes with the vampire logo."

"Great. So you're a franchise?"

"After a fashion."

They stayed that way for a moment, for a reason neither one of them could comprehend. They didn't want to move, and saw no reason to, but equally saw no logical reason why they should be standing there.

Finally, a reason to move struck them; yelling from down the street, and sirens. Apparently, the cops had arrived. There was a cluster of three gunshot bursts, and a few loud *booms*.

Marco frowned and looked over his shoulder. The cops had brought out a shotgun, and the idiot muggers were apparently still interested in getting away.

"Morons."

The two of them both went to their right, picking a rock off of the sidewalk. They turned as one, arms cocked, rocks ready to throw. As one, they hurled the stones.

Marco's landed in the right shoulder of his shooter. Amanda's blow landed in the right side of hers. Both of them crumpled.

Amanda looked to Marco. "I think it is time for us to go."

"Couldn't agree with you more."

Five minutes later, they were two miles away, with Marco slowing down to catch his breath. He bent over, hands on his knees, and coughed. "Well, that was fun. Sorry, I'm a little slow."

Amanda smiled, patting him on the back. "Don't apologize. You're still alive. You can burn through the additional strength my bite gives you. So, do not rely on it, okay?"

"Gotcha." He glanced at the date on his watch. "Listen, can you eat? Real food, I mean?"

She nodded. "I can. As noted, I keep my body functions going—breath and heart and other things I do not strictly need. Eating keeps my body generating some of its own blood. It keeps me from getting too hungry. Why?"

Marco glanced up from the pavement, trying to catch her eye. "It's going to be Christmas in a few weeks. You object to hanging out with the family?"

The vampire was silent a moment. She couldn't remember the last time anyone had invited her to Christmas dinner… or anywhere, for that matter. "Why?"

"Well, there are more suicides during the holidays than there are at any other point in the year. I naturally assume that, after the first three dozen Christmases alone, it becomes tempting to walk out into the early morning sunlight and get a tan."

Amanda smiled at him. He was tired, and not even trying to put up a false front. There was no ulterior motive in him.

"Besides," he said, "we're the only friends we have."

Chapter 7:

Vampire Christmas

December 24th

Amanda Colt knocked on the door to the Brooklyn brownstone. Marco opened the door. He had been standing there every time he had a spare moment. He thought ahead, but he didn't think far enough ahead to realize that she would probably have figured out that he was waiting for her to knock.

Marco gave a slight bow to go with his smile. "Welcome. Come on in, dinner should be soon…ish."

She nodded slightly, looking over his simple outfit: dark green pants, red polo shirt. "You look very Christmas-y."

"Sort of the idea." He stepped to the side of the door so she could come in. Closing the door behind her, he allowed himself to be hugged.

Amanda held onto him as he returned the hug. They both relaxed a little, enjoying each other's warmth. She could hear the blood in his veins and smell him plainly; a clean smell of thoroughly washed skin, but nothing chemical or artificial. Did he do that to make certain not to offend?

They disengaged at the same time, each forcing themselves to be relaxed and comfortable. Marco did it so well. Amanda couldn't pick up on what he felt, and she could read most kinesthetic signs and indications from human beings easily.

Marco led Amanda into the apartment. To the left was the sitting room, the next room over was the living room, then the dining room. The living room was wide and laid out for comfort, with a decorated Christmas tree in the corner. It was a nice, neat home, with comfortable furnishings. There was no art on the walls, except for a few family photographs. This was not an overly sentimental household. More like Nero Wolfe's brownstone.

She took a deep breath, and then paused. She could smell stuffed mushrooms, shrimp, and enough types of seafood for a small Italian army…or a Sunday dinner. But she couldn't smell anyone else in the house.

"Am I early?" she asked, looking around, in case her nose deceived her.

Marco shook his head. "Not particularly. The family is out working. They'll be here in another thirty minutes or so. Thankfully, most of the food is prepared far enough in advance that they can let me near appliances."

"Is that generally a problem?"

"You've seen me in action. Think of MacGyver. In a kitchen. With a gas oven." He was about to say something more, then stopped and shook his head. "Long story, never mind.

Would you like a beer? Some vodka? Something else?"

"Beer would be fine."

"Guinness okay?"

"*Da*. Just nothing German. I have not enjoyed that since Dresden."

"Guinness. Gotcha." He came back quickly, bottle in hand. "With or without a glass?"

"Bottle is good. Less temptation to use fangs."

"Ah, understood."

Marco handed her a bottle, then sat down on the couch, across from Amanda in the armchair. "So, I've been thinking."

"Yes?" Amanda asked. That phrase had all sorts of possibilities. Was he thinking of opening up to her? Was he thinking of amending the "let's be friends" agreement?

"What happens at the far end of the vampire spectrum?

Amanda started. Of all the possibilities running through her head, this wasn't what she expected. "Oh? I am sorry, what?"

"We never exactly went into end results in regards to vampires? What happens when a vampire hits sainthood?" He took a sip of Guinness. "Or just plain good and damned?"

She was not expecting this sort of conversation at Christmas. "Why do you ask?"

Marco leaned forward on the couch and gathered his thoughts, putting as much brainpower as he could to avoid thinking about Amanda. Despite all of his excellent control, strict discipline, and thorough knowledge of what she was and what she could do, he was still a teenage male left alone in the same house, and the same room, with a woman as beautiful as Amanda. He could still smell her perfume from the hug: a light, vanilla base, and he even caught the slight chemical odor of unscented shampoo.

Thinking about vampires and philosophy would be far safer for him than anything else. "What you have seems to be a system that operates somewhere along the way of Aristotle's four kinds of people. Those people who knew the good, wanted the good, and did good were virtuous—in Vampire terms, let's say sainthood. Those who know the good, *wanted* the good, but fell short were continent—which would be most vampires, who are like most people. They don't get the negative religious side effects, but they aren't perfect."

Marco took another pull at the bottle. He knew he was rambling and sounded pedantic. He only had the option of going into a rational, long-winded conversation he could focus on, or risk letting his heartbeat and respiration go up, and he didn't want Amanda to ask why his body was acting funny. "I assume that most of the vampires who are affected by crosses and such are incontinent: they know the good but want and do the bad. The last one is vicious—they know, want, and do only the bad. I'll call them demonic. Which begs the question: what happens when you become the perfect evil? Or simply perfect?"

Amanda shrugged. "Oh, we do not know if they have ever happened. Those stories that have mentioned them are mostly rumors." She laughed. "I like to think that the saintly ones have been taken up into Heaven, and that the ones from Hell are dragged there and allowed to take over. Vampires are, in some ways, like high school girls," she said, making it sound like *gyrls* with a rolled R. "They gossip without stop."

"Remind me to never become a vampire then." He smiled, awkwardly, this time, watching her lips. They avoided being Angelina Jolie full and settled for not being anemic. And pink. No lipstick, just naturally pink.

Why am I staring at her lips?

He was about to say something else when the front door opened. "I'm here," Doctor Catalano said loudly from the hallway. "You can disengage lip-lock."

Marco rolled his eyes. "Excuse him, he thinks he's funny." He leaned backwards so he could see into the hallway. "I thought you'd be a little later."

The doctor nodded, stopping long enough to throw one of the locks closed. "So did I. My patient decided to die on me instead of letting me continue with his major, lifesaving surgery." He slipped off his coat and folded it in front of him, stopping a moment. "I hate to say this, Marco, but one of your friends died."

Marco flinched. "I'm sorry, um, who?"

Robert Catalano stepped into the living room and unbuttoned his suit jacket. "One of the lizard people was murdered."

Amanda looked to Marco. "I assume he means one of the Dragon street gang."

"I still object to the label," the senior Catalano muttered, undoing his tie, and undid the top button. "Especially when they bust some heads, then break out the zip-ties the *local cops* give them and *call* 911. Their idea of a gang war is to see who can turn over *more criminals to the cops*." He growled. "A real street gang isn't something to aspire to."

"Anyway," Marco said, interrupting his father's rant, "who died?"

Robert frowned and whipped off the tie. "A fellow named Nissin?"

Marco let out a sigh of relief and gave a light laugh. "Oh. *Red!* I thought it was someone *important*. Geez. Nissin was kicked out of the Dragons a year ago, easily. Brutal, thuggish little creep. If he got torn apart, we're all a little better this Christmas season."

Doctor Robert Catalano rolled his eyes. "Oh, well, you should keep me apprised of these things. I wouldn't have wasted my time trying to save his sorry ass on Christmas Eve."

Amanda smiled. "I see where you get it from."

Father and son looked to her. "Get what?" they asked.

She rolled her eyes. "Never mind. So, why is he called Red?"

Marco chuckled. "Nissin is a type of fish. In fact, it's Japanese for a herring."

Amanda looked at him a moment, then decided to ignore the joke. She turned to Robert Catalano. "So, Doctor, what is up?"

"Nothing out of the ordinary."

"A murder is considered ordinary?"

"They aren't. Well, they *weren't* ordinary, not until a month or two ago. They seem fairly common now, which makes me wonder what's going on. However, I don't take too much notice. We haven't gotten much in the way of attention from the police, and we haven't had that many people brought into the hospital, all told—"

The knock on the door stopped him mid-sentence. "Rob," called a deep, masculine voice, "it's Don."

Marco rose from the couch, strode past his father, and opened the door.

Officer Donald "Duck" Tolbert of the NYPD stood in his full uniform. He was a tall, light-skinned officer of Jamaican heritage, two generations back. "Hey, Marco. I hope I'm not interrupting anything."

Marco waved him in, closing the door behind him. "Not yet. What's up?"

Tolbert stepped into the hallway, moving for the living room without spoken invitation, and took the area in with a sweep of his eyes. They lingered a moment on Amanda. "You must be the girlfriend, Ms. Amanda Colt."

"No. I am not anyone's girlfriend."

The cop looked at the doctor, who smiled and shrugged.

"So, I'm a little preemptive," the MD said. "I still don't

understand why not."

"Maybe there's no chemistry," Tolbert joked.

"If they want chemistry, I can work on home explosives," Robert answered with a smile. "No offense, Don, but it's Christmas, Theresa should be home soon, and I want to know what you want so I can get rid of you as soon as possible."

"I just wanted you to be on the lookout for anything out of the ordinary. There have been five murders tonight alone."

He glanced to Marco. "Chat with your friends about what crimes they try to stop."

Marco's mouth dropped open. "What do you mean *murders*? I've only heard about *attacks*. As in assault, mugging, that sort of thing."

"Those are the ones who make it to the ER," Tolbert answered. "The others just go to the morgue. The homicide rate in this area of Brooklyn has nearly tripled. It hasn't made it out to the rest of the world just yet, mainly because it's just *us*, not the rest of the city. But we can't keep this under wraps much longer. You know how the much the media lusts for blood."

Marco frowned thoughtfully. "Serial killer?"

"That's the theory." He smiled. "Couldn't exactly be vampires, now could it?"

Amanda edged to the front of the chair, acting as natural as possible. "What makes you say that?"

"A lot of the attacks go right for major arteries, hence the nickname for the guy. We've been calling him the Prince of Darkness back at the station, since all of the attacks take place between sundown and sunrise. Just, don't tell anyone in the media. Or anyone at all, for that matter. Trying to stave off the press as long as we can."

"I *meant*," Amanda said, "why *not* vampires?"

Tolbert blinked, studying her a moment, trying to consider if her accent meant there was a language barrier he hadn't accounted for.

"Aside from the fact that vampires don't exist?"

She nodded. "Exactly. Why *one* person?"

The light dawned on Tolbert's face, and he grinned. "Ah. You mean why not a *group* of attackers hunting like a pack of vampires? Because there's no reason to think otherwise. There have been no multiple attacks at the same time. There isn't any posing of the body for a gang or cult thing. This means we're dealing with one productive serial killer. If the body count keeps going up, the media gets a hold of it, and then we're all screwed."

Marco cut in. "I'm surprised they haven't already."

Officer Tolbert chuckled. "That's because most of the bodies are people we don't like. They're mostly professional scumbags. There have only been one or two civilians caught in the crossfire. Your gang wannabes don't count as civilians. They want to be in the line of fire, let them. It can be on their own head."

"So," Amanda concluded, her voice as always almost a friendly purr, "your good news this Christmas is that you're lacking large body counts of people who matter?"

"Pretty much," the cop agreed. "Though I'd rather we stop this fellow before he runs out of criminals and goes after people who do matter."

"This I understand."

Marco nodded. "Ditto."

Robert sighed. It was late, he just finished his shift, and the Italian dinner in the kitchen smelled great. "Anything else, Don?"

The large officer nodded. "Yeah. Tell the gang leaders Frick and Frack to make sure their guys go in pairs. This psycho has taken out at least one veteran, and I don't mean some tank driver or machinist. I mean a real-live 'I reupped five times because I kill people for fun' SEAL. There were no defensive wounds on any of the bodies—"

"And since it's impossible for *all* of them to have known their killer," Marco finished, "you assume that it means he's really, really good at this."

"Precision cuts," Amanda added, "as well as blitz attack. Do you think your killer is trained?"

"I'd bet on it," Tolbert replied. He sighed, then shrugged. "I just came by for the friendly warning. You all keep safe, you hear?"

Robert Catalano nodded. "Quack quack, Donald."

After Donald Tolbert left, Robert turned to his son and their guest. "Well, that was nice and lighthearted."

Amanda looked at Marco. "I know where you get your sarcasm from."

At one in the morning, Christmas Day, Robert Catalano looked at his watch, yawned, and rose from the dining room table. "No offense, but I'm going to join your mother. Have fun, and stay as long as you'd like. Try not to wake us, though."

Marco leaned back in the dining room chair. "We'll try not to."

"Don't worry," Amanda said politely, "I am generally not a screamer."

Both men looked at her askance. She looked from one to the other, blinked, and thought of another way to say it. "I am generally quiet? I do not raise my voice."

Marco laughed. "That's better."

"Says you," Robert answered.

His father wandered off. Marco looked around the corner and waited for the sound of footsteps to fade. He turned back to Amanda and said, "So, what was the question about vampires before? You think that friends of yours might be in the neighborhood?"

Amanda shook her head. "*Nyet*, I doubt it. Most vampires try not to kill like this. We do not need much blood to stay alive. Attacks like this would draw attention and would require multiple vampires. But coordination like this would be highly unusual."

"Why? Vampires don't run in packs?"

"They can, but they are rarely so coordinated. There are vampires who stay in groups, but they are, let's say, incontinent. They do not play well together. Serial killer would be more likely. Always more likely. Also, vampires who *could* coordinate like this, they would not act so blatantly, unless…"

"Unless?"

"Unless there were so many of them, they needed to feast. Often."

Marco frowned. "That would be bad."

"It would."

"Heh. Remind me to start carrying my rosary all the time."

Amanda nodded. "Indeed. That would be wise."

"You know me."

"True," she agreed, raising a partially-finished glass of wine, "I do know you. I am glad to."

Marco grabbed his own glass and tapped it against hers. "Same here, Ms. Amanda Colt. Same here." They sipped the wine, and his little smile turned on at her intensely. "Well, there's one line that's obviously not true."

"What?"

"As Dracula has said in numerous films: 'I do not drink…wine.'"

She smiled. "Of course I drink wine. Otherwise, it would be rude…And where would I get most of my blood?"

Marco stared at her, trying to process the link between wine and blood. Then he nearly coughed up a lung. "You get blood from the cup *at Mass*? You go to Church so they can turn wine into the blood of God for daily *dosing*?"

She smiled but didn't answer his question. "By the way, do you want your Christmas present now or later?"

"Now could be good."

"Wait here."

She blinked out of existence. He blinked, wondering what happened with her. *Obviously, she's very fast.*

Time to be fast, too.

Marco turned around, then moved for his room. There was one shelf of his closet that had smaller items of importance to him: a knife, a dress shirt covered in blood, and Amanda's gift.

He had considered long and hard what to get her. Fred Saberhagen

novels—swords and vampires—were nice, but she probably had all of them in first editions and autographed to her personally. History was out of the question, she had lived it. So there was only one thing he could get for a vampire who had to be over eighty years old (It was a rough estimate. It had been months, but he couldn't imagine asking for her exact age. It would be rude).

He walked into the dining room as she reappeared in her chair. "Something for you," he said. "Now that I know how often you go to mass, this might be of interest."

"And for you."

She took the small package, while he took one only slightly larger.

She unwrapped a golden crucifix, three inches long, beautifully decorated along the sides. "It's lovely."

He gave a little dismissive wave. "Eh, well, it's nowhere near as beautiful as you are." He said it casually, simple and straight forward–it was not a compliment, just a simple statement of fact.

Amanda smiled, uncertain of how to take such an offhand compliment. "And gold?"

"You're a creature of legend and myth. That left out silver and cold iron."

"Your turn," she said, motioning at the gift in his hands.

Her gift to him was a rosary that ended in a golden Celtic crucifix. Marco studied the piece.

"Marble cubes instead of beads. With brass connections? Neat."

"They're made of Connemara marble from Ireland." Amanda clutched the cross to her chest. "Thank you."

He kissed the cross on the rosary and held it up to her as though saluting her. "You too."

Marco sipped again, studying Amanda over the rim of the glass, and then looked through the glass, which distorted her.

How much of what she had told him was the truth? How much of her thoughts on the attacks in Brooklyn was theory, and how much was fact, and how much of it was misleading? How much did she know, what did she suspect, and what was she not telling him?

Of course, a line of thought like that led to another, obvious question that he hadn't given much thought to before. After months of knowing this vampire, how well did he know her?

About as well as she knows me. Very little.

Chapter 8:

Old Friends

January 1st

The week after New Year's was always what Marco called "fun," a sarcastic way of saying "Shoot me now, these people should be allowed to die for the greater glory of the gene pool."

Gomers, short for Get Out of My Emergency Room, were the bane of most hospitals. They were generally accepted as people who should have been deemed too dumb to live. New Year's Eve into New Year's Day was generally a time for gomers by the bushel. Drunks, druggies, nutcases—all of whom earned a driver's license out of a Cracker Jack box—arrived in the ER en mass. This is why Marco was dragged into the picture early in the morning on New Year's Day.

When one particular gomer came in with wounds fitting the general method of the theorized serial killer, Marco was the one to note something odd. The wounds on the arms were similar, but a little off. It was as though someone had clamped down on the arm with a hand. The marks would be similar, but a thumb impression didn't look like the marks from the other fingers.

Maybe it was because of Amanda being a vampire, or because Amanda suggested swabbing. Maybe it was the cleanliness of the outside of the forearm, maybe it was an intuitive leap, but the first thing Marco did was grab a swab and wipe down the cut on the outside of the arm, away from the bite marks.

The reason he gave was simple. "They're bite marks," he told his father when questioned, "so the incisors would dig into the major veins on the inside of the arm. The outside of the arm was still bitten, and still bled, but it's cleaner than the other side. Why? Because he licked it clean. We've got saliva."

Robert Catalano rolled his eyes. "Great. It's good to the last drop. This son of a bitch thinks he's a damned vampire."

"Exactly."

The swab of the wound was taken to the lab and plated as if it would grow an everyday organism.

Marco stepped outside of the clinic and breathed in the crisp winter air. The sounds of the evening were merry, and the driving hazardous, but what the heck, it was home. The wonderful world of Brooklyn.

Now what? he thought, considering his options. *His father would spend the evening indoors, the rest of the evening an exercise in waiting to fall asleep. Step one would be to get home, you twit.*

"Hello, Marco."

Marco slid into a defensive stance and turned towards the sound of the voice. Amanda was there in a little winter ensemble. A white knit cap highlighted the red-gold locks pouring over her shoulder. A matching scarf encircled her graceful neck, the rest of her body hidden under a down coat. She looked so bundled up it was cute.

"I didn't know vampires needed to dress warm for the winter."

"We don't, but it helps save energy on internal temperature regulation."

"Ah, gotcha."

Amanda moved closer to him and put an arm around his waist. "Come. I will walk you home."

Marco grinned and put an arm around her shoulders in return. "What's the matter? Have nothing else to do tonight?"

"Nope. You are lucky winner."

He kissed her on the top of her cap. "Yup. So, why has your accent been thickening lately? You're dropping more articles. I know that 'the' and 'an' are not in the Russian language, but your use of them fluctuates."

Amanda sighed. "I know. Accents and speech patterns tend to stick after a certain age. I try, but it does not always work." She gave him a little squeeze. "How was your evening?"

He laughed. "You're kidding, right? If this weren't winter break, I would have been halfway into insanity wondering what I'd do about the reading. As it is, a night in the ER like this makes me want to knock heads together."

"I can understand that."

"You've done hospital duty?"

"For one of my degrees."

Marco rolled his eye and laughed. "Of course it was. Why would I think otherwise?"

"No idea," she said, pronouncing it like i-di-a. "You should know better by now."

"Probably," he said casually. "You'll just have to hang around me until I get the hint."

"Considering your intellect thus far, that should be soon."

Marco kept looking straight ahead, and muttered, "I

don't know. Sometimes I'm a slow learner."

Amanda settled in against him as they walked away from the clinic. He was so nice and warm. His heartbeat suddenly increased. His heartbeat hadn't sped up this fast even when he learned she was a vampire.

"What is the matter?"

"Nothing," he said, the tone contra-indicative.

She knew something was wrong. No matter the heart rate. He isn't smiling.

Amanda's eyes darted to the surrounding area. If she discounted the drivers–she could only see the back of their heads–then that left pedestrians. Assuming it wasn't someone that Marco spotted already passing by them, that left the couple heading towards them.

The man was standard frat boy jock. He may have had an intellectual scholarship somewhere, but she wouldn't place money on it. The woman was short, busty, and cheerful. She was Filipino, with a broad smile, and features that made her seem Eurasian. From the volume of her babble, Amanda could tell that the woman was a soprano, with hair such a dark shade of brown it was almost black. If she were categorizing by stereotype, she was "cheerleader."

Marco increased his pace, and Amanda easily kept up. It wasn't hard for her to figure out what he was doing—the faster he walked, the less time the other woman had to notice him.

However, the cheerleader glanced away from the man she was with, looking briefly ahead. Then her eyes locked onto Marco like laser-guided missiles. There was a second where all other activity on her face stopped, and even the cadence of her step fell off. The dark brown eyes then flicked to Amanda. The vampire smiled, gave her a little New York nod of "Sorry, we made eye contact, it won't happen again," and looked away. But Amanda could feel that the cheerleader kept staring. Marco's pace only slowed while they passed the brunette.

Amanda said nothing, but she was certainly going to ask about this encounter. Soon. Though she already suspected who the woman was.

"Marco," the soprano voice called out.

Amanda felt him wince, and she did the same. If this was the encounter that Marco wanted to avoid, it must have been for good reason. This could become unpleasant.

Amanda held him a little more firmly as she turned in mid-stride, taking him with her. Marco knew enough to go with it, and not resist. He didn't even pretend that he had just spotted the cheerleader.

He simply looked at her and said, "Lily."

Marco said it with enough weight that Amanda thought he would announce Armageddon, and in much the same fashion. Amanda didn't react, merely thinking to herself, *I hate being right.* Finally she smiled at Lily; she practically beamed. "Oh, Lily. Marco has told me so much about you," she lied.

Lily blinked in surprise; a smile frozen on her face as though it were a default position. "It's good to see you again, Marco. You're in better shape than high school."

"This time last year, I believe," Marco answered. "That's when we last saw each other."

Lily glanced at Amanda. The vampire smiled, and took her free hand to place it on Marco's chest, fingers splayed in a friendly pat. She was trying to signal a mark of ownership.

Lily answered with a bright smile. "You're his new girlfriend?" she asked, the emphasis on new.

Amanda merely smiled at the girl. "I am girl. I am his friend." She took the hand off his chest and offered it to Lily. "Amanda Colt."

"Lily Sparks."

Marco looked at the man Lily was with. "Hey Carlos," he said, his voice flat. "How have you been? Hang out in the Village much, anymore?"

Frat boy looked nervous, and took a step back, trying to take Lily with him.

"I'll see you around, Marco," Lily added, her voice having changed to something softer, with a certain hush to it.

Amanda smiled and waved to her. To Marco, she lowered her voice when she said, "That was fun. She may still want you."

Marco finished waving and turned around so he wouldn't have to keep his face neutral anymore. "What do you mean?"

"I made possessive movements, indicating my ownership of you," Amanda explained, her Russian accent thickening over the awkward wording, "and her response was to modify her voice to attempt seduction. It is universal and consistent."

Marco looked over his shoulder at the fleeing couple and scoffed. He shook his head and looked back to Amanda. "I'd rather have you, here, now, as a friend, than have her climb into my lap, naked. Come on, I think it's time to get out of here."

January 2nd

"Marco, get in here, would you?" Marco followed the sound of his father's voice and entered the microbiology lab. His father held up a blood culture plate and looked right at him. "What do you think?"

Marco glanced at the plate. Blood agar plates were used to grow bacteria, usually off of swabs from wounds, or for throats. They were red, encased in a plastic shell and lid. What grew on the plate could then be sampled and put under a microscope for identification. In this case, the blood culture looked like it had been poked full of holes.

"Somebody had fun with a set of scissors?" Marco suggested, examining the sample. "A small set of scissors?"

"This had the culture from one of the victims."

Marco winced, his mind racing as fast as possible. So it was something that could eat holes in a blood culture plate, and he had been dancing around the issue of vampires for the last few weeks. "Did someone break in?"

His father shook his head. "Not unless they could reach through the case. It was locked."

"I suppose this means that the Invisible Man couldn't have done it either, doesn't it?"

"No, he couldn't have," Robert said with all seriousness. "The security cameras show that the door on the incubator never opened."

"Goody." Marco sighed and thought himself an idiot for even suggesting the next idea that popped into his head. It was the only theory, however, that fit what he saw. "So we should assume that whatever this is eats blood?"

Robert nodded. "That seems to be the case. The next step is to take a look at the viral plates."

"You want me to look at those?"

"That would help. I already sent some samples to the CDC. If it eats blood, I can only hope this is as rare as a flesh-eating bacteria. Otherwise, this could get bad in a hurry."

Marco nodded. "I'm on it."

Marco looked into the microscope, examining what his father had tried to culture. He immediately saw the problem, or at least one of the problems, with the blood culture plates. It certainly wasn't a bacteria. It was most definitely a virus. *Well, that explains why I had to turn up the magnification so damned high.*

Marco had spent plenty of time looking at viruses, trying to memorize them like the local cop would go through a book of mug shots. This didn't match any of them. *Maybe it's time to call Amanda, if only to see if she's run across anything like this in the time she's been around.*

The sound of crashing glass from down the hall broke Marco's focus. He jerked away from the microscope, listening for the next sound. This part of the building was locked right now. Like most labs, it had a biometric security system. No one whose palm-prints didn't match the scanner could get through the door.

Glancing over the lab, Marco looked over his options. He wasn't encouraged. No scalpels. Mostly glass tubes, pens, and slides. The microscope was heavy, but unwieldy. If he went with his usual assumption that things would go wrong in the worst possible way, then the sound would be that of invaders. People too stupid to know better about where anything should go, like viruses instead of valuable hospital supplies.

Maybe I should just point them to the methadone and the pain killers, let them off themselves with an overdose down the road. Though, if they can get past security, this may not be as pleasant as an addict.

Marco leaned against the stool and waited. The lights were on and attracted all manner of pests. Druggies were no different.

The intruder entered the lab. Dark hair, Hispanic, but seriously pale. Almost dead. It was the sort of person you crossed the street to avoid and kept looking over your shoulder until he departed. Obviously, a long term substance abuser.

"Sorry," Marco said, surprising the intruder by both his presence and his matter-of-fact reaction. "Wrong part of the building. You want the area with the armed guards and the security. This is the micro lab."

The intruder studied Marco; an amusing insect too stupid to know he was in trouble. He grinned with a broad smile. "I'm here for your father, Marco Catalano. I have business with him."

Hm, what's worse? Marco thought. *That he knows Dad, or knows me?* "Sorry, he's out. What business?"

The intruder's mouth twitched, as though he considered smiling, but didn't quite remember how. "He's been asking questions. Inconvenient questions. Questions that shouldn't be asked."

"Yes, that's generally what happens when questions are inconvenient. People ask them," Marco replied, his smile never once flickering, his own sincerely amused. He slipped the toe of his shoe around the chair leg. "It is a family trait, I suppose. Always getting in trouble. It never fails. Seriously. But, sorry, my father isn't here right now. You'll just have to call back later. Maybe leave a memo, because I'm not your secretary."

"If you won't tell him anything, then I guess you'll serve as my message."

He growled, and Marco didn't wait for him to make a move. He swept the stool with his foot, sending the chair right into the man's face. With a quick burst forward, he followed up with a kick to the groin. Simple body mechanics force the intruder to bend over. Marco drove his elbow down into the back of his head. Marco wasted no time in grabbing the stool, bringing it up, then down on the same spot his elbow had landed.

This last attack sent the intruder sprawling. Then he pushed off into a roll, almost flying across the room. Marco blinked, holding the chair aloft still.

The intruder turned. He bore long incisors, his eyes glowing red.

Vampire. I should've guessed. This could be a problem.

Chapter 9:
Hospital Visit

When Marco Catalano started training in Krav Maga, he didn't expect to put it to the test against a vampire who had broken into the microbiology lab. He had to keep his cool, however. There was only one way out of the lab, and the vampire had already fought a path inside. Outrunning this guy would be impossible.

"Oh, you're a vampire, is that all?" Marco said, then dropped the stool, and stuck both hands in his pockets. His eternal smile didn't flicker. "Why didn't you say so? Come on then, what's keeping you?"

Within seconds, Marco went through every possible combination of what the vampire could do next. *Simple lunge and slash. Throw beaker and charge. Try for stupid ninja move, kicking off of the wall—unlikely. Roll towards me to close the distance, or even spring up behind me.*

Oh, wait, he's bending his knees and leaning back. Despite all super-speed these guys have, they have no concept that, yes, they are still telegraphing their every move.

The vampire smiled a split second before he lunged for Marco, his arms out in an attempt to swat him like an ant. Marco sidestepped him, and the vampire charged right into a cabinet. He never saw it coming when Marco's hands launched out of his pockets, whipping out a set of rosary beads around the vampire's throat. Marco grabbed both ends and pulled with all his strength. The snap and hiss of burning flesh was instantaneous.

The vampire gagged and coughed, thrashing at Marco behind him. He tried to grab, kick, snap, and claw, but the burst of frantic energy quickly slipped away, countered by the power of the rosary. The vampire was left with normal strength, as generated by human muscles. He tried to twist, charging towards Marco. Marco merely turned out of the way, and swung the vampire around, staying behind him.

Marco crossed his hands, crossing the rosary over itself, and locking the vampire's neck in the improvised garrote. He threw his shoulder into the vampire's back, pushing the creature to its knees. A knee to the vampire's spine, laid him flat on the floor, face down. The burning continued, even as the vampire finally stopped flailing.

Marco paused for a moment before jerking back on the chain. There were questions that needed to be answered. Why his father? Why Marco? What questions could Robert Catalano have asked that could get the attention of vampires?

The first, the only, thing that came to mind was the strange element of the blood work done on the victims. More precisely, the microscopic traces left in the wound tracks. Since the attacks had become more ferocious by the day, there was only one place he could turn to for help.

It also happened to be the first person he was angry at right now.

Marco gave a final jerk on the rosary. The holy artifact had already been burning through the flesh of the vampire. The last yank fully decapitated the creature of darkness. His head rolled off of its shoulders and turned to dust as it hit the floor.

When Marco Catalano rose from the floor, he was not smiling.

As Marco made his way to Amanda Colt's apartment, he felt the rage boiling within him. It burned his veins, his brain, and made his heart race. There was one thought in his head. It echoed over and over, bouncing around his skull like bells in a church tower. *Amanda lied to me. She lied to me. I trusted her and she lied to me...*

Someone was coming out of the apartment building when Marco stormed up to the door. He brushed past the resident and pushed into the building. He took the stairs two at a time and focused all of his annoyance on one goal–getting to Amanda's apartment.

When he reached his destination, he didn't knock, but he raised a knee, kicking the door instead. The impact was loud enough to sound like a shot. The door was well constructed; he knew it wouldn't give, but that wasn't the point.

The door opened. Amanda stood there in a plush white robe, her hair turned dark red from water. The scent of shampoo and soap was fresh. Most men in his position would have been startled speechless by the sheer sexiness quotient. This kind of radiant, angelic beauty only appeared in Hollywood and commercials for soap products. Marco ignored it all and pushed into her apartment.

Amanda smiled despite registering the dramatic change in his usual demeanor and closed the door. "Is something wrong?"

Marco stared at her wall of weapons. He tried to keep his temper, as he said through gritted teeth, "The truth."

She arched a brow. She readjusted her robe a little tighter around her and wrapped her arms in a hug over her chest. Any other day, Marco would have seen the stance as adorable.

"About what?"

"About what?" he roared. He whirled about. He was completely oblivious to anything adorable. "That vampires were snacking on friends of mine. You asked my father to swab wound tracks. You must have at least suspected that they were bite marks. 'Oh, it couldn't be a gang of vampires, they're not that coordinated,'" he mocked, mimicking her statement from Christmas Eve. "By the way, thanks for the rosary, it came in handy when a goddamn vampire tried to eat me!"

She was genuinely surprised. "Someone attacked you?"

Marco nodded, his eyes wide as he moved in on her. "Yeah, and you know why? Because my father sent off samples of our swabs to the CDC when those samples ate the blood in the culture plates."

"Oh. I see how that would be a problem."

"Oh, no," Marco said, the sarcasm dripping from his words. "That? That wasn't a problem. The problem is that they came looking for my father!"

He stepped closer to Amanda, deliberately violating her personal space, though she didn't move. "Let's face it. He isn't exactly up on the whole vampire thing. The next time he might not be that lucky. I would like it if my family isn't eaten in the meantime. Do you understand that? I don't like secrets when they can get family killed. You said no, vampires couldn't be behind this spree of killings. And then, after I swab a victim, surprise, vampire."

Without even a blink, or a perceptible change in respiration, Amanda met his eyes. "Is Lily a secret that could get me killed?"

Marco stopped dead. His dark blue eyes turned darker; storm clouds signaled an oncoming squall. "Don't go there. Don't even try it."

"I know. But it is a fact. You had friends before me, Marco. Now you don't. I find that odd. Is something there that is going to harm me?"

Only if you get close to me. Only if I start to give a damn about you. If that happens, then, oh yes, very much so. People die.

His outward appearance didn't change as he said, "I find it irrelevant to the topic of my father almost being eaten tonight because you didn't give me all the information we need."

"We?" She stepped closer to him, the two of them almost chest to chest. "What would you tell your father? There are vampires? That someone he wants for your girlfriend is one of them? If he mentioned that to CDC, things would get complicated, da?"

Marco scoffed. "So what? He likes you. We tell him you're a bloodsucker, he'd probably point you at people to dine on."

"What if he thinks that I am the killer?"

"Don't be stupid. I know it's a five-vampire team—one for the neck, and one for each arm and leg. If I can see that, so can he."

"There are FBI profilers who could not reach that conclusion so easily," she said, her anger turning to curiosity. "How did you know that?"

Right then he knew he was starting to reveal parts of himself that he didn't want Amanda to see. Marco's fury immediately calmed, pulling it back before things got messy. "Five bite marks, five vampires. You say they don't need much, so a vampire wouldn't need more than one bite—a human body has five quarts of blood. Simultaneous bites allow for even distribution, even if they only take half of that. I suspect the reason we have the survivors we do is related to the healing properties of the vampire virus within the saliva. One bite from you lets me throw manhole covers like

Frisbees, so five bites should theoretically give someone the strength to live through losing half their blood supply.

"Given that the number of attacks per night is escalating," he continued, "that means that the number of groups is escalating. Not to mention that they are highly organized, if they can kill like clockwork…completely opposite from what you've previously told me, I might add. Given the quality of the people they've attacked, that means only two things: one, they want to stay low key and are smart enough to kill only the local scum nobody's going to miss; and two, they aren't local, otherwise, they would know not to go after the Dragon-Tiger crowd. Which means that they're in the line of fire, too."

Amanda took a breath, then let it out slowly. "I did not know for certain. I even suspected, but I could not be sure. What would you have done, Marco, if I'd known something and I told you? Increase security? Go hunting? We would need armies to patrol, like street cops. I am not telling the police to look for vampires. I suggest you do not, either."

Marco stared at her for a long moment, as though she'd gone completely insane. Because being a vampire wasn't crazy enough. Then he burst out into a loud belly laugh that made him double over.

It was Amanda's turn to look at him like he was insane. "What is so funny?"

"You want to protect me?" he said, roaring with laughter. "You want to protect me!"

When his laughter finally died down, he took a deep breath. "Hi, have we met?"

"I know you are a good fighter. And you know some police officers–"

"Who said anything about going to the police?" he said, an evil smile slowly spreading across his face. It was much like his usual one, and it, too, didn't flicker. "I have a small army of gang wannabes. I think it's time for me to use them."

Amanda was taken aback. "Do you truly believe that they would do this?"

Marco nodded. "Yes."

"Because they fear you?"

"Because I have earned their respect. I have taken the tactics and discipline I learned, and I used it to mold them into an effective fighting force. They owe me."

"They also fear you."

"They respect me." He paused a moment, and the smile stayed fixed. "And they fear me. I believe in the power of feudalism, Amanda. In this situation, I am the feudal lord. Come on. We're going to call Vega and

Nyugen, get them and their lazy gang-bangers in shape. Then we're going to sic them on the forces of darkness."

Amanda cocked her head, her still-dripping hair falling to one side like a curtain on a crooked rod. "May I at least dry my hair first? Maybe get dressed?"

For the first time, Marco looked her up and down, as though he hadn't noticed her state of dress. "Nah, go out like that. It'll at least get their attention."

January 3rd 3:00 a.m.

Hector Vega and Zeng Nyugen gazed at Marco and Amanda bleary-eyed, as the four of them sat together in the hospital waiting room.

"Three in the morning, dude? Really?" The leader of the Tigers was dressed in a hand-tooled brown leather jacket. His shorter counterpart wore a high-gloss, black-leather jacket that resembled plastic. "Are you nuts, man?"

Amanda had changed into a long-sleeved gold sweater and jeans. She could dress faster than Marco could leave her apartment.

Vega glanced around the waiting room. Despite the time, there were still people hanging around. "Could we take this outside?"

Marco looked around the few patients waiting to be seen. "We can do it somewhere else. Not outside, though."

Zeng stepped closer to Marco, dropping his voice. "Marco, we don't need to talk around her. In fact, she may not want to know."

"Amanda needs to tag along. Trust me. She can take care of herself. And anyone who gets in her way."

As they walked and talked, the two leaders were looking at Marco as though he had grown three heads and a tail. They hardly looked at Amanda since Marco started speaking, and that was an achievement.

"Marco," Zeng said, "no disrespect man, but what the hell?"

"Seriously," Vega added, "vampires? I know these dudes have been vicious, but still—"

Marco's glance was enough to cut off both of their complaints.

"What? You want evidence? You want proof? I'll give you proof. I'll give you solid, flesh and blood proof that you two can choke on. So can the rest of your guys."

Amanda internally cringed. *Is he going to expose me right here, in front of all of them?*

"Come here," Marco said, then pushed into another room. It was a patient room, but empty. However, it had a TV and a DVD player. Marco slipped out a DVD from his coat pocket, and then put it into the player. He leaned against the wall and crossed his arms. "There are some things they won't miss in the security office."

The film was Marco, looking through a microscope until he stopped and looked around. Then someone walked in. After a brief scuffle, the other guy went out of frame, then back into frame, only to have Marco garrote him with a rosary, and the body turned to ashes.

"Now, unless you think that I spent a lot of time and energy putting together a movie production so I can screw with you guys, I think this is fairly compelling evidence that I'm not lying to you. It's time to apply Marco's straight razor."

Amanda chimed in. "What is that?"

"That the simplest solution to accept my story rather than to be on my bad side."

Vega nervously stretched his neck to one side, then the other. "Yeah, okay, they're vampires. So what?"

Zeng rolled his shoulders, trying to hide his discomfort at the new concept. "They're vampires. How does that help us, other than letting us know we're screwed? Seriously? These are killers. We don't know how to deal with this kind of... thing."

"That's okay, because I do." He started to move outside, backing up into the door, using his butt to press the push bar. "Come on. You two have work to do."

Zeng crossed his arms over his chest. "Yeah? And the first step is?"

Marco held the door open. "You're going to get all of your thugs and smart-ass fellas together as soon as possible. You're going to meet me when I get out of classes. We're going to meet in Washington Square Park. I know it's the city, but if you guys can't face up to the thugs who inhabit the area, you should all give up and go home."

"Then what?" Vega asked him. Marco's eyes flashed. "I'm going to teach you to fight monsters." He jerked his head to one side. "Come. We have an army of darkness to fight, and no Bruce Campbell to do it with."

Amanda smiled to herself as followed the other two out the door. She enjoyed watching Marco at work. His words were sharp and fast and precise. There would be no misunderstanding should he have to kill someone. The inflection was enough, but his words took the extra step.

He moved through the hall with speed, as though he owned the place. He knew where he was going, a man on a mission, so blocking his path was unwise. Those that wouldn't, or couldn't, move fast enough, he stepped around with grace.

It is odd, Amanda thought. *He is almost more military than men I've died with in world wars.*

It was almost like he was eager to go to war with something. He was elegant, and graceful, and for the first time his movements matched her first impression of him—that he was more like a dancer than a wrestler.

"Where are you going to find the time?" Zeng asked, catching up to him. "Aren't you supposed to be this hotshot med student?"

Marco came down on the forward foot, and pivoted, scooping Zeng up by the lapels of his leather jacket and brought him up against the wall. Marco held Zeng there, bringing them eye-to-eye. "I'm not a med student. I'm a Physician Assistant student. Get it right, and don't insult me like that."

Vega hung back, and Amanda could smell his fear, which had the bitter taste of adrenaline and the sour taste of sweat. It was odd how they both reacted to him. *Why were these two so afraid?* She figured she might as well ask. "Why are they so afraid of you?"

He didn't even look at her as he answered. "They're not afraid. They are merely wary of my currently energetic condition."

He dropped Zeng and said, "Come on, there's work to be done!"

The three of them let him go bounding off. Amanda rolled her eyes and turned to the gang leaders curiously. "Would you two like to tell me why you're so worried about him?"

Zeng snickered. "You want the list?"

Vega nodded. "He's a scary dude. You want it in fifty words or less?"

If these two are going to be like that, I will have to make do. Amanda shrugged. "That would be nice."

"Have him tell you about the thing with Lily," Zeng said.

"Only, do it nicely," his counterpart put in, "and don't tell him we suggested it."

"Seriously, don't."

"You're the one dating him," Hector told her.

"So you can get away with it," the Dragon leader agreed.

Amanda looked from one to the other. "We are not dating."

The two gang leaders shared a glance. Their silence said more than any smart-mouth response could have.

She rolled her eyes, and followed after Marco, considering what little information she had. *Lily again? If she was not already gone from Marco's life, I would be worried that there was competition. Then again, what competition? I am not dating him. Nor do I want to. Why would I? He has already made it clear; we are merely friends.*

"Go, catch up to Marco. I suspect he will want his vassals to tag along," Amanda joked. The two of them nodded and left.

Amanda casually walked after them. *Why would Lily be the key to understanding Marco?*

Marco walked into the family brownstone late. He was able to watch the sun come up from the wrong end. "You know, when I asked you to look at the problem," said his father from the living room, "I didn't expect you to take all night."

Marco looked left and chuckled. His father was sitting in the dark, still waiting for him. "I came across some issues."

Doctor Robert Catalano folded the newspaper in front of him, laying it neatly in his lap. "Did some of these issues have something to do with Amanda?"

His father was smart, fine, but if he was serious with that comment about Amanda, it was an intelligence leap of epic proportions. "Why would you think that?"

"Because she's highly intelligent, and I'm certain that you can make the time go faster if she were around."

"Uh huh." Marco thought a moment as he sat into the couch. Was his father still working on playing matchmaker, or did he suspect that something more was really going on? It was hard to tell. "In any event, you don't have a bacteria; you have a virus. Hemophagic, instead of necrotizing fasciitis."

Robert chuckled and shifted at his chair. "You're taking the whole 'flesh eating bacteria' title a little too literally, aren't you?"

"No, I know the difference. I think this virus literally eats blood. Which means that you were right in the first place, the holes in the blood culture plate were done on the microscopic level."

His father the doctor was silent for a moment, thinking this over. "If a microscopic organism can go through that much blood in two days, the virulence must be—"

"I tested it," Marco interjected. "The virus cells have already starved to death. Without blood, they only hang around for a short amount of time." Marco thought a moment, wondering if he could use information he had from Amanda to add to his theory. It couldn't hurt.

"Or, there was just not enough of a virus to make it stick," he suggested, thinking out loud. "It could be something like having a bit of a cold. We're exposed to viruses every day, and few hang around in the body in any strength, or to any effect."

Marco wondered if that could even be possible to attribute that characteristic to something in a lab, and not inside a human being. He wondered why he was so off. Then realized he had been up for almost twenty-four hours. "Am I rambling? Or making any sense?"

"Yes, and sort of, in that order," his father answered.

Chapter 10:

Application Of Fear

January 5th, 6:00 PM

Amanda Colt had long become inured against the long looks of men, and the envious glares of women…well, some women. There were others who tried to hit on her; especially when she was walking through Greenwich Village.

There was a time, not too long ago, when she considered shaving her head, and trying to mar her looks with acid. However, any damage that she had ever taken had healed. It struck her as odd that she made some adjustments to her wardrobe today. She had picked out a white hooded sweater that she had always found a little snug but would help against the cold. She spent nearly an hour with her hair, as opposed to her standard wash and wear evenings. It felt strange to behave this way; she was only going to Washington Square Park to meet Marco.

Washington Square Park was not far from Hudson University. As a park, it didn't rate in the top five in New York City. It was stiff competition when one factored in all five boroughs and the overwhelming grandeur of Central Park. As a park, however, it would suffice. As a training ground, even better. Hooligans from other parts of the city gravitated towards Washington Square.

As Amanda closed in, she spotted Marco Catalano from a distance, sitting on the edge of the fountain. A backpack sat next to him on the fountain, and a briefcase sat on the ground. He was early, pocketknife in one hand and an old chair leg in the other. The leg was thicker than his wrist, and over a foot long.

It was pleasant to watch him work. His eyes were focused on the chair leg, as though he were working on a mathematical problem. She tried to remember the last time she met a man that detail-oriented. She was even more amused as she sauntered up to him, and he didn't even look up.

"Are you whittling?" she asked.

Marco jerked out of his concentration and blinked at her a few times. "Can you think of a better hobby to have right now?"

She motioned to the chair leg. "Where did you get that?"

"Oh, you'd be surprised what New Yorkers will throw out. The chair had four perfectly good legs, though the back was broken."

She slid next to him on the edge of the water fountain. "You want to make that a knife?"

He shrugged and put some more details on the leg. "Knife, short sword, something like that. I prefer it be something I can throw."

"Humans can dodge throwing knives, what makes you

think that vampires cannot?"

"That assumes I'm only going to encounter smart vampires, and no humans."

"So, have you had to deal with many muggers? Aside from our first outing?"

Marco's hands kept moving, though his eyes no longer focused on the task. His eyes were somewhere else, something Amanda did not know about.

Another mugger Marco had to deal with? she thought.

"Of course," he finally answered, surprisingly casual. "You saw me deal with those two the night we had The Talk. Did you think I was unskilled? After all, I live in Brooklyn, where only the strong survive."

"*Da.* I saw that shirt. By the way, the others are here."

Marco looked up, then around, then squinted at what Amanda knew to be Los Tigres and the Dragons, led by their respective heads. "I'm going to ask you to bite me again sometime soon. I miss having twenty-fifteen eyesight."

She smiled to herself, and leaned in close to him, her lips almost kissing his ear. "All you have to do is ask."

Marco blinked, taken off guard, then shivered. He cleared his throat. "By the way, I should probably ask, vampire anatomy is no different from regular human, right?"

"Oh yes," she said, her voice low.

"Good, I'll need that for the pressure points," he said, stretching his neck, deliberately moving his head further away from her. It meant exposing his neck, but it took his ear out of her lip range.

Amanda blinked, then settled back, away from him. "Oh! Yes, of course. Um, that should work."

"Good." He stood as Hector and the others came close. "Hey there, everybody, how are you?"

He looked over the collection of other men. Maybe a third of them were younger than twenty, but most of them seemed interested in staying in the "gangs" for as long as they could—possibly a matter of boredom on a Friday night. Stay in and read a book, or kick some ass? What a choice.

Some of them had jobs in EMS, others in the fire department, and a few moved far away from jobs that could be considered "street level." The least blue collar worker was Kellen Capone, who was the oldest, at thirty-five, and the foreman at a construction company. He was adopted when Vega's crew had discovered him beating two thugs into another incarnation with a piece of rebar.

"Everyone up to speed?" Marco asked.

"Ye-up," Kellen answered. He looked around the others and smiled. "You kids sure are interesting."

"You have no idea," Marco said dryly. He looked over the crowd and winced. This was going to become crowded rather fast. "Does anyone here have combat experience?"

No one was surprised that Kellen raised a finger. "I spent some time in the reserves, that count?"

"Close enough. Anyone else? Fist fights? Schoolyard scuffles? Mild training in an obscure martial art when you were ten? Anyone?"

There were more than a few volunteers from the crowd. He sent back anyone whose idea of a scuffle was five guys beating down two muggers. However, a quarter of them had put time in the military, including actual military service. He nodded, trying to keep all of them in mind.

He finally turned to Amanda and whispered, "How much of this do you want to handle?"

She shrugged. "You are the human."

"Gee, thanks. Big help you are." He looked back to them with his customary, amused smile. "Anyway, Vampires 101. Let's start with everything you have ever needed to know

about vampires, you learned from Bram Stoker."

"Who?" one of the younger ones said.

Marco rolled his eyes and sighed. "Screw you, Marvel Comics. Okay. Vampires are not cute biological anomalies. They do not sparkle. They do not glitter. They are not shiny unless they are on fire. They are more like the ones from Buffy the Vampire Slayer, and less like what you see in the Blade movies.

You can fend them off with any holy object. You kill them with decapitation, with fire, and with a nice solid stake to the heart."

One of the smartasses laughed. "You want us to go shopping at the meat market now?"

Vega smacked him upside the head. "Wooden stakes, for nailing things down."

Marco held up the wooden chair leg, which already looked like it was on the way to becoming a short sword. "In this case, nail them through the heart."

Amanda nodded. "Metal does not damage them as badly as wood does. Damage inflicted by wood will take them longer to recover from, unless you are cutting off a limb with a bladed weapon. Also, do not go through the ribcage if you can avoid it."

Marco grinned broadly. "Exactly. If you can stab them at an upward angle, you can go underneath the ribcage to the heart."

Hector Vega looked over his gang and smiled. He asked Marco, "How do you feel about machetes?"

"I assume you are not stabbing with it?"

"It sure as hell ain't a fencing foil."

"Sure. Just make sure you're cutting off heads. Religious artifacts are good to carry. Crucifixes—not crosses, I mean the one with the person hanging off of it. In my case—"

Marco reached into his shirt and pulled out what he wore around his neck, a rosary—"a rosary is not jewelry, it is a religious artifact. It makes it harder for someone to rip your throat out. I suggest you don't get that close if you can avoid it."

"I ain't Catholic," one of Zeng's people in the back said. "I'm a Uighur Muslim, a Turk."

Marco looked at the guy in the middle of the Dragons. "Funny, you don't look Turkish."

Zeng waved it away. "That's what they call his people in China. Turks."

Amanda cut in now. "It doesn't matter what you are. This is not a matter of faith. The object itself is what is important. God can come into the world of His own accord; a booby trap, if you want. A cross is easier to use as a weapon than smacking someone with a Torah."

"Exactly," Marco said, backing her up gratefully.

Amanda smiled at him, about to say something else, but hesitated. Out of the corner of her eye, she noted a small band forming near the arch leading to Washington Square. They didn't look like they wanted to join in with Marco and company. In fact, they looked decidedly like the folks that Zeng and Hector's people would beat up on a regular basis.

As more people joined, they started flashing hand gestures at each other. *That sure isn't ASL. Gang signs, great.* Her eyes flickered to Marco's, and she gave him a slight nod.

"I love working with you," he said under his breath, so softly that even Amanda had trouble hearing him. Marco flashed her a smile, then looked back to the crowd of Dragons and Tigers. "Now, in addition to crosses and such, holy water is also recommended." He bent down, and picked up his bag, taking out a glass bottle of what had been a Starbucks iced coffee. The bottle just barely came out the top of his hand, filled with water. "Filled fresh with water from the baptismal font at St. Patrick's Cathedral. Who here has played baseball?"

Easily a third of the crowd raised their hands. Marco nodded.

"Good. When you're out in squads, you guys should carry at least a six pack of these with you every night. In fact, I'd say carry twelve. Just pretend they're baseballs and throw them at full force and direct impact. Now, we may need an intermission, as I think we have company."

"What da hell do you think you're doing in our park?"

"Right on cue," he muttered, again for Amanda's ears only. He looked over at the approaching gathering of thugs. They were the punks who had massed on the border of the park. It was time for them to make their mark, push around some people, the usual macho idiocy that started whatever bar fights alcohol didn't.

"We're just having a LARP," Marco said.

The leader of the gathering blinked. "You're doing what?"

"LARP-ing. Live action role playing game. Mostly vampire."

The punk smiled. "Really? Well then, we wouldn't want to mess with your game, now would we?"

Marco's smile turned into a grin. He grinned in a way that made even Amanda nervous. "No, you wouldn't."

"Yeah, we wouldn't…bitch."

Marco looked at Amanda. "I sincerely hope he wasn't referring to you. Otherwise I would be quite put out."

"Really?" the thug asked. "Wouldn't want that. Might

upset yo' 'ho."

Even Amanda had to smile at that one. "Does he believe himself to be pirate?" she asked, her Russian accent thickening. "Yo ho, yo ho, like that?"

Marco shrugged, playing off her. "Honestly, I have no idea."

Zeng and Vega had taken their top two officers in their respective gangs and moved themselves into position between their people and the newcomers. "You don't want to do this, man," Zeng said to the thug.

"Or what?" the adversarial punk said

"I believe," Marco said, his diction becoming more and more acute as he became angrier, "that Mister Nguyen wants to say that you wouldn't like me when I'm angry."

The punk laughed. "Really?" He made a series of hand gestures. Marco chuckled, and the leader's eyes narrowed. "What's so funny?"

A quick glance made Marco chuckle. "You're wearing blue."

"So?"

Marco stepped into the fellow, his shoulders hunching up and down slightly, mirroring the other man's posture in grotesque parody. "You think you gangsta, son?"

With some well-practiced flailing of his arms, the other one angrily replied, "Who you calling son, punk? I know I's gangsta."

Amanda listened as the two of them started slipping into what sounded like an urban regional accent. The deterioration on both of them was startling. She was tempted to intercede but didn't want to interrupt Marco's play.

"You born in the city?" Marco asked.

"O' course."

"Then I say again," Marco replied, his diction taking a sharp turn for the better. "You are wearing blue."

The thug looked down at his clothing, as if to confirm this fact. He looked back up to Marco. "And?"

"That is a color of the Crips."

"So, bee-atch?"

"So, son, born in New York, you're using West Coast hand gestures."

The aggressor blinked and took a step back. Amanda could almost feel his momentum deteriorating. But does that mean he backs down, or does he become more aggressive?

"You calling me a liar?"

Marco's smile quirked, and his brows arched. "If your posse here knew anything, then you would have already been in a dumpster for being a poser."

The thug scoffed. "How about I beat you in front of your ho?"

Marco went deadly still. Vega and Zeng both tensed. Several of the other Tiger-Dragon gang members took a step back. Amanda had no idea what they were expecting. Did they believe Marco would literally explode, leveling the surrounding city block?

Marco's voice came out, low and simple, even light, like a gentle whisper. "I believe you want to be more polite."

"You do, huh?"

He nodded, his manner level and cool-headed. "Oh yes." There was a tightening in the eyes, and the back foot tensed. Marco's smile widened.

The thug launched a knee for Marco's groin, but Marco had already been in motion, his own leg coming up. The knee glanced off of Marco's leg, and slid off to one side, moving right past Marco.

Then it was his move.

The leg Marco used to deflect the kick was what he used to lunge forward. He drove in with an elbow, smashing through cartilage and bones in thug's nose. He brought back a hammer blow with the same hand, right into his target's face.

He followed up with a left roundhouse punch that launched teeth into the air, as well as a mist of blood. Marco's hands shot forward, grabbing the back of his attacker's head, and pulled, making it meet his knee in a sickening crunch. The punk's head snapped back up. This brought it into a perfect position for Marco's downward elbow.

The wannabe Crip sprawled out on the concrete. Marco stepped on the back of his neck. Marco's eyes were alight with adrenaline, his grin baring teeth that appeared particularly sharp and flesh-rending. His eyes swept over the man's crew, back and forth across the bunch of them. His breath was already heavy, as though he had taken a quick sprint instead of a few strikes.

When Marco spoke next, it came out low, tightly controlled. "Come on, that the best you guys have? Huh? That it? Nah, surely you must have something better that you can give me. If this is the best you have, then you are all a sorry band of wimps and weaklings."

Amanda stepped forward, and gently laid a hand on his shoulder. She wasn't quite afraid that he would bite her hand off, but she wasn't entirely certain at this point. "I do not think you need to antagonize them."

"Oh, I have no intention of doing that, but they would be better off backing away." His eyes flicked to the thugs, and in a louder voice, "In fact, I think it would be a good idea if they backed away now and take their trash with them."

Chapter 11:

Train Ride

The meeting in Washington Square Park had disbanded after Marco Catalano's impromptu performance. It was agreed that they were going to gather later on, sometime next week, after everyone had brought their own supplies. Practice would begin soon after.

Marco also added, "Everyone be certain to hold on to any Styrofoam packing peanuts you have."

After a confused look, he explained. "It's a key ingredient in homemade napalm."

As soon as it was over and they all scattered, Amanda leaned over to him and said, "I think that went well."

Marco nodded slowly, barely controlled. His respiration was up, and she could hear the blood pumping in his veins like a high-pressure valve. Amanda noticed he remained angry and staring. *Might as well ask now, while he's already angry, instead of ruining a good mood later.*

"Who was Lily? What happened with her?"

Marco went stiff, and his control became perfect as he slowly turned to look at her. He stopped smiling altogether. With slow, measured words, almost like there were periods after every word, he said, "Do you really want to do this now?"

She didn't waver. "Yes, I do."

Marco's right eye twitched. "Then come with me."

He walked for five blocks without saying another word. He carried his backpack like it was a rucksack in a war zone, filled with books and old chair legs. After several strange turns, they ended up in a dark alley in the middle of Greenwich Village, the primary area in New York for the overall lasciviousness and lechery of every conceivable kink. Marco stepped into the alley and leaned up against the wall. He stared at the ground, as though expecting it to bleed.

"Lily was my friend in high school," he said flatly. He didn't look up from the spot on the alley floor. "She was adventurous. She liked my uniform. She liked my sword—the one on my hip, thank you. She was fun and she was funny, and she was smart.

"That night, she became clingy. And affectionate. And very, very loving. She tried dragging me into this alley, and I went with her willingly." He gave Amanda a quick glance, and an even quicker smile, one that was so fleeting even the vampire wasn't certain that he had smiled. "It was a situation I'd never been in before. Never been kissed. Seventeen, and never had a girlfriend…until her, that is. I had no idea what to do."

He looked back to the alley. "So, while she was trying…or I was trying…just to get the angles right on proper lip lock, someone wanted to mug us. He tried his best, I'm sure. It was a simple matter to take the knife out of his control, but he kept pulling back on it. So, I let him have it. Then I went to work. Hurting him. A lot. I even bit him. I was out of control. By the time I was done, he gave out a death rattle.

"When I turned back to her, well, she looked at me like I was something out of a horror movie. Vega and Zeng were close by, and they weren't that much better. He wanted to hurt us, so I hurt him first. Vega and Zeng got me and Lily out of there, and they dealt with the cops. They claimed that they offed him in self-defense. He was a meth-head, so no one missed him, and no one cared that he was gone. End of story. Apparently, there was enough of a record on the guy that the DA didn't even bother asking about it."

He smiled wryly. "Apparently, Lily didn't appreciate my efforts on her behalf, and not only broke off contact with me, but quickly spread it throughout Xavier that I was a complete and utter psychopath. What friends I had stopped talking to me, except for

Zeng and Vega. I went from mild popularity among a small group to total isolation in a matter of days. The whiplash was so fast, I thought I would have a broken neck."

Marco stopped there, and he considered going farther. He thought of the last conversation he had with Lily, where she told him what he looked like, what she believed was going on in his head. Marco told her she was right. Then Marco never heard from her again.

As he thought this over, Amanda studied him, and could almost feel his anguish. When she had changed, she lost her family, so she knew the pain of isolation. Over time, with her ability to hear the blood flowing in someone's veins, she could read emotions, even if they were well concealed. She could hear Marco's heart break. The bitch Lily, and all of Marco's "friends," had hurt him deeply.

"Anyway," he continued, excerpting the end of the story, "that was a year ago now. Everyone knows that I have no problem killing someone who threatens me or mine. There were a few at Xavier who understood, mostly professors who were ex-military."

"Ah. So, what was she like?"

Marco blinked, surprised that after the whole story, this was the question she had. "You saw her. Five-foot-three, Filipino. Standard cheerleader type, only with a brain. Or at least, what I thought was a brain. Why do you ask? You want to go out for a quick bite?"

She smiled. "It is not impossible. Sometime."

Marco shrugged, and stepped out of the alley, then turned north. "Time to get on a train. It's time to get home. Meanwhile, I should invest in turpentine."

"The world's most flammable substance? You wish to make firebombs?"

"Either that or set fire to my textbooks."

"From last semester?"

"Nah, from this semester. I got the textbooks for the classes before last semester ended. I'm nearly done with them. What, you thought that I could spend all of my time playing stake-the-vampire and not study? Granted, not much is new to me. I've only been hanging out in my father's hospital since I was five."

"You, being you, started picking things up from anyone who would be willing to teach you."

"Close enough. I'm going to take the train home. You want to join me for the ride?"

Amanda didn't have to think about it for even a split second. If vampires were truly roaming around in packs of five, there was no way she was going to leave Marco to wander Brooklyn by himself. "Why not?"

Marco and Amanda sat next to each other on the train heading for Brooklyn. They claimed the two-seat bench on the train, even though the standard three- and five-seaters were empty. Marco claimed it was to allow for people pouring in. Amanda claimed to agree.

Marco put his arm up along the top of the seat, keeping his arm above Amanda's shoulders, only barely touching her hair. He could smell her light perfume, but mostly her shampoo. Why didn't his shampoos ever smell half as good? He used her washroom on occasion, and noticed she used the same no-name stuff he did, and yet…

Marco flashed back to only an hour ago, when he asked about biting him again. When Amanda leaned over and whispered into his ear, "All you have to do is ask." Oh damn, the sensation that whisper sent through his entire central nervous system was like nothing he had ever felt before. It was all he could do to change the subject and pretend it hadn't affected him.

Marco once again reconsidered the let's be friends verdict. And once again, he ran the mental mathematics on their general social interaction, adding in as many variables as he could come up with. She was, easily, five times his age, and age discrepancies were usually a problem in normal relationships. Not to mention, she was friendly, personable and sociable.

He had a mind like a computer, and social skills to match. After all, "All I have to do is ask" means that she will turn me into a physical equal via the parasitic microbes that make up her condition. On the one hand, I could just ask her out and we can get it all out of the way. She can shut me down and we can return to normal… unless and screw up out interactions. Besides, if the Lily situation is anything to go by, it will be yet another flaming train wreck. There's a reason the military doesn't have those in a relationship work together. That's less of a flaming train wreck and more of a flaming F-16 in the sandbox. The result was a negative infinity and crashed the calculator.

"Why Brooklyn?" Amanda said. "Would not the Bronx or Manhattan be better for vampires to do their hunting? Maybe Staten Island?"

Marco blinked, and chuckled. "I suspect, in part, because Brooklyn and Queens are where New York goes to die. Most of the cemeteries are in those two boroughs."

Amanda suddenly stiffened slightly. "We are in the last car?"

"Second-to. Why?"

The door from the adjoining car slid open, and several well-built, pale men and women stepped into their car. Amanda slid from the seat, and Marco followed. He held his hands behind his back, undoing the Velcro cuffs on his winter jacket.

Marco recognized the vampire just off of the leader. His father had reported him dead on the operating table on Christmas Eve. "Hello, Nissin."

The vampire stopped. He was Asian, short and stocky, like a barrel with arms and legs, with a head like a soccer ball. He straightened out his black leather jacket and smirked. "Hey, Marco. You don't look so impressive anymore."

Marco didn't take his eyes off of Nissin as he leaned over to Amanda and said, "Death hasn't improved Red any. Looks or fashion sense."

Nissin smiled. "I'm going to enjoy draining you, bitch."

Amanda leaned forward. "I do hope you are not referring to me."

Nissin stepped forward, to just within kick range of Marco. The vampire was fast enough to rip Marco's throat out in an instant should he decide to. "So what if I am? You gonna stop me?"

Marco could see that the leader of the group was growing annoyed with Nissin's posturing. The leader stepped towards them.

Marco threw his arms forward. Two squirt guns came out of his sleeves and into his hands, and he fired. One gun was aimed at Nissin's eyes, the second at the leader. Neither expected the first blast, and the pain distracted them long enough for a second squirt. Marco's knee came up, almost to his chest, and his foot punched out, kicking Nissin into his leader, and they both sprawled back into their little gang behind.

Marco swung his aim to the left as Amanda shot forward to the right. She grabbed one of the poles and swung around it, driving her feet into the vampire on the far right, kicking him out the window and into an oncoming train. She kicked off of the wall and grabbed the head of one of them, swinging around his body like on the pole, knocking most of them off of their feet, and twisting his head off. The body turned to dust before it hit the floor.

One of the vampires on Marco's side leapt over the seating, letting her coat slough off the holy water. She swept his guns aside and lunged for his throat with her fangs. The teeth went for his throat. She couldn't proceed further. It was like pressing two magnets together on the same polarity, she was stopped dead.

That's why Marco wore his rosary around his neck.

While she tried to pass the barrier provided by the rosary, the vampire saw Marco's eyes. The last time she saw eyes that cold and dark was the last night she drew breath.

Marco dropped the gun in his left hand. The right hand came up and squirted several blasts into her face. As the squirt gun fired, Marco's left hand slipped up the right sleeve, and came out with a wooden stake. He jammed it into her skull like an icepick, pulled it out, and quickly put the squirt gun to the wound and pulled the trigger, emptying holy water into the newly open space in her brain. The woman fell aside, screaming and thrashing in pain as the holy water ate away at her gray matter like acid.

Marco stepped past the woman, leaving her for dead, even as she screamed. There were five more to deal with, sprawled over the ground, not counting a blinded Nissin and their leader on top. The leader rolled to his feet – Amanda grabbed his head and twisted, not breaking his neck, but throwing him into another vampire as he tried to rise. Nissin scrambled to his feet, thrashing wildly, not trying to use his advanced senses to locate Marco.

Being dead hasn't made him smarter, Marco thought.

One of the others leapt from the floor and charged Amanda. She grabbed him in mid-air and hurled him out the train window, aiming for the third rail. He didn't make it that far, struck by one of the many iron girders in the subway. However, since the train was going at a speed in excess of fifty miles an hour, the vampire was essentially doing the same speed when his chest hit the girder. The vampire's momentum was stopped dead. His head, on the other hand, kept moving without him.

Marco moved to assist; his eyes locked on the other vampires. As he passed the hunched-over Nissin, Marco casually stabbed down into his back, aiming for the spinal cord.

You might be all sorts of things, but try moving without a nervous system, he thought as he kept moving.

Another female vampire, still knocked on the floor after Amanda's second whirl around the car, spotted Marco. Her eyes dropped to his squirt gun. She pushed to her feet and lunged.

Marco saw the move, and didn't even hesitate as he sidestepped, bringing his right arm up in a clothesline as the vampire leapt for him.

The vampire only noted Marco's move when she had already committed to the leap. Her confusion about trying to clothesline a vampire was brief –

instead of a spear-hand ending the straight arm, it was a fist wrapped around the stake. The vampire only noticed it when she slammed herself upon it.

Marco chuckled at the brief look of shock on her face before she turned to dust.

Amanda pulled two stakes out from holsters in her coat. She twisted to stab out with the right, across her body, then twisted the other way, stabbing with her left, each stab an instant kill. A third enemy leapt for her as she finished her second stab. Amanda countered with a kick to the knee, bringing him low, before slashing his jugular, then his carotid, and finally stabbing him in the heart through the back.

Amanda turned to the leader, whose eyes had been corroded by the holy water. "We should interrogate him."

"This should be fun."

The vampire chuckled, reached into his pocket, and pulled out what looked like a pocket watch. Marco's eyes widened, and he leapt forward.

The leader of the group had swallowed the contents of the "watch," and was already choking when Marco slammed into him.

Marco grimaced and pushed off of the vampire. "Ignore him, he's already dead."

Amanda leaned over and picked up the "watch." "Ug. It's actually a pyx."

Marco took it from her hand as she offered it to him to see. "A container for carrying communion wafers? He used communion as a suicide pill?"

Marco dropped the pyx and grabbed Nissin by the collar with one hand and held the squirt gun in his ear with the other. He pulled Nissin up off the floor, the damage to his spine causing him to scream. Marco jammed the squirt gun in so Nissin would pay attention. "Want to tell me what you've been doing with your afterlife, Nissin? Or would you just like me to leave you on the tracks for the next train to come by?"

Nissin laughed; a rasping, gurgling thing that Marco couldn't decipher. "You're all going to die. Every last one of you."

Marco frowned. He didn't even need the threat to be spelled out. Nissin had last been seen–alive– threatening revenge on, well, almost everybody in Marco's immediate sphere of influence. He glanced at Amanda. "I think I know who suggested that the vampires start eating my gang members."

Nissin gurgled again. "They know everything about you. They know who you are. Where you live. Who…you… love…ha!"

Marco stared at him with empty eyes, and then snarled. With a roar, he slammed Nissin to the ground, stood, and stomped on the damaged spine. Marco kept stomping, and Nissin kept screaming. The stake twisted in his spine, and in his guts, every time Marco hit him. After twenty seconds of this, Marco dropped to one knee, pulled out another bottle of holy water and snarled.

"You want to hurt me, you little prick? How's this for pain?" Marco twisted the cap off, then stuck the bottleneck into Nissin's mouth, and poured the holy water down his throat. It was hard for Nissin to scream and drown at the same time, but he managed. His skin snapped and burned and sizzled like meat on fry pan. It burned away the back of his head, his throat, and finally his neck.

When Nissin disintegrated, Marco rose. He looked to Amanda and said, "We're on the wrong train."

"Why?"

"Nissin was with the lizards about five minutes before they threw his sorry ass out. He can say that he told the vampires whatever he likes, but he knows damn little about me. In fact, there's only one thing he could have told about me that these vampires wouldn't be able to find out themselves."

Amanda had a bad feeling. "What would that be?"

Marco merely stared at Amanda for a long moment. "The person he thinks I love. There's only one person he ever knew about. They're going to kill Lily."

Chapter 12:

Meeting The Ex

"Why Lily?"

"To start with, Nissin was an idiot, and being a vampire didn't up his IQ any. Back when he was with the gangs, he saw Lily around me all the time. He hasn't seen me since. Therefore, she's the only candidate he could possibly know of."

Amanda studied Marco closely. "Are there any others?"

"Of course," he said in a complete deadpan, "because I only hang out with the most beautiful women in the entire city."

Amanda paused, uncertain if that was a compliment. In her experience, she was the only person he was friends with, as well as the only woman.

"You're going to have to bite me," he told her.

Amanda Colt looked away from the train door. She had been posed in front of it like a runner about to go into a sprint. She was so intently focused on the doors, she hadn't heard Marco's statement, despite her advanced hearing.

"What did you say?" she asked.

"I said that you're going to have to bite me. I've done the math, but I can't predict how many people they'll send to get her. I can't run fast enough to match your speed, and if they slow you down enough, this train ride is for nothing."

"This assumes they have sent anyone yet."

"Oh, Nissin was already bragging. If they're already bragging, they've probably already started their evil plan. I would at least send two people if it's a simple assassination, but there could be five of them in a standard meal formation."

"Meal formation?"

"Given the way they've been attacking, do you have a better way to phrase it?"

Amanda opened her mouth, ready to come up with an entire list of better ways to phrase it, but simply sighed, and shook her head. "Never mind."

"Yeah." He sighed, more tired than anything else. "The annoying thing is, I don't even like her. But knowing me shouldn't be a capital offense."

Amanda straightened up and strode over to him. She still made it look like a sashay even though she was being as straightforward as possible about it. "I would not like you to suffer too much blood loss, Marco, so I will not drink. Da?"

"Sure."

Marco stepped forward and wrapped his arms around her in a hug. Had anyone asked him, he would have said that it was so Amanda could easily stabilize and steady him while she bit him. She wrapped her arms around him, and she would have said something similar.

Marco cocked his head to one side, exposing his neck to her.

Amanda's lips first touched his neck, like a light kiss. Then her fangs came out, and quickly penetrated his skin, driving directly into the carotid artery. The first time she did this, she rushed, and she was in a near frenzy. Now, with only a few drops of his blood, his warmth filled her. He was good and solid against her; she enjoyed that feeling, a sensation that she had been without for decades, until him. He wouldn't run from her, wouldn't try to kill her. He was there, and he was hers, for as long as they could stand each other. His scent was all around her, the scent of a friend, or of something more. The smell of home.

Marco felt a pinch at his neck, like someone sticking a needle into him at the blood bank. Like at the blood bank, the pain faded quickly; the only sensation he was really aware of was Amanda's lips against his skin, sending electrical currents up and down his body.

Every few seconds, the tip of Amanda's tongue went along his neck; the rational part of Marco's brain told him she was merely providing more saliva, and thus more of the vampire virus. There was a part of him, somewhere mid-thorax, that didn't care but pulled at him to look at it as something more. The feel of her body against his…was more than he could think about right now.

Then the vampire virus hit him. What little pain there now faded completely into the background, and he could feel her strength flow into him. He could even more acutely feel her body against his.

They both stayed there for a long time, neither one wanting to break apart. When Amanda finally pulled away, she gave his neck a final lick…to seal the wounds closed, of course. Still in the grip of the afterglow, they stared at each other.

Then they noticed that the train was slowing.

Amanda Colt didn't wait for the doors to open before she left the train–the moment the train platform was in sight, she pried the door open with her fingers and was out the door. The train hadn't even slowed to a stop yet.

Marco had given her Lily's Astoria address and told her to go ahead without him. Even with the vampire strain giving him strength, he couldn't move as fast as she could.

The house was one in a standard row of brown-brick buildings in Queens. The homes were all interlinked for blocks at a time, looking more like apartment buildings than one-family homes. The front stairs were shared by every two front doors, creating a top landing that was almost a small patio. Within a minute of coming up from the subway, Amanda was at the front door of Lily's house. She rang the doorbell, then sat on the low wall beside the door, keeping one eye on the street and one eye on the door.

The door opened slightly, then all way. The bouncy cheerleader looked at Amanda and frowned. "What do you want?"

"Marco has made some enemies."

"I'm, like, *so* shocked."

Amanda's eyes narrowed at the dripping sarcasm. *How could Marco have ever had anything to do with this fickle little fool?*

"He believes they might be coming to do you harm." Lily let out a little gasp and glanced out the door into the street, as though expecting someone to be right behind Amanda. "Who has he pissed off now?"

"Do you know Nissin?

Lily blinked. "That fool? Yeah. I met him once, and that was enough, thanks. Why?"

"He has his own gang, and he seems to not like Marco."

"That's nothing new. Marco has that effect on people. I'm surprised you haven't done anything to him yet."

Amanda gave Lily a small smile, calculated to be just visible to a perceptive person, easily confused with an unconscious micro-expression. "What makes you think I have not?"

Lily's eyes flared, and Amanda kept her expression as passive as possible. This woman had rejected Marco but was obviously struck at the prospect that another woman may already have taken him. "You wouldn't—"

"I called the guys!"

Lily turned her gaze down the block, towards the sound of Marco's voice. Amanda merely glanced his way, and then scoping out the street again. With a light jog, Marco made it to the stairs, his backpack over one shoulder, briefcase in hand.

Amanda noticed that both of them were unzipped.

"Now that we know Nissin has his own little gang of thugs," he said, coming up the steps, "I'm going to have some of the lizards and pussy cats come in, and have this place protected, sundown to sunup."

Lily scoffed. "Yeah, because no one would do anything in broad daylight in New York."

Marco and Amanda exchanged a knowing, amused look. He said, "I figure we can spare a couple of guys for a few hours a day. The worst that can happen is they get bored."

Amanda nodded. She glanced at Lily, whose expression had softened. She quickly flipped her hair and deliberately, and obviously–to Amanda, anyway– sashayed towards Marco. Even he raised an eyebrow at her approach, as much surprised as Amanda was not.

The screech of tires on the street caught their attention. Marco and Amanda turned as one towards the sound. A van had stopped dead, parked half-on, half-off the sidewalk, as though they were going to use a driveway to leap the curb, and gave up halfway through.

Four men stepped out of the van, and they started moving towards the trio in a brisk, military formation.

The vampires had arrived.

Unlike the incident in the train, Marco wasted no time putting his plan in action. He tossed Amanda his backpack, and said, "Lily, get inside."

Amanda caught the backpack easily, while Lily stood there a moment, confused. One moment she was on her way to seducing Marco in front of Amanda Colt, and the next she was told to go inside and hide. She was smart, but not quick enough to adapt to the sudden atmosphere shift.

Marco had already turned towards the oncoming vampires.

A van *and* a five-vampire team—four on the street, one behind the wheel—meant that they had intended to kidnap Lily, and either torture her somewhere else, or use her to get to Marco or his father.

They really were pissed off that dad sent samples to the CDC, weren't they?

"You guys want to go home now."

The largest vampire, the one in front of the vampiric v-formation, grinned broadly. "We'll simply take all of you back with us."

Marco rolled his eyes. "To what purpose? Hold me, you get my father's attention, sure, but he's already sent samples to the CDC. What would be the point?"

"Nissin told us *you* were the threat. That if anyone would have caught on to us, it would have been *you*."

He frowned. *Well, that would explain why they were waiting for me on the subway. Did Nissin know that I was going to Hudson U? If so, then that means he definitely would have known the train I'd be on. I wonder if they arranged it so that they could isolate Amanda and me. It's the only reason I can think of for having that subway car all to ourselves. But do they know of Amanda? I can't see how they could; no vampire we've encountered has left alive.* "You folks really want to start something in public?"

The big one was almost at the top step. "At our speeds, who will notice? Who would believe?"

"Well, if you're going to be like that about it –"

He reached into his briefcase and came out with a Frappuccino bottle full of holy water and tossed it into the leader's face. It shattered, and the vampire's face sizzled and steamed like he'd been splashed with acid.

Marco took two steps forward, and kicked the larger vampire right in the groin, doubling him over. He then dropped an elbow to the back of his head, followed it up with a knee to the face, and then shoved him down the stairs into one of his compatriots.

Before Marco even had time to take his next step, Amanda was already in motion. She pulled a matching bottle from the backpack he tossed her and leaped for the vampire nearest her. A hammer fist to his forehead knocked his head back, and she simply rammed the bottle down his throat, making him ingest all of the holy water within.

Marco leaped from the top step, drawing his stakes as he did so. He landed knees first into the vampire he attacked, pinning both him and the female vampire beneath him. A stab into the first vampire disintegrated his body, and Marco dropped down onto the woman, and stabbed her without even needing to move.

Amanda leaped past the vampire she just "drowned" in holy water. She threw both of her stakes. One of them lodged in the tire of the van, the other in the chest of the last vampire standing.

Marco and Amanda closed on the van, each going for a door – Amanda for the driver's side, Marco for the passenger's. The driver decided that the human would be the easier fight than the vampire, and he leaped out, heading for Marco.

Marco predicted he would.

Marco dropped to one knee, letting the assailant fly right over him. He turned, pleased to see the vampire landed where he should have. The vampire rolled over onto his back, revealing what he had landed on…Marco's briefcase, which he had tossed aside at the start of the confrontation. Marco had made certain to leave the half-sharpened chair leg point-side up, at the mouth of the case. The vampire gave out a gasp as he disintegrated.

Marco looked around. All of the attackers had been dusted, and it had only been a matter of seconds. No one was rushing out to see what had happened, so no one was going to call the police.

Amanda appeared at his side. "It seems she listened to you." He stared at Amanda for a few seconds, trying to think of what she meant. Marco looked for Lily and discovered that the door was now closed and locked.

"Well, that was fun. I guess we should wait for some of our guys to show up from Brooklyn." Marco looked off into the distance. He continued speaking, as though talking to himself, thinking through the reason. "At the very least, they can serve as an early warning system. I know a few of the guys can handle guns. If some of these fangs come in and knock on the door, a crossbow from across the street will do just as well as a stake to the heart. It's not like these vampires have shown a lot of counter-surveillance techniques thus far. Also, they hired Nissin, so they'll take anybody."

Amanda nodded, then looked at him strangely. "Why? We are keeping a permanent guard here?"

"Why not? Seriously, we can afford two guys, and I'd rather not have anyone get killed because they're tangentially connected to me, even if it is her."

The door opened, and Lily came out. She looked around and didn't see anyone but the two of them. Had the street been brighter lit, she might have seen that there were sets of clothes on the street without people in them, only large, people-shaped piles of dust. "What happened?"

"They ran. They even left their car," Marco explained. He took the steps up in two strides, stopping at the landing. "I don't think we'll have to worry about them anymore, but just in case, we've got two of the guys coming by."

"Oh," she said, sounding almost disappointed. "Are you sure you can't stay?"

His smile was a little tight this time. "Nah, I have to get Amanda home before she turns into a pumpkin."

Lily's smile turned into a forced grin. "She could stay, too." Marco looked over his shoulder at Amanda, and arched his brows, his expression clearly asking, *What the hell?*

Amanda shrugged. She didn't know either. He looked back, and said, "Funny, I didn't think you'd want me anywhere near you on purpose."

Lily reached out and touched his arm. "Well, since we broke up, I think…well, I think I was wrong. It's always useful for…um…"

The muscles holding Marco's smile up tightened visibly. "You mean it's always useful to have *someone like me*? Yes, I'm *sure* it is."

Before Lily could face a full verbal onslaught, Marco's cell phone rang. He pulled it from his inside jacket pocket and flipped it open quickly. "Speak."

"It's Vega. I got two of my guys in the area already, one visiting his *abuela*. You know Roman?"

"I believe so. Big guy, army family? Marines tossed him out after he spent six tours in whatever sandbox they'd let him play in?"

"That's him."

"Good. If the cops swing by, tell them that the attackers were scared off." Marco thought a moment, switching from rage to his plan. There were a bunch of annoying drug pushers who ended up in the East River after graduation, and they hadn't surfaced yet– Marco had wrapped them thoroughly. "Give them the description of those guys from early last summer."

"I can do that. Anything else?"

"No." Marco looked straight at Lily as he spoke into the phone. "I'm leaving."

Marco closed the phone with a snap as he turned and started down the stairs. He met Amanda's eye and nodded towards the direction of the subway.

He was halfway down the stairs when Lily called out, "I never meant to hurt you!"

Marco stopped dead on the last step and looked over his shoulder at her. "Leaving me without a word was your choice. You can associate with whomever you like. Telling everyone at Xavier I was a freak, though; that proves I can't trust you. Ever. And that I shouldn't have trusted you to start with."

Marco and Amanda started walking again.

When they were two blocks away, Amanda said, "She really wants you back."

"So?"

"She might repent."

"So?"

"She is cute."

"So?"

"You have anything else to say?"

"Nope." Marco walked in silence for a few moments. "She stabbed me in the back so hard, the sword tip came out my chest. I'd never trust her again after such an egregious violation. Lucky for her, that doesn't mean I want to see her dead."

"So, why are they putting this much energy into you?" Amanda asked once they were back on the train.

Marco frowned and leaned back in the seat. "I'm not sure. Okay, fine, Nissin may have hated my guts, but that's no reason for anyone in a vampire hierarchy to *believe* the newest person in the gang when he started ranting. It's probably because they sent a guy after my father, and he didn't come back. Add Nissin saying that I had something to do with it, and then, tag, I'm it."

"Which leads to another troubling 'something.'"

"Which is?"

"That there *is* a hierarchy," she said, making it sound like *higher-arr-key*.

"Wasn't that implied by the way they've been organized?"

She raised a brow, a small amused smile on the edge of her lips. "With networked intelligence? *Nyet*, this is more organized."

Marco considered it a moment. "You have a point. Which means we're probably in even more trouble, and we need to step up training on the gangs, and…"

Amanda frowned. "And…?"

"This is too much without someone noticing." Marco stared at the subway map in front of him, his eyes losing focus as he concentrated on the matter at hand. "It's not like we're the only ones on the planet with a brain cell between us, right? This is too organized without prior experience. This has happened before, and I'd bet a lot of times before. That's not possible without *someone* seeing *something*."

She nodded but said nothing. She bit her lip, gazing at the same map as Marco.

After a long moment of silence, he finally turned to her.

"What?" she asked.

"Under the heading of *someone* who could have noticed something like this happening before, there happens to be someone right next to me who's been around a while."

"I'm not *from* New York, remember."

"But what do you know about this kind of thing happening anywhere?"

"Hmm…I have heard of this before," she said slowly. "On occasion. It happens. But not enough for someone to be this proficient. There are usually villagers with pitchforks involved."

Marco chuckled a little, but then his smile faded, disappearing with fatigue. "Oh, please, this is New York at the dawn of the twenty-first century. No one believes in vampires, the supernatural, God. We're living in one great, big, atheistic culture. Go to San Francisco and they'll believe in practically anything. But this is New York. You might as well have a muezzin with a call to prayer of *Dawkins-hu Akbar*, so you can get all of the atheists to come and talk about how they hate everybody."

"You do not like atheists?"

"Oh, I don't care about atheists, one way or another. I'm a Libertarian Catholic. My God is quite forgiving; if you're going to go to Hell, you more or less have to put some effort into it. As for me, you leave me alone, I leave you alone. I mind people who inflict their beliefs on me when I'm leaving them the hell alone. This includes everybody who tells me my religion is harming them even though I've never met them before. They can go screw themselves."

"Okay, point taken. And this relates to our vampire issue, how?"

"My point is that whoever did this knows that no one in New York is going to think 'vampire' except as a last resort. Even then, there are a whole slew of people who would shrug it off and ignore the whole thing. Most of Manhattan, I suspect. Still, someone has to have noticed this sort of thing before, somewhere, somewhen. You know of anyone in particular?"

"There is Mikhail, but anything I know about him is rumor."

He nodded, his eyes closed. Fatigue was starting to set in already…had he burned through that much of the vampire virus in his system, or was it just the adrenaline letdown?

Also, it was a metaphysical virus, so maybe his emotional drama was a physical drain.

Any other day he would have pressed for details on this Mikhail, but not today. Not now.

"So, not a close personal friend. Understood." He rolled over onto his side. "I think I want to go home right now, stay in bed, and not get up for a day."

Amanda smiled. "I am not going to object."

"Didn't think you would. I'm also a semester ahead on all of my reading, so I should be good as far as classes go."

"Ah."

Marco sighed and closed his eyes. "Would you like to stay with me?"

Amanda blinked, a little shocked. "What?"

"I have blackout curtains in the house somewhere. I wouldn't mind…you know, if you just stayed over. Slept a little." He opened one eye to look at her and smiled weakly. "Only sleeping, obviously."

She finally took a breath. "I would like to, but I do not have my earth with me."

There was a moment of silence. One traditional "rule" that most vampire fiction ignored was the requirement that vampires sleep in the dirt of their native land. In the case of Amanda, she was old enough that she didn't need to sleep with buckets of Earth in, on, and around her. She used Ziploc bags for the last twenty years. Though she had plenty of Russian soil over in a warehouse on Long Island.

Marco frowned. "That was one rule I never understood. Why the dirt?"

"At a guess…I have *nyet* idea."

"Oh well." Marco closed his eyes. "I'm just wondering why there isn't someone else who's caught on. I mean, hell, who *would* have caught on after a while? Granted, that needs an organization that's been around for years, who file reports, keep them over time, have people who analyze stuff that is so out of date it's virtually obsolete…"

Marco's eyes snapped open, and he sat up straight. "We need a church."

Amanda cocked her head to one side. "Any one in particular?"

"Catholic, of course. They're the only ones I know with a long-term headquarters…and I'm not walking into a synagogue with a rosary wrapped around my neck."

Amanda nodded as the train came to a stop. "I presume that you wish to wait for morning?"

Marco glanced at his watch. "Yeah, I can't imagine a rectory that's going to like me knocking on their door at this hour." He stood as the door opened. "At least come with me? I'm sure my father would like to say hello, assuming he's home."

"Sure. Why not?"

They exited to the fresh night air of the Brooklyn Street. Marco wondered what it smelled like to a vampire. With a burst of speed, the two of them made it to Marco's door in moments, mostly because they could.

He skidded to a stop just before the first step, and Amanda left some shoe rubber on the sidewalk.

Officer Donald "Duck" Tolbert was passed out next to the stoop, his blue uniform covered in blood.

Chapter 13:

Elementary, My Dear Dracula

Amanda remembered Officer Donald "Duck" Tolbert from the Christmas dinner with Marco and the Catalano family. The large black officer had the air of a minister and smelled good enough to eat. A blood-type A-positive, and a good vintage, too.

Now, he looked quite different. His blue uniform shirt was covered in blood, his face slashed, his call radio crushed.

His gun lay next to him, the slide locked open and empty.

Marco knelt next to him, felt for a pulse, surprised when he found one. "It's actually quite good. What do you think?"

Amanda took a deep breath, then listened a moment.

"By the coagulation, he has been here for two hours, maybe more. It looks worse than it is."

"He should have been *home* three hours ago. His, not mine."

"How often does he drop by?"

"Often enough that he could have been off-duty when he arrived here." He moved and grabbed one arm, Amanda grabbed the other, and they both hauled Tolbert to his feet.

He looked across Tolbert at Amanda. "All this blood isn't affecting you?"

"Only the way you would look at food after spending all day at a buffet."

Marco winced. "Try not to vomit on him, then."

Maneuvering Tolbert up the stairs was easy. Marco quickly unlocked the door and relocked it while Amanda carried the cop into the sitting room. "Look after him," he whispered. "I'm going to go see if anyone is awake. If not, I'll patch Donald up myself."

After a quick walk through, Marco couldn't find the lights on in any part of the house aside from the main hall. He muttered a silent curse and went directly for the first aid kit.

He returned to the sitting room and found that Amanda was already washing the blood away. It seemed the source of most of the blood was the massive gash alongside Tolbert's head.

Amanda tossed some damp, blackish-red paper towels into the garbage. "No pun intended," she began, saying it like *in ten did*, "but it will suck to be him in the morning."

Marco nodded and moved closer. Suddenly Officer Tolbert sat up with a start and a shout, making even Amanda flinch.

Tolbert's eyes looked around, taking in the scenery. "I don't remember getting inside the house."

"You didn't," Marco told him. "You got to the stairs. You'll be fine, though. What hit you?"

"Something weird."

Marco's mouth bunched up. "Yes, that's helpful. Because nothing 'weird' *ever* happens in New York."

Tolbert gave Marco a look that told the student that the cop would be quite all right. Maybe even better after kicking Marco's ass. "I shot a creep. Two of them. They were attacking a guy in the street. I drew down. I told them to freeze. Then they tossed something at me, threw my aim off. I got one of them in the throat, should've taken his head clean off. Then he…sort of just…was gone. Just…gone. I think

I emptied most of the rest of my magazine into the second guy. Bam, same thing. Though I think he took three rounds in the head. It was like a freaking monster movie."

Marco and Amanda exchanged a glance. "Amanda, can I speak with you a moment, please?"

The two moved to the doorframe, standing on the threshold. "Should we tell him?" he asked. "Or should we pass it off as him taking a hit to the head?"

Tolbert groaned. "Guys, I'm brain-damaged, not deaf. Are you guys trying to avoid telling me there are vampires? Because, right now, I would accept that as an explanation."

The two of them turned to look at him at the same time.

"Sorry?" Marco asked.

Tolbert slowly swung his feet off the couch onto the floor. Even that required him to get his bearings. "There are a whole bunch of people being attacked, *at night*, with the only wounds being bite marks along the major veins. There are attackers who become dusty when you blow their head off. How stupid do you people think I am?" He slowly raised a palm and pressed it into his eye, rubbing as though trying to keep it from popping out of his head. "My problem is that I couldn't prove this around the station house. I tell anyone, they're going to put me into a rubber room for eval."

The two of them exchanged another look.

Tolbert looked at them, then rolled his eyes and sighed. "You to want to tell me something else now, or are you going to have a conversation without letting me in on it?"

"The DVD?" she asked.

Marco nodded.

Tolbert stood up. "The what now?"

"We have a DVD of a disintegrating vampire," he told the cop. "The problem is that you can do anything on a laptop nowadays."

Amanda nodded. "Exactly. You would have to have it verified as true in forensics, but then, how do you control the flow of information?"

"It gets out, people start being set on fire," Marco noted.

"Goths being shot with arrows in the street," Amanda added.

"Environmentalist lawyers trying to make vampires an endangered species."

Both the vampire and the police officer looked at Marco.

"Really?" Tolbert asked. "Of all the bad things you think could happen, lawyers are in your top five?"

He shrugged. "My father's a doctor, so of course I hate lawyers. Lawyers are like the top ten evils of the universe, with evils number one through ten being different varieties of lawyers. But unfortunately, I think they'd actually try that."

Tolbert frowned. "Okay, I see your point. I've seen enough lawyers get career gang bangers off for fun and profit that I don't doubt a future where vampires are protected predators. But, yeah, we're going to have trouble selling this to anyone, no matter how much evidence we have. And if it was *proven?* Oy."

"Just imagine if it got out to the general public." Marco winced. "Keeping regular people still long enough to explain it to them, calmly, and reasonably, would require nailing them to the floor, locking their faces in place with a collar, and put them on Ritalin to control the ADD of the average New Yorker."

Tolbert smiled. "Makes you wonder why they had to come here."

Amanda laughed. "Really? Why not? Groups of people who walk around in the middle of the night, who are pale, and bloodless, and occasionally having red eyes?"

Marco nodded. "Sounds like a night in the Village, don't it? We're a heavily-populated area with enough transients, illegal aliens, hookers, and organized criminals that there's a buffet line of people who won't be missed. Try having *one* strange murder in the middle of, oh, hell, *Iowa.*"

Amanda agreed. "In rural areas, people notice strange things. Would not be as easy to make people disappear as any neighborhood in five boroughs."

"Yeah," Tolbert said. "And who'd noticed a few more violent sociopaths in Crown Heights and Brighton Beach? Oh, yeah, and some of our citizens carry machetes, and others *routinely* dismember victims. For fun. Not to mention various hazards of city life."

Marco frowned. "True." He glanced to Amanda. "I don't think it's easy to fall on the third rail and burst into flames in the middle of Utah. Though if they ate a few Mormons, I wouldn't mind too much."

The cop and the vampire gave Marco another look. He shrugged. "Have you ever *met* a door-to-door Mormon? Those guys are *creepy*. Blonde-haired, blue-eyed, and always *perky* and *cheerful*. I feel like they've always stepped out of an Ira Levine novel."

"*Stepford Wives*," she supplied. "*Not* with Nicole Kidman."

Marco sighed and shook his head. "Okay, I can prove that Mormons are creepy in two words: sparkly vampires."

Amanda hissed. "Do not even *discuss* those books."

Tolbert rolled his eyes and groaned in pain. "Ow…hey, guys, I should ask. How much work have you two been putting into this?"

"Enough to start putting together an anti-vampire army, and killing people in the middle of my clinic," said Doctor Robert Catalano from the staircase, blue bathrobe wrapped tightly around him. He stopped on the bottom landing and looked at the three of them in the sitting room.

"The next time you turn someone into a great big pile of dust in the middle of my micro lab, Marco," his father said, "dispose of the clothing, and delete the digital backup on the security cameras."

"Good to know, Dad," Marco said, fidgeting nervously. "I'll take notes."

Robert looked at Tolbert and nodded towards the living room. "Donald, I'm going to have the kids here move into the living room so they can have a chat, and we're going to start putting your head back together."

He walked down the rest of the way, hands still in robe, and stopped between the two of them, and leaned over close.

At a very soft whisper, he said, "Shouldn't your girlfriend get home before sunrise? We'd hate for her to burst into flames in the middle of the sitting room. Insurance wouldn't cover it."

Amanda left for her evening classes. After Officer Tolbert was patched up and sent to bed in the guest room. Marco stayed up with his father in the kitchen.

Doctor Robert Catalano only started getting his hands under the water before Marco asked, "How?"

"To which part?" his father asked, not looking away from the soap.

"How did you know Amanda was a vampire?"

"You know my methods, Marco," he said, in an impersonation of Basil Rathbone as Sherlock Holmes.

Marco restrained a sigh. "You mentioned the clothes at the clinic in the micro lab. I remember throwing them into the garbage. You found them and decided to look for the deleted security footage."

"Not to mention you did a number on the stool in the lab," the doctor told him. "You smacked the guy so hard, I could see marks in the wood."

"The beaten up stool led you to the clothing, which led you to the security footage, which led you to think vampires."

"Correct. When you calculate the rate of speed that the virus consumed material in the blood plates, that would mean anyone infected with it would have to be transfused, or they might even ingest blood directly. The human body couldn't take it otherwise. Which leads into all of the gang violence and other nocturnal activities of the average criminal lately."

"But Amanda?" Marco asked his father. He leaned against the kitchen counter while the doctor scrubbed. "There are hints at her being a vampire, but proof?"

"That was, I admit, more of a supposition." He flicked his hands into the sink and reached for a towel. "Amanda never showed up in daylight, and when she came in, she always smelled faintly of suntan lotion, even in fall and winter. She was pale, bloodless, and you two don't talk dating, so there had to be a good reason for it. Not to mention, *your* hours are getting later and later. When vampire is an option, my conclusion isn't too much of a stretch."

Marco nodded but stayed silent.

Robert looked at Marco now. "Since you're still breathing, I'm assuming she hasn't been snacking on you, and since I'm still breathing, I assume that she's not in the running for the Bram Stoker award for evil. So, what am I missing about vampires?"

"Do you remember RPGs?"

"Rocket Propelled Grenades, or Role-Playing Games?"

"The latter."

"I remember some of them," Doctor Catalano said, "back when you played. Why?"

"Let's just say that alignment truly does affect powers and vulnerabilities. Everything we know about Dracula is true, but only for those who share Dracula's alignment. There is no *Buffy the Vampire Slayer* automatic evil."

Robert Catalano smiled wryly. "I'll be sure to keep up with my garlic tablets and keep my rosary on me at all times."

"That would be a good start. Mostly the rosary."

"Good to know." He put the towel off to the side and studied Marco a moment. "You do realize that going up against the forces of darkness with a street gang you organized may not be enough, don't you?"

"What makes you think I'm organizing the street gangs?"

"You're a little predictable, Marco. I don't remember the last time you had a problem that you thought that you couldn't handle yourself. After all, you *do* like claiming to be the feudal lord of Brooklyn."

"Yeah, well, people want to come and screw with my neighborhood, they had best come prepared for a smack down."

"So, what *are* you going to do? I hope it's more than just reorganizing your pet gang lords."

"I'm going to pay a visit to the church tomorrow," he said.

"I figure that if anyone's going to notice something strange in the long-term, it would be Rome."

Robert nodded. "I've heard dumber ideas. Just for curiosity's sake, have you asked Amanda about the history of vampires?"

"Not specifically…do you have something in particular you want to know? I mean, I don't know for sure how old she is, but I am pretty sure she didn't invent vampires. Who knows how much she has actually studied vampiric history."

"Well, start with the Enlightenment."

Marco arched a brow, remembering that he had made much the same argument. "What's your reason?"

"Because if I were a vampire, I would be happy to pop out of my coffin at a time when people started to drop God and pick up the symbol of Lucifer as a symbol of 'change' and 'bringing the light.' Not to mention, a belief in vampires spiked during the same time period. Now that I know that vampires exist, the belief in vampires might have been encouraged by the actual *appearance* of vampires."

Marco nodded. "That was pretty much my reasoning. Heck, meeting a vampire helped my belief in them."

"Well, that, and Vlad Dracul was around during the Renaissance, so the Enlightenment just makes sense."

Marco winced. "Well, that can't be good. I wonder what impact that would have had elsewhere."

"There was always the French revolution." Doctor Catalano smiled and nodded. "I'm back to bed. Be sure to get Officer Tolbert up in the morning if I can't."

January 6th

The Church of St. Anthony - St. Alphonsus was a Catholic church in the midst of Greenpoint. Built in the 1850s, it looked like it could be the pinnacle of construction back then. It had a tall, 240-foot spire as black as iron that shot straight up to the sky, with a red brick face trimmed in white limestone. The inside was cavernous and Gothic, like the architect attempted to construct a small St. Patrick's Cathedral in a space not half as large.

The priest of this particular church was a slightly pudgy, older black man. His hair had not yet started to gray, but he was already mildly wrinkled. He had thick plastic frames for his glasses, though the lenses weren't that thick. "Bill Rodgers," Marco began, "meet Amanda Colt."

"Ah!" the priest exclaimed, his voice practically booming throughout the small church, "you finally got a girlfriend you could bring around to meet me, eh?" He looked towards Amanda and shook her hand with both of his. "How are you? Bill Rodgers. Pastor of this fine parish."

Amanda smiled. "Charmed, but I am not his girlfriend."

He looked back to Marco. "Why not?"

"We're just friends."

"Ack. Not that again." With a boyish grin, Rodgers backed away and waved them in. "So, Marco, what brings you down here with your 'just friend'?"

"We're interested in vampires," Marco said without any hesitation. His smile was stuck on entertained.

Rodgers stopped, turned, and blinked. "Really? Why?"

"Da, really," Amanda answered.

"Because it's come up lately," Marco added.

"We want the church's official position on them," she concluded.

Rodgers looked from one to the other and shrugged. "They're a nasty bedtime story. Something to scare little children with. They're not real, and never have been, and never will be. Does that satisfy you?"

"No," Marco told him directly. "Because things have been happening lately that concern us."

"Deeply," Amanda added.

Rodgers sat back, against the arm of a pew, and crossed his arms, resigning himself to suffering through this discussion. "Such as?"

Marco leaned against a pew of his own. "Packs of vampires roaming the city, draining people on a synchronized schedule, starting with the usual dregs, ending with cops. Things like that."

Rodgers nodded and looked back and forth between the two of them. "So, what do you expect me to say about it?"

"Let's say that we want the church's *unofficial* position on vampires. How does that sound to you?"

Rodgers gave them a loud, booming laugh. "It sounds utterly ridiculous!"

The priest stared at them both for a long moment, and Marco had the sense that it was going to be the stare just before a lecture about how stupid belief in vampires really was.

If this was a bust, the next stop was Amanda's parish, to see if that local pastor would be more knowledgeable. Then they would have to start blindly seeking out other priests, making them a handsome couple of abject nutcases who asked random priests about the existence of vampires.

That would essentially be the point where the two of them would be completely screwed, unless Amanda wanted to flash her fangs at the priests they were asking and encourage them to kick the question up the chain of command.

But the reason for coming here was simple: bodies were dropping in Brooklyn. Attacks were happening *in Greenpoint*. The local priest was the first person Marco could think of.

The priest's look softened, and he said, "I really wish you hadn't decided to do this, Marco."

The younger man blinked, and a sudden thrill of worry shot through him. He straightened, and slid his back foot behind him, sliding into a fighting stance, even if his hands were up against his chest instead of covering his face. Even Amanda straightened next to him.

"Do *what*, exactly?" Marco asked, his eyes flicking around the church to see if there might be any place to hide from Amanda's senses.

"Ask questions," Rodgers told him. "Branch out. Because, now, we have to do something about you."

Amanda and Marco exchanged a look. She was the one who asked, "Who is this 'we' you speak of?"

From the darkened corner of the church came sudden motion. Thermal-lined camouflage sheets fell to the floor, revealing the men and weapons behind them. There were crossbows, and assault weapons, shotguns, and a flamethrower.

"And there is a man with a sniper rifle in the choir loft above you," Rodgers explained. "Just in case you get any ideas."

Marco frowned. "I'm starting to think that we shouldn't have called ahead."

Chapter 14:

The Attack Of The Vatican Ninjas

Marco considered his options as he looked around the Catholic Church of St. Anthony – St. Alphonsus. He took in the weapons arrayed against them, and he didn't like the odds. The crossbows he didn't mind, or the shotgun. However, the assault weapons were most likely the biggest concern. The flamethrower looked particularly menacing.

Marco spared Amanda a glance as he tried to track all of them at once. "I count eight in front of us. You?"

"I cannot tell. At least ten. I cannot sense more."

"Anti-vampire squad," Marco concluded. "Their camouflage was so good, you couldn't even see it."

Amanda nodded slightly, wondering exactly how this would go. If these Vatican ninjas wanted everyone on their side to get out of there alive, then they would have shot Marco and Amanda before they revealed themselves. But no one made a motion beyond dropping the camouflage. In fact, had their intent been to kill the vampire and her friend, a shot with a .50-

caliber sniper rifle would have taken her head off, and Marco would have been close behind.

Which means what?

Marco didn't even look in Rodgers' direction when he said, "So, what are you and your Vatican ninjas going to do with us?"

Father Rodgers was quite somber. "That completely depends on you, young man."

Amanda shook her head and let out a faint growl. "Oh, enough. We are impressed. Either this show of force is for intimidation or for recruitment. Marco is not much of a joiner, and I am not intimidated."

Marco chuckled. "You think *I* am? Really? How many vampires have I killed?"

"Okay. Okay."

"Also, if this were a recruitment drive, that means they have an idea of how experienced we are already."

She shook her head. "I do not believe they have an accurate picture of how much experience we have."

"Neither do I."

Things happened so fast, no one could really track it, but the Vatican ninjas came close.

Amanda and Marco darted in two different directions at the same time, almost as if they had rehearsed.

Amanda went for the priest, grabbing Rodgers and hurling him by the shoulders, sending him at the ninja with the flamethrower like a handball. The man saw him coming, and turned off the flame, bracing for impact as the priest slammed into him. The vampire didn't even stop moving after she hurled the priest but was in motion a split second after he had left her hands. She went for the ninja on her left, darting for him, and leaping over his line of fire, coming down on him from above like a lion on prey in the Serengeti.

Marco darted to the back of the church, moving faster than either of the ninjas behind him could have expected, still affected by Amanda's bite on the train the night before.

The ninja off to the right side of the church tried to lead Marco as a target, but the young man dove for the floor, going straight into a roll, underneath his line of sight. When he came to a stop, he sprang up, launching two palms into the chins of both ninjas at the back door of the church. He sprinted past them, heading right for the stairs.

Amanda sprang off of the ninja in the left of the church, then shot up the left aisle, heading straight for the altar. She dipped down into a pew as several arrows shot in her direction. Springing up, she darted around a pillar, then leaped onto the altar, sweeping the legs out from underneath one commando and driving her forearm into another shooter. She hurled that one into a third gunman, then dove into a roll, cutting the legs out from underneath a fourth gunman.

The sniper in the loft above was confused, trying to track both Amanda and Marco. By the time he had decided that Marco was the one concern he could tend to, the blond was already out of his line of sight.

The sniper then swiveled around, aiming for the stairs up into the choir loft.

The barrel swung neatly into Marco's hands.

Marco pulled back on the sniper rifle, then slammed the butt of the gun into the sniper's face. Without any preamble, Marco swung the rifle back around so that it faced the Vatican ninjas.

"So, do we pass?" Marco's voice rang out as he drew a bead on the backpack for the flamethrower. "Or does this have to get messy?"

Rodgers rose from the altar and dusted himself off. "Well, Marco, I think we should talk, don't you?"

"I think I'm good from up here," Marco shouted back. Amanda placed a hand on Marco's shoulder. He hadn't even seen her move from the altar. "Marco, we can go down now."

Marco's face showed a definite strain. There was more effort to restrain himself than Amanda had seen in all the time she had known him. She could even feel his muscles tensing.

"Put it down, Marco," she said calmly. "Killing in church is not a good way to start any conversation."

The hand on the rifle's grip opened, as though the gun had become red hot, and he swung the rifle off to the side.

"Okay. Let's go down and iron out some details."

Father Rodgers poured out the tea into the cups on the counter, his back to Marco and Amanda as they sat at the kitchen table in the small rectory off of Rodgers' church. The kitchen was small, barely big enough for the three of them, so the rest of the "Vatican ninjas" were stationed outside, in the hall.

"Lucky for you, this parish is understaffed," Marco said.

"Nothing lucky about it," Rodgers answered. "When Rome caught on to the ever-growing string of murders, everyone else was transferred out, and the soldiers moved in."

He grabbed two of the mugs, then took them over to the table. "Don't you remember the massive transfer right before Christmas?"

"I wondered where they had all gone." He leaned back in the chair. "So, Vatican ninjas. I expect that they aren't a new thing?"

Rodgers shook his head as he took a seat across from them. "Not at all. The organization is a few hundred years old. A subdivision of the Swiss Guards…mostly because Rome needed to secure itself before it could do anything about the rest of the world."

Marco nodded with a bit of a grunt.

Amanda said, "So, what would you like to tell us?"

Rodgers placed the mug on the table, a slight tremor making the cup shake. "Where would you like me to start?

There's a lot of material to cover."

"In the beginning would be good," Marco said.

"In the beginning was the Word."

"A little more recent than that."

"I can't do that," Rodgers said seriously. "If you want the beginning of vampires, then we have to start there."

Amanda leaned back in her chair and looked to Marco. "You were the one who mentioned Lilith to me back when this first started."

Marco frowned. "The original tale being that she was the prototype for Eve, only she malfunctioned…and when something God makes goes bad, they go really bad. Lucifer is a case in point. I'm not being literal about this, I hope."

"I doubt it. No one has been for literalism within the Catholic church since the early days. By the time of Augustine, it was considered outdated theology."

"But," Amanda interjected, "what if the tale of Lilith was a way to account for vampires?"

Marco cut in. "In which case, considering how old the story is, that's not good news for us."

Rodgers quoted, "'And in the days before Noah, giants walked the Earth'…if you remember. They also survived the flood. So, you can expect that they would be most resilient."

Marco held up a hand. "Okay, stop. You're now throwing out random quotes from Genesis. Those giants who walked the earth were the 'Nephilim.' Again, *giants*. If we're not taking things literally, connecting the Nephilim to vampires is a little much, isn't it?"

Amanda shrugged. "Not if they were *my* ancestors."

Rodgers nodded. "There are more than enough lines in the Bible that imply a distinction between them and human beings."

Marco groaned, then put his head against the table, rapping his forehead against the surface a few times. "So, now I'm going to be fighting creatures out of Bible mythology. Okay, fine, these guys want to come to my neighborhood, screw with my people, I'm going to show them that Brooklyn is the last place on Earth they want to try to invade. So, are your Vatican ninjas on loan or something?"

"That's not really how it works."

Marco laughed. "Actually, I don't care how it works. You know me, Father. I've been coming to your church for as long as I've been alive. I'm going to eradicate this vermin, with or without your help. Or your Vatican ninjas, or–"

"We would want to send you for training," the priest interrupted.

"–the NYPD, or…" Marco's rant slowed to a stop. "I'm sorry, what did you say?"

"They are offering you 'Vatican Ninja' training," Amanda said with a smile.

"Why me?"

"You mean other than your belief in something others wouldn't believe, your willingness to risk your life to fight this scourge, and your skill in combat?" Rodgers turned to Amanda. "How many has he killed in personal combat?"

"Two or three last night on the train, another two in Astoria with some additional aid from me."

Marco nodded and leaned back in the chair. His eyes focused on the crucifix on the wall, using it as most Catholics should: a focal point, something to concentrate on. After a long moment, he said, "No."

Even Amanda was surprised. "Really?"

He frowned, thoughtfully, his eyes not wavering from the cross. "I still have an education to work on, and I'd like to get it. Fancy ninjas aside, you can't waive classes, and let me just take tests and labs. I don't think you're that tight with the government. Any government. How about I make you a deal: you give me tactical support when needed, and we can talk about me joining your little gang of rogues when I graduate, or if I'm ever allowed any free time in the meanwhile.

Better?"

"If that is our only option, I suppose we have to take it. However, if you don't mind, we have another matter we'd like to discuss with you." He picked up a bible from next to the chair and opened it. One of the bookmarks was a photo of a well-dressed, clean-cut fellow. "Have you seen this man kicking around Greenpoint?"

"Nope. Sorry. Why, should I have?"

"He's dead right now," the priest told him casually.

"That would be why I haven't seen him." Marco took the photo and slid it over to Amanda. "You?"

She studied it for a long moment. "*Nyet.* I don't think so. But from this alone, what is the American Phrase? He smells like FBI?"

Marco nodded, his smile amused. "Oh yes. He's almost certainly a fed."

The vampire looked at the priest. "*Should* we know him?"

"Not necessarily." Rogers took the photograph back. "He was an FBI agent; you have that right. He's been in Greenpoint recently, and now he's disappeared."

"What makes you think that it has anything to do with us?"

"It may not," Rodgers said, "but be advised to not take any chances. This guy had years of training and now…? Anyway, who would have thought 'vampires' when the assaults first started in Brooklyn?"

Marco nodded, standing up. "Okay, I'm going to want the number for your tactical team, and I'm going to need a copy of the photo of your dead fed so I can spread it around the neighborhood to see if anyone has any information."

Amanda rose with him. "We still have much to do. Educating the locals on vampiric self-defense, organizing them into patrol forces that follow schedules…"

Rodgers nodded and pushed himself to his feet. "Understood."

He reached out his hand, and Marco took it. "Be careful out there, Marco. I hate holding funerals for people I baptized."

"Gotcha." Marco was about to walk out, then stopped. "By the way, this is going to sound strange, but have you ever heard of a connection between the Enlightenment and vampires? I know it sounds stupid, but–"

Father Rodgers eyes lit up, and he barked a laugh. "Ah! The origins of the great vampire uprising of the eighteenth century! I'm surprised you know about it, not many people do."

"I didn't. It was just a guess."

"Well, let's just say that there was a good reason that they used Lucifer as the symbol of the Enlightenment, and it wasn't just because he was a symbol of 'change' and 'light.' It's why the Illuminati and the Masons were banned."

Marco made a face. "I was at a lodge meeting once. They drank beer and had awful venison steaks. There are just some things that shouldn't be done to decent meat."

Amanda put her hand on his arm. "European Masons are not the same as American Masons. Trust me. They never were, really. In Europe, to be a Grand Mason, you had to experience one ceremony where they rammed a sword through a mockup of the Pope's miter."

"Goody," Marco said, completely deadpan. "Now, what was the great vampire uprising?"

"It was well disguised," the priest told him, "but the demonic influences were evident in the public decapitations. Peasants would run in and catch freshly flowing blood with their bread, and eat it, in one of the most obvious perversions of the Eucharist ever witnessed."

Marco put his hands up in the classic "time out" signal.

"Wait, public rituals of blood sacrifices? When the hell was this?"

"Most people called it the French Revolution."

Chapter 15:
Things Can Get Worse

March 13th, 8:00 a.m.

Over two months after Marco and Amanda's run-in with the Vatican Ninjas of St. Anthony–St. Alphonsus Church, Doctor Robert Catalano finished tightening his tie and glanced down at the coffee table in the sitting room.

The entire table was covered by a spread of wooden knives. Most of them were small knives, not even six inches long. He frowned, picked one up, and balanced it on his finger. The center of balance was in the middle of the knife, so they were for throwing.

Then there was a large, machete-sized wooden knife, which also had perfect center of balance.

He thinks he's going to throw this? He leaned towards the entrance to the sitting room. "Marco? What exactly are you working on now?"

After listening to a small herd of elephants on the stairs as Marco sprinted down, he heard his son say, "Anything in particular?"

Marco was on the stairs, both hands braced on the banister, his feet on two different steps, as though he was about to sprint back up at any moment. Robert nodded towards the weaponry on the table. "When did you join the Boy Scouts?"

Marco rolled his eyes and let out a burst of air that sounded like *psssht*. "When Hell froze over. That's when. Remember that one summer camp you sent me to?"

The doctor smiled. He remembered it very, very well. There was a bully at that summer camp. An ambulance was involved. Lawyers had been threatened…then there was something about waterboarding in the lake…

"The camp we had to come exfiltrate you from? I remember.

Why?"

"I picked up whittling." Marco flipped a mental coin and decided that this conversation was going to take a while, so he came all the way down the stairs. "Obviously."

"Throwing knives, and a throwing *Bowie knife*?" Robert Catalano asked, still mildly incredulous. "Where do you even *get* the wood for this?"

"You'd be surprised at the quality of materials thrown

out." Robert nodded, reached for his jacket, and paused. "You know, I believe there's an old wooden broomstick that never made it to the curbside trash. You wouldn't know anything about that, would you?"

"Waste not, want not." He gave his father an easy shrug.

"Look at it this way. Our environmentalist neighbors will take great comfort to know that we are responsibly reusing garbage to a good purpose."

"Please. If you were any more Right, you'd be Attila the Hun."

"Really? He was a revolutionary, so that makes him more of a left-winger, doesn't it?"

Marco's father looked at his watch, then waved his son to a couch. "We need to talk."

Marco moved from the hall into the sitting room. "Funny, you don't even look like a girlfriend." He slid into the couch, leaned back.

Robert took a moment and thought about whether or not he wanted to stand or sit for this, but standing wouldn't give him an advantage with Marco, so might as well be comfortable. Once seated, he began, "I'm a little worried about you. You've been training your gang folk to deal with vampires, and from what I've seen, you haven't been able to stop them. I'm still seeing the same amount of people coming into the ER, with the same wounds, and I'm trying to remember the last time you talked to me about something like, oh, I don't know, your *classes*. You are still going to them, aren't you?"

"Of course. When I miss one, I just make sure to have someone record them. Trust me, I'm not missing anything."

"What about the turpentine you picked up lately?" Robert asked knowingly. "I don't think you've taken to painting."

"Turpentine is one of the world's most flammable substances, right?" He reached up one sleeve and pulled out a stake.

Robert looked at him askance.

Marco explained, "I want to be cautious. The sheaths were easy to make out of old canvas bags." He leaned forward, pointing to a round, clove-shaped piece of paper taped to the stake. "Now, this is a stake covered in turpentine. See this little thing on the side? It's one of those contact firecrackers, the kind that go off if you throw them on the sidewalk. In this case, when trying to stab through, oh, an entire *ribcage* is too much. You just line this up with the fleshy part of a vampire's body, and, well…" He looked over, saw one of his old textbooks on a table next to the couch, and stabbed it.

The stake went up in flames so fast, Marco's hand barely had time to pull away, and he had let go the moment it penetrated. Marco reached over, behind the couch, and came back with a bucket of water. He merely slid the burning textbook into the bucket.

"That was easy."

"You just happened to have a disposable textbook lying around to set on fire, and a bucket of water? Marco, no. Just…no." He studied the book for a moment and considered something. "You know, I think that book's been lying around for a few days. Possibly a week or two. I remember thinking that you had already taken that course last summer…"

Marco shrugged. "You know how I like to plan ahead."

"Fine. In which case, I want a full report of exactly what you've been doing."

"Me? Not much. I've coordinated the gangs into patrols, so that they're essentially within three blocks of potential screams at any one time. I've arranged for them to start taking up hobbies like archery, and, thankfully, we've got some guys who are former army and marines. Two were retired out, and by that I mean they got shot, or wounded, or just plain cycled stateside. They've been helpful. It's not like I'm running these guys with some training I got at Xavier."

"Yet, you still terrify them?"

Marco shifted in the couch. "I do have a certain skill set in violent activities that makes me…a source of concern, should I flip out on them."

"That leads me to another question. These former military members of yours were good at their jobs, would you say? Then how did they get in with the Dragons and Tigers? How do you manage to not have a power struggle in a group of people who, I assume, are natural-born alpha males?"

"Dad, you remember back when I took Krav Maga?"

"Since you were, what, ten? Of course, I remember. Why?"

"Let's say I kept my hand in."

Robert winced at the memory of Marco's time studying Krav Maga. The combat system of the Israeli Defense Force had only five levels before the system counted "expert" levels.

Between ten and fifteen years of age, Marco had covered several levels, and Robert remembered having to work on black eyes and bruises that would cover entire limbs. Marco even learned a dislocated shoulder trick out of a *Lethal Weapon* movie.

"Uh huh. Should I ask what level you're up to now?"

Marco considered a moment, then shook his head. "No, you shouldn't. Anyway, all that to say that my skills make me the clear leader of the group. Back to what we've been up to though. We're working on the arrows, which are easy to carry around, since they're not technically a concealed weapon. Lord knows there are enough cosplay conventions going on in New York at any one time to not be that noticeable. That, and the NYPD are slowly becoming aware that the escalating problem requires escalation of force. We've even got a few guys who are going for tricks like breathing fire. In short, the reason there are people coming into the ER is that they aren't being brought into the morgue. The body count you recall, was starting to grow in December."

"They've stopped growing," Robert realized. He nodded, thinking it over a moment. "But you realize that you haven't actually stopped the bleeding, you've just controlled it."

Marco nodded. "That's something I intend to do with Amanda tonight. Now that we have people to watch our backs, and we don't have to worry about the ER being flooded nightly, we're going to get some information about the source of this problem and figure it out once and for all."

The doctor studied his son a moment, and the gorge between them, symbolized neatly by the table full of knives. "Tell me once more about alignment."

"What?"

"Assume that I don't play video games. What should I expect from, say, someone who had gone to the dark side?"

"The more choices you make, the more to the dark side you go, or the light. The more evil you do, the more sensitive a vampire is to holy objects. They're generally harder to kill, otherwise, and more powers come with that sort of vile behavior, but we've generally run into more of the Incontinents than anything else."

"Incontinent? It sounds more like a diagnosis of constipation."

Marco rolled his eyes. "Aristotle's definition of 'incontinent'– those who know the good, want the good, but generally tend towards the bad. Outward signs trend more towards a pale, pasty appearance, like a drug user going through withdrawal."

"Why is that, anyway?" Robert asked. "Why are vampires the picture of Dorian Gray?"

"Remember how I used to be able to tell a lot about people just by looking at them? I always thought something was off? Some people would call it profiling, no matter if it were two Caucasians looking at each other. Sure, a lot of people are deeper than they look, but how many more than that are shallow creatures with no depths to plumb? More than I can count, certainly."

"But physical changes?" Robert frowned. "I guess if you want to go with things like the hands of a carpenter, or the belly of a champion eater…"

"More or less. Vampires are people, only their bodies are more tightly linked to their souls, so positive alignment is reflected positively. Therefore, the more evil ones *look* evil. Break out the crosses, and go to town."

"Okay, but what about Amanda?"

Marco's entire body postured tensed, as though he was about to leap out of the chair. "What about her?"

"You're working with her almost nightly. I'm sure you've already tested to see if she's affected by holy artifacts. What else are you doing with her?"

"What? Nothing. We're friends, I told you that."

Robert scoffed. "You also told me that you had no reason for discussing vampires. Have you had a Defining the Relationship discussion that actually ended in 'Let's just be friends'?"

"No," Marco answered quickly. "I preempted it. There's no reason for us to be attracted to each other, no reason we should be more than friends, nor any reason that the two of us should stop working together. To even hint that there may be something more…No. That would change everything."

Marco rose, his entire face going neutral. "I have to go, get ready for the day."

Robert sighed. He knew Marco had shut down completely for this conversation. "Marco, what exactly will you and Amanda be doing tonight, anyway?"

"Oh, just hitting some bars."

"Well, that's not too bad."

"Vampire bars."

March 13th, 5:00 p.m.

Marco arrived at Amanda Colt's door earlier than she expected. The sun was still up, and she was about to feed when the door-bell rang.

She buzzed Marco in and moved for her refrigerator. In addition to her own blood-creating organs, Amanda preferred taking the wine at Church. A healthy sip was usually enough to satisfy her for a week, but if the two of them got into trouble that evening, she would need the extra fluids to heal any damage she might take. On the one hand, she wanted to have faith in the Lord thy God. On the other, she wasn't about to test Him, either.

Amanda took out a quart container of blood she had taken from the expired blood at the local hospitals. She took a healthy sip from the top, and grimaced. Part of the problem with expired blood was that it tasted expired.

She flipped open the cabinet above the refrigerator and pulled out a bottle of imported Russian vodka to top off the blood.

Yes, she was over a hundred years old and dead for most of that time, but, damn it, she was still *Russian*.

Amanda sipped again, smiled at the proportions, and capped the bottle. She started to drink it like some humans would a protein shake.

She turned, and headed towards the living room, wondering what took Marco so long to get to her door. She was surprised to find him standing by the collection of weapons against the wall.

Amanda almost gagged on the blood. She had forgotten that she had given him a key shortly after their run-in with Officer Tolbert in January.

It shocked her how handsome Marco looked. She had told him to dress up for the occasion in business casual, and he had. He wore a well-cut sports jacket, and a dark blue polo shirt, and his blond hair was immaculately brushed in place.

"No rush," he said, "we have time."

She gulped hard. "How did you know I was behind you?"

"I came in, and you're in the apartment." He turned and gave her his little smile. "Sun's still up. There's nowhere to run." He looked at her a moment, and she worried for a moment that he was focused on the quart in her hand, but his eyes were on her face.

Marco took several strides towards her, stopped within arm's reach, and lifted one finger to the side of her mouth.

"You missed some," he muttered, and wiped the smudge of blood with his index finger.

Amanda moved forward, and her lips closed down on his fingertip, surprising both of them. She sucked the blood off.

Marco slid his hand along her cheek, lightly caressing it with his thumb. His hand lingered for a moment. His eyes met hers, and he leaned in close.

Amanda wondered if Marco was about to change his "let's just be friends" stance.

His lips touched her forehead, and he leaned back. His hand moved to her shoulder and gave it a light squeeze. "So, what's on the agenda for this evening?"

Amanda blinked, disappointed, and surprised at her disappointment.

"We are, um, right…do you know of Mount Sinai?"

"The Hospital? Who doesn't? It's about, what, twenty blocks from here? On Central Park East." He studied her a moment. "Why, we're going to see someone on staff?"

She shook her head. "*Nyet.* Near there. The Blood Bank," she finished, quickly taking another hit from her quart container.

"Wonders never cease," he muttered. "Well, it'll be a healthy stretch of the legs."

Amanda nearly choked on the blood again. "Twenty blocks?"

"It would take about as long just for the green line to pick us up from the train station, and I'd much rather go walking with you."

"Sweet of you, and depressingly true about the speed of the train. I think it has been that way since I first arrived in the city." Amanda made a show out of looking him over. "You look nice."

He scoffed. "I'm dressed in mail-order clothing. I see no point in wearing something expensive if I may have to burn it in the morning. Though, given the area, I suddenly feel under-dressed."

"You prefer a whole military uniform from Xavier?"

Marco nodded. "It came with a sword."

Amanda laughed. "Indeed. Why did you not become military after attending Xavier?"

"I'm sorry?"

"You went into their ROTC program," she said. "You had uniforms, swords, but you did not go into a formal military. Were you waiting for something? Your degree?"

Marco sighed, looked off to the side, then looked back. "Actually, it's more a matter of weight. When I gave up my Krav Maga studies, fencing couldn't give me the same exercise value. I gained some fat, lost some muscle mass, and the army has pretty stringent strange standards. I figured I would lose the weight while I got my degree, then join up."

Amanda looked at Marco's body, then reached up and poked his stomach with a finger. He wasn't solid muscle, but darn, he was close. "I think you're done."

"Yeah, well, now I have vampires to deal with. I'll be a little busy."

"True, but at least you are fighting darkness in more ways than one."

"I just never thought it would be this close to home. I always thought it would be a little sandier."

"But then again, you are *nyet*, um, am I thinking of team player?"

Marco laughed. "Oh, wow, you have no idea how accurate that is."

"That is no answer."

"Nope, it isn't." He looked off at her Van Gogh reproduction.

"Were you in town when September 11th happened?"

Amanda shook her head. "I was up north."

"I had a great view of the city that day. I could see across the water and stare at it. A great storm cloud had come to ground level and settled over the city." His vision grew distant and unfocused, lost in a haze of memory as he stared into the white swirls of Van Gogh's *Starry Night*, and his voice followed him. "It was horrific. I could see dots falling out of the windows. It wasn't hard to figure out that they were people who decided they didn't want to burn. It was something so big, so vile, that it broke through all of the post-modern gibberish where we were 'beyond good and evil.' The ash came down so thick, it was like snow. Some people in New Jersey, they had *parties*. Can you believe that? *Parties?* For mass murder."

He looked to Amanda once more, his eyes hardening. "Right then, I decided that I wanted to hunt those bastards down and kill them like the dogs they are. I wanted to kill those responsible. I wanted to kill those who *helped* them, those who *planned* it, and everybody who felt *happy* about it. I wanted to hunt them down and kill them all."

"How old were you?" she asked.

"I was young. Very young." His look turned distant. "Oh, and if I had the time, and the energy, I would join the military now, or when I get out of college. But seriously, when are we going to be rid of all of these vampires?"

"We will."

He shook his head, ready to change the topic. "Speaking of, anyway, let's go."

"Would you like me to bite you before we leave?" she asked quickly. "We know that we are heading into a hazardous situation. Want me to enhance you?"

Amanda winced at how fast the words came out, as though she were eager to taste him again. Was she that transparent? Did it come out as whiny? She wanted her lips on his skin more than her teeth in his throat. His blood was nothing special; it tasted like copper, like all blood did. But it was him. Even having him hold her as she drank was worth the bite.

Marco shook his head, though. "As much as I would like the little added boost, I would hate for them to smell it on me when I walk in. I would especially hate to antagonize them, letting them think I'm only a threat when you've bitten me. If any of them were interested in revenge, they'd simply try hunting me down later on."

Amanda frowned. "But that would make you vulnerable."

"Not much. Try and hit me."

Amanda blinked, furrowed her pretty brows, and then shot out with a right palm to Marco's chest, a strike she knew would not incapacitate him, but would make him know he was hit.

But the moment she lashed out, Marco had already twisted his upper body out of the way, grabbed her wrist with his right hand, and swiveled his left elbow into her upper arm, above the elbow. Had that been an actual strike, at full force, her arm would have been broken.

"Fighting is just three-dimensional chess," he said, "like fencing."

"Let us hope that other vampires are as predictable as I am," she told him.

"Oh, Amanda, I'm never totally certain what you're going to do next."

Chapter 16:

Bar Hopping

March 13th, 6:00 p.m.

The Blood Bank was upscale. It would have to be, being near Fifth Avenue. Since no one wanted a large influx of humans walking in the front door, the sign was only eight-and a-half by eleven. It was large enough for vampires to see, but dark red lettering on a black background was difficult for most humans to notice.

The bar ran the length of the room. There was a full stock of standard alcohol, though the bottles of blood were under the counter, in case there was the odd human walked in and happened to survive. Under the bar was every conceivable flavor of blood, from A-positive to O-negative, diabetics for the extra sweetness, and even the blood of cancer patients for those who wanted to "taste their suffering"—there was actually only a real impact from the patients on radiation therapy, and that gave a *real* kick to it. Behind the bar was not a mirror, but a giant television screen. Tiny cameras embedded in the shelving were connected to the large screen, "reflecting" the room.

Amanda walked into the Blood Bank in a nice, black business suit. She looked around, amused at the styles she saw. Black velvet dresses with underwire bodices were strangely in fashion.

Marco leaned into her and whispered, "Too many Anne Rice novels?"

Three of the nearest women in the same outfit turned to glare at him. One in particular, a blonde with a tightly wrapped bun of a hairdo, looked him over. She glanced to Amanda and said, "Oh deary, you brought your own wet bar? How tacky."

The background chatter of the bar died down at the comment, drawing attention to the newcomers, and, more importantly, to Marco's decidedly human scent.

Amanda shook her head. "To use him for snack time would be to bite off more than I could chew."

The blonde smiled broadly and started to slink her away across the room. "I don't think I will have that problem."

"I'm actually here to ask a few questions," Marco said, his voice loud enough to broadcast to the room.

The woman in the black velvet Anne Rice getup stopped, looked him over, and scoffed. "What could you possibly ask from us, you Happy Meal with legs?"

Amanda put a hand on his shoulder, both to restrain his next remark and to mark her possession of Marco to the room. "There are problems in Brooklyn. We want to know what any here may have heard. Particularly if it involves the Vampire known as Mikhail. He is supposedly known for starting nests like the one that has popped up."

The bar was silent. The blonde was particularly annoyed, if her scowl was anything to go by.

Marco looked them over. "What? You guys all afraid of one stinking vampire? Please. You want to worry about someone you should fear, it's me."

The blonde rolled her eyes. "We don't care about you, or your little girlfriend. Girl, take your pet home before he gets eaten by something with bigger teeth than he has."

Marco moved forward, going for the center of the floor, while Amanda moved to the bar counter, keeping an eye on the patrons. He kept his eyes on the blonde the entire time.

When he arrived at the center of the room, he noticed that the other vampires had formed a semi-circle around him.

Most had probably sensed the crosses on him, so they kept their distance for now.

"Say what you like," he said, his voice deliberately projecting, "at least *she* doesn't have a bad dye job."

The blonde's fingers became white, turning into a fist. Her lips pursed so tightly that they turned white. Her hand blurred.

Marco *moved*.

Her hand had gone for the nearest bottle to hand, a bottle of Absolut Vodka, as Marco thought it might. When her hand moved, Marco had already twisted his body to one side, certain that she would be hurling it for his center line: either in the head, or in the middle of his chest.

The bottle shot past him, and Marco didn't turn his attention to the blonde, but to the bottle. It had smashed on the other side of the room in a perfect example of a Polish firing squad. One vampire—one of the few who had completely ignored them until now—took the bottle to the side of the head.

Knowing vampire reflexes as he did, Marco's first thought was to drop to one knee in a full genuflect. A fraction of a second later, the assaulted vampire sailed over Marco's head, missing him entirely, but landing on the blonde.

Marco's computer-like brain crunched the variations.

The blonde could throw him at me.
The blonde could throw him into the crowd and lunge for me.
The blonde could stop to engage him; this is unlikely.

The blonde could throw him aside and throw something else at me.

Conclusion: Be somewhere else.

The blonde tossed her attacker aside, into the rest of the crowd, and lunged for Marco on her own.

Marco was already in the process of leaping to one side, drawing one of his special stakes. As she passed him, he stabbed into her side. The firecracker snapped in a small explosion, setting the turpentine ablaze, making her black velvet dress catch fire.

Marco came up in a roll and turned to the blonde in time for her to start putting herself out. He took the opportunity to look through the crowd for signs of anyone who wanted to join in on this little assault. Most of the looks he got were bewildered glances of vampires who had trouble believing that a human was able to do this.

The blonde was almost done extinguishing the fire when Marco saw his opening.

He darted in. The side of her velvet dress had largely burned away, showing the underwire beneath. Marco dove under her obvious backhanded swing, and grabbed her dress, his grasp feeling parts of the wire beneath the velvet. He slid forward, dragging her forward only one step, and he plugged the exposed wire into an outlet in the wall.

Marco let go immediately and rolled away, to his feet.

The blonde stood there as the electricity coursed through her body. She was frozen there, a rictus grin on her face as the electricity forced all of her muscles to contract. Her body started to smoke and smolder. She couldn't even scream as her body incinerated itself.

"And that," Marco said aloud, "is why you don't read Anne Rice novels for fashion advice. It makes you a fire hazard when you're as flammable as a vampire."

Marco turned his back against the wall and surveyed the room. The gaze of every vampire was on him. He felt himself tense, waiting for any one of these predators to pounce.

From the other side of the room, there was the sound of a pump-action shotgun being racked.

Marco blinked, not expecting a weapon in a vampire bar. The gun was pointed at Amanda's head.

"This is filled with silver buckshot," the bartender began, in a loud voice and heavy brogue. "With alternating shells of wood flechette. So, I wish to ask ye all, who wants to get shredded to pieces?"

Marco and Amanda exchanged a glance. "We just want information. That's all. We don't want trouble.

Think about it; if we did, we would have led with a flamethrower from both ends of the bar. We came to talk."

The bartender raised a brow, the barrel of the shotgun shifting back to Marco. "Oh? Really?"

Marco studied the vampire a moment, considering exactly what sort of person would be running a vampire bar. Especially who would hold onto a shotgun underneath the counter in a neighborhood this ritzy, with clientele to match. Add the brogue, the build like a refrigerator, the short haircut, and an unfashionable, bushy mustache, and Marco came up with one conclusion.

Irish cop…circa 1850, when they were being drafted right off of the boat. He'll likely listen to reason; we may be able to avoid further violence.

"Look, we're basically trying to do some police work. Help us gather some information, and we'll go away. The equation is that simple."

"Of course it is," the bartender said. There was enough skepticism in his voice to level several city blocks. His eyes darted to his left, and the shotgun swung up. "Rosenthal, if you consider going after the prick because the late lamented Kathleen hit you by accident, I'm going to blow off parts of your body and cauterize it with holy water so it don't grow back. Are we understood, lad?"

He looked back to Marco, and then Amanda. He had the expression of someone weighing his options between telling them what they wanted to know and wondering how much it would take to clean their blood off of the wood paneling. "As for you, all I can tell you is that there've been some noises about something big coming down lately. Mostly noises around Mount Olivet Cemetery, in Queens. Now, the both of you get the hell out of my bar."

Marco nodded. "Thanks for the lead."

He strode towards Amanda, keeping an eye on the other vampires in the room, thinking. *Come to think about it, no one even considered moving to the rescue of what's-her-name. She must have been really popular. Anne Rice must be the source of all annoying vampires. Unless, of course, they sparkle.*

Amanda leaned toward the bartender before rejoining Marco. "Yes, thank you. While I think of it, I must to ask: NYPD? 1850s?"

The bartender gave her a smile. "1860s, but yes, thank you. I still go to church every Sunday, so don't come back with any holy water, thinking you're something special."

Marco nodded, flashing him a smile. "Good to know, though I'm sure now that we wouldn't ever need it with you anyway. Thank you, sir. We'll be leaving now."

When Amanda and Marco made it out to the street, Marco laughed. "Well, that was fun! Wasn't it?" He looked to Amanda, and saw she wasn't smiling. "Wasn't it? Um…is something wrong? Amanda?"

They walked in silence for over a block. When she thought they were far enough away, Amanda grabbed Marco by the shoulder and dragged him against the wall. "What were you *thinking*?"

Marco was thrown by her uncharacteristically violent outburst. He met her deep brown eyes and found them hard and angry. He blinked, genuinely confused. "That vampires don't want to answer questions unless they don't have a choice in the matter?"

"You could have been *killed*!"

Marco rolled his eyes and scoffed. "*Feh.* Nah, you would have saved my ass if I even looked like I was in the slightest bit of trouble. Besides, did you really think she was dressed for optimal movement in that outfit? Please."

Amanda stared at him a long moment, growled in frustration, and turned away, leaving Marco confused.

"We will call those Vatican ninjas," Amanda said, as she walked away, glancing over her shoulder, "tell them the tip we got and see what they find."

Marco sprinted a little to catch up. "Gotcha, sure. Whatever you want," he said, trying to smooth over whatever the hell was bothering her. "I wouldn't trust our gang wannabes to do a quiet recon, either. What do you want to do now? Try some other bars?"

Amanda spared him an angry glance. "I think it is time for you to go home."

Chapter 17:

A Quiet Talk

March 13th, 7:00 p.m.

Amanda Colt didn't have any rational thought about the depth of her anger. After all, Marco had only risked his life in a one-on-one confrontation with a vampire, without any support, or additional strength that came with her bite.

It was only one vampire! she tried to reason with herself. *He managed to handle multiple vampires in the ordeal on the subway car, back in January, so what's the deal? Then again, I was watching his back then, and this time it was a room full of vampires. Not even I could have protected him if they had all decided to join in the fray.*

He thinks that I would have had his back against her. Doesn't he realize I was too busy watching everyone else? Still, it had only been her. He can deal with one vampire. Shouldn't that be enough?

But why does he have to go do these things? Why can't he just let me protect him? What is his problem? Does he have a death wish?

Why am I so upset about this?

Amanda shook her head, frustrated and angry, and uncertain. She wanted to talk with someone. Heck, anyone would do.

I guess there is only one option.

Doctor Robert Catalano looked up from his desk at the hospital. He hadn't heard the door open, or even the chair squeak. He saw something out of the corner of his eye and looked up.

There was Amanda Colt, sitting in the chair across from him. "Hello."

He smiled awkwardly. "Um, hi."

It was strange being in the room with someone his son was so obviously enamored of. Especially left alone with her. Trying to gauge how to handle her was something he wasn't good with, even when Marco was dating Lily.

Amanda's presence in his hospital made him wonder if Marco was injured, or if he had done the injuring. Again. After the first dozen times Marco had stepped into a situation that did not involve him, but he would settle anyway, Robert had taken a more Zen-like approach to his son. He wouldn't worry about anything until he had all the facts before him.

"Is Marco with you?"

"He should be home by now."

"Ah. Good." The silence was about as awkward as a hippo in a tutu. If Marco was all right, what could she possibly want to talk about? Unless she was going to ask if she could make a move on Marco, which would be odd, but not the strangest thing he'd have seen that year. "Um. Can I help you with something, Amanda?"

"Any news on casualties?"

He frowned and leaned back in his chair. "Marco's right. I crunched some numbers, and the dead and wounded have actually leveled off since January. I suspect the more you train those gang losers, both numbers will dip."

Amanda smiled. "You do not like them, do you? The Dragons and *Los Tigres*."

"They have their uses, but I think they're more likely to hurt themselves than their enemies. If holy relics didn't work, we'd be tending to *them* more days than not." He waved it away. "Never mind them. What about you?"

"Me?"

Robert leaned forward on his desk and smiled. "Let me put it this way: are you biting my son?"

She gaped at him a moment. "I have not bit him since January, and he asked me to."

He held up a hand to stop her. "Obviously, I need to elaborate. What are your intentions towards Marco?"

"I--I do not know what you mean," she lied. *Isn't this why I'm here?* she asked herself. *I know you've been on your own a long time, but someone can't help you process if you close up.*

"You're kidding me, aren't you? I see the way you look at him. Either your goal is to kiss him until he's brain damaged or wring his neck. I'm not certain which."

"I understand." Amanda's natural grace, apparent even when sitting, escaped her. She shuffled a little in her chair, unsettled. "You realize I have never been in love before? When I was young, I grew up among people who I could not love. When I became vampire, I became busy. Too busy." Her gaze drifted away, to a distant past. With cordite in the air, and blood on the snow. "In all my time, I have never found someone like Marco. He is intense. He is strong willed. He is intelligent. He is…almost as lonely as I am. But, do I *love* him? I cannot say. I have never been. I never had time."

"Ah." Robert frowned and thought over her dilemma. From what little he'd been able to gather, this woman was older than he was, but came off as being at the same point of development as Marco. "Well, have you ever considered asking why his last relationship fell apart?"

Amanda Colt stood outside the house in Astoria, Queens, and felt like an idiot. She briefly wondered if this is what it had been like for the average teenager in high school–talking to other women about previous boyfriends, gossip, exchanging stupid little quirks and stupid little stories like stupid little people.

Maybe I am taking this too seriously, she thought to herself as she knocked on the door of Lily Sparks, Marco's ex-girlfriend.

Lily opened the door slowly. The young girl looked at Amanda as though she knew what the vampire was. Amanda didn't comment on the girl's outfit, which was a t-shirt one size too small, no visible bra, and read *Shuck me, Suck me, Eat me Raw*, and, in smaller print underneath, (*New England Oysters*). Lily had on a tartan skirt, worn to mid-thigh, that Amanda thought was too short for this weather, and pigtails that cut her age in half.

Catholic school girl outfit? Truly? Amanda thought but was careful not to let show on her face.

Lily eyed her warily. "Yes?"

"I would like to talk with you."

"What about?"

"Marco, of course." *What else do we have in common?*

Lily considered it a moment, then nodded, opening the door wide. Amanda strode inside without an invitation, grateful that her intentions were still pure. If she had come there with even the subconscious inclination to make this tart into lunch, she would have required a verbal invitation.

The house was surprisingly spacious. The living room had a couch opposite the television, an arm chair at right angles to the couch, and even another corner couch diagonally opposite to it. Amanda took the couch in order to take the least threatening position. Lily took the armchair.

"So," Lily asked, "what about Marco? Does he have more enemies after me?"

"What?"

"That's what you came to tell me last time."

"Oh, no. Nothing like that."

Lily exhaled, giving away her prior nervousness. "Whew. Okay, then what?"

"Why did you two break up?"

Lily blinked in surprise. Clearly, she was not expecting this. "He told you that we were a couple? He *said* that?"

"That was the best term that he had for it," Amanda explained slowly, racking her brain to remember if Marco had actually used that term. "He implied that you were more than just casually interested in him. At least during the night of the incident."

Lily squirmed in the chair a little, and Amanda could hear her heart rate spiking. "What did he tell you about that?"

"There was a mugging. Marco dealt with it. He added some poetic license—too much, I think—but that was all." Amanda added a slight glower to give the impression that Lily would make a great fertilizer for a backyard.

"I never meant to hurt him," Lily rushed to explain. "You have to understand that."

"Of course," Amanda lied, not understanding, even a little.

"When I saw what Marco did to that guy…well, you know Marco. When you're around him, you just get this feeling that's he's so…so…"

"Intense?" Amanda prompted. "Focused?"

"Dangerous," Lily answered, a thrill of excitement entering her voice. "He was able to take anyone in a fight. I saw him once or twice. He had a uniform, and a sword, and was just so beautiful in full dress. He didn't have all of the social graces, but I could fix that. I did fix that. I brought him out of his shell. I showed other people he was interesting. Okay, he's not generally that much to look at, but just the sense you get when you're around him. In that uniform, he looked great. He looked perfect. I just wanted to grab his sword and…"

What does this have to do with the price of caviar in the Black Sea? "What does this have to do with…?" Amanda deliberately trailed off.

"I always *knew* there was something about Marco," Lily said. "I just didn't see what it was until that night. I don't know how much he told you, but we were out with a few friends. I had a few drinks. I wanted him *so* much. I wanted a sample. To hold him, touch him, kiss him…I would have had him, too, if it weren't for that…" Her voice was a mixture of excitement and frustration.

Amanda said nothing but could only think. *Yes, and you would have gotten some that night if it weren't for that meddling mugger and his stupid dog…oh, wait, wrong story. It never occurred to you that Marco was too much of a gentleman to have sex with you that easily? You self-absorbed, egotistic—*

"The guy came out of nowhere," Lily continued. "He pulled a knife. He grabbed me. He threatened Marco. Marco, he just swooped in. He actually took the knife away from the guy. Marco grabbed the guy's wrist, twisted, and plucked the knife out of his hand like it was nothing."

Lily's excitement peaked now. She reported this entire incident like it was so cool. Amanda heard the heart spike like Lily was turned on by all of this.

A hundred years old, I still do not understand some fetishes.

Then Lily's excitement bottomed out. "The guy fought back, and Marco…Marco hurt him. It looked less like the guy was actually fighting Marco, and more like he was thrashing. But he clipped Marco, and Marco kept hurting him. And twisting. And beating." She winced, and her heart rate spiked again. Amanda could only guess that it was at a particular image.

"Like I said," Lily continued, far more sober, "I always knew there was something dangerous in Marco. But this was different. When I watched him tear that man apart, I saw something in him. It was dark and cold and *hungry*. It scared the crap out of me. I couldn't handle it. I freaked out. I think I told anybody who would listen."

"All of Xavier?" Amanda asked.

"I guess," Lily said, more embarrassed at being called on it than ashamed or guilty.

Amanda was not the type of vampire who had strong telepathic tendencies, but even she could tell that Lily wasn't as sorry about what she did to Marco as she was sorry she committed such a *faux pas*. She was sorry she had freaked out, and sorry she lost her chance with Marco. There *may* have been sorrow that she had hurt him, but if there was any such guilt, it was buried underneath all of the other, shallow reasons.

Add to that her description of "fixing" Marco's social graces ... helping him acquire a circle of friends ... and then scuttling all of that? That just meant that Marco had been twice burnt by this little *suki*.

Amanda nodded and stood. She had learned more about Lily than she had Marco, but at least it was something.

"Thank you. That was all I wanted to hear. I am sorry for wasting your time. I will leave you be. I can't imagine that you would ever see me again."

Lily got up and followed Amanda to the door. "Could you tell Marco I'm sorry?"

Amanda opened the door and spared the girl a glance.

"He *knows* you're sorry. You are very sorry." She took two steps outside and paused. When she walked up, she remembered that one of the Tigers, a man named Roman, was in the area. At least two members of the Tiger-Dragon crowd were supposed to be there at all times.

Now she could detect no one.

Amanda felt Lily move behind her, almost out of the door. "Get back inside," she ordered. "Now."

Amanda felt it coming a moment before it hit her. She tried to get out of the way, but it was no use. Someone was on the roof, but came down, landing on her, feet first. Amanda was driven face down into the bricks of the stairs. By the time she rolled to her feet, the vampire had already jumped away.

Lily was no longer in the doorway. The vampire had her.

Amanda spotted the vampire already down the block. She pushed to her feet and gave chase, when another vampire got in her way.

Amanda slid to a stop, studying the bigger vampire. His face was visibly deformed, as though he had lost a battle with a fencer numerous times. The man's hair was slicked back and jet black, and his skin coloring was stark white. His eyes were covered by sunglasses, and he stared at Amanda with a wide, toothy grin.

"Were you water tortured with actual holy water?" she asked.

He just grinned. Amanda's eye twitched. Lily was being taken further away by the second, to a place she couldn't fathom, and Amanda didn't have the time for a stand-up fight.

She leaped away, diving diagonally, past the scarred vampire, rolled to her feet, and started running after the vampire with Lily.

The scarred one kept pace with her.

Amanda mentally swore to herself as the vampire with

Lily headed south, for Brooklyn. It was going to be a foot race, and she wasn't entirely certain that she could win it. She had the advantage of not carrying someone, but the disadvantage of being chased herself.

The kidnapping vampire went up along the elevated train, running along the tracks with Lily under his arm like she was a football. He moved fast for someone with the build of a linebacker, at a speed fast approaching that of sound.

Scarface was right behind her and catching up.

Amanda paid no mind. She would catch up to the monster who had Lily, no matter the cost. Not for Lily's sake. Not for the sake of stopping the monster.

Not to avenge the almost certainly dead gang members back at Lily's home. But because Marco would be hurt if she failed.

Amanda actually put on extra speed she didn't know she was holding back. She felt like she was flying. She followed the kidnapper around a curve and was suddenly shoved to one side.

Scarface had caught up to her.

Since Scarface knew what way his fellow vampire was going, he could anticipate where she would be, and took a shortcut between two points.

The shove wasn't a problem. Amanda could almost certainly get back on track and onto the path again in no time.

If it weren't for the oncoming train.

Chapter 18:
The Ashes Of An Old Flame

March 13th, 9:00 p.m.

Amanda Colt looked at the oncoming train and tried not to panic. After running along elevated train tracks at a speed that outperformed trains, a solid shove from Scarface sent her flying on a direct collision course. The ground was out of reach, so that would be no help.

Her only point of contact with something solid would be when the train hit her.

There were some basic tricks for someone who was solidly on a path of good or evil. As she explained to Marco all those months ago, when the soul and the body were as closely intertwined as a vampire's were, it allowed for complete control over the body, down to reshaping the molecular components.

So, with a nanosecond to do it, Amanda let her body become mist.

Without her in them, her clothes were tossed in the air, and floated aside in the draft generated by the train. It was bad enough that the train hit her mist form, but the winds generated by the train's movement essentially ripped Amanda apart and scattered her in all directions.

It wasn't a pleasant feeling as her entire being scattered over half a mile of track. While she couldn't be harmed in this form by anything short of the morning sun or fire, it wasn't her fastest moving form.

Amanda had to fight hard in order to pull herself together, drawing in every last molecule of her being into one, solid form. It also had to be done at street level, lest an oncoming train scatter her even further.

All told, it took an hour for Amanda to gather herself in one place before she could drift up, between the tracks, and slide back into her clothes.

The vampires, and Lily, were gone.

Amanda Colt showed up at Marco Catalano's doorstep feeling tired. She raised her hand to knock at the front door, but it opened before she laid a hand on it. Marco still wore the suit jacket and polo shirt from earlier in the evening.

Marco stared at her and said, "What's wrong? Are you all right?"

Amanda smiled weakly. "What makes you ask?"

He took her arm and led her inside. "The guys on station in Astoria called in to tell me that you showed up to Lily's house. Vega called me directly. However, since then, they haven't called in, they're not answering calls or text messages."

He led her into the living room and gave her the armchair.

"So I figure I know what happened to them. They're dead, and you look like you've been hit by a truck."

"A train. The number seven, I think."

Marco knelt down in front of her, running his hands over her arms and back, as though being hit by a train would be the same as looking for stab wounds. "I so seriously hope you were in mist form at the time."

"Yes." Amanda was about to say more, but Marco's hands rested on her shoulders, and held her lightly. She enjoyed the feel of his hands on her body, no matter where they were.

It was strange, but she hadn't been touched all that often in the last fifty years or so. She sighed and forced herself to say, "Marco, they took Lily."

"I know." Marco sighed. "Well, I figured. If she were unharmed, you would have called here first thing. If she were dead, I suspect it would be over your undead body."

"You are so sure of that?"

"I like to think so. I suspect you can be as relentless as I am. If they're going to hold her hostage, they'll call. If not, they'll get through some other way. It's only eleven. I expect that's like noon on a Saturday to most vampires. Come on, let me make you something to drink."

He started to rise, and she grabbed his hand, almost pulling her to him. "You are not upset?" she asked.

"Why should I be?" He gave her shoulder a reassuring squeeze. "Amanda, you got hit by a frigging *train* to save her. I'd rather not have you as a smear on the side of the number seven."

"But she meant something to you once."

Marco paused. His eyes drifted over her shoulder, spacing out. "Yes. Once. She meant the world to me. Then she meant nothing."

He paused, looking deep into her Frangelico eyes. His hand slid up her neck, and cupped her cheek, just before he leaned down, and kissed her on the forehead. "You did good, love," he whispered. "You did good."

Amanda's hand came up of its own accord and slid around the back of Marco's neck, keeping him that close. She looked up at him with a wary smile. "Marco, I–"

She was interrupted by the sound of a *thump*.

They exchanged a look. That was the sound of something slammed up against the front door of the house. Both of them were tense and facing the door in an instant.

Marco moved first, keeping against the right wall of the hallway. Amanda took the left wall, both moving for the front. Marco got to the front door first and opened it.

Lily Sparks was on the top landing, her body having been slammed up against the front door. Her clothes weren't so much in disarray as they were shredded. Her modesty was barely protected by the scraps that clung to her body.

Without a word, Marco knelt down and grabbed her.

She moaned slightly, and she was still warm, so Marco didn't even bother checking for a pulse. He scooped her up and brought her inside.

Amanda kept watch outside until she could shut the door. "They are gone."

"Good," Marco said, his voice completely clinical. "I'm going to need some fluids, and we're going to start pumping her full of enough vitamins and juices to make her want to puke." He moved into the sitting room, laying her out on the couch.

Lily stirred, groaning. "Marco?"

"Yeah, it's me. Just stay still, Lily," he said. He looked at his watch, then grabbed her wrist to take her pulse. There wasn't any. "Oh crap."

Amanda moved to hold Lily down, but the newborn vampire was feral, and fast. She leaped for Marco immediately, and they were both taken in a roll straight to the other side of the room. Lily was on top, and Marco's left hand pressed under her chin to keep her fangs off of him. The rosary dangled only millimeters away, to no effect.

"The rosary," Marco grunted. He punched Lily with his right hand while his left kept her at bay. "Isn't" – punch – "working." Punch. "She's too new."

"I need you, Marco," Lily groaned, even as he tried to push her away. His right hand pushed against her breast bone in an effort to throw her off of him. He would have bucked, but that would dislodge her from her position, and he couldn't risk losing control of her teeth.

Amanda leaped onto Lily's back, but Lily rammed her head straight back, crushing Amanda's nose. As with any human, Amanda's eyes started to tear up. Lily delivered a casual rear uppercut elbow to the chin that sent her flying backwards. Amanda landed head first into the wooden coffee table. Had it been metal, she would have bounced back without missing a beat. Had she been human, the impact would have cracked her head open. Instead, she was only knocked out.

This left Marco alone with a feral vampire who wanted his body, probably *a la carte*.

Lily's move allowed Marco to thrust his forearm into her throat, but since she didn't have to breathe, and didn't have blood flowing in her veins, it didn't help much. *Her body must have kept some residual heat, meaning she hasn't been dead that long. She hasn't learned how to continue maintaining her bodily functions yet.*

Marco grimaced and said, "This is what I get for teaching you some Krav."

Lily's hands flailed at Marco's face. Had she had any brains about it at all, she would have broken his arm with two hands, then have her way with him.

And she'd probably kill me in the process, since she's new at this.

Then Marco met her eyes.

If there was a *Bram Stoker's Guide to Vampyres*, rule number one would *not* be "Don't invite them into your house."

That would be rule number *two*.

Nor would rule number one be "Don't tell a vampire 'Bite me.'"

That was a rule approximately a few dozen down the line. Had Bram Stoker survived his tuberculosis long enough to write down a list of rules about his most famous creation, Rule Number One would be very simple.

Don't look them in the eye. Never, *ever* look them in the eye.

When Marco met Lily's eyes, the vampire's eyes bored into his brain. A feral vampire trying to enter a human brain was much like an animal trying to operate a computer system. It went wild, flailing around, growling and snarling, barking at every flashing light in Marco's brain. Likewise, Marco could see everything in her mind. They were wild flashes, as frantic and as untamed as her physical attack. There were flickers and bleeps and images of lust and heat and skin, and what amounted to a pornographic fetish movie, or a Lady Gaga music video.

Then, those images, those memories, faded away, and all of those and similar thoughts focused on Marco. It was only a split second, but more than enough to have allowed her to get lucky, if Lily were smarter or quicker about it.

It was time to end this. And her, if need be.

"I don't want to hurt you," Marco said, "but if you make me, I will."

"I want you, Marco," she growled. "She wants you, too, but I won't let her have you. You're *mine*. Mikhail told me I could have you. If I have to, I'll kill her."

Marco's vision narrowed, and the edges of his eyesight became blurry. He leaned forward as much as possible, still keeping Lily at half an arm's length. He reached back with his arm, digging his elbow into the carpet, then drove his fist into Lily's face. She fell back, relieving the pressure from Marco long enough for him to buck and roll her off of him.

Marco leaped back, grabbing a wooden chair. He whirled back in time for Lily to leap after him. Her chest hit the chair leg first, driving it deep into her body. Lily blinked twice, looking into Marco's eyes. With one last, weak breath, she pleaded, "Marco…"

His eyes went as cold as Alaskan skies, and as dark as storm clouds. "I would have tried to save you. But you threatened Amanda. All because you want me. You don't come back from that. You were a soul-sucking monster before you became a vampire."

He growled and swung the chair, lifting Lily off her feet, and throwing her into a wall.

"Now go to Hell."

He drew his second flammable stake of the evening, stepped forward, and thrust it into her throat. The stake burst into flames, and Lily caught fire.

Marco grabbed the chair with both hands and swung her again, away from the wall, as she went up in a sudden blaze that turned her, her clothes, and the legs of the chair, to ash.

He smiled as he watched her burn. He only wished that he could have watched her suffer more.

Later, he would think about how he should have felt put off. This was a failure. He didn't protect Lily. But then, Lily was already a failure to him. He had cared for her so deeply, the betrayal of trust had made him want to crawl into his work and die there. There were more than enough times where he had wanted to murder her horribly, but they were always theoretical. He had wanted her to suffer the way she had made him suffer, and now, looking at the ashes of his old flame, he felt that setting her alight was just a good start.

Marco waved the chair a little bit to put out the flames, dropped the chair, and moved to Amanda. He turned her over, checked the back of her head, and contemplated how to check a vampire for concussion.

Amanda's eyes flashed open, and she sat up quickly, searching the sitting room. There was a wrecked chair, some ashes on the floor, but the only one in the room was Marco, and she had a pounding headache. "Where is she?"

Marco leaned forward, trying to probe through the thick hair to check the back of her head. "She made a real ash out of herself."

If she were anyone else, she would presume his flippant comment might have better hid his real emotions. She could see them though, and Amanda gave him a look of infinite pity, placing her hand on his shoulder. "I am so sorry. She gave you no choice."

Marco froze a moment, for a reason she couldn't guess at. Was there another reason to kill her?

Marco gave her a little shrug. "She had to be put down. She was violent. She couldn't be restrained or reasoned with."

"But can you blame her? She was–"

Marco shook his head. "I said nothing about blame. If we could have restrained her, she might have been reasoned with, eventually." He patted her back, and then rubbed her shoulders. Amanda enjoyed sampling even that much of his touch.

"Come on," he said, "let's get you on your feet. You've had an eventful evening, and you're a little banged up."

"As though you should talk? You have killed two vampires and an ex-girlfriend."

"I wasn't the one thrown in front of a train. As far as killing an ex…" He smiled weakly. "Well, I'm just living the dream."

He is already joking about this? "That is an odd attitude, considering."

Marco gestured to a seat, and she took it. He sat next to her. "Do you know why Lily went crazy?"

Amanda paused a moment. She could come up with a few theories. "I can make some guesses if you want."

"Me first. This is just a guess, a complete shot in the dark. True or false: A potential side-effect of becoming a vampire can be an enhancement of whatever initial attributes, personality traits, and vices one had while alive."

Amanda nodded slowly. "It is possible. It has happened."

"Amanda, when Lily tried to grab me, I couldn't tell if she was going to eat me or screw me. She was basically driven insane by her own internal vices." Marco slumped into the couch. "I think my body is going to object to the adrenaline I'm feeding it."

"If we keep this up, that is not impossible." She sighed and spared him a look. "So, what did Rodgers say when you called him about Mount Olivet cemetery?"

"Nuts, I didn't think to call them. Give me a few minutes, and I'll give them the news."

Amanda nodded, and just stared up at the ceiling. She knew Marco had been hurt by this woman, but she had been murdered once, and he was forced to kill her again, only permanently. Yet here he was, relatively calm, more interested in planning a nap than revenge. This man threatened his own people for staring at her too hard, but this didn't provoke more than a sigh?

"You know, I am surprised at your reaction."

"Hmm?"

"I thought you would be taking Lily's death harder than this."

"You mean just because she's an ex? Sort of?" He gave a little wave of his hand. "Nah. Lily has been dead to me for over a year now. This was just a formality. What? Were you expecting a murderous rampage?"

Amanda winced at how his words sounded.

Wow. That is cold, even for Marco.

"Yes."

"Well, if it makes you feel any better, I'm not going to let them think they got away with it." His casual, calm demeanor faded. "They killed two of my men tonight, and they killed someone under my protection. They can't pull this sort of stuff without retaliation. As I said, I'm the feudal lord, and they are my vassals. I'm going to deliver the message loud and clear."

This was more like what she had expected. A readiness, a desire to wreak havoc on those who had hurt him and his. But this was over men he had lost, and not the woman he was…intimate with. Really? "Oh? How?"

"How many vampire bars are there?"

She thought it over a moment. "Few dozen. Why?"

"I think there are some vampires who are going to need to find another place to hang out. I have a chem lab, and I'm not afraid to use it."

March 14th, 8:00 a.m.

Marco stood outside The Blood Bank, staring over the facade, and chuckled. The place was so ordinary and bland, it was almost out of place for something this close to Central Park. The black storefront was solid stone, without even a window, and the door matched the storefront.

"If these guys were any more of a cliché, it would be painful," Marco muttered to himself. He hiked the backpack up on his shoulders, squaring himself to the door. He smiled, knocked on the solid wooden door, and waited for a reply.

"No one here, go away," came a light brogue. Marco thought it sounded like the bartender from the other night.

"You're going to want to let me in, now, buddy, or else."

"Or else what?"

"Or I'll huff, and I'll puff, and I'll blow your door in."

There was a pause. After a moment, several locks were thrown open. Another moment later, the bartender said, "Come in."

Marco twisted the doorknob, and pushed the door open just enough to be shoved. He took a step back, against the doorway, and launched a side kick, popping the door open.

The bartender had the pump-action shotgun in his hands, but not aimed at Marco – he was cautious, not hostile. The human nodded, and stepped inside, closing the door behind him. "Good, I was hoping that would be your answer."

The bartender, who Marco swore dressed like every bartender stereotype from the start of the last century, grunted.

"Don't be so certain of what my answer is until I give it. *Now* what do you want? You already got your answers here the other night, so give me one good reason why I shouldn't fill you full of flechette and bottle your blood for my customers?"

"The church-going vampire? Um, no. I don't think so."

"What are you, crazy?"

"No," Marco said patiently, his heartbeat spiking so much even he could detect it. "Do you know who I am?

"I know your name. Otherwise, I don't care. I'd like to run my business and be left alone."

"I understand that, and sympathize. Last night, two of my men were killed. The woman they were protecting was turned into a vampire, and I was forced to kill her. That woman was special to me. She was the first person in the 'real world' who made me suspect that I was human. So, right now, I'm sort of pissed."

The vampire looked him over strangely. "Made you feel human?"

Marco looked right at him, his gaze intense and unwavering. "You try being isolated by your IQ and your mannerisms practically from when you were born. And then, at some point, you meet one who treats you like you're actually someone, a person, and not like a freak. You ever have someone like that?"

The bartender smiled. "I married her in 1923."

Considering that you would have been sixty years a vampire by then, I can see you understand the freak feeling.

"Yeah. Well, this person was someone I cared about once. She was taken from me with as little care and consideration as your average car wreck. I want my vengeance to be swift and painful. So, I want the names of your competition."

The vampire started. "Really?"

"Really. You're an Irish cop from the really old school. What bars would you like to see go out of business? You know the ones I mean. What bars have *humans* on tap? Where do they make people disappear?"

The bartender smiled. "You just might be a decent bloke after all. Well, if you're going to be like that about it, I may know a place or three…"

Marco left The Blood Bank with three new names of vampire establishments. He came to a stop a block away. When he had walked into The Blood Bank, he had let his mouth do all of his thinking for him. Everything he had said about Lily was the truth. From kindergarten until the day he met Lily, he had been a freak. There were years he was too fat to be considered "normal," or his interests didn't line up with everyone else's, or he was too smart to be considered "cool."

Then there was Lily. A friend who was with him for four years of high school. She had helped him gain friends, and she had been the one who pointed out to all the world, "Hey, this guy is interesting!" Sure, in the end, it all went wrong. But she was the first person who actually made Marco feel like someone who was not a relative that gave a damn about him.

There was a tear in his eye that was genuine, and a part of him that hurt greatly.

But his smile remained. The ever amused, eternal smile. Some people thought he used it to cover up some flaw in his head; some thought it *was* the flaw in his head. Some thought he smiled to hide the pain he had gone through in his life. Some believed that he smiled because he had a nervous condition.

But, despite his pain, despite everything going on in his head at any one time, Marco's smile was genuine. His amusement at the world was genuine.

He was now of a mind to share his hurt with the undead.

Time for them to cry.
He had enough explosives to do the job.

Chapter 19:

Sniper Fodder

March 14, 9:00 p.m.

"Wow, you're fairly old, aren't you?" Amanda Colt started. She wasn't used to people hearing her sneak up on them. She had stopped only two meters behind the Vatican ninja and his rooftop perch. "How did you know I was here?"

The Vatican ninja with the sniper rifle spared her a glance over his shoulder.

"Two eye holes on that rifle?" she asked. "I get that one is for the scope, but the other…"

"I have a motion sensor," he told her. "It's the only reason I knew you were there."

"I see." She looked him over. The man wasn't much to look at, more wiry and spry than anything else. He wasn't going to outweigh Arnold Schwarzenegger, maybe not even Chuck Norris. His "ninja" outfit was in the standard format for what would be considered "traditional" ninja garb—if one ignored the tactical pouches and the sniper rifle—with one major difference: it was a striped garment of dark blue and green.

"I thought Swiss Guard colors wore blue and gold," Amanda said as she moved next to the sniper, sitting down on the ledge, facing away from the street.

He looked back through the scope, down at the bar known as The Platelet. "Yes, well, gold is too visible for camouflage, and solid black is too dark. Green works better. We've noticed that, since blue is on a different spectral wavelength, it breaks up our form." He frowned a little as he readjusted his scope. "From a distance, that is."

Amanda pushed a strand of hair behind her ear. "Why did you ask if I was old?"

"I've killed my fair share of vampires. I can hear most of the less experienced ones. You have to be one of the older ones," he muttered. "What are you doing here, anyway?"

Amanda looked over her shoulder, down at street level. "Same reason you are: Marco."

"Hmm." The ninja-sniper looked up from the scope so he could get a broader look at the street. "You know, for a teenager, he's amazingly focused."

"So, you followed him?"

The ninja didn't even look at her. "Rodgers heard about the death of someone named Lily Sparks. He was under the impression that *Herr* Catalano might do something…rash, I believe was the term. So, what exactly does Marco think he's doing?"

"Did you ever see the movie *M*?"

The ninja swept the street once through his telescopic site. After a second sweep, he said, "Long time ago. German film… Fritz Lang? Peter Lorre as a child molester and killer. To catch him, the police leaned on organized crime so that they hunted down the killer themselves." The sniper drifted off, then looked up from the scope and spared her a shocked glance. "You're kidding? Please tell me you're kidding."

She shook her head. "Nope. Marco believes that having the vampires *not* involved in the killing spree in Brooklyn do our work for us would be an asset. At least they would not consider giving shelter to those responsible."

"We hope." He went back to his scope and fell into silence.

After a few minutes, when Amanda heard his heartbeat slow down so much, she thought he might have been asleep, he asked, "So, what is it with you and Catalano?"

The vampire nearly fell off the roof. She caught herself so fast, the ninja-sniper didn't notice, but it was a near thing. "What about us? We are just friends."

The ninja-sniper stopped his sweep and spared her a long look. "He has more restraint that I thought he would."

Amanda's eyes widened. "What do you mean? He told *me* that, before he even knew about vampires."

"Is he gay?"

"No. Sex does not need to come into it."

"No, it doesn't. But you're saying he hasn't even tried?" The ninja-sniper went back to his scope. "Either he knew what you were ahead of time, or he has a personal history I don't want to imagine."

"What of you?" she asked. "How many non-Swiss are there in the Vatican ninjas?"

He didn't look up when he answered, "What makes you think I'm not Swiss?"

"Your eyes are brown," she stated. "Your skin is naturally bronzed, not tanned. It is more Mediterranean or Middle Eastern than Swiss."

The only response the ninja-sniper made at first was a small bit of his mask moving. He was smiling. "Persian, actually," he corrected. "Still Catholic, but let us just say that the Middle East knows vampires well."

She nodded. "*Da.* Ghuls."

He chuckled. "If you're going to use a plural, *and* the original pronunciation, you should call them *ghilan*. You are, technically, a *ghouleh*—a female ghul." He stopped to focus in on a target, considered it a moment, then moved on. "You've never turned into a hyena, have you?"

Amanda smiled, then shook her head. "No, I have not. By the way, I am Amanda Colt. You are?"

Not looking up from his scope, he said, "Ibrahim Javaherian. My friends call me Abe. My teammates call me Bram."

That's your code name? As in Stoker? "Ah. How did you get into this sort of thing?"

"Family business. My brother's a lawyer, but my sister teaches close quarters combat. Trust me, when you're on the anti-Vampire team of the Swiss Guard, you take your job seriously."

"Indeed." She frowned a little and leaned over to take a closer look at his weapon. "What are you using, anyway? I never heard of a bullet that can kill a vampire."

"You haven't been living in the age of modern weaponry much, have you, Miss Amanda?" He chuckled, even as the muzzle panned around. "This is the Barrett M82, fifty-cal. It will shoot through engine blocks, walls, and will remove whole limbs. Including the head. Say goodbye to any vampire who gets on the wrong end of this. It would probably remove the heart, if I do it right."

Amanda nodded, then hesitated. There was something approaching. "How do you feel about close-range weapons?"

"I have a few, though I prefer not to use them."

"You are about to."

Ibrahim chuckled, then reached down to his belt. He tapped something on the buckle. "We'll see."

He turned around, leaving his rifle in position, propped up on its tripod.

By that time, not only was Amanda already on her feet and ready for battle, they had visitors.

Scattered around the roof were vampires, ten in all. Four had guns, three had swords, and the other three were unarmed. The leader placed himself in the middle of the roof, hands empty. He was rather well-dressed, in Joss Whedon Chic: long black leather duster, and everything else solid black. The leader of this particular pack was somewhat handsome; Amanda would have joked that he was tall dark and Hindu, but he could have been Sikh for all she knew. His looks were aristocratic, with a sharp nose, smooth features, and proper posture.

"I would sooner recommend Armani if you're going to hold yourself like a human being," Ibrahim said to the newcomer.

The leader of the pack smiled. "This *is* Armani," he said, his voice about as overdramatic as his features; as smooth as a well-oiled motor, and his accent was more British than American. "They do leather."

"Kinky," Ibrahim said, his delivery deadpan.

The male vampire looked from Amanda, to the Vatican ninja, to his sniper rifle. "My name is Mister Kalsey. May I help the two of you?"

"Kalsey?" Ibrahim asked. "That's Sikh, then?" He glanced to Amanda. "Sikh and ye shall find."

Amanda cut in. "We are here to protect someone bearing messages to your employers."

Kalsey smiled tolerantly. "I have no employers, Miss. I am the owner of The Platelet. Any and all messages can be delivered to me directly."

"Mikhail," the ninja Ibrahim said without hesitation. "We think he's in New York."

Kalsey's smiled vanished. "If he is, then I have no knowledge of it. You have delivered your message, now go away."

Amanda held up a hand. "That is not it. We want him. You can give him to us. Or find him for us. Or else."

Kalsey sighed, his tolerance fading fast. "Or else what?"

Ibrahim took a step forward, more for cutting off Amanda than a tactical necessity. "Two things; one, you are all standing on bouncing Betties. Land mines."

Amanda looked at the ninja. She thought back to when she warned him about the incoming vampires. He had tapped on his belt. Could he have just armed booby traps?

Kalsey laughed. "You are bluffing," he announced confidently. "Any such mine, detonated at this range, would kill you before it would kill us."

"Well, I've been killed before." Amanda shrugged. "There is one other thing."

Behind them, on the street, The Platelet exploded in a massive inferno. The door came off of its hinges and flew out into the street. The flames were so bright, Amanda could see white flashes against her hand. That was less from what Marco had done, and more from the intense heat given off by vampires on fire.

"Or else that," she concluded.

Kalsey growled, then waved his men forward.

That was their mistake.

Ibrahim was as good as his word. The vampires without guns stepped off the mines covered by the roof gravel, and explosive devices leapt up into the air, around crotch height, and exploded, though not with shrapnel. With water. Holy water.

All of the vampires were splashed. The ones armed with guns were hit even worse. They had been standing on the wall around the roof so they could have the high ground, and the best vantage for shooting. When they were first hit with the holy water, they screamed and fell back, right off the roof.

When Kalsey raised his hands, Ibrahim drew his sidearm, a Desert Eagle semiautomatic handgun, loaded with .50 caliber bullets. Some were solid, "jacketed" bullets, and others had hollow points. The hollow points were sealed off with melted wax from church candles; the wax sealed in the holy water.

The holy water from the bouncing Betties slowed the vampires enough that Ibrahim fired off eight of the nine rounds in the magazine – two for each of the sword-wielding vampires. He dropped it and drew an oak knife from his belt as the two unarmed henchmen closed.

The vampire went after Ibrahim with a quick but careless lunge. The Vatican ninja leapt for him, thrusting forward with the pommel of his dagger, which was in the shape of a cross. The vampire staggered back, stunned. Ibrahim recoiled, and thrust forward with the dagger, sliding it up, under the ribcage, and into the heart. The vampire dissolved into a pile of dusty and expensive clothes.

The other one went for Amanda at the same time. Amanda only sidestepped. She grabbed the vampire on his way past and dragged him with her as she charged the edge of the roof. She let go of him, guiding him straight for the inferno pouring out of the bar's front door, going at the speed of a bullet.

The Vatican ninja and the vampire turned to Kalsey at the same time.

The dapper vampire smiled at them both, and leapt back, landing near one of the fallen swords. It was a long cavalry sword, the type one would have seen a British cavalry officer carry. "I hope you both aren't thinking of killing me. That would be a mistake of epic proportions."

Amanda sighed and shook her head. "That would be counterproductive."

Kalsey smiled. "But if I kill you two, the little punk who destroyed my bar would be defenseless. No more threat, and I don't have to go against Mikhail the Bear."

We never gave him the nickname.

Amanda snickered. "He destroyed your bar without effort. Without help from us. Totally on his own. We only watched. Do not think that he would not destroy you first."

"Really? Let's see how cocky you are when I cut you both to pieces."

Ibrahim wasn't Marco Catalano, but he apparently could also do math. Without even a look in Amanda's direction, he tossed her his dagger as he leapt for his Barrett.

Amanda caught the knife using solely her peripheral vision, then charged Kalsey. His sword was longer, and sure to cut her before she could close. Her dagger was against the inside of her forearm, but at least it was made of wood.

Kalsey's first swing was a full baseball swing, meant to take Amanda's head clean off. In fact, had it connected the right way, he could have cut her in half at the waist.

Amanda instead dove into a roll, going under his swing. Her knife arced through the air, slashing across Kalsey's femoral artery, and she leaped away.

Kalsey let out a little gasp. He wasn't used to pain, and staggered. It had only been a few seconds since the slash, but one leg of his expensive pants was already soaked with his own blood. Between the cross on the dagger, and the wooden blade, the wound wouldn't heal quickly. He tried slowing his heartbeat to cut down on the blood loss, but he had already lost too much.

He growled, and lunged for Amanda, who was on the other end of the roof. It took only a split second, but for a vampire, it was practically slow motion.

Amanda smiled at Kalsey's charge. It was standard fighting for soldiers forever. Most warriors didn't fence, they *fought*. In her case, she had been playing what Marco termed "three-dimensional chess" with fencers for the last fifty years. Kalsey broadcast his next move so far in advance, he might as well have sent it Western Union.

Amanda dashed directly at Kalsey. His sword was raised high, ready to cut her straight down the middle. Kalsey swung down, as Amanda sidestepped out of the way, her dagger slashing through his clothes, and into his stomach, ripping apart the aorta, and most of the other arteries that made a stomach wound fatal. Kalsey doubled over, and Amanda slashed down for his exposed neck, cutting through the carotid artery.

Kalsey tried lifting up the sword, and fell flat to the roof, unconscious.

Ibrahim approached slowly, looking at Kalsey through the scope of his rifle. "I think that did it."

Amanda nodded. "*Da*. We need him alive to spread the word. Otherwise it would look strange that the bar merely exploded."

Ibrahim smiled. "In which case, I think it's time that he takes his medicine." He lowered the rifle and reached for another compartment.

"What are you doing?" Amanda asked, looking at the bottle of pills he came up with.

He tossed her the pills and said, "Have you ever heard of micro pharmaceuticals? It uses nanotechnology as a delivery system for medication."

"And?"

"Well, how else are you going to make holy water into a binary poison?" he asked. He reached down, grabbed Kalsey, and flipped him over. The vampire groaned as he fell on his back like a turtle. Amanda handed Ibrahim one pill, and the ninja knelt down next to him, and then dropped it into Kalsey's open mouth. Since Kalsey didn't need to breathe, the ninja couldn't merely hold his mouth shut and make him swallow.

Ibrahim frowned, took his dagger back from Amanda, and slit his own thumb open. A drop of blood made it into Kalsey's mouth, and the vampire reflexively swallowed, taking the pill into his body.

The ninja grinned, and stared just above the vampire's eyes, never into them. "Listen, friend. Do you know what we just did to you?"

"It's poison," Amanda added. "If you come near me, or Marco, or if you fail to meet our demands, my friend here will slip you the other half of the poison."

Ibrahim nodded. "That pill you swallowed? It's filled with holy water, encapsulated within nano-capsules. They'll float in your bloodstream, cling to arterial walls, you'll be stuck with it forever. We can get to you anytime we want. Do you know what would happen then? Your veins would be on fire. Your blood would boil. You would spend your nights, and even your days, screaming in agony, until, at long last, you simply *die*."

The Vatican ninja, trained by Catholic priests, said, "Or you could go the redemption route. To do that would require that you do what we ask anyway."

"Indeed." She knelt on Kalsey's other side, across from Ibrahim. "We want you to refuse aid and comfort to Mikhail. We want you to spread the word throughout the community. Any death in Brooklyn will result in reprisals. There will be plenty of death. The kind you do not return from."

Ibrahim patted him on the arm. "Have a good day, buddy."

Chapter 20:

Snack Food

March 14, 9:30 p.m.

When Amanda and Ibrahim walked down the fire stairs of the building, they moved slowly, in no rush. Amanda didn't want to leave the ninja behind.

"So, I have to ask," he began, "What did Marco use to blow up the bar? That was white-hot fire in there. You don't just pick that stuff up on the street."

Amanda smiled and shook her head. "Marco used a relatively simple explosive system. Do you know that you can make nitroglycerin at home?"

The ninja-sniper scoffed, only it sounded more like a laugh. "Yeah. Sure. If your home is a chem lab."

"There are days he practically does live there," Amanda told him. "In this case, he separated the chemicals with wax, and strapped the test tube to the package of gasoline and Styrofoam."

Ibrahim reached out and grabbed Amanda's shoulder. "Wait, you're telling me that he used nitroglycerin as a detonator on *homemade napalm*?"

Amanda casually shrugged off his hand. "Given Marco, he most likely used two packages. One on the liquor supply, and another on whatever was the most crowded part of the vampire crowd. The vampires were the white fire. They burn hot."

"Heh. I thought that prick was dangerous when he took my rifle." The ninja studied her for a moment. "Though you aren't a slouch either. Have you ever had much in the way of combat experience?"

Amanda merely turned and started walking. Ibrahim looked after her a moment and started again. "You know, there are stories about a Vatican vampire. One who worked with the teams long ago. She was pretty. With reddish hair. She was Russian. Know anything about that?"

Amanda laughed and gave him a glance over her shoulder. "Is that not like asking me my age?"

The ninja laughed. "More like carbon dating a corpse."

Amanda's smile faded. "Come. Let us follow Marco to his next bar before someone does something *else* stupid tonight. After all, Marco wishes to burn down *three* vampire bars tonight."

April 4th, 5 PM

Marco Catalano, Amanda Colt, and Father Rodgers sat around the small wooden table in the middle of the rectory dining room. The older black gentleman leaned back in his chair, a glass of Johnny Walker Black in his hand.

"I am truly sorry to hear about Lily, Marco," Rodgers told him, his voice just above conversational volume–he was old enough to have preached in churches that never had a microphone.

"That they would make this personal is something new. This is more like organized crime than anything I've seen from vampires."

Marco nodded thoughtfully. His brow furrowed with thought. "Ditto. I don't recall vampires playing well with others. Should I just eject everything I learned about vampires from Bram Stoker, and start anew?"

Rodgers allowed himself one short, booming laugh. "Ah, Bram. Yes. Pity he fell to his prey." He shook his head and paused before he took another sip. "And they said it was Tuberculosis. Ha!"

Marco and Amanda shared a look. "Do we want to ask?"

Amanda shook her head. "I think we already have our

answer."

"Yeah, that's what I thought." He looked back to Rodgers.

"Does anything we discussed last time fit with any other data?"

The priest nodded. He took a sip of his scotch, put it down, and straightened. "Back when you first approached us, you mentioned to me a name: Mikhail."

Amanda nodded. "I had heard of one called Mikhail the Bear. A master vampire who liked to nest. Often. He usually nests, clusters a family, trains a replacement to be his equal, and then moves on to repeat the cycle."

"Now he's here," Rodgers said, a flat statement.

Marco raised a finger. "Point of order. How do we know *for certain*? I heard the name twice, once from Amanda as a rumor, and once from Lily while she was insane. That's hardly two reliable sources. It may not be 100% of one source."

Rodgers gave him a half-smile. He and Amanda both knew that Kalsey, the vampire bar owner of The

Platelet, had dropped the name when Amanda prompted him. It was decided that it was best if Marco didn't know that there was a guardian angel over him last night. "You mean aside from the description of the vampire who ran off with Lily? What did you say, Amanda? He was built like a bear?"

"That is good description."

"Everything else fits his pattern. He's come in and set himself up. There are routines, patterns almost militaristic in fashion. The last time that any Vatican troops caught on to a nest of Mikhail's, it didn't end well."

"Should I ask?"

"Tunguska."

Amanda had to hold up her hand at this one. "Wait. *Nyet.* That event in Tunguska resulted from something above? One air burst. Comet? Meteor? Something?"

Marco coughed as though he choked on something. "Whatever it was, it was more powerful than the Hiroshima atomic bomb. About a thousand times more powerful. A thirty megaton airburst that leveled over eight hundred square miles. Are you telling me that one vampire did all of that?"

The priest held up his hands in mock surrender. "I only know that the last time we heard from that particular group of Vatican operatives, they were headed towards Tunguska. That's *it*."

Marco rolled his eyes. "Okay. So you're certain that this fits in with his usual M.O.?"

Rodgers frowned. "If this is Mikhail, then I have no idea what he's doing. He hasn't touched a city this size…at least, not since cities this size came into existence, and going after FBI agents is completely out of bounds for him."

Amanda blinked, leaned forward, putting a hand up. "Agents? More than one? There was only one in January."

"Didn't you read the updates I sent you both?"

The vampire and her man exchanged a glance, and as one they pulled out their cell phones, tapped a few buttons, and frowned briefly.

Rodgers rubbed at his forehead. "Tell me that it didn't go to spam."

"Okay," Amanda told him, saying it like *Oh. Kay.*

"We won't," Marco added.

The priest sighed and took another healthy sip. "We're now on FBI agent number four by now. Possibly five."

Marco frowned, releasing a heavy breath. "Okay. We don't know what the FBI agents were doing in Greenpoint in the first place. Right?"

"I don't," Amanda confirmed. She looked to Rodgers. "You?"

He shook his head.

She nodded. "So, no. We do not know."

"We know that if Mikhail likes his secrecy," Marco said, "killing the Feds meant that he didn't have any choice in the matter. If he doesn't generally do cities, then there's a reason why he's *here*." He sighed, and leaned back, almost as though he were bored and falling asleep. "What are the geographic profiles of the attacks? How far through Brooklyn are they?"

The priest shrugged. "There seem to be some disappearances in Queens, but for Brooklyn, they're stymied around Greenpoint."

Marco's eyes snapped open, and he sat up straight. "You're joking."

Amanda shrugged. "That is good? Yes?"

"Oh, great, wonderful. But I didn't think we'd actually *halt* all progress."

Father Rodgers smiled. "Aside from the occasional death in the middle of Bensonhurst, there hasn't been an issue outside of this area."

Amanda and Marco both looked at him. "What?" she asked.

Marco concurred. "Why Bensonhurst?"

"It is farther into Brooklyn," she continued.

"Why jump so far on the map if they're securing whole regions at a time?" Marco sprang to his feet and started to pace, a feeling of dread coming over him. "Right now, we're fighting them piecemeal, not wholesale. Not to mention that we're at least aware of something going on in Queens, if only because of the Mount Olivet tip we got from our bar-hopping sojourn. If we provoke them enough, they'll probably try coming in force." He waved it away, as though brushing off someone else's objection, and resumed pacing. "Doesn't matter, had to happen eventually, but I didn't think that we'd have this much success so soon. If they kill any more FBI agents, we're going to have a boatload of *them* storming around the area, which is so many kinds of not good."

Amanda smiled, as though she thought this mental brain activity binge was cute. "*Da.* Having them see men with arrows, wooden stakes, and playing with fire would be bad. We'll be the ones they take in for questioning."

"Take one FBI incursion, add the Queens issue, and the curious incident of Bensonhurst...Why Bensonhurst?"

"Why Howard Beach?" Rogers countered.

"What about them?"

"If Bensonhurst is the aberration in Brooklyn," Rodgers elaborated, "then Howard Beach is the one for Queens."

"But that's the other end of the universe, comparatively speaking." He rolled his eyes at his own slowness, and said, "Bensonhurst is the midst of Brooklyn, as opposed to Greenpoint, which is the end nearest Manhattan."

Amanda chimed in. "But there is something they have in common."

Marco blinked a few more times, his pacing completely halted. "Mafia ties. Bensonhurst, realm of the Gotti clan; Howard Beach, also with connections. It works."

"Though I should ask," Amanda added, "why not *Brighton* Beach? They have some more vile mobsters lately, with mafiosky, Eastern European mafia."

Marco ran his fingers through his hair. "Yes, but the Russians are too out of control. The Italian version isn't much better, but they do as they're told. Okay, so we have issues with Queens, the mafia, possibly the Feds, and, soon enough, a massive first strike on our resources."

Rodgers cocked his head to one side. "What was Lily then?"

"A warning," Marco said. "One we're going to completely ignore. We're going to keep killing the bastards."

Rodgers frowned. "If you can."

Marco chuckled. "Don't underestimate the power of utter nutcases in large groups."

"Speaking of which, several bars were blown up last month. The Recovery Room? The Bloody Mary? The Platelet?"

"Homemade napalm."

Rodgers coughed, nearly spilling his drink.

Marco chuckled. "Oh, that reminds me. We've brought you four bottles of Johnny Walker Blue, and several of Black, which looks like it was bottled when they started working on the Blue."

Marco looked off to one side and drifted off. *What would FBI agents be doing in Greenpoint, anyway? At least with the Secret Service, I can make up a reason, such as counterfeiting. The DEA would be hanging around the docks. But the FBI? What would be around here that they would be interested in? We don't have terrorists, unless you count the occasional tinfoil helmet squadron. So, if we can find out why they're here, maybe we can find out why the vampires are here.*

"Father, do you have any contacts with the FBI? We're going to need to know what they're doing here, and I'm not sure I can convince them with my charm."

Rodgers shook his head. "I'm only in contact with the Vatican strike team. I'll have to send word to the Cardinal and find out what he can do."

Marco's cell phone rang. "Hi, dad," he answered, then paused. A moment later, he said, "Sure, I'll be right over."

Marco cleared his throat and looked at Rodgers. "Well, I have to go over to the clinic now. Someone is making my father an offer he can't refuse."

"Are they trying to buy it from him?"

"I mean the Mafia have my father hostage."

Chapter 21:

Negotiations, Vampire Style

April 4th, 7PM

Amanda Colt sat across from Marco Catalano in the back of the Vatican-Ninja assault van. She watched Marco's face. There was a new expression, something she'd never seen on him before. Worry. Of course, he tried to hide it, even from her. She was good at this, however. Years of practice helped, and he was too upset to hide it well. He kept his right hand low and out of sight, next to his thigh. It was in a fist so tight it had gone fish-belly white.

She leaned forward and touched his knee. "It will be all right."

Marco's face whipped toward her, and his smile, this time, looked more like a twitch. "Of course it will. It's only a bunch of mobsters with my father, and not two weeks after losing Lily." She hadn't realized that Lily's death had truly affected him. At all. *At least that is comforting. I think.* She motioned towards the others in the van. "But we have backup."

Six of the Vatican Ninjas were in the van. Two were in the front seat, and the rest were getting their weapons locked and loaded. When the word had come to mount up for a human situation, they had ditched their dark striped pajamas for street clothes.

"That's nice." He looked to the ninjas. "How many of you have ever done a hostage takeover with vampires?"

One who was tall, dark, and Persian, looked to one who was pale and red-haired. "Last year? Black September idiot?"

The redhead shrugged. "I think so."

Amanda almost smiled. She recognized the voice of the Persian; that was Ibrahim, the ninja-sniper from the other night. Without his mask on, he was quite handsome. His dark hair was cut short. His skin was the type of dusky bronze that could have been from half the Mediterranean, and there was not one sharp angle in his face, only smooth curves.

Marco scoffed. "Please, the Israelis wiped out Black September for what they did at the Munich Olympics."

Ibrahim smiled. "A .22 to the head doesn't work if the guy's a vampire. Trust me."

Marco frowned. "Uh huh. Marco Catalano, nutcase amateur. You are ninja…?"

"Ibrahim Javaherian."

"Uh huh. Can I just call you Abe?"

"Call me Bram."

Marco rolled his eyes. "Of course. Have we met?"

"You hit me with my own sniper rifle."

Marco blinked, mouth open a moment before anything came out of it. "Ah. Sorry."

"Quite all right. I haven't shot you yet, have I?"

Amanda looked back to Marco and slid forward enough so she could grab his shoulder and pulled him closer so they could meet eye-to-eye, at six inches distance. His eyes had gone from dark blue to simply dark. "Marco. I know you are worried. But we will get your father out of there alive."

He gave another, horrible, twitching smile. "I know we will. I don't want to lose him, too. He's one of the few people who actually understands me. He's possibly my best friend."

His breathing was starting to come quick and shallow, like a build up to hyperventilation. "You know what was the best part of Lily?"

Amanda gave a little shrug. "What?"

"Lily made me feel human. Just like you." He took a deep, slow breath. "I love you, Amanda Colt."

Amanda was taken so off guard, her heart stopped. Literally; she actually forgot to instruct her heart to continue beating.

He gave another horrid grin. "As a friend, of course, as per our non-involvement treaty."

Amanda thought she hid her urge to rip out Marco's throat exceptionally well. She didn't even growl.

The van came to a stop. "We're here," Ibrahim said. "Get out. We'll get into position, so take your time."

Amanda nodded, and leaped out of the van, Marco second. Which was good, because she still felt the urge to push him into traffic.

Marco marched into the clinic, and slowed to a stop, just short of the main hallway, and then suddenly reached forward and grabbed the wall, as though he were overtaken by vertigo.

Amanda was instantly at his side, grabbing his arm. "Are you all right?"

Marco shook his head sharply. His lips were pursed, as in pain, and he gripped the wall as though he would fall over otherwise. "I can't go in like this."

She gave him a comforting squeeze. "It is all right. If you must stay here, I can go in and retrieve him."

Marco shook his head vehemently. "No. I have to do this. I can't always have you watching my back, as much as I'd like to. I mean I can't go in like this." He grimaced, and pounded the wall so hard, Amanda expected a dent.

"Most gangsters take their manners from Scorsese and Coppola films." He swallowed, as though trying to choke down something. "They think they're modern inheritors of Machiavelli, mainly because they have Hollywood films telling them so. If they have any philosophy, that's it. They preach the gospel of fear over love. Amanda, you're going to have to be ready to back my play. I'm going to have to speak their language. You with me?"

"Always."

Marco took several deep breaths and closed his eyes. He straightened and took several more. Then something odd happened. His smell changed.

Amanda blinked. It was odd. It was almost like Marco's entire body chemistry had been shifting over the last few minutes, and he now smelled like a completely different person. Marco stretched his neck a little. "Come on," he said, his voice calm and irritated, like he was about to start dealing with a mosquito instead of a mobster. His amused little smile returned. "Let's go teach those wise guys a lesson in respect."

He strode directly ahead, no hesitation, stepping around anyone who got in his way. He nodded and waved at those people who acknowledged his presence and went straight for the stairs. He took them two at a time and didn't wait to see if Amanda was behind him. She was, but only because she was a vampire who had no problem taking three stairs at a time. When they exited the stairwell, they came out only ten meters from Doctor Robert Catalano's office. The secretary was gone, and there was an obvious Guido parked in front of the office. Marco moved for the office at a brisk pace, not even a run, more like a man in a hurry. The Guido tensed and reached into his jacket.

"Hi, I'm Marco Catalano. I'm expected."

The Guido hesitated, and that's when Marco darted in. He burst forward, his left hand clamping down on the wrist the Guido had in his coat. Marco's right fist came up next to his ear, elbow cocked back all the way, and shot right into the man's nose.

The Guido's head rocked back, smacking into the wall. The arm cocked back again, then smashed forward, this time with the elbow to the face. Marco then shot his hand into the jacket to grab the handgun itself. With the weapon firmly secured, Marco proceeded to shoot his knee into the Guido's groin. Three times.

Marco twisted the gun, the muzzle towards the Guido, then pulled back on the gun, keeping the grip pointed towards himself the entire time. He pulled back, keeping the semi-automatic's barrel in his fist, reached back, and jabbed forward, stabbing the muzzle into the Guido's face over and over again.

Marco grabbed Guido and spun him around, took him by the collar, and used his body as a battering ram for the office door. There were three mobster types watching over his father. Two were undeniably muscle, big-bodied and about as suave as a ball of steel wool. If they used any more product in their hair, they would leave a slime trail.

Marco swung the gun straight to the third man. He was tall, but more elegant than the other two. He didn't seem to have a weapon, and he was relaxed in Doctor Catalano's desk chair like he was there for a business meeting. He leaned back, hands behind his head, relaxed as a beach-goer. This man was less DeNiro and Pacino of Mafia movies, more Michael Rennie of the original *Day the Earth Stood Still*. He was of medium build, with thick cheekbones.

"Hi, Dad," Marco said to his father. "You okay?"

Robert Catalano sat in the guest chair. He seemed unharmed and stared at the gun in Marco's hand. "I think so. Though I may be hallucinating."

Marco's little smile was perfectly in place this time. "I believe you were expecting me?" Marco asked the others as Amanda smoothly slid into place next to him.

The third man smiled easily. "Yes, we were." He casually waved a finger at the Guido Marco had just used as a blunt instrument. "And you, Mikey, you should be more careful."

He looked to Marco. "My name is Enrico. You do not need to know my last name."

Marco poked his head out from behind his human shield just enough to show the mafioso his smile. "You assume I care."

Amanda could sense that the others in the room were also taken aback by Marco's entrance and attitude. *What was he thinking?*

Enrico showed no signs of noticing this disrespect, and the two hoods–while they obviously took notice– didn't think it wise to rush the man with a gun on their boss. "We've had some associates hurt in a fashion reminiscent of what's been happening in Greenpoint. We understand from one of your boys that you know what's been going on around here lately."

Marco raised one eyebrow slightly. "Which of my boys would that be?"

Enrico waved it away, as though he were dismissing a dessert tray at a restaurant. "It did not take long to make Mister Vega talk to us."

Amanda found it odd to imagine hoods like these managing to find their way into Hector Vega's neighborhood, kidnapping him, and vanishing, all without Marco hearing of it from Vega's Tigers.

Marco's eyes narrowed. "Let him go."

"Why should we?"

"What did you hear about some bombings lately?"

"Some bars were destroyed in the city last month. Why?"

"That is what happens to people who hurt those who belong to me." Marco jerked back on Guido's collar, starting to choke him with his own shirt. "*My* men. *My* women. They are *mine*. They belong to *me*, and I don't take kindly to those who would break my toys."

Enrico leaned forward, his eyes narrowing into slits. For the first time, he seemed annoyed. "Do you know who and what I am, little man?"

"No, but I know your next residence. I hear Mount Olivet cemetery is nice this time of year."

Amanda noted facial tics in the mobster's face. "I don't take kindly to threats."

"Threats? Did anyone else hear a threat?" He smacked Guido upside the head with the butt of the gun, leveling it immediately on Enrico again. "Did you hear a threat, schmuck?"

"You think you're funny," Enrico asked. "Don't you?"

"You're the clown who thought he could intimidate me in my own playground."

Enrico narrowed his eyes. "This is Brooklyn. We own it."

"I'll be sure to tell the Russians in Brighton Beach," Marco replied immediately. "Didn't they carve up one of your boys last year?"

Enrico's eyes glanced to the thug nearest Doctor Catalano. "I'm going to have my men start hurting your father–"

"Because evidently you're unable to do it yourself," Marco spat.

Enrico stood, using his height in an attempt to be imposing.

"Don't make me do something I may regret."

"Too late," Marco answered. "You're here."

"Listen. You're either going to cooperate or–"

"That's just what I was going to say," Marco interrupted, adjusting his aim somewhere around the man's belt buckle. "Give me my father and Vega, and you can walk out of here. Alternately, you can be carried out."

"Who do you think you're dealing with?"

"Someone not nearly as frightening as what I've been dealing with for the last few months."

"And what might that be?"

"You beat the crap out of Vega enough to get here to me, so you already know."

Enrico scoffed. "He tried to tell us some fairy tale about vampires. No matter how many bones we broke."

Mar co reared back with the pistol and cracked Guido over the head. The human shield fell over like a tree. Marco readjusted his hold on the gun to a two-handed grip. His eyes went dark, and his voice dropped an octave. "Then you already know the answer."

Enrico rolled his eyes. "Now I'm just going to start hurting your father."

"No you're not."

The mobster smiled. "Or else what? You'll have your girlfriend beat me up?"

"No. I'll let her eat you and your men."

Guido Number Two, nearest Marco's father, chortled. "I'd let her eat my sausage any night."

Amanda didn't even need to look at Marco. She could feel the frisson of rage next to her like a sudden flare. She caught only a glimpse of his face in the window. Whatever it was, the situation, the comment, everything together, finally sent Marco into "tilt."

"Amanda," he said, his voice suddenly deathly calm. "You feel like Italian tonight?"

"Nah," she answered. "Too much *bruschetta* in their diet. Gives me heartburn."

"Pity. Try not to kill them, if you can. They might feel like talking after."

Enrico growled this time. "Now, *look*, kid—"

"Something's been killing your men," Marco interrupted.

All three mobsters tensed. Enrico leaned over the desk, hands down on the blotter. "What did you say?"

"Something is killing your men. They are assassinating wiseguys. Vampires."

Enrico grit his teeth. "Shoot him in the kneecap." Marco detected motion on the right, flicked the gun that way, and fired. The bullet grazed the thug, and Marco redirected back to Enrico. Marco didn't say that he was shooting for the wall next to the thug's head.

"Heel, boy." Marco took one hand off the gun and put it around Amanda's waist. He drew her to him, hip to hip. It didn't even take her a second to follow

Marco's lead. He was playing the tough guy, the feudal lord, Alpha male, macho B.S. What macho fellow would have a woman like Amanda along with him without having her fawn over him? Her arm went around his upper back, her head lolled against his shoulder, and her hand pawed at his chest.

On one hand, it felt good to be this close to him. She hadn't really had this much physical contact with Marco since she had to bite him on the train to Astoria. He was just as warm and as comforting as she remembered, even if his scent had changed. On the other hand, she felt like the model for some trashy romance novel.

"This young woman is more than just some Russian sex kitten. There's a mirror in the bathroom over there, just off of the office. Go get it. I'll be happy to show you proof."

Amanda smiled, lolled her head up to Marco's face. "What do you vant me to do, darlink?" she asked in the worst cartoon Russian accent she could recall.

Marco's breathing blipped. *Did he just stifle a laugh?* She thought and had to stifle a giggle then of her own. Then she wondered if the three armed mafioso also noticed…and if they noticed, would they kill Marco and his father before Amanda could do anything about it?

Chapter 22:

The Oncoming Storm

April 4th, 7:30PM

It took everything Marco had not to laugh at Amanda when she asked him, in that awful, *Rocky and Bullwinkle* Russian accent, "What do you vant me to do, darlink?"

Then again, it was possibly bad form to start laughing in front of the mobster and his two henchmen…technically three henchmen, but one was sprawled out on the floor.

While he had a gun he had confiscated from the Guido on the floor, and he had Amanda next to him—draped over him, to be exact—that would take out two of them. Would that be enough to take out all of them before they did something stupid?

And if I get my head blown off, it might be what I deserve for calling her a Russian sex kitten. What the Hell was I thinking?

"Just stay next to me for the moment. No reason to eat the nice men just yet." He looked to the remaining two musclemen. "Like I said, go get the mirror. And if you try anything, I still have a gun on your boss."

Guido Number Three went into the office bathroom. After some grunting and a sharp crack, he came back with the mirror and thumped it down on the desk, pointing it at Marco and Amanda.

Both Marco and Amanda smiled. The mirror showed exactly what he knew it would: just Marco. To add to the effect, she stroked his chest, ruffling his shirt – which made the reflection look like it was shifting all on its own…and made Marco's own heartbeat skip a little.

Crap, why does she have to feel so good against my body? He couldn't believe how much she affected him.

Guido Number Two and the boss blinked in surprise, unable to say a word. Guido Number Three looked at the mirror, then back to Marco.

"I think it's time that we all sat down and talked," Marco said. "Don't you?"

Enrico scowled, backing away from the mirror. "No." He was no longer squared off against Marco, but at an angle, in a combat stance that would be proper for holding a gun–a Weaver stance–and the stately mobster's hand started to slide up the front of his suit. "I think we should just ice the both of you."

Marco arched his brow, forgetting his tough guy act a moment. "Ice? Are we back in the twenties? If you really want to do this, I should probably mention my tactical team."

Enrico paused. He looked from one thug to another, then back to Marco with a smirk. "Really? You're going to try to bluff me, punk? You're a worthless kid. You don't have anything out there, not even the cops."

"I just took out one of your guys on guard, and he saw me coming. Where do you think I get that sort of training? I brought a bunch of Vatican ninjas with us, and they seem rather high-tech. I'm going to assume they have something as simple as a laser microphone. So I'm going to suggest that they shoot out a window, just above your heads."

A bullet clipped one Guido, then the other, felling them both. They barely heard the plink of shattered glass.

Marco smiled and said, "Or, that could work. Enrico, if you could look at the back of your head, you might find a little red dot. Now come on. We'll sit down, explain the situation, and then I'll make you an offer that you can't refuse."

April 4th, 10:00PM

Doctor Robert Catalano laughed as he sat down in his office chair with a solid thud. He combed his fingers through his salt-and-pepper hair and looked from his son to Amanda and back again.

"So, Marco," his father began, "when did you inherit a strike team?"

"You see, when I went down to talk to the local church, things got…interesting."

Amanda nodded in agreement. "It is why we called Father Rodgers immediately after Enrico decided to play nice with us."

Marco added. "He would be better at coordinating any alliance and explaining things." He tried another smile, and it faltered. He was even starting to sound tired, as well as look it.

"I should hope so," Doctor Catalano said.

Amanda nodded, and looked at Marco, concerned. "Indeed. Speaking of which, what did you do back there?"

"Hmm?"

Doctor Catalano laughed. "I think she means your trick where you decided to come in like an eighties action hero and tried to out-mob the wiseguys."

"Wiseguys?" Marco snickered. "None of the guys in there I'd characterize as 'wise.' As far as changing like that? I've always become whatever I need to be. It's like method acting.

There have been cases of actors becoming the parts they play almost since the start of Hollywood. Simply put? I'm adaptable."

Amanda was tempted to ask him just how could he so completely alter his body chemistry and give himself a different scent in a matter of minutes. Who was that flexible?

There was a knock on the door, and Marco almost wished that he had kept the mafioso's handgun. Amanda didn't move but sniffed the air a little. "Come in, Bram."

The door opened, and in came the dusky, smooth-featured Persian Vatican ninja-sniper.

Marco visibly relaxed. "Oh, Bram, hi. Dad, this is Ibrahim Javaherian, the sniper attached to the Vatican Ninja team, and the guy who helped us before. Bram, this is my father, Robert Catalano."

The sniper nodded. "A pleasure." He looked to Amanda. "We have a problem."

She straightened in the chair. "What is it?"

"The FBI has just found another dead agent."

Marco winced. "Oh nuts."

Doctor Catalano knocked on his desktop like it was a door. "Excuse me. What FBI agent? What do you mean by another?"

Amanda gave Ibrahim a brief glare. "Thanks."

"Short version?" Marco started. "FBI agents keep popping up in Greenpoint, and they quickly pop up in the East River."

Ibrahim interjected, "Actually, a back alley—"

"Thank you, Bram," Marco and Amanda said at the same time, loudly.

The sniper held up his hands in surrender.

Robert shook his head. "That makes no sense. This isn't Brighton Beach or Bensonhurst. We don't have anything around here for the FBI to look at."

Marco and Amanda shrugged in sync. Even the Vatican ninja started at how in tune they were.

"That's not the major problem," Ibrahim said. "You see, they're going to be sending one of their best."

Marco frowned thoughtfully. "Define best?"

"Okay, how do I put this?" Ibrahim looked off to the side, obviously trying to encapsulate the depth of the problem. "He works for the government as their own private Harry Dresden–"

Marco barked a laugh. The idea of the government hiring a wizard private investigator was amusing. "It must be cheaper than putting together its own 'X-Files' unit."

The Vatican ninja ignored the crack. "There may be about a dozen people within the Federal government who knows who, what, how, and why he's in government, but let's say that we know who he is. He's good with locks and, as some have put it, he's good with 'things transcending everyday human experience.'"

"Are you saying that this is a true sorcerer?" Amanda asked.

"No. It may just be a matter that he has the correct amount of both knowledge and luck. It would be hard to explain any more than that."

Doctor Catalano shook his head, then turned to his computer. He called up Brave and asked, "What's his name?"

"Merle Kraft," Ibrahim answered. "But it's not like you can find a government agent for the supernatural on Facebook–"

"Merle Kraft, San Francisco," Robert Catalano read. "Owner of the Art of Kraft magic shop in the Embarcadero. One second." He tapped a few more keys. "The Art of Kraft magic shop has two other stores. There's Tal Kraft, of New Orleans, who owns one store, and a Dalf Kraft of Boston, whose store is

'Dark Krafts.'" Robert looked at Ibrahim with his dark eyes and said, "What was that about not being able to find him?"

"That must be his cover."

"Maybe." Robert tapped a few more keys. "Hmm, I don't think they're related." He turned the screen to them. Three internet windows were open, each had a photo. One was a large black fellow in a long, loose-fitting dress shirt; the second was a "black Irish" Caucasian dressed in an opera cape, top hat and dress suit, looking like a classical magician; the third was a short Eurasian in a dark blue windbreaker.

"Those are the three Krafts who run the stores," the Doctor told them.

Marco leaned forward while Amanda could see perfectly well from where she was. After a moment, they both said, "They're related."

"How do you figure?" Ibrahim asked.

"Elementary, my dear ninja," Marco stated.

"They have the same eyes," Amanda completed.

Marco looked to her. "Dark blue?"

"Midnight blue, I think," she concurred. "Which one is Merle?"

"The Eurasian."

Marco leaned forward, studying the short one. Black hair, dark blue eyes. He held himself casually and confidently. He was relaxed, he knew where he was, and what he was, and if you didn't like it, he didn't care.

"Merle Kraft. Secret Agent Man, is he? Makes you wonder who he dragged into the world of the weird." He glanced at Ibrahim with an amused smile. "I mean government work, not vampires. Right now, I think that politicians are a worse enemy than vampires."

Amanda giggled. "I have met a few. I can believe that. I have met vampires who suck less blood than politicians."

The ninja-sniper rolled his eyes. "Has anyone suggested that you two deserve each other?"

Marco's father cut in. "Ah, Mister Javaherian, you've pretty much said what I've been thinking for the past few months."

"Please, call me Bram."

"How about you go find someone to stake?" Marco said.

"It shouldn't be that hard, the UN is right across the bay from Greenpoint. You should be able to find a few blood suckers there." He stopped short. "Son of a bitch. Do you think that's why the FBI keeps sending agents here?"

Amanda cocked her head. "Because of its position to the United Nations? Not impossible. Why would vampires want to kill them, though?"

"Bad timing?"

"Well, if they're parked near a nest of vampires, that would be more stupid than anything else, for the vampires, of course, not the FBI."

Marco looked at Ibrahim. "When is this expert coming?"

"Tomorrow."

Marco grimaced. "Lovely. I have to ask. How good is your ability to shape shift?"

Amanda shrugged. "I can match Dracula in the novel. Why do you ask?"

"Because if this guy is as good as he seems to be, we're going to need something he won't expect. A vampire."

April 5th, 6:00 PM

Merle Kraft sat back on his haunches as he looked into the open maw of a gouged out throat. It was a remarkably dry wound, almost no blood at all.

"What's that white thing in the middle, Mister Kraft?" a cop asked over his shoulder.

Merle didn't even look at him as he answered. "Call me Merle. You say Mister, I expect my father. And the white thing is the agent's spinal column."

Even worse, it was an oddly intact spinal column. Literally, there wasn't even a scratch on the vertebra. Merle wondered aloud, "Exactly how did the bastard rip out the throat without even leaving tool marks on the bone? The gouge goes straight to the bone, but there's not a scratch? The skin is ragged, so the throat was torn out, not surgically cut. And where's all the blood? There's the initial spatter pattern on the wall, but after that? Normally I'd say they moved the body, but that's arterial spray. If it's his, he was killed right here."

Merle shifted positions to make certain that the cop didn't notice anything distinguishing about him. It wasn't usually a worry; most people don't notice him, since he was a 5'6" Eurasian, but those who did only remembered the oddity of dark midnight blue eyes in a face that should belong to a samurai.

"Well, you know what they say, Merle," another voice added, "it's good to the last drop."

Merle didn't even look over at the FBI agent who thought she was Joe Friday: Stetson fedora, raincoat, dressed in grays, offsetting her silver locks. Only her quick hazel eyes showed signs of life.

"Odd, Agent Demers," he answered, "that I got on the plane from San Francisco thinking I'd left all of those jokes behind me. I would have thought this wasn't something you'd joke about."

"How do you think we keep sane?"

The cop raised a brow. "Are we?"

Merle smiled and looked up at him. "Thanks, Officer Nolan, I can take this from here."

He nodded and walked off. Merle stood, hands in the pockets of his blue windbreaker. "So, you drag me to New York City, commandeer a crime scene and isolate it for over twelve hours so I can see the body in situ in the middle of a Brooklyn Street?"

"It's more of a back alley, actually." Demers stepped forward, stopping so that the distance between them barely left enough room for the corpse. There was no blood pool for her to avoid stepping in. "Merle, I'm not going to kid you. He wasn't my best man. In fact, my best man disappeared following leads on the same case."

"What do you think it is? Al-Qaeda in New York?" he asked, half-joking.

"No, it's not Al-Qaeda," Demers answered. "Not that we can tell. It's something…else."

"So you didn't call me because of the manner of the murder. You called because you have a bad feeling about all of this, and you want the expert in the 'exceedingly strange' to stake the bogeyman."

Her eyes twinkled. "Sort of like that. I know you've been busy looking into those Goths in San Francisco, and I'm sorry to pull you off of them, but—"

"Spare me. You think you're the only person to yank me off a personal project? For a guy who's only supposed to be known by only a dozen guys in the District, I'm very wanted."

A small grin from her. "Dead or alive, I would presume."

"Well, if it's dead, then I double my fee." Merle looked down at the body. "So, I'm guessing he was stripped of all ID?"

Demers' hazel eyes flickered to the corpse's pockets. "Not all. He has the standard issue implant under his skin with his medical history and a contact number."

"Ah. Basically an 'If found, please return to the FBI' label."

"You could say that. Should I leave you with the body, Merle?"

"Unless you've got something else to add."

"Nothing PERT couldn't come up with. If you find anything…"

"I'll let you know. Count on it."

This is going to be a nightmare. The FBI Physical Evidence Retrieval Team is pretty good. If they couldn't find anything relevant, what do they expect me to do, divine something?

She turned and started to walk away. Halfway down the alley, she turned back. "I know you like working alone, but still…"

He waved her off. "Don't worry, I'm in no rush. Besides, if you really need my help, then you won't be able to assist. I'll tell the morgue to pick up the body when I'm done."

Merle Kraft watched her turn the corner. He muttered to the air, "Dalf, what are you up to now?"

A deep chuckle came from the darkness. "Why do you always blame these things on me, Merlin?"

"Well, it helps that you usually are the problem."

Merle didn't even bother looking towards the darkness behind him. He knew exactly what he'd find. His half-brother, Dalf Kraft. He was eternally in his mid-twenties with midnight blue eyes and a pale, though charming, face. He wore a black cape around his shoulders that terminated above his ankles, a black shirt like a Catholic priest and a deep, blood red tie. His raven black hair parted deftly on the right and he smiled like a wolf about to dine. His cheekbones hinted of Slav-Celtic ancestry, but neither confirmed nor denied. As always, he carried a cane with a silver wolf's head handle.

"So, Dalf, how quickly do you travel? I was brought here on a super-sonic jet. If you weren't responsible, how did you get here so fast from Boston?"

Dalf's melodic voice floated from the darkness. "I travel at the speed of shadows."

"Sure, Dalf." He turned to face his half-brother.

The only visible part of Dalf was his midnight blue eyes that glittered with an unseen light illuminating nothing but the irises. The color made it hard for even those to be seen against the dark. It was the only thing that hinted at their relationship to each other. When one mother is descended from samurai, and the other is a Boston Irish something, the eyes are the only thing they had in common, physically.

"So, you want to tell me what did this, brother of mine?"

The form in the darkness gasped in mock injury. "You wound me, brother. Whatever did I do to you to make you think I would have any knowledge of such an event?"

Merle raised a brow. "That's rhetorical, yes?"

The Boston Kraft laughed through his mouth. It was a soft laugh, static-like, with the texture of a serpent's hiss. "Of course it is. Do you truly think I would answer you?"

"Never know if I don't try. It may make my life easier. You're always referring to your employer as someone who pays well."

"Oh yes. Besides, I'd rather take the other side's money, Merlin. My Master pays much better than a government salary."

Usually, Merle would worry when his brother talked about who he worked for, but at this point, the San Francisco Kraft brother was too cranky to give a damn. "Any advice?"

The silver-tipper magician's cane rose to point at Merle's throat like a rapier. "Go home, hide under your bed, and pray that your God prevents you from being swallowed into Hell."

"Well, aren't you the over-dramatic one?"

Dalf 's teeth now showed in the darkness, though there was no glimmer of a light source for his Cheshire smile. "There is nothing of this Earth to prepare you for the hell you'll have to contend with. Even if you survive the coming storm, it will be nothing compared with the rest of the hurricane."

Merle frowned. *He's more cryptic than usual.* "So…what, I'm about to face a conspiracy out of an old Anne Rice novel?"

"No, my brother, I will not give you the game. But I warned you."

"Whatever. You want to help, I welcome it. If not, go back to Hell, or Boston, or wherever you keep your coffin."

Dalf clucked his tongue. "Do not waste your breath becoming irritated at me. I am simply an enforcer for the Army of Darkness, Merle. I can only do so much before I'm…fired…for mutiny."

Merle ignored him and crouched down to further investigate the wounds on the body. "Yeah, well, I still remember one of my last targets being reduced to a pile of ash. Where were you during that fracas, anyway?"

"Eating."

Merle glanced up to confirm his suspicions. Dalf had disappeared. Like the Cheshire cat, he was probably gone before he spoke his last word.

We have this down to a science, Merle thought, *although this is the first time he's deliberately told me to run and hide.*

Merle rolled his eyes. The relationship between them was always odd. At best, each tried not to acknowledge the other existed. Thankfully, their respective locations made it easy to avoid one another. *He keeps to Boston, for all I know nostalgic for the good old days of Salem. I stay in San Francisco, the width of the continent just barely far enough for my taste. Unfortunately, my job deals with what the government calls strange, and Dalf should have his own entry in the Oxford English Dictionary.*

Merle sighed, moving around the body once more, trying to figure out what the heck went on there. The arterial spray on the wall meant he was killed here—Mental note, make sure it is his blood—but if that were the case, what was used to catch the blood after the initial slash? Where were the tool marks to show what had torn his whole throat out?

At this point, I would even accept evidence of teeth marks as a help.

Chapter 23:

Saturday Bite In Brooklyn

April 5th, 8:00 PM

On the roof across the street, Amanda Colt noticed Merle Kraft didn't seem to care *why* anyone took the blood of the dead FBI Agent. However, Amanda didn't wonder about his lack of curiosity. After all, she had been to San Francisco.

Amanda knew, however, the moment anyone suggested a theory of vampires, superiors within the government would write the murder off as a nutcase killing a random human being who just happened to be an FBI agent.

As Merle Kraft walked out of the alley, Special Agent in Charge Alice Demers was still there, waiting for him, hands in her coat pockets. "As you can imagine, the moment news of this gets out, you'll be gone, and we'll be told to wrap it up."

"I know, Al. I'm sure that the Attorney General doesn't like such things."

Alice Demers' smile reached her hazel eyes. "You really think that an Attorney General would give this any thought? I mean, the corpse's blood is missing. What's the first thing you think of?"

"You're reading my mind."

"Large print," she replied dryly.

"With any luck, it'll take them a while to get their act together on this, which buys us time. Though, you're right, I don't think anyone that high up is going to care about a murder in the back end of…what is this neighborhood called again?"

"Greenpoint," she answered. "Merle, look west."

Merle smiled. Not six blocks away from where he stood was Turtle Bay, and on the other side of the bay was the Isle of Manhattan. More importantly, there stood the esteemed institution of the United Nations. "I should be able to wrap this up soon enough. Now my question is, why'd you call me? If I were you, I'd say this was some nut playing Dracula. Typical loser psycho."

She nodded. "But you're not me. What's this telling you?"

He blinked in surprise. "It's that obvious something's very wrong here?"

"More than usual, anyway. Last time I heard from my guy, he said he was on to something big."

"Such as?"

"He didn't say. He just said that he was close to…" She looked at her watch. "Come with me to my office, I want to show you something."

Amanda followed after them, leaping from one rooftop to the other. She didn't have to worry about being spotted. It was dark and no one ever looked up in this town…or in any other, actually, unless they were tourists.

The joys of living in the city, she thought. *You can act like Batman, and no one notices. You can even dress like Batman, and no one would notice…Didn't I do that once?*

She looked on, noting that the shorter man and the FBI agent, Demers, were heading for a car. That was all right, she had her own transportation.

April 5th, 8:30 PM

Marco Catalano turned his family's sitting room into his own personal study, and he was doing something he hadn't done in years.

He was studying.

It wasn't that he had any individual test to study for, or a difficult subject to overcome. He knew all of the material. He knew more than some of the professors. He observed more surgical operations than medical students.

Marco was studying because he didn't have anything else to do.

He couldn't follow Merle Kraft around like Amanda could. If the assessment of the Vatican Ninjas was worth anything, Marco's presence was only going to give the game away. Marco hated that he couldn't help her.

If Merle were really good, could he notice Amanda? Could he kill her? Marco frowned and shook his head. *Nah, that's impossible,* he told himself, more to push down any sense of worry than because he was certain.

He flipped through a book. *Then again, I could take her in fencing. But I'm a freaking computer! I'm really freakish, which gives me the advantage.*

Marco slammed the book closed and hurled it aside. *But so's this guy!*

"So, what about Amanda?"

Marco's head snapped towards his father. "What?"

"You're throwing things. I haven't seen you that pissed off in a while." While Marco had taken the couch, and spread his work over the coffee table and the cushions, Robert took the arm chair at right angles.

"What's up?" his father asked. "Lovers' quarrel?"

Marco grimaced. "I'm not going to even dignify that comment with a response. The government agent who specializes in weird stuff has arrived, and Amanda is tracking him."

"And you're stuck at home while she's having all the fun?"

"It isn't that."

"You don't think Amanda can take him?" Robert asked.

He gave out a light growl. "I don't know. Bram and the other ninjas talked him up a bit last night. These guys kill vampires for a living, so when they say that he's good, I assume that means *vampire-killing* good. So, yeah, I admit I'm a little worried."

"You love her?"

Marco blinked. "I'm sorry, what?"

"I'm tired of having conversations like this with you. It's getting wearisome."

"Then don't ask."

Robert sighed and ran his fingers through his hair. "Look, you hang out with this woman more than you do with your classmates. More even than Zheng and Vega. Seems to me, she's the only person you hang out with at all. If you're going to tell me again that you two are 'just friends,' at least try to be convincing, and without pyrotechnics."

Marco stared at his father for a long moment, the tension evident on his face, and all through his body. He took a long moment, trying to decide if he'd open up at last, or if he'd keep up the façade. Finally he relaxed, letting out a slow breath. "I don't know. I try not to think about it."

"You're going to go with that? Truly? You can't stop thinking about a million things, but this rather important issue you can turn off?"

Marco looked down at the textbooks and shifted through them as though looking for something. "I haven't given it any thought. I mean, I *have*. None of the conclusions are satisfactory though, so I push the question aside. You know what I'm like, Dad. Would you truly wish for someone to fall in love with me?"

"Marco, I know your previous dating attempts have been–"

"Disastrous?"

"–but that doesn't mean every relationship will be like that."

Marco let out a sigh of frustration. "You don't seem to get it. I'm not worried about something going wrong with Amanda, I'm worried there's something wrong with me. Let's face it, on a good day, I'm abnormal. On bad days, I'm not safe to be around."

"So when you say you haven't thought about being in love with Amanda…"

"It isn't a matter of if I love her. It doesn't matter how I feel. I cannot even *consider* it. It's safer for everyone that way. Heck, take me and my … issues, out of the equation. Just look at most military regulations about fraternization. Life's easier on the battlefield when you don't have to worry about a relationship leading to fragging."

"Have you ever considered how she feels about it?"

Marco paused, confused. "Of course I have. That's why I don't say anything. If she came out and confessed that she loved me tomorrow, that would be interesting."

Robert gave his head a little shake, incredulous. "Interesting? That's it? Just interesting?"

Marco's smile slipped. "The day she tells me she loves me is the day I have to tell her everything about me. And that's the day I fear worse than vampires. That's the day she stops talking to me once and for all."

Merle Kraft settled into the chair in FBI Special Agent Alice Demers' office. "So, what am I looking at?"

Demers handed him a glass of Kahlua from her full bar stashed under her desk. SAC Demers was a leftover from the old boys' school, and she had more testosterone than half of them.

Most of the time she reminds me of a secretary out of a Raymond Chandler novel, Merle thought, *straightforward, as blunt as a piece of concrete, and armed.*

I'm certain I'm catching a whiff of cigar smoke from the "smoke-filled backrooms" of yore. It might be something in the wood.

As if to emphasize Merle's point, she kept on her trench coat, even indoors.

"You're looking at intercepts going to Kojo Annan," Demers answered him.

"Son of former Secretary-General Kofi Annan? Of the UN?"

"The same. He ran the old oil-for-food program. You've heard of it?"

"It always sounded like a nice little racket to me, even before there were questions about the project.

Iraqi dictator Saddam Hussein was theoretically limited to selling oil that would generate enough revenue to feed the populace of Iraq. Though about eighty-thousand a year starved to death under Saddam. Between everything we heard before and after Saddam fell, my bet is it was really an oil-for-*money* program.

Considering that Saddam provided suicide bomber life insurance—$20,000 to the families of suicide bombers—as well as built himself multiple palaces designed on those of Joseph Stalin, I never thought it took a genius to figure out where the cash was going. Given the 'success' of the program, you're looking at fraud?"

He twirled one of her letter openers between his fingers. "So, he was a player with money and international contacts. You figure he wanted to be a Bond villain when he grew up?"

Her eyes narrowed, then she opened a desk drawer. "How'd you get my letter opener?"

Merle paused, looking at it between his fingers. "Oh, sorry." He flipped it from one finger to the other and out of sight.

"I have to find out how you did that," she muttered.

Merle gave Demers an inscrutable little smile. "So, you want me to look into Kujo while I'm at this?"

"One thing at a time. Find the killer first, and we can get to the Annan family later. And his name's Kojo, not Kujo."

"Oh, like Kojo the Executioner from *Star Trek*?"

She shook her head. "That was Cronos the Executioner."

Merle shrugged. "Whatever. I at least got you to admit you know *Star Trek*."

Demers turned, grabbed a *Star Trek* novel from behind her to rub his face in the obvious, but when she turned back, Merle's glass was empty, Demers' office door was locked from the inside, and Merlin Emery Kraft was gone.

She sighed. "Who does he think he is? Batman?"

Actually, I always wanted to be Mandrake the Magician, Merle thought.

Amanda perched on top of the Soviet Embassy— *No, it's the* Russian *embassy, you idiot. The Soviets fell years ago*— across the street from the FBI's New York branch.

Gee, the FBI building across the street from the Soviet Embassy, how subtle. Then again, it's New York. Our idea of subtle involves a baseball bat. Then again, it's the same in Brighton Beach.

From her perch, she could see a young blonde woman enter the FBI headquarters. She could hear the woman's pulse rate accelerate, smell the woman's anxiety, her fear, her…

Hormones?

A petite, athletic, golden-haired woman stood in the doorway of the FBI headquarters of New York City. Strands of brassy hair fell smoothly to the nape of her neck. Rich blue eyes set over smooth Celtic cheekbones locked onto Merle Kraft immediately. She wore a lightweight black sweatshirt with a zipper in front, opened partly at the neck, revealing creamy skin he knew so well, with a pair of black jeans. Merle hadn't accounted for her when trying for a getaway from the building.

Detective Kristen Kelly caught his arm as he tried to leave. "Hi, Merle."

He blinked, pretty sure his irises dilated to ringlets. "Kristen, um, hi."

"Are you going to tell me why you stole my murder case from me?"

"Murder case?"

"Dead body? Alley? Greenpoint?"

"Oh, that. He was an FBI agent, Kristen. They get their own, you know that."

She nodded. "Certainly. But why you? They think it was a vampire and wanted you to look at it?"

He smiled. There are days Merle still wondered whether or not she simply teased him about his job, or if she knew the truth, and merely expressed that knowledge in a jocular manner. "Well, um, I'm not sure. He was working on something, so I guess I'll need to look at both the murder and finish off whatever it is he's been working on. Is Captain McShane interested in this as well, or just you, since it was yours?"

"Where do we start?"

"We?" Merle blinked. "Like heck. You know you've been removed. So has the NYPD; it's—"

"I'm your local contact, darling."

Merle froze, stunned. *Wow, I dug myself in deep on that one.* "Oh, um, great! Perfect. I guess I'll see you tomorrow then, bright and early."

"Where are you staying?"

"Probably at the airport hotel. It's easier that way."

She shook her head. "You're coming with me."

"Why?"

She put her hands on her hips. "Because Arthur wants to see his father before he forgets what you look like."

Because Detective Kristen Kelley, NYPD, didn't trust him to find his own way home, Merle Kraft's ex-wife secured him to the passenger seat of her car and drove to their home.

Her home, you idiot, he thought. "You didn't move?"

"Why would we? The place was small enough to begin with. It can fit me and Arthur. With your black bag crap, I'd think the government would pay you more. Whereabouts are you now?"

If only she knew that half the time the black bag is a body bag. "I own a magic shop in San Francisco. I live above the shop. It supplements the income nowadays."

She laughed. "You mean it's cheap and the government pays for it as your cover?"

He looked out the window for a moment, affirming her answer. "So, what did you think of my last offer?"

"Moving out to San Francisco?" She stared out into the street for the space of several streetlights. "It's an idea, but wouldn't it simply be easier for you to move than anything else? I can't say I see many advantages."

"It's quieter than New York. It's also smaller. You might not even consider it a real city."

"Sold."

Merle studied her. "That was too easy. What's the catch?"

"There are enough days that Dalf has stopped by unannounced that I think it's worthwhile to be on a different coast."

His eyes narrowed. "My *brother* Dalf? He *visits*?"

She nodded slightly, keeping her eyes fixed on the road. "He came to see Arthur."

His fingers flexed. "I'm going to kill him."

"You've bought stock in silver bullets lately?"

He gave a tight-lipped smile. "You finally believe that Dalf works for the forces of Hell?"

"I've seen his eyes glow red," Kristen told Merle. She stared at the stoplight, and didn't look at Merle, even though they both knew it was a long light. "It was after we took his picture, and I don't think it had anything to do with the camera flash."

Merle thought about it over, trying to make sense of it.

Didn't most cameras remove red eye from photos nowadays? Heck, couldn't it be done at home? "How could you tell?"

Kristen gave him a look. "They were glowing for the next minute after the picture was taken."

"Did he come out on the film?"

"It wasn't film," Kristen explained. "It was digital. The camera hasn't worked since. I'm just assuming he's a monster straight from Hell and writing him off right now."

"Good idea. Not even I know what he is, really. And I'm afraid to ask."

"So, what do you have on the dead Fed?" she asked.

Yeah, that's as good a note as any to change subjects on.

"Wiretaps on Kojo Annan."

"Lemme guess, food-for-oil?"

Merle Kraft smiled. "Wow, that wasn't even hard, was it?"

"Hell no, that's the only thing Kujo did that's worth mentioning."

"His name's Kojo, not Kujo."

"Oh, like Kojo the Executioner from *Star Trek*?"

"That was Cronos the Executioner."

She smiled. "Whatever."

These are the days when Merle remembered why they got married. Whenever he talked with her, he was hard-pressed to remember why they got divorced in the first place.

"To tell you the truth, Kris, I'm not even certain where to start. Fine, Kujo's been a bad boy…so what? If he skimmed a few billion here and there. Who cares? I mean, the Kurds made noises about food-for-oil for years before Saddam was overthrown, and no one cared enough to blink funny at it. Even after there was a full-scale investigation, no one did anything about it. What would they do about it? Blow up Turtle Bay? Exile the UN? Please, no one has the balls."

Kristen looked at him. "True enough."

"So what was this Fed doing in Greenpoint?"

"Well, his home was within sight of the UN building, in Greenpoint."

They looked at each other simultaneously, and Kristen performed a sharp J-turn, driving back immediately the way she had come, heading straight for Turtle Bay and Greenpoint.

"Laser mic," they said as one.

A laser microphone, or electronic ear, as some people might call it, could basically be pointed at a window a block away and pick up everything going on in that room. Granted, there were some problems with it, especially if you were too far away. The last thing someone wanted was to be listening to a conversation going on across the river and then get a foghorn blasted into their ear because a ship drifted into the path of the laser beam.

Merle opened his files and turned to the agent's folder. "He's got an apartment above a clam restaurant in Greenpoint."

She nodded. "I think I know that one. That's on the bay, within bullet strike of the building—hell, you could hit that place with a handgun."

"Even better." *Well, I couldn't hit that place with a handgun. I can't shoot worth a damn.*

Chapter 24:
Dance With The Devil

April 5th, 9:00 PM

Merle Kraft was halfway out of the car before Kristen even hit the brakes. "Stay here, watch my back, and make sure no one follows me up. Ring my cell if you see anyone coming. I'll put it on vibrate so it doesn't attract attention."

Personally, he thought the reason sounded good, and not at all like he was being protective. *I don't want to tell her that if I find a blood-drinking freak in the apartment, I want her at a safe distance.*

Merle ran to the front of the restaurant and leaped over the small gate locking off the al fresco area. He landed on a table before grabbing the awning and swinging himself up to the windowsill of the apartment. He entered the apartment without seeming to open the window.

The next window over had the laser mic, attached to a computer and a digital recorder.

Both of which were in pieces, one part currently in each hand of a towering man in black leather jacket and black jeans. He wore sunglasses over his eyes, and the rest of his face was covered in scars. The man's hair was slicked back and jet black against his stark white skin. "Let me guess, bad night in Romania?"

Scarface glared, then hurled the last mic fragments to two different corners of the room before leaping on the government agent.

Merle barely managed to leap out of the way, and Scarface kept flying through the air, and would have gone through the wall had he not pushed off of it with his hands. Scarface landed on his feet and turned on him.

"Did you by chance eat an FBI agent lately?" Merle asked.

Scarface smiled, revealing teeth that were crusty and stained with dried blood.

Amanda slowed to a stop on the rooftop, and just in time, too. She didn't want to miss this little encounter. She could track the entire fight from her position.

Amanda's entire thought process stopped dead when she saw who Merle Kraft was fighting. It was the vampire who had pushed her in front of a train during her attempt to save Lily Sparks.

Scarface ran forward, and Merle disappeared from view, reappearing behind him. Kraft grabbed Scarface's leg in mid-step and pulled, flattening him to the floor. Kraft was about to leap on him and restrain him, but Scarface rolled onto his back and jackknifed onto his feet, leading forward with a right jab.

Merle ducked it by the enamel of his teeth, then sprang up, delivering a left jab to his kidney, and a reverse spin kick to the back of Scarface's head, a blow which should have blinded if not killed him.

Scarface merely stumbled forward a little. Merle pushed off one foot to deliver another spin kick to the small of the man's back. There was an audible crack, which Kraft expected, and Scarface's legs went out from under him. It was logical for him to have a broken spine after an attack like that.

Kraft slid into fighting position, grateful he hadn't gone for the man's neck, otherwise there would be a problem getting him to talk.

Breathe, breathe…that's better, he thought. *And why are you braced for impact? He's not going anywhere.*

Kraft relaxed, then moved forward, dropping to a crouch next to Scarface's head. "So, why did you kill him?"

Scarface looked up at him, glaring.

Snap. Merle looked up, and thus was unprepared for the sharp uppercut that sent him sprawling across the room.

When the stars cleared from his vision, Scarface was looming over him...Standing over him. But didn't I just break his spine?

Scarface smiled, baring eerily sharp teeth, and took his time bending over Merle. Kraft curled his knees to his chest, then lashed out with both feet into each of the giant's knees, bending them backwards. Scarface collapsed backwards, a growl coming from his throat. Merle flipped onto his feet, grabbing the leg off a ruined side table.

"Fine, then how about I just drive a stake through your heart and be done with it? Oy, you are no help at all."

Scarface rolled away from Merle. Scarface rolled to his feet and smiled at Kraft. He looked at the wooden table leg warily, and then shrugged.

The larger man turned and leaped through the window, landing on his feet like a cat, not even slowing down for a second.

Amanda was tempted to intervene, but she had no idea how either Merle or Kristen Kelly would respond to the sudden appearance of someone leaping off a roof. She didn't relish the idea of getting a bullet in the head.

Scarface landed nearly in front of Kristen Kelly's car. He smiled at the blonde and ripped the gate off its hinges, raising it over his head, ready to smash the car in.

"Don't kill him!" Merle yelled. "We need him alive."

Kristen opened the door and rolled out, drawing her gun as the gate came down on the hood. She fired twice, taking out both knees.

Not only was he still standing, he was advancing.

Kristen glared. "Screw it." She promptly fired three rounds into his heart. Each .45-caliber bullet had enough force to knock a grown man off his feet. Scarface didn't stagger. Kristen stood and then emptied her gun at his chest.

At the same time, Merle raised the table leg like a harpoon and hurled it from the window, going through Scarface's right knee.

The giant finally dropped to one knee, growling in pain. He glared briefly at Kristen, then pulled the table leg through and out of his body.

Kristen reloaded.

Scarface blinked, then twisted and hurled himself into a limping run.

Merle muttered a curse, and then leaped out the window, rolled off the awning, and landed on his feet before running to his ex-wife's side.

He stopped short of hugging her. "Are you all right?"

Kristen leveled her gun at Scarface's back. "I think so. You think he's on something?"

Kraft smiled, then looked at the minimal blood spatter. "I think his blood was around a hundred and fifty proof, and the other fifty was PCP. Even if he's on Meth, E, XTC, Y and Z, he should've been down when I broke his knees…now he should just be dead from the blood loss."

"It's amazing, Merle, you can't shoot to save anyone's life, but you can hurl a table leg like a harpoon so it can hit a dime."

"More like a nickel." He chuckled. "Excuse me a moment, I need to chat with him. He has to at least be slowing down. From the blood loss, if nothing else."

On the rooftop, Amanda watched the engagement with amusement. It was fascinating to see how the short one and his ex-wife interacted with Scarface.

It was even more interesting to note that they were both still alive. *Well, a first time for everything.* She looked over, and down the street.

Scarface ran with a bad limp, his knee not healing after the wooden leg speared him. He was still making good time, however.

Then he felt something.

He looked up at a form on a distant rooftop, sensing that something was watching him. He snorted and kept running, faster this time.

Until he tripped and fell headlong into a garbage bin.

Merle Kraft pulled back his foot and stepped out into the street. "Miss me?"

Scarface looked up. No one could move that fast.

"I'm faster than I look."

The next moment, Merle was flying through the air, hurled by the adversary. He absorbed the impact with his arms and rolled with it, coming to his feet. Merle blinked and saw Scarface, on his feet once more, looming over him like a heavy smog bank.

"You've got to be *kidding* me."

Scarface looked at him and sniffed, as if Merle wasn't worth his time. Then he turned and limped away, this time with less of a limp.

"Screw it," Merle muttered. He looked around the alley and spotted a fallen stop sign that had been taken out by a stray motorist. Maybe half of the original pole for the sign was intact and attached to the metal. He grabbed it and stood.

The sound of the metal scraping along the concrete caught the killer's attention. Scarface turned and glanced at Merle's new weapon.

"I'll give you one shot," Scarface said with a voice as gravelly as a rockslide. He grinned. "Then I kill you."

Merle narrowed his eyes. He raised it as if he was about to bash Scarface's head in and swung it like a baseball bat.

In mid-swing, Merle twisted the radius of the sign ninety degrees, pointing the edge at Scarface's neck. The stop sign became an axe blade and sent Scarface's skull flying.

The blonde police officer came around to the mouth of the alley and stopped, gun drawn. She looked down at the body and wrinkled her nose, lowering her gun. "You cut his head off? I guess that's one way to do it. I thought you wanted him alive."

"That was before I decided he wasn't going to give me any information anyway. Now he gets to wear this year's fashion in body bags."

Kraft crouched by the dead man's side before searching his pockets. His hands stopped and came out with a set of FBI credentials and a badge.

"Well, I guess we don't have to look further for proof that this is our murderer." He stood. "That was almost too easy. I don't even think I've been here for three hours, and already I've solved the problem, or at least part of it."

Kelly raised a brow. "This you call easy? What do you call a normal night out?"

Merle smiled. "You know I can't tell you. They're so top secret I'm to kill myself if I even remember them."

She laughed. "Point taken. You want to leave Scarface here and call it in, or do you want to hang out with the corpse?"

He tucked the contents of Scarface's pockets into the inside of his windbreaker. "Let's head back to the apartment, I want to see if I can salvage anything from the remnants."

"Okay. I'll stay with the body and call—"

Merle turned to her. "*Nyet*, *nien*, heck no, *meschula*. We've already had one freak around here, and I'm keeping you close. Stay with the car and make sure no one dynamites it, but that's all, okay?"

She was about to object that she was a fully-grown, heavily- armed, NYPD officer. Then she recalled how many times she had shot the bastard and changed her mind. "So, what did you find in the apartment?"

"Our friend Mister Freak destroyed the laser mic with what looks like his bare hands. I think the computer went the same way. Also, I'm fairly certain I saw dried blood on his teeth."

Kelly rolled her eyes. "Why can't the freaks just stay in San Francisco?"

His midnight blue eyes flashed dramatically. "Because they pay me to come out here."

Amanda looked down, thinking. *I don't think these are our enemies. Yes, these two might be of use after all.*

April 6th, 12:10 a.m.

FBI Special Agent in Charge Alice Demers looked around the apartment, noting its ruined condition. "Nice work. You're both all right? Nothing wrong? From the amount of damage, I'd expect at least a body."

"Well, we left you one outside. You're right though, I fully expected him to go down here as well. Expected him to go down several times here, as a matter of fact."

Demers looked around the room for a chair, then shrugged and leaned against the wall, her hands in her trench coat pockets. "Anyway, I'm glad this is over quickly."

Kristen smiled. "Nice to know we have our priorities straight. Wouldn't it help to know *why* the guy killed one of yours?"

"Oh, it would help immensely. However, having bagged the killer will at least hold my superiors over until we can get whoever sent the bastard. It's always a good start to get the triggerman."

"Or in this case, the tooth fairy," Kristen muttered.

"Hm?" Demers looked at her quizzically, as if trying to decipher what she meant.

Merle raised a hand. "I think he used his teeth to rip out at least part of the Agent's throat. There was dried blood on his teeth."

The silver-haired woman concentrated. "Well, that would explain some things. The evidence retrieval team swabbed the wound on our guy. Apparently, they found some kind of microscopic…things."

"Things? You mean organisms?"

"They were described to me as some kind of parasite, but that's just a guess."

Kelly furrowed her brow. "A guess? They don't know?"

"They've never seen anything like it before. From your description, I'd say that had something to do with the oddities about your attacker."

Merle chuckled. "Oddities. That's one way to put it."

"Any ideas?"

He shrugged. "There are a range of options. Strange anatomy. Drug use. Body hacking by Doctor Frankenstein. Like the Catholic church and exorcisms, I like to rule out everything else before we jump to a prognosis of demonic possession. I know I specialize in weird, but the deep dark secret is that most of my cases end with variations on Scooby-Doo."

Kristen looked at him. "How so?"

"I once handled a case of someone who'd been stabbed in the heart but didn't die. Found out that his organs were mirrored. Odd, but it happens."

Demers shook her head. "I guess it doesn't matter right now. At the moment, my main concern is about who sent this guy. With any luck, our man used proper protocol and had his laser mic connected to the computer so it could digitize the recording and post it on a secure site."

"You mean you haven't checked if he uploaded it yet? If you don't know already, then it's not going to help much."

"True. We wouldn't know the site, and the Web's a big place, but it'll give us something." Demers' phone rang. She answered, then nodded a few times before saying, "Thanks."

She looked at the two people in front of her. "Sorry to

tell you, but there doesn't seem to be a body left, just a dirty alleyway."

"I was afraid there'd be someone else around." He looked at Kristen. "Aren't you glad you listened to me?"

"So, now what? I get to go home now?"

Alice nodded. "On the first plane out."

"Would you mind if I at least put off the flight until tonight? I'd like to see my son." He turned to Kristen. "You don't mind if I come see Arthur, right?"

She beamed. "Of course."

Demers laughed. "Arthur? You're Merlin and you named him Arthur?"

Merle glared at her and pointed at Kelly. "It was her idea, not mine."

"It makes me wonder who sent the divorce papers. You're *both* nuts."

Chapter 25:

Boston Shaman

April 6th, 12:40 a.m.

Amanda Colt stood in front of Marco's brownstone and considered not going in. She merely stared at the street, wondering how she would come up with a report of the night's events.

And how am I going to convince him that Merle and his lot are not our enemies?

"Are you waiting for something to happen?"

Amanda didn't even look over her shoulder at Ibrahim. "*Nyet.*"

"How did the night go?"

"Surprisingly well, Bram. Merle Kraft seems to be quite good at what he does. He may be useful. They seem to be aware of the parasitic nature of the vampire virus. After all, we never heard back from the CDC after Marco's father sent out the sample in January. I assume the FBI got involved."

"I always wondered why the Catalanos never heard back from them. Even in the form of FBI agents."

Amanda sighed. *It probably set off old alarm bells that no one knows what to do with anymore. Especially not after that*

Fort Dietrich incident. "It is time. I will check. If he is asleep, I will know I tried…"

"One of these days, you two have to get your stories straight on what the two of you are."

"Just friends."

As Amanda sprang for the window at the front of the building, she could just hear Ibrahim mutter, "Yeah, heard that one before."

Amanda ignored him, and slid the window open, then pulled herself into Marco's room. She looked around. It was mostly books and book cases. One would think that he was solely interested in academics.

She crept silently, and noticed the bed was occupied, as she expected. Marco was face up, under blankets. He looked relatively peaceful for once, which was an interesting change.

She was half expecting that his face would be locked into one of intense concentration, or one of his amused smiles, even in his sleep. Stupid, but with Marco, expecting things to happen rationally just didn't seem to be on the agenda.

Amanda stood at the side of his bed and made certain that she didn't breathe for a moment. After realizing that Marco really wasn't going to spring up from a sound sleep, she whispered, "Are you awake?"

Marco's smile slipped into place, and he didn't even open his eyes. "You move perfectly silent, but I can still smell your soap." He sat up in bed, not the least bit self-conscious about Amanda being in his bedroom while he wore only underwear and a t-shirt. "So, find out anything interesting?"

"Merle is someone we should look into."

"Good."

"You don't want to know everything?"

"What in particular do you think I need to know?"

"Everything. He moves quickly. He killed Scarface."

Marco's mouth twitched. "Well, it's something." Amanda then started filling him in, from how preternaturally fast Merle Kraft was, to Scarface being in the perch for the murdered FBI agent, to exactly how Merle had killed him.

Marco cocked his head. "Merle sounds rather interesting. I would love to know exactly what the whole UN thing was about. What they're looking for might be of use."

"I know you're wary of the Feds," she tested, "but Merle seems like someone we want on our side."

He closed his eyes and gave a thoughtful *hmph*. "Maybe if we bring him into the loop, he could give Hector some health insurance."

Amanda nodded. The head of *Los Tigres* had been viciously worked over by Enrico and the rest of his mafia thugs in order to trace the strange happenings going on in both Bensonhurst and Greenpoint.

"How is he doing?" she asked.

"He's still alive and conscious. He won't need physical therapy, so that's something." His eyes opened and he brightened.

"Oh, and we're getting Enrico's thug to foot the bill on Vega's medical arrangements and hospital stay. I encouraged Hector to stay in the hospital for a few days, and, trust me, he is being overbilled."

"How did that happen?"

"Well, I talked to billing and—"

"I mean getting one of the mafia to pay?"

"It helps that the thug I got the drop on is the one who worked Vega over. So Enrico wasn't too fond of him when we made the deal."

"Ahh."

Marco leaned back and thought a moment, eyes closed. "Now, as far as Merle goes, what do you want to do?"

"We should do some more research. I will go up to Boston," Amanda told him. "See what Merle's delinquent brother says about him."

"Is it safe for you to travel by plane?" he asked, suddenly concerned.

Amanda grinned and smacked him on the arm. "It is called the shuttle. One hour up, one hour back. I will spend more time getting to and from the plane than I will be on the plane itself. Relax."

"At least you didn't say *what could go wrong?*" He let out a breath and rubbed his eyes. Apparently, he wasn't as awake as he first implied. "Can I ask you something?"

"Of course."

"Why aren't you involved with anybody? I mean, you're striking, and you're smart, and, heck, I enjoy being with you, and I'm impossible to please."

Amanda gave him a sad little smile. "Maybe I'm a woman that men prefer to keep at arm's length."

Marco's smile turned sad, almost a mirror of hers. He slid his hand over hers and gave it a squeeze. "No. You're not. You're beautiful. And stunning."-

Marco met her eyes and looked into them deeply. There was an odd fire there, one she had never seen burn in him before. It was like everything else about him—but instead of a passionate hate or a passionate determination, this was simply passionate. "Any man would want to be the best version of themselves in order to be worth your affection."

Amanda leaned forward, staring into his eyes. "And what if he already is?"

The light in his eyes, and the heat behind them, started to fade, as his eyes started to droop. He was falling asleep on her, despite his best efforts. "Then you find him, you take his sorry butt," he said as his eyes closed and his head nodded, "you grab him, and you kiss him senseless."

Amanda moved towards him, and he slumped over more. She reached over, grabbed him, and pressed her lips to his…

And he snored.

Marco was asleep.

Amanda leaned over and kissed him gently on the lips. "I'll get you later."

April 9th, Queens, NY. 5:30 PM

Marco Catalano waited in line behind dozens of cars at the departure area of LaGuardia airport. "Bloody idiots," he muttered under his breath, glancing at his car's clock. "You would think that someone would be able to figure out how to drive in an orderly fashion.

You think that I could have you eat some of the taxi drivers?”

Amanda laughed, and lightly swatted his arm. “I could just get out of the car and walk the rest of the way.”

“You’d get run over. Didn’t you have enough problems with the number seven train? You want to take on a horde of angry New York drivers? No.”

“How sweet. I’m immortal and you are still protective. I am only going to Boston.”

“Yeah, well, Boston. Home of the Red Sox. There’s a reason Babe Ruth ran screaming from the area.”

The vampire rolled her eyes. “He did not hate Boston *that* much.”

“How would you–” He stopped short, almost hitting the taxi in front of him. “Wait, you knew Babe Ruth?”

“No. I read the articles at the time.”

“Oh, okay. Amanda? I hate to be rude about this, but just how old are you?”

Amanda smiled. The car stopped, and she leaned over, kissed him on the cheek, and said, “I will see you in a few hours.”

“Nice answer,” he said to her back. She gave him a wave as she closed the door and moved for the front doors.

Thankfully, getting on the Grand Central Parkway to Brooklyn was easier than fighting with the traffic around LaGuardia airport. *There are days where I'd much rather be driving an M1-A1 Abrams tank.*

Marco slipped a CD into the player and cycled through the songs until he found the one cut that exemplified his mood: *Let the Bodies Hit the Floor.*

Marco opened the window, put the speakers on full blast, and started singing along.

Traffic started to clear up shortly thereafter. The looks fellow drivers gave him might have had something to do with it.

It didn't take long to get to his next location: St. Anthony-St. Alphonsus Church. This time, Father Rodgers was already waiting for Marco at the front of his church. "Marco! How are you?"

Marco shrugged as he came up the stairs. "Meh, I'm alive, and still occasionally spending time in daylight. Amanda's gone to Boston, there's not a hell of a lot for me to do."

"I thought you were a student. Why not just study?"

"You're kidding me, right? That's a last resort. I've *memorized* the bloody books and my notes by now. I'm not going back to reread them a third time. Now, let's go inside. I think I need a drink."

Father Rodgers smiled. "Tea?"

"More like scotch. But I'll take what I can get."

Up in Boston, Amanda Colt walked towards the store known as "Dark Krafts." It took her a while to find the store in the Back Bay of Boston. The entire street was one of homes, fancy stores, and numerous other boutiques. Each brown brick building contained two stores, one above street level, and the other below.

The first problem happened when she learned that the online address for the store was totally inaccurate. It had taken a while to find someone who knew enough about the creepy and bizarre. She was bounced from one person to another, from one street to another, until she was finally pointed here.

No one would call the owner anything but "Kraft," until she exhorted them to use the first name. She had almost taken to threats to procure the first name— Dalf. To make certain, she had asked if he was Eastern European, like actor Dolph Lungren. No, this Dalf was a dark Irishman with hair as black as tar in a coal mine and shadowy eyes of midnight blue.

Which meant she was on the right track.

As she approached, she heard the high and harsh opening note of Frank Sinatra's "Witchcraft" floating into the night. As she closed in, the front door opened, and she was met by a set of midnight blue eyes and a pale, charming face. Before she had closed to normal earshot range, he said, "You have been asking about me all over town." His voice was smooth, mellow, with all the quality of fine velvet.

How did he know I would hear that? "Da. You are hard to find, Mister Kraft."

Dalf smiled. "I would be. I take it you have ways of making people talk, Miss Amanda Colt."

Amanda stopped before she took the first step up the stairs. *How did he know my name?* "All I did was follow the darkness. I would like to talk with you about your brother."

The magic store owner gave his head an infinitesimal bow. "This is new. Most people want to talk with him about me. Come in."

Marco sat in the rectory of St. Anthony - St. Alphonsus church, across from Father Rodgers and next to the dark-suited leader of the Vatican Ninjas, Robert Hendershot.

Hendershot was definitely Germanic in background, and he talked with a light German accent. He said he was Swiss, and one of the Guards. He was blond and blue-eyed, and his expression was so neutral, he might as well have been a block of cheese. He also had a dancer's build, quick muscle, not gym muscle, though Hendershot had enough heavy weapons on him that it had to have added a hundred pounds.

"What does your surname mean?" Marco asked.

"It is German," Hendershot said. "It means 'rearguard.' Not many of us tend to survive. You should look up our history. It might teach you manners. And character."

"Buddy, you are the last one to talk about having a character. Everyone who knows me knows I'm a character. Possibly a cartoon character." He rolled his eyes to Father Rodgers. "Next time, bring Bram. I'll take sniper-boy over the cheese head any day."

"He is at Mount Olivet," Hendershot cut in, "keeping an eye on the area, smart-mouth."

"Seen anything yet?"

Hendershot shook his head. "Not yet. It is a big area."

"I know. How many guys do you have?"

"Twenty. Keep in mind, most of them are still in Brooklyn, supporting your people."

Marco's expression went flat and cold. "You are *supporting* my people?"

The ninja Hendershot nodded. "Of course. Why?"

He gave a little cough, and leaned forward, his eyes going even darker. "You realize that if you've been helping my people and no one realized it, you were fully and completely doing the invisibility thing."

"That is part of our job."

"Your invisibility means that your support has been all but meaningless. You have been wasting your time, resources and, more importantly, *my* time. I want *all* of your resources on Olivet."

Hendershot grimaced. "You do not order me around. My orders are to protect life, not stare at *rock*, you American prick."

Marco's eyes went flat and dead. "You're in *my* little pond, buddy. In case you haven't heard, I am the–"

"Feudal lord, I heard," he cut Marco off, rolling his eyes.

"I can be the very model of a modern major general, doesn't matter. My people can take care of themselves."

"Tell that to Mister Vega."

Marco's fingers curled into a fist and uncurled again. "Who I noticed that your lousy protection managed to, oh, not protect."

"You do not get to tell me where to put my men."

"Oh? Really?"

Marco's left hand shot out. Hendershot, being a leader of a highly elite group of commandos that took on vampires on a routine basis, shot his hand up to deflect the punch. It was so telegraphed, it was pathetic. It was so easy to block, he was about to start laughing.

Instead, Marco's left hand recoiled, and the right hand shot out, latching onto Hendershot's wrist. Marco's entire upper body twisted, dragging Hendershot closer, and his left hand jammed against the ninja's elbow, putting him into an arm lock.

The ninja leader threw himself forward, into a roll, which was a standard counter for an arm lock. He was going to push off of the wall, so he didn't run into it like a battering ram.

However, Marco pushed back, jamming the chair against the ninja. "The last thing I want to do is cripple you, but I will be happy to ram the legs of this chair into your back and play vampire with you. Because, guess what, you're really predictable. And I'm smarter than you are. So, how about this – you will either play well with me, or I will–" Marco felt a little stab in his arm. He blinked, looked down at his arm, and saw a dart sticking out of it. He looked up at Father Rodgers, who calmly held a tranquilizer gun in his hand.

Marco looked at the priest. "You, not so predictable." That was the last thing Marco remembered.

"So," Amanda began, "tell me about Merle."

"You want him for what purpose?"

"Vampires," she said without hesitation.

Dalf gave a deep, theatrical nod. "You chose wisely. As for Merle, he is a reliable man. He is … good."

"You make it sound like something dirty."

Dalf grinned. Amanda half-expected him to have vampire fangs. "You would be surprised what I consider dirty."

"How do you know about vampires?"

Dalf 's face didn't change. "Plenty. I also know about Marco Catalano."

Amanda knew something like that was coming. If Dalf knew Amanda's name–well, her current alias–he would have to know Marco's.

Still, how did someone make a name sound salacious, lurid, and almost vile?

"You know Marco. That is good."

"I make it my business to know creatures like Marco."

"What about dead FBI agents?"

Dalf laughed. "You don't read the *New York Times*, do you?" He reached into his opera cape and came out with a collection of paper sheets. They were printed newspaper articles from the *Times'* website.

Amanda frowned, took them, and gave them a glance.

Someone leaked information to the newspaper. They had all sorts of details. They had dead FBI agents in Brooklyn. They had a fuzzy picture of what was undeniably Merle Kraft.

"Why does this say that there are dead British MI-6 intelligence agents in New York?"

"Because there are." Dalf said casually.

"But how would *they* know this?"

Dalf 's voice dropped half an octave. "Obviously, somebody told. I wonder who."

The vampire had the sneaky suspicion that, not only did Dalf Kraft know a lot of things he wasn't supposed to, this was a creature *she* should be worried about.

"This is getting bad."

Dalf's eyes flashed. "Oh *yes!*"

Marco awoke quickly, blinking several times and trying to figure out exactly what was going on. He wasn't in the rectory anymore, but on a bed in his father's hospital. Father Rodgers was right next to him.

"You're awake. Good. We need to talk."

Marco blinked, then looked to make sure he wasn't tied down. He was slightly surprised that, after his outburst in the church, he wasn't. "You didn't want to make sure I wouldn't go postal on you?"

"I knew you wouldn't be so foolish again. However, Marco," he leveled his gaze directly into his parishioner's eyes, "if Commander Hendershot needs convincing, you should have left that to me."

"But did I convince him? Is he going to move his forces to fully cover Mount Olivet?"

"No, and yes. You had a perfectly valid point, but your temper tantrum didn't convince him. I spoke to him."

Marco smiled, chagrined. He pushed himself up into a sitting position. "Oh well. I should have known better. Sorry. I'm usually better at figuring out what I need to be for the occasion. Lately I seem to be stuck on violent."

"Apology accepted. There's another problem."

Marco sighed, then shook his head. "You have got to be kidding me. Now what?"

Rodgers cleared his throat and reached into his suit jacket.

He came back with a cigar. Despite all hospital regulations, he lit it, rather casually, in fact. After a few puffs, he waved out the match. "Remember when you thought there might be something about the United Nations?"

"Of course I do."

"MI-6 seems to think so too."

Since MI-6 was so secret, it hadn't even been formerly acknowledged until the 1990s (despite being in forty years of spy fiction), Marco knew only one way for anyone to know that. "Let me guess, several MI-6 agents were found floating in Turtle Bay."

Marco shut his eyes. It wasn't hard to do the math. The United Nations was on Turtle Bay. That there were people from MI-6 told Marco that there was more than just a little casual corruption going on at the UN.

"The last thing I need is this complication. Fine, something's going on around the UN. Doesn't solve our situation, now *does* it?" He growled in frustration, swinging his legs over the side of the hospital bed. He was angrier at himself and the situation than anything else. "I presume that the dead spies are front page news?"

Father Rodgers nodded. "I read about it in the *New York Times*."

"Okay, so it's public knowledge." He stared off into space for the moment. *Not enough data. Move on.* "Have you seen Hector Vega around here?"

Father Rodgers nodded. "He's asleep."

"Of course."

The light from the hallway was suddenly blocked out. "I had heard you were down for a bit."

The shape of Officer Donald Tolbert filled the doorway like a fog bank. While he was tall, he wasn't overly broad.

Marco looked at the family friend and grinned. He was glad to have a private hospital room. "Yeah, well, they keep trying, but they can't keep me down. Father Rodgers, meet Officer Tolbert. Don, meet Father Rodgers."

Rodgers waved with the cigar. "A pleasure."

Tolbert nodded. "The same, Reverend."

"You both know vampires exist," Marco said, so they both knew this was a safe place to be open, "only Don's experience is a little more recent. Rodgers has his own force of Vatican ninjas hanging around. How about the police? You manage to get anybody on board with us?"

"After a fashion." The black officer looked around for someplace to sit. He didn't like to feel like he was looming.

Since there were no other chairs, and he didn't want to sit on the bed with Marco, he leaned against the wall. "I created an anonymous website a while back, and I posted some ads on Craigslist looking for any cops who had seen strange happenings lately. After fending off spam from Russian fetish prostitutes, I got a collection of cops who have noticed the same problems lately. A lot of the same problems. Many of them were in Greenpoint, Bensonhurst, around Rockaway, and in Maspeth, Queens."

Marco nodded. Greenpoint and Bensonhurst he knew– Bensonhurst had brought the mafioso Enrico down on him–and he'd heard about the area around Rockaway, which included Howard Beach, where mobsters went to dine. Maspeth even made sense because that's where Mount Olivet cemetery was located.

"How many cops do you think you have by now?" he asked.

"We have about a thousand men who are in the know."

Rodgers blanched. "A thousand? That many?"

Marco held up a hand. "Do the math. We have nearly forty *thousand* cops over five boroughs. Guess that half of them do night-shift work. Figure that there will be overlap between where they live, where they patrol, where they hang out, where they have relatives, and factor in everyone who work the streets, from officers to detectives. Add it all up, and you have a decent number of people. Be grateful Tolbert doesn't have a large number around the United Nations."

"About two dozen, mostly homicide people," Tolbert replied. "They mentioned something about British spooks floating in the East River. Why do you ask?"

Marco winced. "When Amanda gets back, we'll need to talk with Merle Kraft, one way or another. Hope she's right, and that we can trust the guy."

Chapter 26:

Enter The Twilight Zone

April 14th, 5:00 p.m. San Francisco

Merle Kraft would remember this day like most New Yorkers would remember September 11, 2001. It started just as clear and calm and as dull a day in San Francisco as it was in New York, but the rest of the day turned out to be something else entirely.

Merle entered his magic store early, rolling out of bed and into his back room. Many customers only came at night because, after all, it's San Francisco, and some of the locals really did think they were vampires.

There were certain things he really didn't want to sell them.

At five o'clock that evening, the sun hid behind the Pacific like the coward it was, and Merle's business really heated up—literally. A pothead ignored the "no smoking" sign and lit up near the magnesium flash powder.

After making sure his store didn't blow up, Merle tossed the jackass out, making sure to empty the guy's wallet to pay for the damages.

Five minutes later, *she* walked in.

The cascading red-gold hair caught his attention first, even more than the curves of her body under her fitted sweater.

Granted, it is a nice form with curves that a Volvo would hug.
She smiled. "Accident?"

Figured. White Russian skin, Russian accent.

"Pothead and flash powder are not a fun mix." Merle tossed away the last of the powder box. "Now, what can I do

for you? Help you find something?"

She nodded and her eyes wandered over him. He knew the look. *Short Asian guy with midnight blue eyes, how'd that happen?*

She surprised him by asking, "You're Merle Kraft? I have heard that you are the one to talk with about…strange things."

He chuckled. "Strange…that's pretty much San Francisco."

"I meant stranger. Would it help if I said your brother sent me?"

Merle winced. "Depends, which one? I've got dozens."

"Dalf."

Do I get my knife, or retreat? he thought.

"Something bad?" she asked. "Your irises dilated."

"Did Dalf tell you to use his name?"

"*Da*. Why?"

Merle Kraft relaxed; this woman was not an enemy, at least. "That probably means he wants you dead. So, what can I help you with?"

"You were in New York lately, weren't you?" Amanda asked. "There are more bodies. Look them up if you do not believe me. Several MI-6 agents have also been…eaten."

"Eaten?"

"*Da*, eaten. Throats ripped out and blood drunk."

"Why me?"

"Why not? Besides, it is either you or Dalf."

"Good point. I'll start packing."

She smiled sweetly. "Good."

"Beforehand, a little information?"

"Of course."

"Who are you?"

"Amanda Colt."

Merle raised a brow. *Colt? As in Sam Colt?* He gave what could only be termed an "automatic" response. "Have any relatives in Pennsylvania?"

"You sound like my friend. He asked about that as well."

"Smart man." *Lucky man, too, if he's your friend.* "How did you manage to find my brother?"

"I have…connections…to the underworld."

"Where Dalf is concerned, that could mean you hold séances to discuss events in Hell with Jack the Ripper."

Amanda smiled, which made his knees weak. *I'm human, all right?*

"Not quite that bad."

"I should hope not." He looked this Amanda Colt over again, visibly this time. "You live in New York, I guess, but Dalf 's in Boston. For someone to have connections that deep, I'd expect you to have fangs, horns, and claws."

She flinched. Merle waved a hand. "I mean I'd expect you to have the full set of Goth implants, but from what I can tell, you're all natural." *Is she ever.*

"I should hope so," she stated.

Merle folded his arms. "So, where do you fit in all of this?"

"In Brooklyn, we have been dealing with certain difficulties for some time, long before the police or FBI caught on. You might be the first person to help us deal with it."

He braced for impact. "What are these difficulties?"

"Do you believe in…well, what do you believe in?"

"I believe in whatever my meager government paycheck will pay me to believe. Except for honest politicians. Anything in particular?"

"What about vampires?"

Gee, vampires, why am I not surprised? Question is, does she merely believe that we're dealing with vampires, or does she have proof? Play along in either event.

After years in San Francisco, Merle knew how to deal

with dangerous loonies. "You know, you'd figure that vampires would pick someplace that *looked* sort of like Hell. The Sudan, perhaps. Not like anyone'd miss a few more bodies, especially those of the Christians. Granted, if they ate a few slavers, no one would cry too much either. Then there's LA. Stuff all the vamps in there and let the whole city burn to the ground. But New York?" He shook his head. "You'd figure they'd have enough sense to be afraid of Mayor Giuliani, at least. If they thought he came down on squeegee men hard…"

Amanda started laughing. "You know, that sounds like something Marco would say. Except Giuliani is no longer mayor."

"Marco…Polo?"

"Catalano."

Merle nodded slowly. "Ah. What part of New York are you in?"

"Greenpoint."

"Okay, and why do you need me? Why not talk to Dalf?"

Amanda raised an eyebrow. "He's evil, you're not? Did I get that backwards?"

"True enough." Merle took a deep breath. "I should've known it was going to be one of those days. When will you be ready to head out?"

"Now."

Wow, she didn't waste time, did she? "I suppose you already have our plane tickets."

"On the redeye before dawn."

Merle furrowed his brows in confusion. "Isn't the point of the redeye to leave California when you're about to go to sleep, and land in New York as you wake up? In the daytime?"

"I am not a morning person. Your ticket is in first class, by the way."

He gave her a smile that made him seem more confused than he usually was. "Wow, thanks. Both of us?"

"No," Amanda said hesitantly. "I'm in…a different class."

She can't afford two first-class tickets. Well, that was nice of her. "Thanks, I appreciate it. Just give me a bit to gather some things, would you?"

She nodded, and Merle went into the back supposedly to pack, and closed the sound-proofed door. He flipped open a cell phone, dialing his favorite cop.

"Detective Kristen Kelly," his ex-wife answered.

"Hey, Kris, how are you?"

"I'm…fine. How are you, Merle?"

"A little busy, believe it or not."

"Have the creatures of San Francisco finally raised a zombie plague for you?" Kristen asked with a laugh.

Wow, that is so many kinds of not funny. "No, if that were the case, I would call brother Tal, tell him to come out of New Orleans and get his tuchus up here. Actually, the creatures are coming out of New York to see me now. Can you look up two names for me?"

"Anything to improve our relations with the feds, or whatever you are, but why can't you look them up?"

"I'd like street cop input." *The fact that I really like talking to Kristen has nothing to do with it. Honest.* "Marco Catalano and Amanda Colt. Apparently, they're both residents of Greenpoint."

"Wait a second, Greenpoint?" she said, pronouncing it

Greenpernt like a proper New York native. "I think I know about Catalano. Brooklyn. Real smartass. The borough cops don't know whether to smack him or invite him to doughnuts."

"Charming. What is he, then? Drug lord with a sense of humor? Benevolent hemorrhoid? Candy striper? What?"

"He's a college student who plays nice with local gangs and cops. You want his FBI file?" Kristen asked.

Merle frowned, thinking. *Of course. Marco Catalano has an FBI file. So does everybody. Kristen has an FBI file. I have an FBI file, but the last person who read it went insane...*

Just kidding. I hope. "Maybe later," he told her.

Hector Vega had accepted the dirty looks from the nurses as he dealt out the cards. He had no problem using his rolling food tray for playing cards. The nurses did. Maybe they just disapproved of poker in general.

However, as time went on, he and Zeng Nyugen got tired of getting their heads handed to them by Marco. The man had a poker face like a gargoyle.

Hector turned to Zeng on his right, then Marco on his left. Both were perched on stools high enough for their hands to be level with the tray.

Zeng nodded and looked at Marco over his cards. He knew one thing that might break his poker face. "So, why did Amanda go to San Francisco and not you?"

Marco's poker face didn't even dent as he tossed a few more dollars on the table. "I had a test. She had the money for a ticket. I wasn't in a position to argue. I'll see you and raise you five."

"I'll see that," Hector said. "When did she leave then? She's going to California. I would have thought it would be about nine in the morning."

Marco's face didn't even twitch. "She left a few hours ago."

Zeng arched a brow. "Isn't it customary to leave in the morning? She'll get there in darkness. I'll see you both and raise ten."

Marco looked at Zeng with the predatory gleam in his eye that would usually make him want to curl up into a corner and cry. *Now it almost seemed…playful? Like a cat playing with a mouse, I'm sure. Though, for some reason, I'm almost certain he just wants my money.*

Without hesitation, Marco said, "I'll see you, raise you twenty."

Zeng blinked. "Okay. Listen, you have something going on with her, right? Something? Anything?"

Hector nodded and smiled easily. "Yeah. Hey, we're not trying to mess with you. We've both known you a long time now. She's good for you, bro. I haven't felt like you were going to kill me in weeks. I'll see that and raise an additional five."

Marco's smile broadened. "If you don't count what I'm going to do to you right now. Zeng, you're up."

"You're starting to threaten us again. Only during poker."

Zeng smirked. "I think you're bluffing. All in."

"Brave words for a man who's almost out of cash," Marco said. "Fine. All in."

"Aw guys," Hector said. "I'm wounded enough, I don't have to take this abuse. I fold."

"Wise man." Marco looked at Zeng and turned over his four aces. "You wanted a reaction from me, Zeng. You got it."

In San Francisco, on the phone with his ex-wife, Merle Kraft sighed. "What about the other one? Colt?"

"Not sure…let's see. Okay, I've got an address in upper Manhattan, a name, social security number, and a birth date. She should be about twenty-one. There's no evidence of employment, no real background though. Merle, the last time I saw something like this, it was for a WitSec client."

That made no sense. "Witness Protection guarding a *Russian*?"

"Russian mafia case? Possibly CIA? They were allowed by the INS to bring in over 500 people per year with fake visas and nationalization paperwork before it became ICE. Whatever they say she is on paper here, she really isn't."

"Of course she isn't. Why would she be? Any thoughts?"

Kristen paused a moment. "I've heard of Marco. He might be an ass, but he's our ass. He's a decent guy. And there are a lot of cops starting to think something is up."

"Anything in particular?"

"You'll never believe this, but they're talking, cults. Maybe even vampires."

"Of course they are," Merle said with a sigh. *There are days when my life reads like a* Twilight Zone *script, only without the chain-smoking, black-and-white narrator.*

"Merle?"

"Hm?"

"Vampires don't really exist, do they? Dalf isn't one, last time I checked. I always just assumed he was Hellspawn of some sort."

Merle sighed. "Right now, it wouldn't surprise me."

Chapter 27:

Filling In The New Guy

April 15th, 6 PM. JFK Airport, New York City

Merle disembarked with a rucksack over one shoulder. He invisibly weaved his way through the airport terminus, his blue eyes darting from face to face, hoping to catch a glimpse of Amanda Colt. While they had been in two different sections, he thought he'd at least see her getting on and off.

"This the one we want?" a deep voice asked.

Merle pivoted in mid-stride to the new voice. Eight feet away was a tall, athletic, blond man with deep blue eyes wearing gray slacks and a red polo shirt.

This face carried an almost permanent smile that reminded Merle of Sabatini's line: "He was born with the gift of laughter, and the sense that the world was mad." Next to him was Amanda Colt. *Okay, this must be the legendary smartass Marco, but how'd she get off the plane ahead of me?*

Amanda smiled. "Yup, that's him."

The other fellow held out his hand. "Marco Catalano."

Merle looked over the two people in front of the car, refusing to get into the car without assurance. He had done enough background research to be nervous. Marco Catalano was no one to worry about. Amanda's social security number, however, looked about as kosher as a pig in an Israeli deli.

"So, how did you two kids get wrapped up in this?" Merle asked. "Vampires, and all?"

Marco chuckled. "You must have an open mind about such things."

"You can't imagine."

Amanda cut in. "Having briefly encountered your brother, I believe I can."

Marco explained that his father had run into strange blood work in the hospital during an attack on several of "The locals."

Amanda nodded. "The two street gangs that inhabit the clinic's neighborhood. They're more like the neighborhood watch than gangbangers, even though they like trying to act the part. They keep their boom boxes on low because they don't like headaches, and both gangs answer to some really cranky local preachers."

Marco rolled his eyes and looked forward. "Hector Vega took over *Los Tigres* when his older brother abdicated leadership and went out for his law degree. Hector describes it as going from being a big cat to a bigger reptile. Zeng Nguyen, Hector's counterpart in the Dragons, came up through the ranks."

"And neither one," Amanda said, "will tell me who makes those designer jackets for them."

Marco continued. "For months, people have been attacked in a blitz-attack fashion, leaving gashes on their throat, wrists, and inner thighs. It's been going on for months. Some have suggested serial killers, some have suggested gang initiation–"

"But you think vampires, got it." Merle settled back in the car seat, enjoying the slow ride. "I can see why no one bothered telling me about the local attacks. The FBI agents were killed in a neat, surgical fashion. All of the blood was drained, but it was from only one wound. They were assassinations. Not the sort of attacks you're talking about."

"We thought as much."

"But wait," Marco added. "It gets better, especially when I was attacked. One jumped me at the clinic.

You'd think that they'd be nicer about someone merely being curious."

Amanda sighed, almost lovingly, in Merle's opinion, and said, "You sent samples to CDC."

Merle raised his hand to stop the two of them. "Back up a second. May I ask how he found you? Also, how exactly did you get mixed up in local gang garbage?"

Marco Catalano smirked. "I've had my share of…altercations."

Merle nodded, reflecting on the FBI file that Kristen had emailed him before he left San Francisco.

Amanda looked over and smiled at him. "He calls it aggressive negotiations."

"No," Marco corrected her. "I call it do no harm but get their attention first."

"You said something about your attacker not taking kindly to your questions?"

Marco looked over his shoulder at Kraft, since they were stopped in traffic yet again. He described his first fist fight, with the vampire in the lab, and ended with the rosary as garrote.

Merle tried to piece together everything they told him. He recalled what Kristen had said; there was a collection of NYPD believers who considered "vampire" a reasonable operating theory for some of the stranger things going on in their neighborhoods.

He decided to test the waters and see just how much these kids knew. "I'm just surprised that the local police haven't caught onto this."

Amanda gave Merle a strange look. "You mean you have not heard of the police Craigslist page for vampire encounters?"

So, they have heard. Were they involved in making it? "Do they get many hookers soliciting them for vampire roleplaying?"

"Not anymore," Marco said, also amused.

"So," Merle said, "what have you people been doing before you knocked on my door? In fact, I'm even surprised that you're bothering with me, if you have local cops on your side."

Amanda shook her head. "Not always. It just happened."

"Sort of just happened," Marco corrected. "An officer friend of the family was attacked a few months ago. He's been putting together this little society ever since."

"Before that, we have been relying on the locals."

Merle winced. He tried to imagine local gang members as hapless as the ones described against anything big, mean and organized, vampires or not. "That must be going over well."

"We have few problems," Amanda answered him.

"Surprisingly," Marco added. "I think it helps that we have veterans scattered throughout the gangs, and one southerner who was transferred into the Fighting 69th army unit. He came here with the rest of the fellas on leave once and decided to stay. He brought his hunting bow and arrow set. A bow with an eighty-pound pull. He's been known to hit two at once."

Merle gave a short laugh. "I can believe it."

"All this isn't even counting the mafia."

Merle straightened in the back seat. "Wait, I'm sorry?"

Amanda explained. "We had some problems with mafia thugs recently, too. They heard we had success against the attacks, and they …"

"Moved against us," Marco added simply. "We came to…"

"An understanding," Amanda finished for him.

Marco cleared his throat. "Should we mention the Vatican ninjas?"

"The Vatican what?" Merle asked. This conversation was going to give him whiplash.

"Vatican strike team," Amanda corrected. She looked back to Merle with a little smile. "You might say that we came to an agreement with them by accident. They saw what we were doing in the area, and they decided to get our attention."

"Oh, they got our attention all right," Marco muttered.

"Okay, so, what do you need me for? You have a small army, and considering the differences in their methods, I can't see any reason for your vampires and mine to be related."

He visibly winced. "Oy, I can't believe I just said 'my vampires' and 'your vampires.' But, still, I can't see the connection. How do you know they're not just two different groups of vampires in the same area? This is New York. You could have a million vampires, and they wouldn't even be twenty percent of the population."

Marco cleared his throat and started edging his way towards the off-ramp. "Freaking Van Wyck." He stopped in the next lane only an inch from the car in front of him. It was like he was daring the other drivers to hit him. "One thing at a time."

"Yes, we do have manpower," Amanda said, "but we do not have all the intelligence contacts we need. We know they are here, we know they are acting strategically, but we do not know what their purpose is. We know they are related because, at one point, they retaliated against us."

"Me, actually," Marco said, his voice darkening.

"You mean besides the original assassin in the clinic?"

Marco nodded.

"What did they do?"

"They kidnapped an ex-girlfriend of mine, thinking I still…whatever. That part doesn't matter." Marco directed the car into the next lane, in front of the next driver, who apparently didn't want to give one bit of ground. He managed to get through, stomping down on the pedal so he could get on the exit ramp. It looked like he was taking local streets all the way to Brooklyn. He didn't have much consideration for the traffic laws, the speed laws, or possibly the laws of man and God. "Amanda saw the kidnapping, and she tried to prevent it, but she was stopped by an old friend of yours."

There was only one person Merle could think of that might possibly have any relation to Marco's problem, the one enemy Merle ran into in New York last time. "The guy I decapitated with the stop sign?"

Amanda nodded. "Exactly."

Merle leaned back, keeping his face implacably calm. It wouldn't do to show that he was freaking out inside. *Vampires, just what I needed. I'm not sure what's worse—if Marco and his girlfriend are telling the truth, and there are vampires, or if they're nuts and have me in the car with them.*

"Indeed. Now, what did the assassin in the clinic mean when he said you'd be a message? To whom? Your father?" Even as Merle asked, he knew the answer, thinking back to the anomalous organisms the lab had found in the dead FBI agent's blood.

Marco turned the wheel, moving around an annoyingly slow car. He shot past an intersection. "You found organisms in your victim's wound track, didn't you? What you found are in vampire's saliva. They help keep the victim alive after the initial blood drain. From what we can gather, they're not parasitic, more like symbiotic."

"Microbial symbiotes?"

Marco nodded, then his eyes locked on a car moving in to cut him off. He veered the other way, dodging him. "Of course. You've heard of mitochondrial DNA, right? Mitochondria are the things that basically power blood cells within the human body. But they're not actually us. They even have different DNA from the human host they inhabit."

"So you're saying that mitochondria are microbial symbiotes?"

"*Da,*" Amanda confirmed. "When a vampire leaves a victim alive, the microbes from their saliva remain. Microbes only live for a few days, and those few days are fun for the one bitten, but after..." She paused, as though thinking of the right word. "Poof, all dead. The microbes, I mean. The human generally survives, unless he was drained or had his throat ripped out."

Merle Kraft cocked his head. "What do you mean, about those few days being fun?"

"I've been bit before," Marco answered casually. "For the next few days, I was able to hurl a manhole cover, single-handed. If you're wondering, no one can become a vampire because of a simple bite. Lord knows I'm not one."

Amanda nodded. "Which would explain why vampires are created by drinking the blood of another vampire. It's the only way to get enough of a concentration of the microbes for vampirism to take effect."

Merle raised a brow. This was all being delivered to him in an oddly controlled and casual way, as though this was normal. "So vampires are not the Dark Side of the Force, they just got a bad bunch of midichlorians? And you thought *I'd* believe this."

"You tangled with a vampire," Amanda explained. "From what we've gathered, Scarface was a number two man."

Marco nodded. "We've been gathering data, and from what we can tell about the social structure of this group, we've figured there is some sort of 'master vampire,' with the age and power to create one of these packs of animals. They're obviously directed, coordinated. After all, they took out an FBI agent. They usually go after people that wouldn't be missed: homeless people, prostitutes—"

"Gang members," Amanda finished. "These vampires obviously did not keep up much with local events, or they would have known that going after the Dragons and *Los Tigres* was a mistake. We never thought they would perform CSHs."

Merle smiled at the term; CSH stood for "Community-Service Homicide." *One drug dealer kills another. That is community service.*

"We figured," Marco said, "that's also the reason vampires get a bad rap as being unwavering evil. Most vampires who create other vampires aren't nice guys. The only reason we have so many vampires biting for the other side is that *those* vampires make sure that those they turn *into* vampires will be as evil as they are."

Merle had images of Kristen running into one of those freaks. He was suddenly invested in the situation. "Now, go back to the whole Master Vampire thing?"

"We know his name is Mikhail," Amanda told him. This time, she didn't try looking back at him. She just stared straight out the window. "We know that he has done this before, and he has total control over his people. He's strong and makes certain his people stay in line."

"Which is why we haven't had any police officers killed yet?"

Marco answered, "We figure that vamps don't want to get into too much trouble with the cops. If they do, someone may decide to go hunting with napalm."

Amanda laughed. "Someone other than Marco."

"Okay, I grant your reasoning thus far. But why target the FBI?"

Amanda leaned back, stretching her long body gracefully. "What was he doing?"

"I can't say. That's classified. I can tell you he was doing surveillance."

"With a laser mic, maybe?" Marco asked. "If that's the case, the vampire probably picked up on it."

Merle studied his hosts. *Let's say I take all of this at face value. What was a vampire doing inside the United Nations?*

"Gotcha. So, have you done anything else against the vampires?"

"Waged war. Set some bars on fire. Interrogated some with fire and holy water. Waged a kind of terrorist campaign against them. You know, that sort of thing. They're easy enough to keep out of our homes, at least. If you don't want to rely on the requirement of an invite, you can nail crosses everywhere, or get a mezuzah. From what I could tell, we can keep those bloodsuckers out of the clinic and other enclosed, public places."

Merle couldn't resist. "Lawyers, too?"

Marco ignored him. "Anyway, we found out about your little excursion around here. We looked you up. That was when we turned to your brother in Boston for a little help. You sure you two are related?"

"Well, I can tell you the family first thought something was wrong with him when we watched *Star Wars*. My brother Tal liked Luke, I liked Yoda, and Dalf rooted for Darth Vader."

Marco raised an eyebrow. "Obviously, that was before *Episode I*...one more thing." He reached for the glove compartment and took out two glass Arizona Iced Tea bottles.

"Fresh from the baptismal font at St. Alphonsus. Guaranteed to melt vampires and keep away those nasty sunspots."

Amanda chimed in. "Also, while we've been holding our own, they're probably making vampires faster than we can kill them. They have a list of those who will not be missed, and it is *not* little."

Merle took a breath. If these people were crazy, it was his job to verify or deny. "Very well, I guess we should start by taking me to the area of most of the attacks."

Ms. Colt nodded. "I'll do it."

"I'll drop you two off, then circle back to the house."

Marco looked into Amanda's eyes with concern, placing a hand on her arm. "Are you going to be alright?"

"Of course. Aren't I always?"

Marco glanced back in the mirror. "Um, Mister Kraft?"

"Hm?"

"You have any backup?"

"Usually not, why?"

"Because someone is following us."

Chapter 28:

Once Bitten

April 15th, 6:30PM, Van Wyck Expressway, New York City

Marco considered evasive maneuvers but decided against it. He looked into the rear view mirror at his guest and said, "So, Merle, you want to look at our tail and decide if you know them?"

Merle blinked and looked over the back seat. "Gimme a minute, I need to make a phone call. Oy, *mein Gott.*" He slid back down into his seat, and pulled a cell phone from his windbreaker, then hit redial.

"Hey Merle, how are you doing?" Kristen Kelly answered.

"Land in New York, yet?"

"Hey, *meschula.* I shouldn't ask, but are you following me from the airport?"

Kristen paused for a long moment. "Should I ask how you know?"

"My *driver* told me."

"Ouch. Sorry about that. His little maneuver getting off of the Van Wyck was sudden. I didn't see that coming."

"Don't worry," Merle said, casting a glance at Marco, "I don't think that *he* saw that coming."

Kristen laughed. "I just figured it would be a good idea to make certain you were in one piece…and stayed that way."

"Thanks for that. I think I'll stay alive." *I would be more worried about you, considering everything I've been told. Unfortunately, I have no way to disprove anything they've told me.*

"The last thing I need is a dead ex," Kristen said.

Merle smiled. "All the same, we should probably go our separate ways on this one. That way, Arthur doesn't become an orphan."

"Understood."

After he hung up, Marco said, "You speak Yiddish?"

Merle shrugged. "I'm sure that you do too."

"Yes, but I'm a New York native. It's practically one of our three dozen second languages. You're from San Francisco."

"You you're surprised because I'm Asian?"

Marco shrugged as he made a turn. "If you wish."

"I live in San Francisco. I'm *from* here. Anyway, now that I know that this whole mess is due to vampires, I guess I should start by reexamining the crime scene."

"Then I should drop you both off here and start making some calls. Feeding time should be any moment now."

Merle scoffed as Marco pulled over. "Feeding time, huh?"

"You'll find out soon enough."

Merle waited a moment before continuing the conversation. He spent the time admiring how utterly fluid her moments were, almost as though she were boneless. She looked exceptionally good.

She's not my Kristen, though. "So," Merle asked once they were out of earshot of Marco's car, "how did you know I've taken down the number two guy in the local vampire crew?"

Amanda paused for a split second; just enough for Merle to not fully believe her answer. "Because we have good contacts, and you took a while to put him down. Marco can deal with most vampires because of sheer skill…and his ability to play 3D chess in his head."

"You mean he thinks three moves ahead of the vampires he fights?"

"More like five moves. He is good at what he does, Mister Kraft. He's an excellent student as well. Were he older, he could work with the EMTs in tandem with his Hudson U. studies. God knows he's tended to me a few times. Of course, he has enough on his plate at the moment."

Merle raised a brow. By her tone, and her gushing, he concluded she would have liked him to tend to her in more personal ways. "So, you two are close?"

"Very," she confirmed, but stopped short when she caught his drift. "Oh, but not quite *that* close."

"I take it you would like to be?"

Amanda Colt looked ahead. "We're almost there."

Merle nodded, then paused. He sensed something wrong in the air, and Amanda paused as well. "We're being followed," he casually told her. "You know?"

She nodded, and tensed, a ball of energy waiting to spring. Merle looked the other direction, hoping to cover her back. She supposedly fought vampires, so street muggers shouldn't be a problem. If they *were* muggers.

Merle turned around to take in his surroundings. From here, he could see the Italian restaurant where the FBI had taken over the top floor to spy on the United Nations. Merle could even see the UN from street level.

He spotted the alley where the dead FBI agent was initially found. He also saw where he had killed off that pesky psycho with the bad scarring, who may have been a vampire.

Then their company started emerging from the shadows. There were seven of them in all. One carried a chain. One had a knife. A few were empty-handed.

Amanda muttered, "They found some new friends, I see, and are back to their old ways."

Merle blinked, then leaned over to her, not taking his eyes off of the miscreants. "You know these guys?"

"They jumped me and Marco last year," she answered. "Evidently, they can't take a hint."

These two have been taking on vampires, and they've left muggers standing? "So, they're just muggers, I presume."

Amanda nodded.

Merle smiled as one leaped out of an alley with a lead pipe. "Your money or–"

Merle came at the mugger, shoulder first, sending his entire body weight into the charge. The impact took the man off of his feet. Merle's left arm wrapped around the arm holding the pipe, and his right elbow smashed the attacker's throat. With ease and skill, Merle twisted the pipe out of his hand and cracked it across his skull.

The next one didn't have half a chance as Merle threw the lead bar like a throwing knife, hitting him between the eyes.

There was a third with a chain, like any good stereotype, and he swung. Merle casually ducked, then kicked the mugger's scrotum practically up into his abdomen.

Merle turned to see how Amanda was doing, and it looked for a moment like he should help her—a mugger had his arms around her in what looked like a bear hug. Upon closer examination, Merle saw something wrong. To start with, he wasn't holding her up. She was holding him up.

Second, there were several dead bodies on the ground, all of them with their throats torn out. She dropped the assailant and turned to Merle, her lips stained with blood.

Oh darn.

Merle did the logical thing and ran for the nearest residence and entered it easily. He figured that a vampire was still a vampire and couldn't follow into a home without being invited.

Merle smiled, sat in a chair, and decided to wait until sunup.

"Nice trick. How did you get in?"

Amanda Colt stood on the other side of the room from Merle. He rolled backwards out of the chair, coming to a defensive position.

She smiled at him and leaned against a far wall. "Ever read Thomas Aquinas?

Merle blinked back his surprise. She hadn't attacked him. "I'm being asked about a Catholic philosopher by a vampire?"

She looked at him with those warm brown eyes of hers. "Answer my question," she said with all the seriousness of a kindergarten teacher trying not to laugh at a student.

Merle Kraft cocked his head, still expecting to be eaten. "I know a little bit about him, why?"

"Get comfortable. This will take a while."

After Amanda finished explaining "good" vampires and "bad" vampires, Merle sighed. Vampires. UN corruption. Oil deals... what the Hell did I wander into here? "Come on," he muttered, "let's get out of here before someone decides to shoot us for trespassing. I suppose I should ask if there's anything else we're missing?"

Amanda smiled. "Unless you want to help us figure out what the vampires are doing in a local cemetery."

Merle smiled. "Oh, I can come up with a solution to that. Use you as bait."

Chapter 29:

The Mount Olivet Incident

April 15th, 11:59 PM

Mount Olivet Cemetery in Maspeth, Queens, is both well-situated and badly situated. To start with, it is one massive cemetery right next to All Faith's Cemetery.

On two sides of the two cemeteries run high traffic roads: Metropolitan Avenue, a heavily-trafficked two-lane road with parking on both sides of the road, as well as a major bus route. It was a horror to drive, easily jammed, and overflowing with traffic. In tactical terms, it was a ready-made bottleneck for any poor fool who needed to use the road.

On another corner was the heavily-trafficked local street, 69th. This road was an outlet for traffic coming from Queens Center Mall, a major shopping center with five levels of parking structure, as well as a major public transit hub for multiple subways and buses.

The other two streets were relatively quiet and peaceful...comparatively, anyway. Elliot Avenue was another two-lane road, also with a major bus route. However, Elliot Avenue had Mount Olivet on one side, All Faiths on the other, and connected two residential neighborhoods.

The cross-street that meets up with Elliot Avenue is the one-lane Mount Olivet Crescent, which separates Mount Olivet from a row of homes. How would you like to live across the street from that?

On the other end of Mount Olivet, there was Grand Avenue, and a row of houses, where the cemetery bordered the backyards.

Marco and Amanda came in from the quiet end of Elliot Avenue. The street was poorly lit and strangely quiet, even for a cemetery.

Then again, what do you expect at this time of night? Amanda thought.

As she walked along the uneven ground, she tried not to frown. The ground was dug up and replanted so many times, the soil was uneven.

Also, she didn't like the layout of the cemetery. It was built on the side of a hill, and it didn't even out between Grand Avenue and Elliot Avenue at the top of the hill.

She glanced to Marco. His arm was around her shoulders. She liked the idea of posing as boyfriend and girlfriend, even if he thought it was a bad idea.

"Are you going to tell me that they aren't going to know Amanda's a vampire?" Marco had asked the

Vatican Ninjas, and Merle Kraft, when the government agent had first proposed the idea. "Even worse, don't you think that everyone there wouldn't recognize me? Let's face it, I've made an impression."

The lead ninja, Hendershot, laughed at that. "You mean that you might be easily identifiable to those vampires who you met, and you *left alive?* Are there really many of those?"

"And," Amanda suggested, "if you stay close enough to me, your scent should hide anything that I might give off."

However, now that Marco and Amanda were in the actual cemetery, Marco had no trouble draping himself all over her. If she didn't know any better, she would think that he was more like a horny teenager than the man he was. His arm around her shoulder, his lips were almost constantly making contact with her somewhere. He kissed her covered shoulder, her cheek, her neck, practically anything he could reach.

Amanda felt giddy at his boyish enthusiasm. He was playful without an underlying current of intensity. He seemed, for once, to truly relax.

They wandered through the graveyard for a while, mostly with Marco being flirtatious and affectionate. Not that she was complaining.

Amanda was caught off guard when Marco swung her around towards one of the flatter tombstones. It was just broad and flat enough for a person to stretch out on, if someone could find marble particularly comfortable.

But Marco laid her out on the marble like it was a wedding bed, and wrapped his arms around her in a warm, more-than-friendly embrace. His eyes burned into hers with an intensity even he had rarely shown. She would have gone so far as to call it passionate. They stared long and hard into each other's gaze.

Suddenly, Amanda heard his voice in her head.

"If I whispered to you right now, could vampire hearing pick up on it?"

Amanda blinked in surprise. He had just reversed a vampire's mind-penetrating gaze and focused his way into her own mind.

Amanda scarcely believed that such a thing was possible. She managed to nod.

Marco smiled with his eyes, and his hug tightened. His face buried itself in her neck. He said, in one of the softest, most gentle voices she had ever heard him use, "Oh God, you have no idea how much I love you. I love how you feel against me. I love your hair. I love how you tolerate me, no matter what I've done." He kissed her neck softly, where her neck met her shoulder. "I love your mind," he kissed a little further up her neck, "your walk," and again, "the way you speak," and once more with feeling, and a small nip of his teeth on her skin.

"I love how the corner of your mouth bunches up when you think something over, and the cute way your brow scrunches up when I do something weird that you're trying to understand. I especially love that it goes away in seconds because you're right there with me." He took a light, gentle nip of her earlobe and tugged on it like a puppy. With his mouth right against her ear, he whispered, "You have no idea the things I want to do with you right now. I would like nothing better than to lay here all night and kiss you senseless."

Marco's voice dropped an octave and became tinged with amusement. "I would like my turn to bite *you* this time." He kissed a spot right behind her ear–especially sensitive because it was a major nerve cluster–and it sent fireworks down her spine. He gave a gentle suck on the skin. "I already know how good you taste."

His embrace tightened around her, and his whisper became harsh, almost strangled. "I want you so desperately, you have no idea."

Amanda restrained a moan and tried not to writhe against the marble. Not only because his kisses hit all of the right nerve points in her neck, but his words were touching her in places she didn't know existed.

Then it hit her.

Marco asked if vampires could hear whispers. This meant he was broadcasting all of his "feelings" to every potential vampire within twenty meters, maybe more.

Which told her that Marco was putting on an act for the benefit of all the potential vampires in the cemetery.

Amanda gave a growl deep in her throat. Two could play that game. Only she wasn't playing.

One of the many things going through Marco Catalano's mind was, *Oh God, the scent of her is driving me insane.*

The feel of her body against his wasn't doing much for his concentration, either. His heart rate had spiked so high, so fast, Marco was terrified that he would give the game away. That Amanda would know that he meant every loving thing he said to her. Things he wouldn't say to her if he thought she would believe him and take him seriously. All of those kisses were "under the guise of an undercover operation." He could do everything short of grope her, and it could all be defended in the name of "their cover."

Marco could tell her everything, and never have to explain.

Granted, there was one thing he was still holding back, but still, it wouldn't fit the image he was projecting to the world: something charming and amorous.

What Marco held back would have ruined the mood. But then, Amanda gave a growl deep in her throat. He blinked. *Has she figured me out? Has she realized I'm using this stake-out as a cover for my own feelings?*

Amanda rolled over, taking Marco with her. Before he knew it, he was flat on his back, Amanda straddling his hips, a look of pure, unrestrained desire on her face. His wrists were pinned to the marble, and he was thoroughly surprised to find himself nose-to-nose with her, Amanda's eyes burrowing into his. Their faces were covered from the entire world by her hair, which fell like a curtain around them.

Wow, Marco thought, *she is a really good actress.*

"Do you have any idea what you do to me?" she purred as she rubbed her body along his. Her breasts pressed into his chest, driving his heart to race like a Ferrari. His hands wrapped around her back, and he had to restrain himself from pressing her closer into his chest, or letting his hands wander. Just the feel of her body atop his was doing things to him that he really hoped she didn't detect.

She lightly pressed her full lips against his. "You make my body react involuntarily to you. I have perfect control, yet when you are near, your proximity controls me." She kissed him again, firmer, and more intense. "I want to bite you every time we meet and hope I don't drain you completely via droplets." She kissed over his jaw, and down to his neck. "I want to run my hands over your body and give you a sample of everything you do to me." Her hands released him and glided down his arms. She felt up his arms and his biceps.

If I didn't know better, she would fool me.

Her hands drifted down his body, over his biceps, down his abs, then back up so she could cup his face in her hands. "Can you imagine the things I want to do to you?"

I can imagine what you're doing to me.

As Merle Kraft watched through his binoculars, he sighed.

"I think we got the short end of the stick on this assignment." Without looking away, he whispered to the ninja on his right, "Are they lying to us, or themselves?"

"Hmm?" Ibrahim, ninja-sniper, grunted in reply. He was already busy scanning the area through his telescopic sight. His 50-caliber sniper rifle was loaded for bear, with enough bullets to drop an elephant, never mind a vampire.

Merle chuckled and lowered his binoculars to he could look at Ibrahim. "You're not going to tell me that these two are 'just friends,' are you?"

"Nope."

"Though what they see in each other is beyond me. She's a vampire, and he's lunch. Fine, she's gorgeous and all, granted, but still. And him? Meh. Whatever they see in each other, these two might as well have a magnetic attraction."

The sniper finally glanced up from his scope in order to look at Merle with something like irritation. "You do realize there are vampires out there, don't you?"

"Hendershot told me all about your low-level white-noise emitters. He told me they were effective at keeping vampires from hearing noises above a whisper, as long as we're in the protective radius. Since I'm wearing the damn thing, I think I'm okay, don't you?"

Ibrahim sighed and settled back at his site. "Well, it is obvious that you're not going to shut up unless we finish this conversation. So, as far as the two of them go, they work together like they were vampire and minion."

"Though in that case, I'd have to ask which one was which. She seems more human than he does, and I've only been around him a few hours."

Ibrahim turned the rifle towards what he thought might have been a bit of motion. He didn't acknowledge Merle's observation but continued his own. "These two think alike, fight alike, and they move like they've been doing this together forever."

Merle nodded to himself, and then went back to looking through the binoculars. "Understood. But if you can see it, and I can see it, why can't the two of them?"

"Possibly too close to the situation," the sniper said without hesitation. "They can see a lot of things coming, but they're already within each other's swing. Make sense?"

"If you want to describe a relationship like a fist fight."

The sniper chuckled. "Funny, I thought you were divorced."

"Don't make me hurt you, sniper boy."

"As if you could, buddy. I fight guys who could eat you for breakfast. Literally."

"Tell that to the last guy I met in a dark alley." Merle watched the two pieces of human bait and frowned. "Are they going to make out with each other, or rape each other on the tombstone?"

"I don't think you can have two people raping each other at the same time…hold up. On their three o'clock."

Merle nodded, instantly sobered. "I see them."

"Congratulations, magician. You picked the right bait."

"Yay me. Now we just have to keep them alive."

Amanda wasn't certain how much more of this she could take. Having Marco near her was one thing. She never imagined how having him *this* close to her would be like. She was close to doing something she was certain she would regret.

Then she heard them coming. They walked on the grass as softly as ants. Amanda's eyes flicked to her right. Marco noticed and followed her gaze, instantly back in control.

There were only three of them.

Amanda didn't know if she wanted to thank the vampires or hurt them.

"Oh, look," one of them said. "Dinner for three with enough for leftovers in the morning." His eyes flicked to her. "And some entertainment in the meantime."

Marco bucked and rolled off of the tombstone, sending Amanda off him. They both landed on their feet, Marco with his back to the vampires.

When Marco spun, he drew out the long wooden knife from the sheath on his back, delivering a backhanded slash through the throat of the vampire who spoke. With a growl, he grabbed the vampire by the jacket lapel and rammed the long blade into the vampire's stomach. The tip of the blade came in at an upward angle, slipping underneath the ribcage, and stabbing into the heart.

Marco gave the vampire a feral grin. "Is this entertaining enough for you?" He gave a little twist as he jerked it out of the vampire. To say the vampire's final facial expression as he turned into dust was shocked would be a bit of an understatement.

The first vampire hadn't turned to dust before Amanda leapt on the vampire to the right of the formation. They went down in a tumble of arms and legs, with Amanda landing on top. The vampire beneath her punched for her face. She deflected it, grabbed the arm, and twisted it so that it went snap, crackle and pop, turning into gravel. Amanda kept the arm and pushed down. The stake hidden up her sleeve went through the vampire and into the ground.

As the first vampire turned to ash, Marco held onto the jacket. Now he threw it at the vampire to his left, covering his face. Marco followed up with a kick to the vampire's groin.

The vampire wouldn't be taken out so easily, and charged into Marco, ramming him against the tombstone. Marco tried to stab down with the knife, but the angle was awkward. The wood of the knife hurt but didn't stop the vampire.

In fact, the vampire came up, threw off the jacket, and he looked annoyed. He also looked terribly disfigured. His fangs came out.

"I'm going to enjoy ripping your throat out," he growled.

Two hands came up and boxed the vampire's ears in with enough force to crush rock. The hands held on, and lifted the vampire off of his feet, then slammed him face down onto the dirt.

Amanda stood over the vampire. Her eyes were literally glowing with rage as she broke the top half off of a tombstone, raised it above her head, and brought it down on the vampire with all the strength in her body.

Marco looked down at the vampire. The shoulders and part of the upper body had been driven into the ground by the impact. "I didn't know that you could kill them with a rock. Where'd you learn that move? Wile E. Coyote?"

Amanda smiled. "Smushing them could be considered decapitation, you know. "He reached for her hand. She took it and pulled him off the tombstone slab they were warming up only a few moments ago. They stood there in an awkward silence for a moment.

Marco blinked. "When did your eyes start glowing?"

She blinked, and the glow faded. "Hmm?"

"Huh. Funny, they were like amber headlights for a moment." He shrugged and looked over the clothing of the dusted vampires. "Oh well, at least we know that it worked. We got a reaction from them. Would have liked one alive, but, eh."

Amanda nodded, then sighed. "*Da.* But I would have thought there would be more than just three of them. Why only three?"

Marco's eyebrows briefly furrowed with thought. "You think it's possible that the bartender was jerking us around about Mount Olivet?"

Amanda shook her head. "I doubt it. Seemed like an honest fellow."

Something shifted. The sound of stone on stone. Something was moving deep in the cemetery. Something heavy.

The sound of a crypt opening.

Marco looked around, and it was closer to the middle of the cemetery—less towards Elliot Avenue, and more towards Metropolitan, at the opposite end of the cemetery from Merle's blind.

"I think we have a location on the others," Marco said. Then a noise came from another direction, somewhere off to the right.

Marco arched a brow. "I guess we have a second location."

A third source of sound came from off to the left, and a fourth from the cemetery next door. And then, there were sounds of groaning stone and metal from all around. Marco slid behind Amanda, going back to back with her. "This is why I hate fishing expeditions."

Amanda nodded as she kept a sharp eye out for the forces coming to kill them. "*Da*. It always ends badly for the bait."

Chapter 30:

The Battle For Queens

April 16th, 12:15 a.m., Mount Olivet Cemetery, Queens, NY

Marco prided himself in being able to find the humor in almost any situation. His life was something he was only vaguely interested in, so he could abstract humor from nearly every scenario. If Horace Walpole was right, that "Life is a comedy to those who think," then it was a good thing that Marco thought all the time.

As he saw vampires crawl out from every crypt and mausoleum, from behind almost every tombstone and rock, he didn't see hundreds of vampires. Marco could see the death of every single man, woman and child in Queens. The young and the old would be drained and discarded, their bodies dashed against the sidewalks and left as carrion. The later teens and adults would be eaten and turned into vampires for the legion. There wouldn't be riots and blood in the street, there wouldn't be time. All Marco saw was a vampire apocalypse.

This wasn't even an army. This was a biblical plague sent to destroy and ravage anyone who got in the way. After slaughtering a city of eight million, what would stop them after they scattered to other cities? Other countries?

This was the end of everything. And the only people between these vampires and the rest of the world happened to be Marco, Amanda, and a handful of Vatican ninjas.

Where the hell did these guys find an entire fricking army?

Marco thought. "If this goes badly," he said, "I want you to know that it's been fun."

"Oh," came a voice to their side, "I wouldn't worry about that."

Amanda and Marco glanced to their side. Merle Kraft stood there, calm in his dark blue windbreaker, rubbing his nails on his jacket as though he were in a Bugs Bunny cartoon.

The encroaching vampire horde stopped about fourteen feet away. Even they wondered where the hell the short man had come from, and why the hell he was so cocky when this was going to be three against hundreds.

"Hi, everyone," Merle said to the vampires, not concerned with the math. "I guess you're all wondering what I'm doing here. How are you doing, fellows? My name is Merle, and I will be your executioner this evening."

The vampires looked around at each other.

"Now, I know what you're all thinking," Merle continued. "'Who is this guy and what does he think he's doing here?' Granted, we're all good at this, but still, numbers matter. Why would I possibly think I had a chance of slaughtering every last one of you?"

"Well, religion is a funny thing. There are interesting rules."

"For example," Merle said, making sure to look at the group like a good public speaker, but looking at the middle of chests, not the eyes, like a good vampire hunter, "holy water. Did you know that holy water doesn't need to be constantly blessed over and over again? As long as there is a certain amount of holy water in the bottom of the container all a priest needs to do is to pour water into it and it *all* becomes holy water. Doesn't even need to be a priest doing the pouring. Anyone can take a gallon of water, and pour it in. Congratulations, it's all holy water."

Merle smiled, taking his time. "Now, if you should take a fifty gallon drum of holy water and connect it to a fire hydrant, with a fire hose on the other end...well then, that would be something to worry about, wouldn't it? I mean, if you're a vampire anyway."

The vampires, as a whole, looked behind them, unsure if this lunatic was bluffing or if he was a threat.

The vampires at the top of the hill, with their backs towards Elliot Avenue, noticed the first Ninja, the redheaded Irishman that Ibrahim was talking to the night the mafia came to visit Marco's father at the hospital.

The redhead gave them a smile and a little wave, and then he opened up with the fire hose.

A standard fire hose utilizes pressures nearing one thousand PSI, enough to blow through a plate-glass window. They could be used for crowd control because it blasted people off their feet and pushed back the masses with little problem.

In the case of these vampires, getting blasted with holy water from a high-pressure hose was like firing at a human being with a high-pressure water saw filled with the most corrosive acid known to man.

"This is the equivalent of heavy artillery, fellas," Merle concluded with flair.

Amanda Colt grabbed both Marco and Merle, dragging them both to the ground behind a tombstone with a cross on it. The stream of water cut through the vampires and split the air in front of them. The cross on the tombstone kept the swarm of vampires from getting too close.

They swarmed down the hill, fleeing the fire hose in the direction of Grand Avenue.

Then ran directly into the path of the flamethrowers wielded by the three Vatican ninjas at the bottom of the hill.

The smartest vampires, and the ones who were able to stop fast enough to avoid the flamethrowers, did not go down the hill, but sideways, heading towards the row of residential brownstones near 65th Street, and towards 69th Street.

Of the residential homes, three had sold out their top floors, and made for great sniping positions for three Vatican ninjas, one of whom was Ibrahim Javaherian.

At the other end of the cemetery, three Vatican ninjas were stationed on the street. All six were armed with heavy, .50-caliber automatic weapons, and Desert Eagle sidearms. The heavy caliber was bad enough, from the vampires' point of view, since the .50 caliber could literally blow someone's head off. Even worse for the vampires, the bullets were silver hollow points, which had all been filled with holy water and sealed with wax from church candles.

At the moment that the vampires had first approached Marco and Amanda, police cars had been called in to secure the area. They were all Officer Donald "Duck" Tolbert's Craigslist pals.

In short, the Vatican Ninjas had secured themselves a perfectly quiet free-fire zone. Even all of the automatic weapons had sound-suppressors attached.

"What the Hell is going on?" Marco growled at Merle over the sounds of vampire's screaming.

"We followed your plan," Merle said.

Amanda blinked and looked at Marco. "What does he mean?"

Marco took a moment and arched a brow. "I submitted a plan to Rodgers a few months ago, not long after we heard the tip about Mount Olivet." His eyes shot to Merle. "You implemented my plan with us as the bait?"

"Sure. It's a good plan. Why not?"

"Because it's not a good plan! It relied heavily on Mount Olivet being the *only* position held by the vampires. It didn't take All Faiths into consideration, and St. John's cemetery is only a few blocks from here. Assuming that these are the only vampires leaves anyone on the outside of the box vulnerable."

The redheaded, Irish ninja with the fire hose had barely heard the movement behind him. He looked over his shoulder in time to watch the vampire grab the fire hydrant feeding the hose.

The ninja, whose name was Timothy Dougherty, turned with the fire hose as the vampire pulled back on the hydrant. The hydrant came out of the ground like a champagne cork just as the final blast from the holy water hose thoroughly drenched him.

The vampire died quickly enough, but the water pressure in the hose fell off sharply.

Dougherty quickly reached for his shotgun, filled with silver buckshot.

It was obviously time to get out of there. He looked back down the hill. There was nothing between him and the trio in the middle of the cemetery. It seemed like as good a rally point as anywhere else.

At the bottom of the hill, the ninjas in charge of the flamethrowers were already moving into the cemetery. The flamethrowers, after all, only had a limited range.

When they heard the crunch of shattered glass and the whine of a dying police siren, two of the three men with the flamethrowers stopped firing and turned around, keeping an eye on the street while the one in the middle moved along the ground, kept an eye out for any vampires who may have hidden behind the tombstones.

On the street level, Robert Hendershot was in charge of the shooters and also heard the dying sounds of a destroyed police car. They were a little quicker on running into the cemetery.

By the time that Dougherty, the flamethrower team, and Hendershot's group had come to the middle of the hillside of Mount Olivet, one thing was perfectly clear.

They were the ones surrounded.

Marco Catalano, Amanda Colt, and Merle Kraft got to their feet by the time the ninjas had gathered around. Marco frowned. "Anyway, if Merle is now quite finished trying to get us all killed, I think we can consider a plan B."

"Your plan *worked*."

Amanda rolled her eyes at both of them. "Captain Hendershot, do you have a protocol for this?"

"Depends. If there are a few dozen, we should be in good shape. If there are a few hundred, then we are in trouble."

Marco motioned towards the homes. "The sniper teams in the brownstones should be perfectly safe, as long as the vampires don't get around to burning them down." He pointed to an area down the hill by the gate, and up the hill, maybe twenty yards up. "There are two lines of tombstones with crosses. The vampires *could* come and destroy them, but that would take time, make them sitting ducks, and take away one of their biggest advantages. We fall back against the gate separating the brownstones from the cemetery, and those crosses will force them to come at us from one direction. They can't come in from behind unless they want to have Bram and his team cut them to pieces."

He glanced at the biggest ninja there, armed with a flamethrower. The only other detail Marco could see through the ninja outfit was the dark brown eyes. "You, what's your name?"

"Von Bieber, sir."

"Okay Von Bieber, stay behind us. If we need to fall back over the fence, I want one flamethrower with something left in the tank." He looked at the other two ninjas with the flamethrowers. "I want you two at the outer edge of a semi-circle. You two will be at the front, with the shooters behind you. We're going to funnel the vampires into a bottleneck."

Merle arched a brow. "I think I know what's in the middle of the bottleneck."

Amanda nodded, catching on quickly. "Exactly. The three of us." She blinked, then looked off into the darkness.

A mist was already starting to roll in…but a mist that moved around every tombstone with a cross on it, taking a strange, winding path through the cemetery. "They are coming."

Marco leaned over to Hendershot. "Unless you really *hate* my tactical arrangements, get into position. I have one more play. Radio up to Bram and tell him to cover my sorry ass."

Marco turned towards the vampires and started to walk out into the darkness. Amanda reached out and grabbed his shoulder. "Marco, what are you doing?"

"What I usually do. I'm just going to talk them all to death." He took her hand in his, gave it a little squeeze, and then gently pulled it off of his shoulder. "Time to have fun."

Marco moved into the darkness slowly, but evenly. It was obviously not fear, but caution. His smile was in place, and his heart rate was so even, Amanda couldn't tell the difference between his heartbeat now and a resting pulse.

He looked out and waited a moment before saying, in a firm, strong voice, "I'm looking for Mikhail the Bear. If he wouldn't mind, I want to have a chat with him."

The mist shifted. It stopped rolling across the graveyard, except for one, snakelike form that headed straight for Marco.

It was visible at fifty feet, and when it closed to forty feet, Marco reached into his back pocket for one of his many rosaries and threw it down on the ground. It landed about thirty feet away. The mist recoiled.

"That's far enough, I think," Marco said.

The mist hesitated and swirled. It slowly grew taller and coalesced into the form of a large man. Mikhail the Bear topped out at six-one and easily 280 pounds. He was bald, with a face that was a rendition of Stephen King's mind on hallucinogens.

If the body of a vampire was the Picture of Dorian Gray, then Mikhail the Bear had participated in a few acts of mass murder, and he was not merely "following orders."

"Marco Catalano?" he said in a thick Russian accent.

Marco nodded. "Pleased to meet you, Mikhail."

"I have wanted to kill you for quite some time."

"Ditto." He looked over Mikhail's black clothing and black leather jacket. "So, nice clothes. It's a cute trick. I've yet to see a vampire take his clothing with him."

"The strongest among us have many tricks."

Marco shook his head. "Maybe someone who's strong for the average vampire, but I suspect that if you were truly the badass you think you are, we would have all been dead by now. In fact, I suspect you would have killed Amanda instead of Lily."

"Lily was far more fun to kill. Especially after she had her way with six of my men."

Marco's smile didn't even flicker. "Lily always did have a bit of a hormone problem. Being dead probably accentuated her natural personality defects. I'm told it happens."

Mikhail did nothing for a moment. Then he cocked his head to one side. "You are most unusual for a human."

He shrugged. "It's the story of my life. I just have a different way of looking at things from everyone else. When possible, I try to understand people better than they understand themselves. Even when they're people I'd rather see dead. Now, in your case, I'm going to bet that, while you're pissed, you're not stupid. You've got men, but we have weapons, and we have the formations. We also have a few tactical advantages right now."

Mikhail grinned, baring his teeth. "Yes, though while I may lose all of my men, I can make more."

"There's your problem," Marco said. "You're totally reliant on the guys behind me being restrained enough to hold their fire while I'm talking to you. Otherwise, you're going to be *a flambe* before you can say 'Why, it's rather warm in here.' You understand me, Count Orlac?"

Mikhail smiled. "I cannot even recall the last time I even heard one of my men reference *Nosferatu*."

"You're breeding from the wrong end of the gene pool, I guess. You get my point though. Any attempt to fight us, and you're going to take heavy losses. You might even be part of them. You may *not* survive. You know this. I know this. Any victory you may have is going to be very Pyrrhic."

"If I withdraw, yet send my men in…"

"I somehow doubt you're going to do that. Let's face it, you've managed unit cohesion throughout decades without a problem. If you send in your forces to be massacred while you stay behind, then I think there are a few hundred *nests'* worth of vampires who'd reconsider your leadership position. Possibly even revoke it."

Mikhail grunted. "Not unreasonable. What do you have in mind?"

"How about this: I give you one chance to kill me. Right here. Right now. No one will see it, and no one will interfere."

"Oh?"

Marco looked up from Mikhail's chest. "Look me in the eye, you son of a bitch."

Mikhail laughed, and then met Marco's eyes.

Marco froze, still and solid as a grave. He didn't move, didn't blink, and didn't waver. There was a long moment when everyone watching them wondered what was going on.

Amanda was the first to figure it out. "You stupid, stupid man."

Marco, for his part, didn't feel a thing. His entire focus was leveled on Mikhail's face.

Most importantly, he was focused on keeping him out. Mikhail mentally hit a wall. Marco's eyes were intense and focused like a shark's—eyes that saw the prey, and leveled on them, but remained dead inside. There was nothing behind them. It was like Marco had completely and utterly sunk back into his brain and walled it off behind a protective shell. He was a solid wall of dark, unfeeling void. For Mikhail, it was like trying to punch through a wall of water—every time he punched at it, the wall reformed. Every time Mikhail slashed at his mind, he never had true penetration. He scrabbled at it, scratched at it, clawed, and battered his mental fists against the wall of Marco's mind, but nothing happened.

Mikhail took a step back, blinked, a look of amusement passing over his face. "Really? Interesting. I know some people who will be interested in you, should you manage to survive."

Marco smiled and flared his eyes. "Oh, I'm sure. Now, withdraw your men and get out of my town, or else this is all going to get rather messy. Am I clear, sir?"

Mikhail smiled. "Oh yes, quite."

Mikhail dissolved into mist, his smile the last thing to vaporize. His mist form swirled backwards, away from Marco, and the rest of the fog bank behind him similarly congealed into nothingness.

"They are gone," Amanda said aloud.

Marco nodded, almost to himself, and then reached into his pocket to grab his cellular phone. "They're gone from here, but that means that they're still alive." He quickly sent a text message.

He looked back at Amanda and the Vatican ninjas. "This night isn't over yet."

"What do you mean?" Merle asked.

Amanda gave a growl deep in her throat. "What he means is that Lily Sparks was dropped on Marco's doorstep. Mikhail knows Marco's name and knows his address."

Merle Kraft winced. "And you just managed to wipe out a good chunk of his army."

Marco nodded. "He was in a bad tactical position, and he saw that if he closed with us, he and his men would be in a fight they might not be able to win. We've hit them where he lived, but he withdrew and took what's left of his local force with him."

Robert Hendershot grimaced. "Just because this was his main force, it does not mean that this was his *only* force."

Marco gave Hendershot a pat on the arm. "Bingo, give the ninja a cigar. Right now that just means that they're going to kick our asses the moment I get home and they think that *they* are the ones in a good tactical position."

"In short, everyone, the situation just got much, much

worse."

Chapter 31:

I Can Kill You With My Mind

April 16th, 1:50AM. Greenpoint, Brooklyn, NY

Marco Catalano, Amanda Colt, and Merle Kraft approached the Catalano household on foot. As predicted, the front door of Marco's home was blocked. At the foot of the stairs stood the familiar form of the towering Mikhail the Bear.

"Oh look, a threat," Marco muttered. "How nice."

Merle held up a hand. "Let me try this time."

Marco, Amanda, and Mikhail looked with surprise at the short government agent.

"Really?" Marco asked.

Mikhail grinned. "Some people just don't know their own limitations."

Marco and Amanda had no time to agree or disagree with Merle's decision.

Merle was already in front of Mikhail, and struck with a kick to the neck that, if Mikhail hadn't been undead, the move would have killed him. He fell back, blinking, and Merle glanced over to Amanda.

She put her left arm forward as a shield. She wielded a stake held like a knife at 11 o'clock on a Friday night in Brooklyn. The enormous vampire reacted by getting into a similar stance, only more professional. It was a stance for a hired killer—more specifically, a trained killer.

Merle frowned. He even knew the martial arts stance— *pentjakt silat,* an Indonesian martial art that made Karate and *taekwondo* look like ballet.

"I am over three hundred years old," the vampire snarled in a deep voice. "I have sired entire colonies. Do you think that in all that time, I could not learn a few simple martial art forms?"

Merle smiled at him. "Join the club, buddy."

The vampire blinked again, eyeing Merle with a mix of skepticism and amusement. Suddenly, he yelped in pain, whirled, and scooped someone up in his hands. He held Marco by the throat, three feet up in the air, and the vampire's back was smoking as if on fire.

Merle hadn't seen that coming. *He has some good maneuvering if he got behind Mikhail while Amanda and I were busy posturing.*

Marco rammed a stake into a spot below the vampire's wrist and flicked a lighter. The stake went ablaze in seconds, and the vampire hurled Marco to the ground before dropping to the street and rolling in an attempt to put out the flames.

"No, no, no!" Marco chided. "Your line is, 'Help me, I'm melting, what a world, what a world!' *Not* turn around and grab the supporting actor. You've had three hundred years and no time to watch movies?"

He held up a hand, and the door to the brownstone opened. A long wooden broom handle came out, landing right in Marco's hand.

Marco glanced at Merle and Amanda a moment and smiled. He pulled a gun from his pocket and pointed it at Merle. He fired. A stream of liquid shot from his squirt gun flew past the agent and hit a vampire a few feet behind him. The vamp took the shot in the eyes. Merle turned and broke his neck, dropping him to the ground.

The bigger vampire rolled to his feet, the fire out. Marco didn't hesitate. He fired two squirts. The holy water blinded his enemy for a moment, and Marco seized the opportunity to toss Merle the broom handle.

Merle caught it and noticed immediately that Marco had sharpened it at one end. Marco pulled out another stake.

"Come here, you reject from *Salem's Lot*," Marco said,

egging his enemy on. "Come and get the pathetic human being. Come on. It's *snack time!*"

Merle cast a glance at Amanda. She stood there, and merely smiled a smile tinged with affection. "At this point," she said under her breath, "I would like to note that my friend is out of his mind. So please, do not try any of this at home."

Another hiss came from behind, and Merle automatically stabbed behind with the handle, ramming another vampire minion through the heart. The government agent whirled, expecting to run into one or two more vampires. Instead, there was a group of a hundred vampires, at least.

"This is going to take a while," Merle muttered.

Marco studied Mikhail the Bear, coming close, two stakes sharpened. One was held point up in his right hand, and the other, point down in his left.

He lunged toward Mikhail, slashing for the eyes.

Mikhail's hand came up and grabbed Marco's wrist.

The vampire looked up, his eyes now glowing a blood red. *I've always made fun of novels that using lines about a villain "seething with malice,"* he thought to himself. *Now I can see it.*

Mikhail growled and pulled Marco off his feet, slamming his back against the wall of his brownstone. The only reason Marco's head wasn't smashed in was that he tucked his chin, taking the impact along his back and shoulders.

Marco stabbed up with the stake. Mikhail intercepted the blade, wrist to wrist.

Mikhail grinned, baring his fangs. "I'm going to rip your arms out of your…" He grimaced in pain. His teeth ground together, his arms started to shake.

Marco's eyes flicked to Mikhail's hands. They were starting to smoke and smolder.

Mikhail growled and tossed him aside. When Marco hit the ground with his arms taking the impact, Mikhail blinked in shock.

The crosses from the rosaries wrapped around Marco's wrists became visible.

"You little bastard."

Marco got to his feet and started doing the math.

He can charge. But no, he's got a few martial arts under his many belts. Charging is too much like brawling…

He can lunge and punch…Likely…

He can burst forward and kick. Not impossible. Less likely, though…

A roundhouse kick? Possible. He can easily advance with it by not recoiling, and he can smash my ribs in.

Definitely a kick then. Punches would be too easy to dodge.

His speed makes kicks hard to avoid. He'll kick off his back foot, which is his right, so I should go to his left and avoid the kick altogether.

Without even another word, Marco burst to the side at the same moment that Mikhail shot forward, launching a roundhouse kick. Instead of a punching motion, as he was trained to do against a groin kick, Marco swung down with the stake, which jammed into Mikhail's shin as the point of Mikhail's boot just grazed Marco's ribs.

Mikhail had to fall back with the stake sticking out of his leg.

Marco spun around with the force of the blow. Even that graze was enough to shatter two of his ribs.

Marco blinked at the searing pain and staggered back. It took an effort on his part to not grab his aching ribs. "You're a fast little sucker, ain't you? I'm going to need to redo my math."

"You will need to redo your ribcage by the time I'm done with you." The vampire roared and lunged in, hands wide.

Without even a second's thought, Marco saw the attack and broke it down.

He's going to swing from the outside, obviously with his right hand. Therefore, he's going for my ribs again, since they're already my weak point. I can work with this.

Marco shot forward, his left arm already down with a low block to the ribs. They met wrist to wrist, the rosary draining strength from the blow. Marco's left arm came up like a bicep curl around the attacker's arm, and his right hand clamped down on the vampire's shoulder. Marco leaned back, his knee coming up into Mikhail's groin. Once, then twice.

Then Mikhail's left arm came up, then chopped down,

breaking Marco's right arm.

Marco screamed and fell back. He tried to work the math on the next strike, but once again, Mikhail was too quick for him.

The next roundhouse kick came in low. Marco had intercepted it like he had been taught at his Krav Maga school, with his shin. However, while a shin-on-shin defense worked against a human, Mikhail's blow snapped Marco's leg like a twig.

Before Marco could fall over, Mikhail grabbed him by the shirt and slammed him up against the wall.

"Your rosaries might stop me from even ripping your throat out," he said, "but that doesn't stop me from punching a hole right through your chest."

Marco did the math. Mikhail was right.
He had been beaten in seconds.

"Oh nuts," Merle said as he looked over the crowd of vampires as they held back, waiting for their boss's fight to end, "and here I left my flamethrower at home."

Merle looked at the whittled broomstick in his hand and sighed. He broke it over his knee, so he had two sharp pieces of wood.

"Does this feel like an odd *Buffy* episode to anyone else?" he muttered.

Amanda gave out a musical laugh. "After a fashion."

Then all hell opened up.

From the rooftops came several packages. Boxes with test tubes taped to them. They exploded on impact with the ground, turning into fireballs.

"Homemade napalm," Amanda said, watching them fall.

"Right."

Gunfire opened up from the roof. Flares shot out from a dozen rooftops, and from down the street, followed shortly thereafter by the sound of machine-guns. Not one, or two, or even three, but dozens, spitting fire.

"Tracer rounds," she added, taking a step back.

Merle looked to her and said, "Really? I know Marco told the Vatican ninjas to take a helicopter to get here ahead of us and the vampires, but still…"

"He also sent a text message."

Merle looked down the streets. From one direction came a bunch of stereotyped Guidos in suits alongside men in NYPD uniforms.

Didn't they say that they had a small confederation of policemen with them? Did they make a deal with the mafia, too?

"Okay, then," he drawled. "Time to make with the hacking and burning–"

Whatever he was about to say next was cut off by another horde of humans charging at the vampires, closing in on the bloodsuckers in a pincer maneuver.

"Now what?"

"These are the local gangs," Amanda explained. "These are friends."

Merle looked over his shoulder for Marco Catalano, knowing he'd like to see his guys in action. Marco, however, was pinned to a wall by Mikhail. His left leg was broken in an obvious fracture, his right arm dangled useless at his side.

"If these guys have things covered, I think Marco may need some help."

Mikhail grimaced, in obvious discomfort at being so close to the rosary around Marco's neck.

"I may not be able to bite you, but I can kill you."

Marco growled low and deep. "Then look me in the eye when you kill me. Look deep into my eyes, dirtbag."

Mikhail did. "I'll hack into your brain and chew through it like tissue paper."

This time, Marco didn't fight him.

When Marco Catalano said he was a genius, he wasn't exaggerating. His focus was always so intense because he observed everything and processed all of it. His mind never filtered or slowed. Like a supercomputer, a hundred little thoughts were ongoing beyond the surface.

During this fight alone, he had been doing a number of things. He had been fighting Mikhail. He had been tracking Amanda, processing his love for her. He had been working strategy while contemplating telling Amanda about his true feelings. He had been considering what to do with the Kraft family, with the United Nations, while trying to process vampire strategy of the killings in Brooklyn. He had also been working the interrelated problems of balancing his four forces, seeing if the Ninjas would lend him some weaponry, if the mafia could be trusted, if they could find more cops, if the gangs would get themselves killed…

Looming large was Amanda. Her brains, her body, her movement, the way her hair flowed, her expressions and warmth and color of her eyes, her laugh, her voice. The way she made him feel human and alive.

Then there was the other part of Marco. The part he wouldn't allow Amanda to see. The part he kept close to the vest. The darkness he would die to protect Amanda from. The darkness he prayed daily to keep at bay, lest it consumed her.

All of this hit Mikhail at once. He had tried to hit Marco's brain like a battering ram. But this time, Marco let him in.

Mikhail's attack turned out to be hitting the guard rail on the roof of a skyscraper. He punched through and then he just started falling. Only this time, there would be no hitting the ground.

The effect was much like popping a 256K IBM into a supercomputer. The walls of water had dropped on top of him. The Red Sea had opened up to let him in, and then began to crush him. Mikhail's mind was a snack, and this time he was the one being eaten.

At the deepest, darkest part of Marco's mind, Mikhail hit bottom. He touched something cold, and hard, and ruthless. Something savage and primeval, and something far more ravenous than Mikhail. It was something that wanted to rip his throat out and watch him die, bleeding on the ground, for no other reason than that he was there, and he was something to kill.

It was something that leaped from the shadows of Marco Catalano's mind, and it was something much more vicious than any vampire Mikhail had ever met.

Then it started to rip him to pieces.

And then it got worse for Mikhail.

Amanda's heart stopped when she saw Marco at Mikhail's mercy. He was broken and beaten, and the only thing she could think to do was to charge the giant vampire.

That was until Mikhail dropped Marco and backed away, screaming in pain. He grabbed his head as though there were something inside trying to break out.

She exchanged a look with Merle Kraft. He looked about as confused as she did.

Mikhail gave his head a final shake, and then whirled on Marco again.

Marco, who simply smiled. Despite having only his right leg and left arm working, he reared up and launched a projectile.

The vampire tried to sweep it aside, smashing a bottle of holy water. The contents spilled all over him. He kept coming and knocked Marco aside. He slammed himself against the wall, putting out the tendrils of smoke.

Merle tapped his foot against the sidewalk, and said, "This is tag team night, right? When it is my turn?"

The vamp grinned, looking forward to besting the mere human. "I have longed to taste of your flesh, Dalf Kraft. I will not let you interfere in my affairs. I have this assignment on the highest authority. Meddle, and I will see you punished by our master."

Merle cocked his head. *It's so nice that my dear brother managed to get a name for himself as Satan's knee breaker. But this guy's just a lackey? He has authority from a "master?" If that is the case, I can only hope that this creature's master is somewhere else and wouldn't come to personally greet me.*

"Wrong Kraft brother. I'm Merle, nice to meet you. I always wanted to meet one of my brother's associates. Which section head are you under?"

Amanda blinked. "What section head?"

"How should I know?" Merle muttered. "I'm making this it up as I go along."

I have no idea how my brother's end of the universe runs, and I'm in no hurry to find out. But odds are, if Mikhail had authority from someone else, someone above him, then odds were, the legions of Hell are organized to some degree.

He tried not to say that his main concern was about whatever human contacts Mikhail had at the United Nations. *One thing at a time.*

"Not Dalf?" Mikhail rumbled. "Pity. I was at least hoping for Tal Kraft. But you'll do."

Nuts. When this is over, I'll have to tell Brother Taliesin he has acquired a fan club outside of his New Orleans nest.

He leaped for Merle, and executed five distinct punch-kick combinations, and seemed frustrated that Kraft kept leaping back each time. Finally, he growled and lunged, and Merle met him in midair, grabbing his shoulders, and flipped over Mikhail's head. On his way down, Merle wrapped a rosary around the vampire's right shoulder and his legs around Mikhail's waist so he could hang on. Mikhail roared in pain as the rosary tightened around his shoulder, which instantly smoked the moment they came in contact. Merle pulled the loop of the rosary right, like a garrote, and literally cut Mikhail's arm off.

The vampire roared in pain and threw himself flat on his back, crushing Merle beneath him.

Okay, so maybe this wasn't the brightest move I'd ever made.

The vampire rolled off the government agent, and they both came to their feet. He snarled. "No more Mister Nice Guy."

He stepped forward, Merle braced for impact. Suddenly, Mikhail fell to the ground.

Amanda Colt stood behind him, a piece of wood in her hand. She shrugged. "I broke the tip of my stake in his C4 vertebrae. He shouldn't be giving you any more trouble."

Merle blinked and turned to Marco. "You're nuts, you know that?"

He gasped and smiled a little. "Your point?"

Merle grabbed the broom handle off the ground. "Right here."

Amanda ran over and crouched at Marco's side. "Idiot. What were you thinking?"

Marco's smile was weak and pained. "It seemed like a good idea at the time."

"Right." Kraft dusted off his pants, then stuck his hands inside his windbreaker. He trotted over to the prone vampire and kicked Mikhail over onto his back. "Now, tell me what the hell you've been up to, my fangy friend."

Marco, deciding he was bad cop, said, "Otherwise, we're going to chain you up, let your spine heal, and then cut off pieces of you one at a time."

A burst of air cut between them, and Mikhail gasped. An arrow stuck out of his heart.

When Mikhail the Bear looked down at his heart, his look of surprise was almost comical. It was amusing right up to the moment where he turned to dust.

Damnit, Merle cursed, *I wanted him alive so I could question him. I wanted him for my investigation.*

Merle turned, dropping to one knee, and pulled his Firestar .45 out of reflex, even though he couldn't even hit the building the shot had come from.

Amanda Colt, however, was already in motion. She disappeared completely. Unfortunately, she came back quickly.

Chapter 32:

Unresolved Issues

April 16th, 2:15AM. Greenpoint, Brooklyn, NY

Amanda felt something amiss, even as the gangs, the Vatican Ninjas, the mafia, and the police finished off the last of the vampires. She whirled, ignoring Merle, and leapt for the apartment building across the street, grabbed a window sill, then leaped up to the roof.

A mop of long red hair framed the face of the most hideous vampire she'd ever seen, and the two viper's eyes glowed green. The creature was at least six feet tall and looked mean.

It stood on the edge of the roof, crossbow aimed toward the street, and Amanda's first instinct was to launch herself at this new creature.

Its first move was to take a swipe at Amanda's stake hand. The strike made the arm go numb and the stake fly over the edge of the roof. She then ducked in time for the backhand to soar over her head and punched for its stomach, and into the vampire's waiting hand.

Wow, this one's fast, was her last thought before the other vampire twisted and sent her sailing onto the street, landing on the sidewalk with a sickening impact.

Marco Catalano, despite having had his left leg and his right arm broken by Mikhail the Bear in single combat, tried to move towards her fallen form. After a brief effort, he growled deep in his throat. "Damnit. Merle, check her pulse."

The government agent still had his weapon up, but whatever it was had vanished. "Pulse?"

Amanda bounced off the ground, her face a mask of rage and fangs, shouting in rage at the rooftop. "The *suki* tossed me! That…I'll get you for this!"

Merle raised a brow and holstered his gun. "She's too far to hear you."

"I can hear gun fire from the Bronx. Trust me, she hears."

She turned to Marco, and carefully rolled him over onto his back. She cradled his head in her lap, though Marco was too out of it to notice. "I think we can heal this, but I'll need to set the bone, okay?"

Marco gave it a moment's thought. "Sure, why not?"

The door to the brownstone opened, and Doctor Robert Catalano came out, with Ibrahim Javaherian at his side.

"I'll do the setting," Marco's father said, "if you don't mind."

Merle sighed. "Whatever. Well, it looks like my lead is dead, in more ways than one. Marco, why did you want me to check Amanda for a pulse? Habit?"

Amanda smiled brightly. "*Nyet.* I have a pulse. I also have a fully working metabolism. My body doesn't need to pump blood, but I have it do so, mainly to keep everything working. I may want to have children someday."

Merle wondered if Marco knew that the vampire of the dark, red-gold hair wanted to have children with him. "You need food?"

"At least blood. I don't know why, but we need it. I tried going without, it's not a pretty sight."

Marco nodded, completely ignoring his father examining his broken leg. "I think it's a version of porphyria, mixed with a touch of inverse progeria."

"In English?"

"Progeria is a disease that makes someone age at four times the normal rate of speed; ten-year-olds looking like they're forty, and physically, they are."

With a quick pull from Doctor Catalano, Marco screamed briefly. It was almost more of a surprise than anything else.

Marco gritted his teeth and continued, focusing on the information rather than the pain. "Porphyria is what King George III had, driving him insane—a cure for that is the ingestion of human blood, which is where part of the myth of vampirism comes from. We figure that the microbial symbiotes that are responsible for vampirism somehow feed off of fresh, living blood, like porphyria."

Merle nodded. Since he lived in San Francisco, he knew something of what he was talking about, he had just never heard the medical terms for them.

"However, there's her ability to elongate her teeth," Marco added. "It really irritates me, because she always has an unfair advantage at bobbing for apples."

The vampire brushed a strand of hair from his forehead. "I do not know what you're talking about. I would never use them for such a thing."

"Then how come you always need to floss out your canines for the next week afterwards?" he objected. His father had his arm and–Marco screamed again.

"I suck out the filling from some of the chocolates," Amanda continued, as though Marco had just had his back cracked by a masseuse, not his leg set. "It is either that, or I eat diabetics for dessert, and you remember what happened to old Tiberius when he drank from too many."

"Yeah, his teeth rotted out. He should've known better than to drink people with too high a blood sugar without brushing." Doctor Catalano gave a quick pull at Marco's arm, setting the break. Marco grimaced and gritted his teeth this time, despite the pain. "Just because he's dead doesn't mean he can forgo the basics."

Merle snickered at the surrealism of it all. "So, Amanda, since you are who you eat, whom do you generally eat?"

Marco and Amanda looked at each other for a moment.

"I sometimes give donations," he explained. "The rest of the time…you can answer it."

"I go to Mass."

"And?"

"Since I mentioned that our physical character is related to our spiritual character, I go frequently. I think I may qualify as a mystic, but I'm not sure, I haven't asked my confessor about this. Technically, that makes me stronger, so I can go without real blood for a week or two."

What was she hiding? "And?"

"I get most of my blood from the Sacred Blood in the chalice at mass. I'm usually the last one up, so I finish the cup."

I guess that answers the debate between Catholics and Protestants as to if the bread and wine literally becomes body and blood, or if they are symbolic.

Merle looked out over at the gang members, the mafia, the cops, and the Vatican ninjas, who all seemed interested in making certain no one had been eaten during the fracas.

"What about them? I can assume they didn't know about your girlfriend before now, did they?"

"I'll talk to them," Marco said, eyes cold. "If any of them decide to do something unwise, I will know, and they will answer to me."

Merle studied Marco a moment. Despite being beaten, bruised, and broken, he still had the distinct impression that he would, indeed, hunt down anyone who took an action against Amanda. He would protect her, anywhere, anytime, no matter his condition.

"Fair enough." He glanced at the ground where Mikhail used to be. "I guess this is all over then."

Marco let out a sharp, sudden laugh. "You're kidding right?"

Merle motioned to the street littered with empty clothes and dusted vampires. "You call this…what?"

Marco tried to sit up, but Amanda pressed down on his shoulders to hold him in place. "Do not move."

Marco sighed, then looked at Merle. "I call this a retaliatory strike. This isn't over. Obviously, Mikhail didn't like us messing up his most ambitious nesting plans, slowing him down and cutting into his personnel. He went after the FBI, and when we made a move on him, he struck back."

"Yes, but if he was being slowed down, that means that he was building up to something."

Marco smiled. "Give the man a cigar. Whatever they were doing at the United Nations, whatever you were looking into, Mikhail was in charge of manpower."

"What?"

Amanda cut in. "We just killed the head of human resources. We have no idea who that redhead was that killed Mikhail just when he was about to talk."

Merle's mouth twitched. "Aw hell. You're saying this is just starting."

"You're not the one in pieces on the ground," Marco muttered. "You don't get to complain. Now, if you don't mind, I think Amanda and I can use some alone time."

Merle arched a brow. So did Doctor Catalano, and so did Ibrahim Javaherian.

Marco frowned and looked at all of them. "Get your minds out of the gutter. If she bites me, I get a hit of her virus. We can see if this will fix me up."

Amanda carefully moved, then picked up Marco as though he weighed about twenty pounds. "Do not worry. I will be happy to bite you."

Marco smiled at the words, considering how they probably sounded to everyone else within earshot. He settled on his right leg and wrapped his good arm around her shoulders. She supported nearly all of his weight. They exchanged a glance, and Marco felt his heart skip a beat.

"You know what?" Merle finally said. "I could use a guy on my coast to organize a team in case I have problems in San Francisco. You seem pretty settled here, but how about we bring you out to my neck of the woods and see what you can do out there? It would be on me. Well, the federal government, anyway. I mean your college education, room, board, expense account, stipend, everything."

Marco blinked back his surprise. Going to California, this time last year, would have meant *nothing* to him. But on what was essentially a government grant? Hell yes. It wasn't like people would miss him. The gangs? Hector and Zeng? They were more afraid of him than anything else. His father always wanted him to get out more. There was nothing in the entire world that would keep him from going to California.

Not one damn thing…except Amanda.

Amanda, who he couldn't figure out. Who he couldn't decide what to do with. Who he couldn't even *think* about without his brain getting jammed up. He didn't know what he wanted from her. Even worse, he didn't know if she wanted something from *him*, something he couldn't give.

Marco's deepest, darkest secret was something that he could never tell Amanda. She had known his incident with the mugger–the violent mugging that had driven a wedge in between him and Lily Sparks, the wedge that would eventually lead to Lily's death–but Amanda didn't know the whole truth. Marco's "secret" was in that mugging. When that mugger had pulled a knife on Lily and Marco, Marco had taken the knife away from him. And then Marco hurt him. And then kept on hurting him. He kept cutting with the knife until there was nothing left of the mugger but a pale corpse rapidly approaching room temperature. That part, Amanda knew.

But Marco *enjoyed* it. He had enjoyed taking a man who wanted to harm someone he loved, and then hurting him. He enjoyed being alive when the mugger was good and dead. He enjoyed the man's screams of anguish as Marco made him pay for the mistake of threatening someone he cared for.

Marco knew what was in his head. He was someone who enjoyed killing. He was a monster. A predator. Yes, even though Marco had a deep faith, and a deeper prayer life, both served to keep the creature within him in check. In the end, one of two things drove Mikhail from his mind. One was his prayer life and his faith. But Marco believed, deep in his heart, that his dark side had driven Mikhail out of his head and saved his life. It was a part of him he was comfortable with, that he enjoyed, and that he didn't want to give up.

It was something that he couldn't tell anyone about. It was why he couldn't be with Amanda. She killed human beings for food. He did it for fun.

As he had his arm around her, he felt her warmth right next to him. Enjoying the feel of her body, the feel of her strength, Marco couldn't help thinking the worst possible thing.

The predator had thoughts on Amanda. *I love her. And I want … her. All of her. And I don't think I can hide it too much longer. I won't be able to hide it at all if she moves the wrong way on my body right now.*

He looked at Merle and said, "I'll think about it."

Amanda felt like someone was slowly ripping out her heart. When Merle Kraft first asked about San Francisco, she was about to laugh…until she realized that Marco had said nothing for a long moment. Then he said he'd think about it.

When they both made it into the sitting room, Amanda helped lay him out on the couch. "You aren't serious, are you?" she asked.

Marco didn't say anything for a moment. "He could be right," he said absently. "He could need help."

She blinked back tears. "You mean that?"

"Oh, maybe. I don't know." He met her eyes. "It's a thought. One thing at a time, though. We don't even know if he *has* a vampire problem in San Francisco."

Marco cocked his head to one side, and she nodded. She leaned forward and kissed his neck. She gave a light lick where the bite would go. It was strange. She even liked the way his skin tasted. How odd was that?

Amanda kissed his neck a second time, and then a third. Marco shifted a little, as though suddenly uncomfortable.

Then she realized that she was doing more kissing than biting. If she kept going like this, she would be exchanging more bodily fluids with Marco than just some blood and saliva.

What am I doing? He's broken on the couch, and all I can think of is taking advantage of him. Amanda's fangs came out, and she bit him quickly, hoping to distract him from the kisses.

This time, she was far too distracted by her own thoughts to dwell on the sensation of biting Marco. Her feelings were obviously starting to bubble towards the surface at some truly inappropriate moments. What that would mean, she didn't want to think about. Coming clean to Marco about her feelings was possibly the worst idea she could come up with. Truly, why would he want to be associated with her after that? Should she do that to him, all she could see were potential problems.

By the time she had withdrawn her fangs, she had come to a conclusion.

She loved him too much to keep him here.

"Maybe you should go to San Francisco."

"Maybe." He looked deep into her eyes and said, "But for now, I'm quite happy to be here with you."

About The Author

Declan Finn lives in a part of New York City unreachable by bus or subway. Who's Who has no record of him, his family, or his education. He has been trained in hand to hand combat and weapons at the most elite schools in Long Island, and figured out nine ways to kill with a pen when he was only fifteen. He escaped a free man from Fordham University's PhD program and has been on the run ever since. There was a brief incident where he was branded a terrorist, but only a court order can unseal those records, and really, why would you want to know?

He can be contacted at DeclanFinnInc@aol.com

Follow him on Facebook and Twitter @APiusManNovel

Read his personal blog: declanfinn.com

Listen to his podcast, The Catholic Geek, on Blog Talk Radio, Sunday evenings at 7:00 pm EST

More From Declan Finn

Love At First Bite
Honor at Stake
Demons are Forever
Live and Let Bite
Good to the last Drop

The Pius Trilogy
A Pius Man
A Pius Legacy
A Pius Stand
Pius Tales
Pius History

The Convention Killings
It Was Only On Stun
Set To Kill

Honor At Stake

If you've enjoyed this title, please check out the rest of the books in this Dragon award nominated series at https://threeravenspublishing.com/love-at-first-bite/.

Or check out some of our other Urban Fantasy titles at https://threeravenspublishing.com/urban-fantasy/
Such as the Lady of Death, Nightshade Series, or Paranormal City

STEPHEN OLIVER
PARANORMAL CITY

J.F. POSTHUMUS
THE FAE'S AMULET
A LADY OF DEATH NOVEL

Or take a look at some of our other award winning series at https://threeravenspublishing.com/series-universes/

Visit us at
Https://www.threeravenspublishing.com and sign up for our newsletter for the latest and greatest news on upcoming titles and events.

www.ingramcontent.com/pod-product-compliance
Lightning Source LLC
Chambersburg PA
CBHW061609210726

48287CB00001B/50